DRAGONFLY
WARRIOR

THE MECHANICA WARS

Sarah,

Hope you enjoy this
steampunk adventure!

Best wishes,

Jay Noel

JAY NOEL

ISBN: 978-0-9912356-0-5

Printed in the United States of America

Published by 4 Wing Press

Edited by Neely Bratcher
Cover Art by Enggar Adirasa
Cover Design by Jennifer Howard
Paperback Layout by Inkstain Interior Book Designing

Visit Jay Noel online at **www.jaynoel.com**.

—For my friends and family that encourage me to keep writing, no matter what.

In the land of dragons,

surrounded by the Eastern Sea,

the mighty King Jiang held the Sky Blade aloft.

His soul was overcome with power as he beheld his vast kingdom.

The King found two paths before him: to create and heal or to destroy and

maim.

The choice was his alone to make.

Unfortunately, his people would suffer for his poor decision.

— FROM *THE KING AND THE SKY BLADE*, AUTHOR UNKNOWN

PROLOGUE

PRINCE KANZE ZENJIRO KNEW HIS mother was going to die one day from the illness that robbed her of her usual vitality. Zen secretly begged the spirits to grant her life long enough to witness him wearing a soldier's uniform. She had deteriorated recently, and his wish seemed more impossible with each passing hour. It was childish anyway, even for a thirteen year old.

A sharp wind swirled around him and dried his tears as he watched the procession of dark clouds pass by above him. He closed his eyes; the dark thoughts contemplating life without his mother began to overcome him.

After only a short moment, a harsh jolt from the airship's landing shook him from his trance. When Zen opened his eyes, he was startled to see that his flight was over. He hadn't realized that they had even left the ground yet. The pilot couldn't open the gondola's wooden door fast enough.

The aeropad near the top of the palace was soaked from the early morning Spring rain. When Zen pushed past the pilot and leaped from the docking airship, the glistening, slick cobblestones made him slip and fall onto the cold wet ground. His body was adept at ignoring pain and obeying the commands from his mind. He wiped away a long strand of black hair that came loose from his topknot and forced his body to continue.

Zen stumbled down the narrow spiral staircase at the end of the landing area, finding himself in the long courtyard. The iron gates at the far end of the garden were already open. His feet slapped hard on the winding stone pathway that took him to the palace entrance. He nearly slipped again as he darted through the gates and careened around turn after turn through the labyrinth of the palace, until he reached his parents' main chamber.

The two guards pushed open the tall wooden double doors to the dark room where Zen's father and a nurse stood at the bedside. The dim chamber's ceiling stretched three stories high, and the lack of furniture accentuated the room's enormity. Heavy fabric curtains were drawn over the tall windows, adding to the gloom. As he entered, Zen stopped when he saw his mother's anguished face. She looked minuscule in the expansive space surrounding her.

Lord Hideaki turned, looking at Zen with bloodshot and watery eyes. "My son, please come quickly."

Zen inhaled, calming his nerves. With each slow step towards the bed his mother's bony visage became clearer. She looked so pale, so fragile. Her sickness had taken away the powerful woman that was once his mother.

She tried to smile and motioned for him to approach. He swept past his father and the nurse, climbing onto the bed and lying next to his mother.

"You are wet," she whispered, moisture building in the corners of her eyes.

Zen laid his head on her pillow. "I fell down."

"Before I leave this life, I want to tell you some important things." Her face contorted for a second, and Zen gently took her hand.

She spoke so softly that Zen was certain no one else heard her. He remained still, keeping his face next to hers. Even near death, she still smelled of vibrant lotus flowers.

"If you so desire, you may become a warrior before your eighteenth year. All I ask is that you wait eight more seasons. Just two years. Your father and I have agreed to allow you to enlist on your fifteenth birthday."

There was a growing darkness in his belly, and a sharp bitter panic rose from his throat. Zen fought back these sensations. He allowed his mind to record every word, every sound, and every shallow crease on his mother's anguished face.

"You were born for greatness, Zen. Generations to come will know of Kanze Zenjiro's heroic deeds. I have seen it in my dreams. I see you as a young man...so handsome."

Zen's grip on her hand tightened, and she smiled again as if she found comfort in his strength. Her eyes fluttered, and she fought off the deep sleep that craved to take her away.

"Be brave." Her breathing became labored, shallow. "Take care of your father. He will need you now more than ever."

He heard his father moving behind him. He caught the swishing of his royal robes. Zen thought he was whispering a prayer.

"Remember and think of me always," his mother said, a single tear escaping and sliding down her face.

3

Zen kissed her hand. "I will, Mother."

Her eyes rolled backwards, her weak breaths coming at longer intervals. The nurse at his right side covered her face to muffle her sobs, and Zen heard the faint agony of his father's breathy cries.

"Zen..." Her voice was barely audible over the sound of wind rattling the closed windows. "You must..."

Her lips barely moved. She gasped and her body tightened, her lungs too weak to expand. She went limp again, and she struggled to speak.

"I must what, Mother?" Zen asked, his eyes blind with tears.

It was only an instant, a moment without pain or agony. Her eyes opened and her face intensified. Her voice, less than a whisper, strengthened to convey her final message.

"You must save the Machine Boy."

Still clutching her hand, Zen watched her eyes empty. She breathed out softly before her spirit left the confines of the material world.

Into the unknown realm.

ONE

ZEN FLICKED HIS SWORD, CLEANING the blood-soaked blade. He stood in a circle of bodies in blue lacquered leather armor. The air was cool, but drops of perspiration ran down the sides of his face. Morning fog enveloped the battlegrounds, and he heard the frantic scurrying of his enemy who had fled into the dense forest in front of him.

He closed his eyes and prayed to the spirits of the four men he had defeated. They had fought bravely, and Zen finished his prayer with a slow bow.

It had been seven years since his mother's death, and Zen wished she was here in the flesh to witness this great victory and celebrate their country's unification. He whispered a prayer to her, asking for strength.

The swaying yellow and orange trees provided cover for the retreating Kaga soldiers. It would be a challenge to flush them out. Several of his own comrades in their traditional, red uniforms ran past him and gave chase, but one of them stopped at Zen's side. It was his commanding officer, General Takeo Yoneda.

Takeo wore faded, red-lacquered leather *nerigawa* with the dragonfly emblem on his chest to signify his blood ties to the Kanze Clan. Zen's own suit was similar in design, but the red hue blazed like fire. The golden dragonfly on his breast plate was of luster, a stark contrast compared to the weathered pitting of Takeo's *nerigawa*.

Above them, Zen spotted a lone Kanze Clan airship. It was a small craft with a singular spherical balloon and carried only a crew of two pilots. It was most likely on its way to spy on the enemy. Distant rolls of violent thunder filled the sky around them, and the dirigible remained decidedly out of range of the Kagas' artillery.

Takeo slid his helmet off. "With our cannons softening the Kagas' front, General Ishimoto's forces are relying on us to do our job. We do not have time to go chasing after the enemy in those woods. But we have no choice. We must clear the path."

Zen took a moment to slide his sword back into its scabbard and reload his two revolvers. "It is only a matter of time. Today will be a glorious day for the Kanze. With this victory, we take the final step to uniting our country. My mother's dream of a unified Nihon is about to become a reality."

Takeo nodded. "Let us hope so. Our victory must be absolute. The Kaga forces must be completely crushed, their will to fight broken. Only then will they be willing to surrender and pledge their allegiance to your father. The Kaga is a proud clan."

The ground shook with the deafening blast beyond the tree line. Takeo put his helmet back on before checking his weapons. Zen inspected both of his revolvers and slid one back into its holster. After a deep breath, Zen felt his anxiety and excitement subside as a determined calm quickly filled his body. More gunfire echoed from the darkness. They exchanged encouraging glances before stepping into the wild wood.

Above them, the thick canopy of trees blocked most of the infant blushes of early sunlight, giving the forest an otherworldly feeling. Takeo kept his rifle level as he led the way deeper into the woods.

The sounds of battle grew louder until an explosion threw dirt in their faces. A Kanze soldier stood up from his hiding place, exposing what remained of his miserable body. Ragged flesh hung in pieces; his blood and shredded armor were indistinguishable from one another. Zen gave his fellow soldier one last short prayer until gunfire whizzed above his head.

Takeo dove behind a tree while Zen crouched low beside him. He took cover behind an outcropping of stone. Zen could only see a few feet through the heavy gloom, but he spotted two dead clansmen near him. Another pair of Kanze soldiers approached Takeo, and they belly-crawled their way to their commanding officer.

"General," one of them whispered, "ten Kaga warriors are positioned north of us. Four of our clansmen are making their way to flank them."

Takeo squinted. "Keep your eyes open for any more of those grenades. Do we have any of our own left?"

"No, General," replied the solider. "We are all out."

Takeo shot Zen a crooked grin. "Should I even bother asking?"

Zen shook his head. "I do not carry them. Ever since I watched Captain Saito's bomb blow up in his hand before throwing it, I have decided not to trust the mechanics of those things. Besides, I have terrible aim."

"You are too young to be so pessimistic, Zenjiro," Takeo said.

More gunshots rang out. After waiting several moments, they heard someone running towards them from the rear. Zen flipped on his back and raised his pistol. The approaching runner was in red armor, and it looked like he might have been unarmed. Zen noticed that more sunlight penetrated the forest. Morning gave way to the rising sun.

"It is Taku." Takeo reached over and pushed Zen's gun away.

Taku threw himself onto the ground next to them. "We tried to surprise them on both sides, but they overwhelmed us. We got two or three of them, but I am the only one of our group to make it out of there. The remaining Kagas have taken refuge at the bottom of a small hill, maybe only forty paces north of our current position."

Takeo tossed the weary soldier a pistol. "Take a deep breath. We will get them."

A deep voice rumbled through the trees. "You Kanze dogs, we will never surrender to you!" The taunt was followed by the roar of Kaga soldiers. The same man yelled, "Come and get us, and we will send you straight to Hell!"

More bullets zipped over Zen's head as the Kagas hollered and cheered again. Hot impatience rose from Zen's chest. A full Kanze regiment was only minutes behind them, and they expected the path to be cleared for a flanking attack on the Kagas' main columns. The timing had to be perfect.

His anger melted into calm, his breaths became deeper and slower.

"What are you doing, Zen?" Takeo asked.

Zen ignored him.

"I promised your mother that I would protect you on the battlefield. Somehow, I have managed to do so the last five years, despite your recklessness. I made the same vow to your father this morning."

Zen felt Takeo grab his arm, but he didn't fight the general's grip.

A familiar hum filled Zen's head, and his mind reached out through the dark woods. He heard everything, even the enemy's movements in the brush from forty paces away. His eyes sharped, which improved his vision in the dim forest. His muscles twitched, coiling like steel cables ready to burst. His body was in the state of full *Ishen* now.

Zen's mind and body languished in reptilian coldness. Inside and out, he was prepared to strike. His desire to kill poured into his icy veins. In the calm before the inner-storm, Zen leaped to his feet, breaking free of Takeo's hand. His powerful legs brought him closer towards the Kagas' position, but he first had to clear the hill. Zen pounced into the air with his pistol in his right hand.

As he hurled his outstretched body over the steep hill, he saw the Kaga soldiers scramble in all directions. His heart pounded against his ribcage, and time stretched and pulled as he took one final deep breath. The enemy appeared in shock when they fumbled with their guns. To him, they moved in slow motion. Zen's movements felt out of sync with real time, as if he existed outside of it.

Zen fanned the hammer of his revolver with his left hand while still in midair; his bullets found their marks as he hit the ground and rolled onto his stomach. Two Kaga men fell dead, but another pair of soldiers fired their unsteady weapons.

Zen emptied his first gun, and his last bullet struck a man between the eyes. The last enemy soldier raised his pistol and made eye contact with Zen. Pistol spent, Zen rolled himself behind a small tree. Three Kaga bullets ripped past him on his left.

The Kaga ran out of bullets, and Zen heard the enemy tear his sword from its scabbard. Zen did likewise, despite having his second pistol fully loaded, and he holstered his empty sidearm. He got to his feet, and with sword drawn, Zen walked out to face him.

"You will not take me alive." The Kaga warrior raised his blade. "I will never bow down to the Kanze. Never. My lord is Nihon's rightful king."

Diffused light now penetrated the forest, and Zen embraced the flow of erupting energy throughout his body. The power of *Ishen* continued to consume his insides, and his senses remained as sharp as his blade.

The enemy soldier stood a shade taller than Zen, but the man possessed long arms. The blue chest piece bore the Kaga symbol, a circle with a square in the center. The man breathed hard, his eyes and sword steady.

"I would rather die than surrender to you, boy."

For one fleeting moment, Zen allowed himself to admire his opponent. A true warrior always chose death over surrender. It would be an honor to take this brave man's life.

The Kaga swung his sword in a crazed fury. The soldier slashed wildly, and his attacks met with Zen's blade. Taking full advantage of his now-enhanced abilities, Zen parried each blow and deflected a sweep towards his legs. He followed with a sharp upwards thrust of his sword's hilt. The butt of the hard metal slammed into the Kaga's face and drew blood from his nose and upper lip.

The enemy reeled backwards, exposing his torso. Zen twirled his blade and plunged the tip through the Kaga's chest. He rammed his *katana* deep into the man's body. The soldier's mouth bubbled with blood, his face twisted, eyes suddenly hollowed before crumpling to the ground.

Takeo and the others descended from the hill. They stepped over the casualties that lay strewn on the ground, their eyes wide and disbelief covering their grimy faces.

One of his comrades whispered, "Incredible."

Zen felt the scrutinizing stares of his fellow soldiers. They exchanged nervous looks among each other, but they remained silent. Zen waited for them to circle around him and congratulate him for his bravery, but they looked at him as if he were a walking spirit.

Breaking the uncomfortable lull, Zen paused to pray over the still bodies of the fallen enemy. The soldiers followed proper decorum with a bow of their heads.

Takeo placed his gloved hand on Zen's back. "I never tire of watching you in battle. It is a thing of beauty, *Dragonfly Warrior*." He closed his eyes and bowed over the dead. "I would have assisted you, but it was obvious you did not need me. I do not know why I even bother promising your father to watch over you. You need no protecting."

Zen flicked his blade once more before putting it away. "Do not call me the *Dragonfly Warrior*."

The *Ishen* faded, and Zen felt all of his senses return to normal. His body loosened, and his lungs felt as if they took a much needed deep breath after being underwater for too long.

"Seriously, Zen. As a general, I should be commanding our brigade against the Kaga column, not out here on the fringes hiding about in the woods and fighting a guerrilla war." Takeo led them down the small hill towards the edge of the forest.

"This is pure combat," Zen insisted. "I prefer this to marching among another five thousand soldiers or being in a mechanized unit, riding around in the confines of a cramped gun carriage or locomobile."

"If you say so." Takeo's angled face hardened. "The way is clear. We will join the approaching regiment and strike from the west. When this day is done, we shall have forged a new country."

The thunderous march of the Kanze soldiers grew louder, and Zen returned his sword to its sheath and reloaded his pistol. In the quiet of the moment, he thought of his lost mother once again.

The wars between the twelve provinces would soon be over.

They will be one country.

One Nihon to stand against the world.

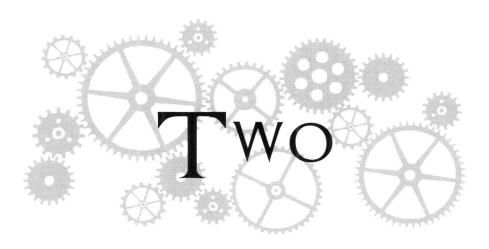

TWO

THE CAPITAL CITY OF THE Kanze Province was recently renamed Tokei, and the various dignitaries and diplomats
representing the twelve major clans of Nihon gathered at
the palace to celebrate the unification. Zen hurried out of his
private chamber to find his father before the festivities began.

Carved from the face of Yamutori Mountain, the main palace overlooked the entire province. Zen found the ornate
stone castle beautiful, but he admired his home beyond mere
aesthetics. It was built for defense against invaders. The sharp
towers jutting from the main structure were fortified with soldiers and artillery. The stone surrounding the palace had never been breached in two millennia.

Zen stood on his small balcony overlooking the city. In the
distance, airships from all over the islands came to transport
visitors to their new capital. Citizens surrounded the mountain to celebrate. The winding street leading to the iron gate of
the palace was filled with revelers dressed in their finest. As

each entourage paraded towards the castle, they were greeted with decorated flags, blossom petals hurled into the air, and exultant cheers from the people.

He watched imperial soldiers hand out small cloth flags on wooden sticks. The new official design of Nihon's flag was stark white, a golden dragonfly within a blood-red circle in the center. The dragonfly commemorated the Kanze Clan's victory and dominance over the other clans, but the red circle symbolized the solidarity of all the states forged through bloodshed.

Today was the first official gathering of the newly formed General Assembly. Representatives from each province were to meet in the palace's Grand Chamber. The final negotiations had gone smoother than expected, with the Kaga Clan offering complete surrender and submission to the Kanze immediately following their defeat two seasons ago. Each subject state had approved the documents sent from the capital.

Today was Unification Day.

Zen sighed. It was also the seventh anniversary of his mother's death.

Thousands of citizens filled the streets below. His mother loved celebrations. His father hated them, but she was always able to persuade him to join in the festivities. With her gone, it would be Zen's job to put his father at ease.

Zen pulled at his stiff, red ceremonial robe. He left the balcony, and with quiet and quick steps, he made his way through the long corridors to his father's study chamber.

Hideaki's door was shut, which meant his father was conferring with officials. He recognized nearly all of his father's administrators and bureaucrats, and he was often asked by Hideaki to sit in on many of his meetings. Just the thought of attempting to endure the endless babble gave Zen a headache. His father argued that eventually, Zen would have to learn to navigate the murky, stormy seas of politics. So far, Zen had managed to circumvent this part of his education.

He leaned against the stone wall to wait for his father to finish whatever business he was tending to. If being king of Nihon meant hours stuck behind a desk arguing with politicians, Zen didn't want any part of it. He thought Takeo was better suited for such things.

After only a few short minutes, the wooden doors swung open and a solider dressed in dark blue exited the study. The strange man wore no clan colors or armor, and his hair was cropped short against a sharp and cold face. It was customary for noblemen to wear their long hair pulled up into a tight top knot, and the stranger looked out of place.

Zen vaguely recognized this man and knew he had visited his father's private study before. He was no politician. He walked with steady strength and purpose. This was a man of action.

The man stopped at the open door and turned to Zen. "Today marks the seventh year since your mother's death," he said without any hint of emotion.

Although the man in blue had not asked a question, Zen replied with a slight nod.

The stranger was about to say something further, but he turned his back and took rapid steps towards the far stairway to the lower level. King Hideaki was sure to have his secrets, which was another reason why Zen despised government affairs. To a true *samurai*, there were no secrets.

Zen watched the man disappear down the stairwell before he entered his father's study.

The chamber possessed a high ceiling, and the rich cherry wood throughout lent a certain sense of warmth to it. Most of the walls were adorned with full bookshelves, and only the large desk and surrounding chairs furnished his father's favorite room. This was his father's refuge, but the king looked tense.

Zen sat in his father's chair and watched the king speak to an imaginary audience.

On this special day, they both wore their ceremonial robes. They were red with an intricate and ancient pattern stitched in gold trim around the seams, the emblem of the all-important dragonfly embroidered on the center of their backs.

Zen's father had not aged, except for the white hairs creeping across the sides of his head, sweeping neatly into a top knot tied with gold twine. Hideaki mumbled the speech that he had worked on for two weeks. Zen was going to say something comforting to his father, but the encounter moments ago with the soldier still bothered him.

"Father, who was that man?" Zen asked.

Hideaki stopped pacing. "What man?"

Zen turned towards the now closed doorway, half expecting the stranger to be standing there. "The man leaving your study just before I entered."

His father's eyes shifted, and Zen now regretted asking.

"Oh, he is a new servant. Foreman. Temporarily filling in. Helping with the preparations for our celebration."

Zen decided to drop the subject. His father was lying. That's what politicians did, after all. Hideaki returned to his pacing and practicing his speech.

"Stop being so nervous. There is no need to rehearse any longer. It is making you more anxious." Zen stood up and blocked the king's path. "Sit down and relax."

Hideaki chuckled. "There was a time when I thought I would never see this day. The tide of war immediately shifted once you stepped onto the battlefield."

"Maybe if I joined sooner, we would have been able to claim victory much sooner."

"Your mother was against it, although she had a change of heart in the end." Hideaki fiddled with the military medals on his robe as he sat behind his desk. "Her spirit would have haunted me forever had I failed to fulfill her wishes." He paused. "I take it you know what today is."

Zen found it difficult to swallow. "Yes, Father."

"It is appropriate that we celebrate the creation of a new Nihon on this day. Difficult to believe it has been seven years. I miss her."

Hideaki glanced down at his papers. Any trace of youth disappeared. His face looked more aged than his fifty-four years. The deep wrinkles of a war-weary king appeared, and it looked as if he was preparing to say something painful.

"We live in unstable times," Hideaki said in a hushed voice. "The world is transforming quickly as all the nations' borders have suddenly become blurry. With the recent defeat of the Russiyan Empire, Iberia has more than doubled its territories across the globe and seems poised to force its will upon the rest of the world."

Zen nodded. "Yes, Father. It is concerning."

"Across the sea, Xia remains divided by civil war, as we too have been for the last twenty years," Hideaki continued. "Without a unified Sun Nation, we do not stand a chance against the Iberians. If Nihon and Xia cannot once again become allies, all is lost."

"I do not think the Xians are willing," Zen said. "Forming such an alliance is probably the last thsing on their minds."

Hideaki stood up and resumed his pacing. "There are reports of an Iberian military gathering at the edge of the western border of Xia. The Western Jins are too occupied with their civil war with the Eastern Sui to take notice. I have sent many representatives to both factions in the last several seasons, but our warnings fall on stubborn ears."

Xia was an expansive country, its land rich of resources and beauty. Zen had studied there in intervals during his youth, but the fighting between the Sui and Jin made it too dangerous for him to remain in the neighboring country for long.

Zen found himself pacing alongside his father. "The Iberians are probably preparing to invade. Let them. If Xia cannot unify itself in time to stop them, then that is Xia's fate. Nihon can stand alone against any invasion."

"Son, the Iberian Empire is employing new technologies, creating weapons never seen before." Hideaki remained restless, taking his seat again. "One of our diplomats recently met with a sea merchant in Western Xia. The trader shared in great detail the weaponry and armaments he witnessed being built in Iberia."

"What did he see?" asked Zen.

"One hand held weapon doing as much damage as a dozen or more soldiers armed with rifles. Monstrous machines walking upright, ripping metal is if it were paper. He called them exomechia. At first I thought this trader was mad, but I have heard similar reports from Russiyan refugees fleeing from Iberian occupation."

Zen tried to imagine such machines, but he could not comprehend that kind of power. He shivered at the thought.

"Master Kyta recently returned from a pilgrimage to Xia with evidence of the kind of weapons Iberia is building," Hideaki said. "She will present her findings to the General Assembly today. If Nihon is to remain free, we must find a way to forge a new Sun Nation. Otherwise Xia, Nihon, and all the Eastern Powers will be slaves to Iberia."

Hideaki stood up. He stepped around his desk and placed his hand on Zen's shoulder. "That is why I must ask you for one more favor."

Zen leaned forward. A knock at the door made both men jump. One of Hideaki's advisers poked his head into the study. "I am sorry for interrupting, Excellency, but the entire General Assembly is ready for you in the Grand Chamber."

Hideaki gathered his notes. The adviser opened the door fully and revealed the soldiers standing at attention inside the vestibule. "Zenjiro, let us not keep our people waiting."

Zen nodded, although his insides churned. What was Hideaki was going to ask of him? At his first opportunity, he planned on stealing a private moment with his father to continue their conversation. However, with the various festivities planned, it would be impossible.

Perhaps reading his son's troubled expression, Hideaki attempted to put him at ease. "It will all make sense in a few moments."

Zen bowed and allowed Hideaki to exit the study first. They followed a procession of advisers through the guarded corridor; the pair came to a stop when they reached a tall set of doors. When the soldiers pushed them open, they were welcomed by warm applause by over two hundred standing dignitaries. Hideaki waved his hand before bowing to the crowd, and his subjects returned the gesture. The Grand

Chamber looked to be filled beyond capacity, the auditorium barely able to contain the nearly three hundred representatives.

Zen stared at the cheering audience, unable to shake the surreal quality he felt as he stood in front of old enemies who were now his countrymen. The hatred fueling the war for twenty years was left on the battlefield, and the blood of his people would now nourish a healing nation.

Standing behind his father, Zen acknowledged to himself that this was the proudest moment in all of his twenty years of life.

THREE

THE GRAND CHAMBER CONTAINED ELEVATED seating facing the stage, which allowed the audience to get a clear view of the marble pulpit at the front. Zen shifted in his seat. His father gave the outward appearance of authority and confidence, but Zen felt Hideaki's unease from the front row.

Hideaki remained on the platform after he delivered his speech. The delegates' applause resounded like raindrops before tapering off as sentries entered the room. Royal guards dressed in red and golden armor directed the delegates to both main exits at the far ends of the Grand Chamber.

Takeo leaned over to Zen, his voice rising above the clamor of the shuffling crowd. "Let us go for a moment. Your father is going to convene his first High Council session. We can wait for them to finish in your father's study."

Zen stood up, bewildered. He wanted to try to catch his father alone to continue their private discussion.

"Your father has requested your presence towards the latter

half of the High Council's conference." Takeo smiled. "Do not worry, he does not mean to throw you to the sharks just yet. It is just a formality."

"I do not understand," Zen allowed himself to be led away, searching for his father up at the pulpit. Hideaki was nowhere to be found. "What does he want of me?"

Takeo shrugged. "I am not privy to such matters, Zenjiro."

"Where is Master Kyta?" Zen asked. His old teacher always had the answers. "I have not seen her at all today."

"She is somewhere behind the stage, assisting your father." Takeo opened the smaller side door and entered the narrow corridor to Hideaki's study. "She will be attending the High Council meeting as well."

They walked to the study together. Zen took his normal seat while Takeo stood by the door. In war, soldiers spent most of their time waiting. Despite Zen being a restless spirit, downtime was a welcome pleasure. He waited at his father's antique desk. He couldn't ignore the foreboding sensation of sinking, of drowning in the realm of politics.

ALTHOUGH NEARLY THIRTY MINUTES HAD passed, it felt like time stood still. Takeo remained silent, waiting for the knock at the door. Zen's own anxiety was understandable, but what worried him was Takeo's transparent attempt at hiding his agitation. The heavy lull was almost too much to bear, and Zen was ready to demand answers when the soft knock finally came.

Takeo pulled the door open and whispered to someone on the other side. He motioned to Zen. "They are ready for us."

Zen supported himself on weak legs and started towards the open doorway. "But am I ready for them?"

"You are ready for anything," Takeo said. "I trained you so."

"A wicked politician is more dangerous than a stealthy assassin," Zen said with a smile.

"I agree."

The two friends made their way through the dark hallway, back into the Grand Chamber. His father remained at the pulpit up on stage, and only a dozen dignitaries remained, all sitting in the front row. Master Kyta was still absent, and Zen sighed. His old teacher's presence was always soothing, and he had hoped her wisdom could break his spell of heavy dread.

At the edge of the large platform below the pulpit, a pictogram projector sat on an old table. Made of brass, wood, and clockworks, its presence struck Zen as curious. He was about to take a seat amongst the Council members, but Takeo touched Zen's elbow. He pointed to the center of the empty stage, and now Zen wallowed in full blown panic. Public speaking was the only thing he feared, and now he fought his nerves to keep steady as he took his place before his father and the High Council.

Hideaki held a scroll as he spoke. "My son. I do apologize for the lack of notice, but I decided to hold an emergency session of our newly formed High Council."

The king unfurled it and raised it in the air. It was a flag, deep purple with a golden winged dragon. He looked out at his council, displaying the foreign banner for them to see.

"This is the Imperial flag of Iberia," Hideaki declared. "Most of you are not familiar with their symbols. They call this animal a *culebre*, a winged beast whose breath is fire and whose hunger for human flesh is insatiable. This is the new enemy threatening our new nation. The Iberians' lust for power will soon advance eastward into a weakened Xia and make its way to Nihon."

Zen felt a drop of sweat roll down his forehead. What did any of this have to do with him? He turned to his right, hoping to catch a hint in Takeo's face, but the general locked his gaze upon the Iberian flag in Hideaki's hand. When Zen turned back to his father, he noticed a familiar thin figure standing next to the king.

Master Kyta looked frail and brittle standing next to Zen's robust father. She was a master of the old ways, and Zen was convinced the old woman would never die. Kyta's white hair fell towards the small of her back, and her tall metal staff assisted her as she walked. Zen noticed the guards dimming the oil lanterns along the perimeter of the chamber. With slow and petite steps, she walked down the marble staircase and stopped at Zen's side. Zen felt his tension evaporate.

"King Hideaki was gracious enough to allow me to address you, my fellow citizens," Kyta said to the High Council. She swiveled towards Zen. "Something terrible is coming our way, and we must be prepared."

Kyta removed a cubical crystal from her robe and hurled it up into the air. Zen hadn't noticed that Takeo had left his side until the general caught the cube and walked to the pictogram projector. Takeo placed the crystal into an opening on the top of the machine and turned a crank. Gears and cogs turned, and the machine illuminated the entire chamber with white projected light.

The projector created a three-dimensional ghostly image

floating above their heads. As the image sharpened, it was revealed to be a man climbing into a machine. The contraption, like armor made from polished steel, stood several feet higher than the man, and it seemed to swallow him whole. The machine possessed interlocking gears and other moving parts at the joints. The steel monster's head was a glass dome where the man was able to see out.

As he moved his limbs, gouts of steam rushed out from two exhaust pipes coming from its shoulders. It raised its right arm, but instead of a hand, it looked to be a barreled weapon. Bursts of fire erupted from the muzzle as hundreds of empty shells spilled onto the ground.

The metal beast lumbered towards a stone wall. It raised its left arm which held a sword-like blade instead of a mechanical hand. With one swift punch, he blasted a hole through the wall. The explosion sent shards of rock in every direction.

Kyta broke the silence with her husky and commanding voice. "The Iberians call this machine an exomechia. It is a type of armor a soldier can climb into, controlling it with his own movements. The exomechia moves with him, like a second skin, yet it increases his strength fifty-fold. The Iberian Empire will bring them to the border it shares with Western Xia."

The pictogram image faded once Takeo stopped turning the projector's crank, and the guards reignited the chamber's gas lamps. Takeo removed the crystal from the small machine and sat near the Council members. Zen wondered if this was his own cue to sit back down, but he couldn't move his legs.

Kyta turned her back on the delegates and spoke to Zen directly. "This footage was recorded twenty days ago. Your father has been reviewing knowledge given by reliable sources near Iberia. If they build an army of these exomechias they will be unstoppable." Kyta bowed and looked up to the pulpit. "Thank you, Excellency, for allowing me to speak."

Hideaki acknowledged his adviser with a slight nod, and Kyta swept across the floor and disappeared into the shadows. Nervous whispers among the council members grew. Takeo wore a worried look as he remained in his seat among the chatter.

"Nearly two thousand years ago, Nihon led the Sun Nation against the invading forces of Byzantia," Hideaki said. "Five hundred years later, the Albions swept across the world, capturing Xian provinces in its wake. Once again Nihon took action, and we cast them out, sending them back to their isle. After liberating our neighbors, we allowed Xia to keep its sovereignty. That was a mistake. Once again, fate is calling us to resurrect this old alliance and stand up to tyranny. We will not make the same mistake again."

The chamber filled with tentative applause. Zen wondered about his father's intentions with Xia. If efforts to bring the Sui and Jin factions together constantly failed, Zen didn't see any other way to secure Xia's allegiance to a new Sun Nation alliance.

Hideaki looked down at Zen, as if reading his mind. "I have been in contact with the kingdoms of the Eastern Powers, and I am confident I will be able to solidify their support. Xia, on the other hand, is another matter. The Western Jin and Eastern Sui remain locked in a stalemate in their century-old civil war. Blinded by their hatred for each other, they fail to see the danger looming from Iberia. That is why our most immediate mission is to find the lost Sky Blade of legend in order to gain Xia's allegiance."

Zen heard a gasp, but he couldn't be sure it wasn't his own.

Kyta walked onto the edge of the stage near the pictogram projector. "The Sky Blade is sure to bring Xia into the fold."

All eyes turned to Zen, and for a moment, his mind went completely blank. He turned to Kyta, then to Hideaki. Words finally came to his brain, and he wondered if addressing his father at this moment was appropriate. Zen raised his face up towards the pulpit.

"Did you say the Sky Blade?" Zen asked. "From the bedtime stories?"

Hideaki opened his mouth to reply, but Kyta spoke first. "Yes, but there is truth behind the stories." The old woman stroked her hair with frail fingers. "The metal extracted from the rock that fell from the heavens is the same material my staff was forged from. The alien metal is extremely powerful. The sword has both the power to destroy or the power to heal. The one chosen to wield the Sky Blade will possess the power to unify the Sun Nation and defeat the Iberian Empire and their machines."

Zen's mind raced. "Or destroy the world, as the story goes."

"That is why the one chosen to find it must be noble and incorruptible," Hideaki said. He left the pulpit and stepped down to meet Zen face to face. "The High Council has chosen *you* to go on this quest."

Zen's breath left him, and his chest quivered. He stared at the faces of the High Council, each man adorned in his respective clan's colors. They wore the look of determination, which didn't make Zen feel any better.

"How will finding the Sky Blade help us?" Zen asked. "It is just a fairy tale."

Hideaki replied, "We are a nation derived from faith, holding steadfast to our traditions. Our faith makes us strong. Too many of us have come to depend on the things we can only see with our eyes and touch with our fingers."

Kyta shuffled towards the center of the stage. "Many of our people have lost their faith. Faith is what weaves Nihon and Xia's fate intricately together for all time. The story of the Sky Blade originated in Xia, and they are a nation of believers. The keeper of the sword is the rightful and sovereign ruler of Xia. It is a most powerful symbol, and one that commands obedience."

Zen nodded, their words starting to make sense. Takeo still looked worried, and Zen wondered if he should be too.

"If we are to successfully defend our homeland, we must rekindle our faith," Kyta continued. "Now is the time to return to the old ways most of us have forsaken."

She struck the wooden floor with her staff and every lamp in the Great Chamber sparked. The flames grew in intensity and illuminated the chamber. "The world is still full of mysteries, and the Sky Blade is the greatest mystery of them all."

Hideaki placed a hand on Zen's shoulder. "Finding the Sky Blade will force the Jin and Sui to end their civil war...to become whole once again. You will rule Xia, as it has been foretold. When you come before the Xian people with the Sky Blade in your grasp, the people will cry out in support of their ordained leader. Then you and I will resurrect the Sun Nation alliance. Together."

Hideaki looked at Zen with exhausted eyes. He produced something shiny with his free hand and lifted the object into the air. "This amulet contains a piece of the same terrestrial rock that fell from the sky and was used to forge the Sky

Blade. Master Kyta has assured me it will assist you in finding this mystical artifact."

Zen noticed the blue stone's glow, its radiant light cascading on his father's face. Hideaki took the amulet's chain in both of his hands, and Zen lowered his head. He felt the cold metal slide down his neck, but the warmth of the pulsating stone soothed him.

"We will honor the traditions of the Sacred Quest," Hideaki continued. "As it was written, the champion to find the Sky Blade must be pure of heart. Zenjiro, you must go alone on this Holy Pilgrimage. As our solitary hero, you will go on this quest with no money, no provisions, and no assistance. You will rely solely on your strength and courage."

Zen struggled to speak, and he spoke loudly to hide his uncertainty. "The world is vast. Where do I start?"

"Master Kyta led our finest scholars in an in-depth study of several Xian scrolls," answered Hideaki. "Within several ancient texts, the authors all describe a wild and vast land where the ancient weapon was hidden. The continent is covered in snow, sand, wheat, many rivers, and lush trees. The Xian king that wielded the Sky Blade abused its power, forcing his people to steal and hide it. We believe the Sky Blade is hidden on Agrios."

Zen had read about the Wild Land, the continent recently named *Agrios* by the Iberian Empire. It was mostly uncharted territory inhabited by bloodthirsty savages. Iberia managed to settle along the eastern coast of Agrios, but the natives fought back any effort to expand foreign colonization.

The chamber fell silent, and everyone waited for Zen to say something. Kyta's metal staff seemed to illuminate, the soft blue glow pulsating in rhythm with the stone around his neck.

"I accept this Sacred Quest," Zen declared.

The dignitaries rose to their feet in applause and left their seats to congratulate him. Hideaki's mouth began to form words, but his tears overwhelmed him. Zen's father put his arms around him, and the two embraced, forsaking proper Nihon etiquette.

Zen missed his mother more than ever, and he wished she were there in the flesh to witness the greatness she predicted.

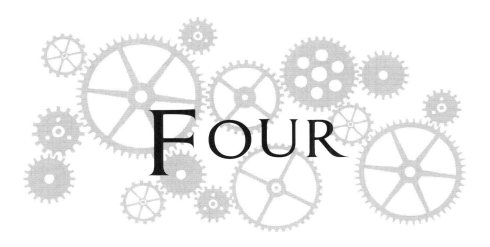

FOUR

THE ROYAL GROUNDS WERE EERILY quiet the morning Zen was to depart. The colorful banners and flags still lined the road from the celebrations five days ago. Zen gazed at the awakening city from his balcony. His mind recorded every pagoda, temple, building, and garden within his wide field of vision. He wondered what cities looked like in Agrios.

Zen packed the night before, and he had placed only the bare necessities in his canvas knapsack. The sacred pilgrimage mandated that he only take with him the things to help sustain him. Other than a couple changes of clothes, Zen packed his armor and gauntlets, a straight razor, a metal canteen, a toothbrush, his pistol cleaning kit, and several boxes of ammunition.

When he reached the courtyard, Zen found Takeo waiting for him near the covered entrance.

"All ready?" Takeo pointed at Zen's full rucksack.

Zen took notice of the new red armor Takeo wore. Two

31

days ago, his father had promoted Takeo to Shogun. It was the highest honor any warrior could ever dream of having, yet his friend didn't celebrate after being chosen. Takeo wasn't the celebrating type.

"I must confess, I have my reservations about your quest," Takeo said. "You are the heir to the throne, so you should not be going on this dangerous mission. Your father and the High Council are not following protocol."

Zen felt his cheeks flush. "We both know I am worthy. Why question this?"

Takeo shook his head. "I do not question your bravery, and I especially do not question your abilities. You are the prince of Nihon. You should remain here. You should be Shogun."

"To be chosen for something as special as this Sacred Quest is all I have ever wanted." Zen slowed his breath and allowed his anger to pass. "This journey encompasses everything I have trained and fought for. For generations to come, when people speak my name, they will recall my victories and heroic deeds. Had I not been chosen, I would have gone on my own. I will not be denied this glory."

Takeo broke the tension with a chuckle. "I am not surprised." He looked down at the amulet Zen wore around his neck. "Regarding your magic charm, I have even further doubts."

"If it was fashioned by Master Kyta, it will work." Zen held the stone up to the sun. It was a swirl of dark colors, dominated by dark gray and blue with glints of silver.

"If you say so," said Takeo with a hint of reluctance in his eyes.

Zen slid the amulet back underneath his shirt. "I am a warrior of faith. That is why I was chosen."

"Of that, I am sure." Takeo turned to him while they walked. "If the Sky Blade is the path to bringing Xia under our kingdom without war, then you must find it. You are our country's greatest, Zen. Perhaps of all time."

Zen swelled with pride. Takeo had been a constant presence in his life since childhood, and he felt homesick already.

Takeo led them to a small road that cut a narrow path through the royal grounds. "It is time, Zenjiro."

"You are not coming to the harbor?" Zen asked, already knowing his friend's answer.

Takeo gestured toward Yamutori Mountain. "I must attend to business at the palace. We have much to do while you go adventuring across the ocean to the Wild Land."

"It has been an honor serving under you, Shogun." Zen felt uneasy with giving him a final goodbye. "I do hope we will be able to share the battlefield once again someday."

"When you first began your training, you were just a boy. It has been my honor to fight at your side and watch you grow into a man." Takeo smiled. "However, I have seen how you get while on the high seas. I believe your first battle will be with seasickness. I pray you do not vomit on yourself."

The two friends shared one final laugh.

"Honor first," said Zen.

"Honor first."

They took hold of each other's forearms before sharing the customary bow. Without saying another word, Takeo left to enter the palace through the main gates. Zen watched him disappear around a corner.

Movement to his far right caught Zen's eye, and he spotted a hooded form lurking behind the lush green foliage. At first, he wondered if it was one of the palace servants tending the garden, but when the lurker pulled back his cape, there was no mistaking the man's blue Kaga armor. Zen hurried toward him, and recognition set in. It was the man who had challenged his father for the right to rule Nihon.

"Governor Kaga," Zen said with a bow. "Are you here to see me off?"

The old man was short, shrunken with age, but his arms remained strong and taut. "Prince Kanze, your quest is a perilous one. Many of Nihon's finest would be trembling in their boots. But not you."

Zen wondered if the governor carried a grudge for his sound defeat. His senses began to heighten, just in case Kaga decided to avenge his loss. "I know no fear, Governor Kaga. This quest is vital to all of us."

"Indeed." Kaga's narrow eyes flashed indecision. "Our clans have been enemies longer than you have been alive. Despite that, my warriors spoke of your honor. Even enemies can respect one another."

Zen bowed at the compliment.

"As a member of the High Council, it was difficult to agree to allow you to go on this quest." Kaga scratched his nose. "I do not know how to say this."

"I am next in line to the crown," Zen said. "Sending me to the Wild Land on a dangerous mission might not be prudent. Yes, I have heard this before."

Governor Kaga sighed. "It is more than that, Your Highness."

A familiar female voice called out Zen's name from afar. Zen turned around to see Kyta waiting at the end the brick walkway on the other end of the courtyard and gestured for him to join her.

"I must go, Governor." Zen bowed.

Kaga bent his body, keeping his eyes pointed downwards as he spoke. "Things are not what they seem, my lord." When he straightened his back, he looked Zen in the eyes. "Be very wary of those you trust most."

The governor pulled the hood over his head and did an abrupt about face before exiting the courtyard. Kaga's cryptic message disturbed him, but for now, he pushed it aside. The quest and Master Kyta awaited him.

Zen secured his backpack before hurrying to the old woman. The two of them strolled in silence together through the tranquil gardens. The cherry blossom trees were in full bloom, and the soothing breeze made it rain down twirling pink petals. They reached the end of the brick-laden road and found themselves at the gravel walkway.

The amulet's sudden heat under his shirt startled him. Against the cool wind, the stone brought welcomed warmth, but this was something more. It felt as if it moved. He stopped to lift it from under his coat, marveling at the soft bluish glow of the stone.

"Master?"

"Your stone is reacting to my presence." Kyta's walking staff continued to glow. "The amulet is also set to your personal vibration, as my staff is to mine. These are our tools, connecting us to the realm of the sacred. During your travels, use the amulet as a guide."

Zen took the pulsating stone in his hand. The chain tightened, and he feared it might break free from his grasp and float towards the old woman. "It will lead me to the Sky Blade?"

Kyta chuckled. "It will lead you to whatever your destiny is to be."

"What will guarantee Xia's allegiance once I find the Sky Blade?" Zen asked.

"There is no guarantee, Zenjiro. Much of Nihon might place its fate in the hands of science and technology, but Xia remains the spiritual epicenter of The East."

Kyta shot him a quizzical look. "Do you see yourself as the one to wield the Sky Blade?"

"Of course I do, Master," Zen answered.

"Good. Only one who is pure can own the mighty sword."

Zen scratched his head. "Pure? The ancient scrolls say that King Jiang was evil. Far from pure. Yet he used the power of the Sky Blade to maim and murder. Enslaving his own people."

"Pure does not necessarily mean righteous," Kyta said. "You must know yourself. Not one shred of doubt about who you are can exist in your heart. King Jiang became a tyrant, because he knew just how black his soul had become. If you are to use the Sky Blade, you must be sure of who you are."

Zen never saw himself as a great philosopher, but he knew himself well enough to know he was worthy of facing such a challenge. However, something about the far western empire intrigued him, and Zen asked, "The Iberian emperor is known to have been a magnificent soldier himself in his youth, and rumor has it that he has become deranged in his old age. Is this true?"

Kyta tightened her robe around her thin neck as the wind picked up. "Emperor Leon Garza was an honorable warrior in his prime. For the last two decades, he has allowed a religious order to influence his actions, forcing his new subjects to submit to his religion. His cruelty has surpassed even the most brutal of dictators. Whether or not the stories are true, it is clear that Emperor Leon wants to force his will upon all of the nations of the world."

Whether Zen found the Sky Blade or not, war with Iberia was inevitable. Yet that didn't bother him as much as Governor Kaga's parting words. He said a short prayer to his mother for strength of conviction.

"Let us go, Zenjiro. Your vessel leaves shortly."

A short distance away, he spotted Kyta's recumbent vehicle parked on the road. The cart was ancient, but somehow Kyta kept the machine running. It lay low, close to the ground. Sitting in the long seat felt like lying on a stiff bed. A cast iron boiler was bolted to the rear, connected to various components and moving parts. As they got closer to Kyta's transport, he watched a dragonfly land on the steering wheel. It remained motionless, oblivious to the world.

"If we hurry, we will be right on time," Kyta said.

They slid into the two seats. Kyta grunted as her stiff bones were forced to crouch and get into position. The old sorceress pushed a brass button on the dashboard and released a heavy lever next to the boiler. The machine spat a plume of smoke from its two exhaust pipes. Zen laughed. It was absurd for one so powerful and influential to be driving such an old jalopy. Kyta could have traveled by carriage complete with her own driver as the other nobles did. After watching his teacher slide the dark goggles over her eyes, he concluded Kyta would never allow herself to enjoy such luxuries.

"You always laugh at my cart," said Kyta as she adjusted various controls on the panel in front of her. With the goggles on, she looked like a crazy bug with mad white hair. "I built this with my own two hands."

The engine resuscitated from near death, forcing Kyta to have to raise her voice above the cacophony. "My own two hands...no enchantment involved whatsoever." She brushed the dragonfly off the steering wheel and watched it fly away in search of prey.

Zen strapped himself in. With an open cockpit, it was sure to be a cold ride against the harsh wind. He placed his large canvas pack on his lap and held onto it, bracing for the trip in the chilly air. Kyta pulled a rusty lever on her side and the boiler spat with a metallic burst. The tires spit gravel as the cart sped down the dirt road leading to the western harbor of Tsuo. They raced towards the ship that waited to take Zen far across the ocean.

FIVE

A MAMMOTH STEAMSHIP BUILT FOR carrying cargo dominated the small harbor. It had traveled from Xia and was now docked in Nihon to pick up passengers and giant crates of goods bound for Agrios. It was the largest ship Zen had ever seen.

Master Kyta's steam cart chugged up to the wharf. It shook and rumbled to a stop. Hideaki, surrounded by his royal guard, gave them a disapproving look. He waved his hand in the air to fan away the black steam puffing from the exhaust. Zen slid out of the seat to greet his father.

"Master Kyta, please allow me to supply you with a carriage. At the very least, a cart that will not explode upon giving it full steam." Hideaki shook his head at her homemade contraption.

"Tinkering is how I find peace," said Kyta as she removed her dark goggles. She leaned on her metal staff and straightened her body.

The area was nearly empty, as Zen's departure was kept a secret from the rest of the populace. The Sacred Journey was more than just a heroic mission. There was to be no fanfare, no celebration for Nihon's greatest hero. The surrounding silence made Zen even more nervous.

Hideaki looked pained as he put his arms around Zen. The guards shifted in agitation, most likely not accustomed to witnessing such a public show of affection among nobility.

"I wanted to send you out into the world to study all the different cultures," Hideaki said in a low voice. "I hoped that maybe Nihon would someday break out of isolation and share itself with the rest of mankind. You were to be my ambassador to the world." He glanced up at the cargo ship. "This is not exactly how I imagined sending you off."

Zen smiled to lessen his father's worry. "I speak fluent Standard, thanks to Master Kyta. And I have studied several international societies."

"There is a vast difference between reading about the world in a book and stepping out into it, Zenjiro." Hideaki's brows crinkled. "You will see many strange things, and you will meet all kinds of unscrupulous people. They will know you are out of place. You will find yourself faced with many temptations we do not have here in Nihon. Stay focused on your Sacred Quest."

"I will, Father."

One of the guards handed Zen his newly repaired sword. He slid it into his scabbard and tied the cord to his leather belt. Zen lifted his pack and slipped each arm through the pair of worn straps.

"I am ready."

Kyta pointed towards the ship. "This galleon will take fourteen days to reach Agrios. From there, where you go is up to you. Remember to pay attention to any signs the spirits should bestow upon you. Listen to your inner voice."

She laid a frail hand on Zen's face. "Agrios is an untamed land filled with violent nomads and tribes. The Iberian Empire has a presence in this country, but their authority is disorganized and scattered."

Hideaki added, "Remember, keep your nobility a secret. We have assured your safe passage with the captain of this frigate directly. Nevertheless, there are many untrustworthy individuals on board this ship. Pirates and thieves."

"I understand," Zen replied. He did look younger than his twenty years, and crooks would surmise that he was an easy target. "I will be careful."

Zen gave everyone one final look before turning and making his way onto the bridge that lead to the top deck with the other passengers and crew. The giant smokestacks chugged rhythmically. Zen followed the steep walkway until he hopped onto the ship's wooden deck.

At first glance, he noticed that most of the crew looked to be from neighboring Xia. Their dark, golden skin looked worn from the many days under the sun. All of them shaved the front of their heads, leaving the rest braided into a long tail.

After closer inspection, several other foreigners scrambled all over the deck and carried out their seafaring duties. Zen leaned against the railing and allowed his pack to fall to the floor. He spotted Master Kyta and his father looking up at him from the pier. The galleon's six smokestacks burst into action with black steam. The whistle blew, signaling the beginning of a voyage for Zen to the other side of the world.

AFTER CHECKING IN WITH THE ship's purser, Zen went to find his assigned room. The tiny cabin housed only a cot, table, and an old gas lamp. The quarters below the upper deck were cramped; the aging walls made poor sound insulation. It was difficult to sleep with the constant din of heavy boots and drunken men on all sides. He was grateful, however, for the privacy, since most of the passengers and crew were assigned larger rooms but bunked with complete strangers.

His door rattled as someone lost his balance in the narrow alley outside. Zen reached for his sword under the cot, but realized it was just a drunken fool stumbling past his door. He took a deep breath and tried to lull himself to sleep.

The gentle rocking of the ship was comforting, and Zen nodded off. That all came to an end when the door blew open. A menacing figure stood in the threshold. Zen sprung to his feet, blade already in his hands.

"You don't get a private cabin, boy!" The figure stepped forward, a lantern in one hand and a revolver in the other.

Others stood behind him, but they were dwarfs compared to this man. "I want your room and whatever else you might have that's valuable."

He had dirty, wavy hair pulled into a loose tail, and his bearded face was pockmarked with scars and divots. The man appeared fierce, but his legs wobbled under his own weight. He looked drunk.

Zen held his sword steady and kept his eyes on the muzzle of the ogre's pistol. "Go, before you regret this," he said to the pirate in a quiet and stern voice. "Go back to your whiskey."

The others in the alley laughed. One of them fell over and

hit the floor with a drunken thud. The giant cocked the hammer of his revolver still aimed at Zen's chest.

"Do you know who I am, boy? I am Zapitoni, wanted in ten countries all across the Iberian Territories. I am practically royalty. Royalty does not bunk with stinky rats. Royalty gets the luxury of a private room. Now leave your things, including that pretty sword of yours, and I'll spare your life."

Zapitoni might have been drunk, but he held his gun firmly. Zen didn't have the time, nor was he in the right state of mind, to reach the calm composure the power of *Ishen* required.

His heart thundered out of his chest while his arm muscles twitched under his skin. He heard the sound of squeaking metal and knew the brute was about to pull the trigger.

Zen lashed out, his blade a blazing arc reflecting the lantern's flickering light. The ear-piercing *boom* of the pistol rang out and silenced the drunkards peeking in from the doorway. Zapitoni fell to his knees. He screamed and cradled his right arm against his chest. Still clutching his pistol, his separated right hand lay on the floor.

When it became obvious the others weren't going to jump into the fight, Zen raised his sword as high as he could under the low ceiling. He held it above Zapitoni's head. The pirate's mates crowded the doorway, stunned and silent. Zapitoni writhed in agony on the floor while swearing in an ancient tongue. The lantern continued to throw light into the room, and Zen noticed the man's once beige shirt was now soaked with scarlet.

"Spare me, boy," Zapitoni whimpered between sobs. "I will pay you whatever you ask. Please have mercy."

"I will, as long as you promise that neither you nor your

friends will bother me for the duration of this voyage." Zen lowered his blade. "Swear to me."

Zapitoni looked to be on the verge of passing out. "I swear. Right boys?" The others grunted in agreement. "Can I please get my hand back?" he mumbled.

Zen stepped back, but kept his blade aloft. "Yes."

They lifted their leader by his arms and led him out of the room. A short stocky fellow entered the cabin, pausing before taking another step. Zen nodded, and the man grabbed Zapitoni's severed hand and scurried away into the darkness. Even when the pirate shut the door behind him, Zen heard them dragging Zapitoni's heavy body down the alley. Zen thought of his father's warning. Agrios was a wild country, not beholden to any laws. Maybe the only thing these savages understood was strength and power. He expected to run into more like Zapitoni in the near future. Despite their promise to leave him alone, these men had no honor.

He flicked his blade and slid his sword back into its scabbard underneath his cot. Zen lay on his back and took deep breaths before deciding to remove his revolver from his bag. He laid the hard steel on his chest. The pirates left the lantern in his cabin, and he watched the dying and dancing flames until he was finally on the verge of sleep.

Before fully surrendering to the world of dreams, he prayed to his mother's spirit. When he finished, he heard her voice in his mind.

You must save the machine boy.

Her dying words had haunted Zen for seven years. Before he could speculate yet again on what she meant, he allowed the gentle lolling of the sea to calm his muscles. Zen thought of his mother's face, trying to recall every detail. It was difficult, and it disturbed him that he wasn't able to remember what she looked like. Zen regretted not bringing a photograph of her.

He drifted again, and in minutes the veil of sleep swept over his weary body.

FOLLOWING THE BECKONING AROMA OF brewed coffee, Zen found the mess deck one floor above his cabin. Only a handful of travelers and sailors sat at the long rectangular tables when he entered. Tacked to a tall counter on the far end of the deck was a sign written in Standard, declaring the cost to eat two meals a day for the voyage was twenty ibers.

Zen's shoulders sagged. How could he aspire to be the greatest hero of Nihon if he couldn't even wrangle up a single breakfast? He turned to leave the mess deck and try his luck topside.

When he turned, he found Zapitoni and his friends blocking the only exit.

"Leaving so soon?" Zapitoni went to stroke his beard, but he frowned when he found no hand at the end of his bandaged arm.

"You could have killed me last night. Luckily, one of my men is an excellent surgeon" He raised his handless arm again as if to remind Zen of their encounter. "If I had been you, I would not have been so merciful."

Zen spotted one of Zapitoni's men draw a long knife from his belt. This pirate was short but wiry, and his eyes were full of hate.

"As I recall, I made you a promise. One I intend to keep." Zapitoni turned to his man with the blade. "Go pay for this young man's meals for the duration of our journey to Agrios." He bent his tall frame towards Zen. "What is your name?"

"Zen."

Zapitoni shooed his associate away. The pirate sheathed his knife and walked past Zen, going straight to the counter as instructed. Zapitoni's followers seemed to relax and filed into the mess deck. Zen, however, kept his right hand on his holstered revolver.

"Will you join me for breakfast?" Zapitoni asked.

Zen's stomach answered him with a stretched out growl.

THE RICH BLACK COFFEE SOOTHED Zen's belly, which was also full of two sea biscuits and several strips of dried beef. Zapitoni and his men ate slowly. They used their mouths more for talking than for eating. Zen caught bits and pieces of one man's story of having survived a horrible shipwreck, and after hearing a similar tale coming from all around the table, Zen assumed Zapitoni and his men were pirates without a ship. That would explain why they were on board a cargo galleon.

Zapitoni, despite his appearance and lacking his dominant hand, proved to be a hospitable host, and he engaged with small talk while they ate their meals.

"Tell me, Zen. Why are you going to Agrios?" Zapitoni asked as he took a final swig of coffee from his tin cup. "That's quite far from home."

Zen thought about his answer for a moment, careful to give

a proper reply without revealing his nobility. "I am searching for something."

"Aren't we all?" Zapitoni slammed his cup on the table. "I'm looking for a new ship. Hit a terrible typhoon off of the southeastern coast of Xia. Lost half of my crew."

The pirates ceased their chatter. Their banter ended with Zapitoni mentioning their recent tragedy. Several bowed their heads in reverence to their fallen comrades, and Zen felt surprised at the show of honor among thieves.

"I seek the Sky Blade," Zen said, cutting through the silence.

Zapitoni cleared his throat. "The Sky Blade?"

Zen felt the bewildered stares from the pirates.

One of them let out a bellowing laugh, and the others followed. Zapitoni took a few slaps to his back from his men, but he refrained from joining in the wild guffaws of his crew. Zen felt his face burning with white-hot rage, but he kept his composure. These were not men mocking him. They were animals. The taunts from such vermin were beneath him, and it wasn't worth his time to kill them for their insolence.

"Forgive my men," Zapitoni said. With an irritated look on his bearded face, he motioned for his crew to leave the mess deck.

The pirates were still snickering when they got up from the table and exited. Zen looked down at his empty plate and cup, not willing to look up at Zapitoni who remained seated across from him.

"I admire your quest," Zapitoni finally said. "If you do find the real Sky Blade, you stand to make quite a bit of money. Now that's a treasure worth finding, right?"

Zen's insides felt twisted, and he had the urge to rush back to his room to be by himself. "Yes."

Zapitoni stood up and straightened his soiled white shirt. "When I was young, I too hunted for lost relics. Piracy is the family business, but I thought I could find my own way. Starvation put an end to my rebellion. I decided to find a steadier stream of income, and I haven't looked back since."

Only shame and doubt filled Zen's heart, and the cold medallion against his chest mocked him in his despair. To be insulted by criminals should not have hurt him, but it did. Zen's faith had been shaken too easily.

"If the treasure hunting doesn't pan out, I think you'd make a wonderful pirate," Zapitoni said. "I'd hire you in a heartbeat. Think about it."

Zen nodded and watched Zapitoni walk away.

SIX

CROSSING THE OCEAN IN FOURTEEN days on board the massive steam galleon left Zen with too much time to think. He tried meditation to clear his mind, but dark thoughts continued to bombard him. Zen had always considered himself a devout person, but he hoped he hadn't left his faith in Nihon.

He ate all of his meals with Zapitoni and his crew, and he found the pirate captain's stories of adventure and thievery exciting. At the very least, it helped Zen pass the time.

After the galleon reached Agrios' most western port, Zapitoni said farewell with a bow and led his crew off the ship. Zen lingered on board for a long while, waiting until the last minute to finally disembark the vessel. Stepping into this new world intensified his festering uncertainty.

Zen was overwhelmed by the bustle of Porticus City. People from a variety of nations wore their native wardrobes, and they filled the crowded market streets. There was an obscene mixture of smells from unknown food, burning coal, and the salty air from the nearby ocean filling the marketplace. The vendors and wandering salespeople greeted Zen with wide eyes and exaggerated amity. Most sold their goods on large carts and called out to passersby to view their wares. Some offered frivolous merchandise like jewelry or artwork. Others peddled more practical items like guns and boots. Zen needed none of these.

What he needed was a sign, direction from divinity. This was a strange land, and not only did Zen feel alone in the midst of thousands of strangers, but he was lost. The solid footing of the earth beneath his boots made him uneasy. During his voyage, Zen's body had become accustomed to the constant turbulence of the violent seas.

He stood in the center of a sea of strangers and tried to decide which direction to travel and what to look for. Zen noticed wrinkled faces eying him. He must have looked as alien to them as they did to him. This was not the time to panic. This was the time to quiet the mind and be open to all possibilities. He grasped the hilt of his sword for comfort. Zen commanded his body to relax and decided to just let things happen, as Master Kyta would have instructed.

THE SUCKERS WEREN'T BITING. AT least that's what Enapay told himself as he watched small groups of fresh faces roam past him and his makeshift ring. Yesterday was profitable, taking in over one thousand ibers. Even though he'd only been back in Porticus City less than a whole season, he knew this business was feast or famine. Today famine reared its bony, starving head.

Enapay studied how the shoppers dressed or moved. There was an art to finding his next victim. The best were the kind that looked like they had money on them, but all of the saps around him looked poor. Enapay made it a practice to scrutinize every potential rube's eyes. If a man walking by possessed a combination of desperation and arrogance, they were prime for the picking. Something had better turn up soon, or he'd have to do something drastic. Maybe it was time to go home after all these years. His people would make sure he had hot meals and a place to stay. To hell with pride.

When a delicate adolescent turned the corner, Enapay knew he had found the perfect target. The foreigner wore plain clothes, but his black hair was folded up into a ball on top of his head. The young man looked like he had made a wrong turn and expected someone to give him directions.

The hint of confusion behind the stranger's narrow angled eyes gave his arrogance away, as if the boy believed he was above everyone else. His long wool coat looked expensive, and it was more than enough to convince Enapay to make his move.

As the foreigner approached, Enapay almost thought twice about luring him to his ring, as if the boy seemed even smaller up close than he did from afar. However, today was not the day to have a conscience.

"You look strong." Enapay pulled as wide of a smile as he could manage.

The foreigner's mouth drew open, and Enapay wondered if the boy could even speak Standard. That would make doing business difficult.

"Would you like to challenge my friend to a stick fight? I'm paying three-to-one." Enapay put a hand on the boy's shoulder and give it a warm pat. "Where are you going to find odds like that? A minimum wager of one hundred ibers is all it takes."

Enapay pointed to the center of the ring where his fellow tribesman Istas stood. The boy turned and glanced at Enapay's fighter. Istas was not just lean, but bordered on malnutrition. The man ate, but he couldn't keep the fat on his long stick-like frame.

Two other friends, Toksu and Sike stood behind Istas. They massaged his skin and bones as they whispered words of insincere encouragement into his big ears. Usually, prospects laughed out loud when presented with their potential opponent, but this boy looked bored.

"What's wrong?" Enapay asked. He lifted his goggles up to make eye contact. "Do you speak Standard? Maybe you speak Ancient? You look like you're from the old Sun Nation. Xian? Nihonese? I can't help you if you only speak Origin."

"Ibers?" the boy asked, his pale smooth face still unmoving.

This was a good sign. Now he was talking money.

"You must be fresh off the boat, huh?" Enapay put his arm around him and pivoted both of them towards the ring. "Ibers ...Iberian currency. All the markets here take it. Sure, few will take *mergos*, but that's nearly worthless now. Everybody takes Iberian money along with the always dependable gold and silver. The barter system is also alive and well in this country."

Right on cue, Istas began doing his dance. It looked ridiculous, and it took effort for Enapay to keep from laughing. His friend looked like an old rag doll being jerked about. Istas played his part perfectly, his sun-tanned face glaring, begging the boy to take him on.

"I do not have any ibers," the adolescent said, his eyes following Istas' dance around the ring.

Sike chuckled and cried, "Enapay, this kid is useless without any cash."

Enapay snapped his fingers at him, furious at his friend for using his real name. Sometimes, he wished he worked alone. He understood, however, that his scheme wouldn't work without the help of his old friends.

Something underneath the foreigner's coat caught his eye, and Enapay's mind worked fast. "What's your name, friend?"

"Zenjiro. You can call me Zen."

Enapay recognized that Zen carried an antique sword under his coat. "Zen, sorry to hear that you've fallen on tough times. Maybe you have something of value you can wager?"

Zen's eyes widened, following Enapay's gaze down to the sword. "This is a family treasure, handed down from my ancestors." He pulled back his coat, revealing the gorgeous weapon. "It is far more valuable than your wager."

The boy was not an idiot. Enapay eyed the silk-wrapped handle and ornate hardwood scabbard. He also caught sight of the boy's hands. His fingers were thick, the palms wide like those of a bear. They didn't fit with the rest of Zen's body. Either Zen had performed grueling, back-breaking labor, or the boy was born with hands that looked as tough as stone. Enapay hesitated, as they were the hands of someone to be feared. But the boy's porcelain face and dainty features were too good to resist. Enapay turned his attention back to the sword.

"I won't argue with you there," Enapay remarked. "That thing looks ancient and expensive."

Istas twirled a fighting stick and struck his own face. Enapay wondered if Istas was playing it up, or if his partner was honestly being his foolish self. He gave a slight shake of his head to tell his tribesman to tone down the idiocy, if that was possible.

"I'll tell you what, you ante up that sword of yours, and if you defeat my champion, I'll pay you ten to one of the original one hundred iber wager."

Istas continued with his clumsy gyrations, and the fighting stick slipped from his long fingers and pounded his exposed big toe. The man shrieked and threw his body onto the floor before grabbing his foot. Enapay was sure his man was no longer acting.

"What do you say?" Enapay asked, now playing to the growing audience around them.

"I agree." Zen removed his gear. He handed everything to an elderly man in the corner. "I trust you will keep my belongings safe?"

The geezer nodded and clutched the large rucksack and other belongings Zen had given him. He attempted to lift it all, but finding it heavy, he dragged it to the wooden benches in the far corner to watch the contest.

The spectators applauded. Several more bystanders stopped in front of the ring, eager to watch a new victim get pummeled. Enapay stepped away after handing Zen another rattan stick before he signaled his men to take their places.

Istas jumped off the canvas platform. Sike followed, which left Toksu alone at the rear of the rectangular elevated platform serving as the fighting arena. The true champion tightened his grip on his weapon and flexed his hardened tattoo-covered arms.

Toksu easily stood nearly seven feet tall. The beast wore a ragged vest which failed to hide the rippling muscles underneath. He held a long worn out stick which he rhythmically tapped on his right hip, hungry for action.

Enapay noticed that Toksu had shaved his head today, leaving a dark strip of coarse hair running down the center. Angry jagged scars decorated his chiseled face. Enapay turned to Zen, not having to guess what the boy must be thinking.

"You tricked me," said Zen, still holding onto his stick. "I thought I was fighting the other man."

Istas shrugged his shoulders and pointed to his foot. "I'm injured."

Zen crossed his arms while the audience grew restless. He turned to the old man holding his belongings, and a dark cloud of doubt blew over his face. Like all the other suckers, Zen walked into the ring anyway. Arrogance was good for business, and most men wouldn't dare walk out now. Even this delicate flower of a boy had some pride.

Zen twirled the stick with the grace of a warrior. It was as if the boy was gauging his weapon's weight and balance. Enapay felt a splinter of apprehension as he stared at the youngster's large and worn hands. But the mere image of this small boy in the ring with Toksu looked almost ridiculous. He felt pity for Zen and the world of pain he was about to enter. Zen's sword could be sold for at last two thousand ibers, and this payoff would more than make up for the day's lack of business.

Toksu's shoulders swayed to the rhythm of an unheard drum beat. It seemed like the entire plaza was watching, and Enapay stood in the center of the ring, wallowing in the crowd's clapping and screaming.

"Any and all attacks and strikes are allowed," he shouted. "The fighter that either knocks out or kills the other is the winner." Enapay pointed to his revolver holstered on his hip. "If you beg for mercy like a coward, I might kill you myself."

This made the blood-thirsty audience howl with laughter.

"Let the contest begin!" Enapay left the center of the stage and took his position next to Sike and Istas.

Zen circled and kept his stick in a defensive position out in front of him. No matter what skill the boy had with the weapon, this was sure to be a swift beating. Maybe there would be enough time to concoct one more bout before dusk. Enapay wondered when the last cargo boat was to arrive and bring him more gullible foreigners.

Toksu worked himself into a silent frenzy; his legs coiled like thick pythons ready to unleash. He and Enapay grew up together, and Toksu was always a god-like specimen built for war. When Enapay had recently returned to Agrios' western coast from his ten year absence, Sike and Istas had not changed much. Toksu, however, looked even scarier now than he did as an adolescent.

All of this was Enapay's idea, and despite his friends' initial reluctance, the amount of money they were making was too good to walk away from. His tribe's Elders forbade this kind of behavior, but he left those laws behind long ago.

Enapay expected to see Zen quivering by this point, but the boy looked unwavering. In fact, his foreign eyes tightened into focus and cold determination. The boyish and placid demeanor vanished, replaced by something else...something that scared Enapay. He looked menacing and strong. Maybe the child was delusional. Toksu would soon remedy that.

"Smash him!" a spectator shouted. "Smash the kid's face

in!"

Toksu lunged forward and swung his stick in a downward arc. Zen glided sideways and evaded the blow. The champion attacked three more times, and Zen parried the swings with his own stick.

Enapay swore he saw the boy's thin lips curl into a wicked smile. He wished he was in the ring to smack that cocky smirk off this boy's face.

Toksu growled and surged again, swinging his weapon rapidly. Without effort, Zen dodged and blocked every strike. Enapay shared Toksu's fury. Not only did the boy avoid punishment, but he seemed to be toying with the giant.

The possibility of defeat crept into his mind, and Enapay couldn't believe what he was watching. Toksu had always annihilated his opponents by now. He noticed Toksu's labored breathing when his fighter backed away from their challenger.

Enapay clapped his hands to get Toksu's attention. "You're wasting all your energy! I told you not to eat so much for breakfast."

Toksu struggled to suck in air. Zen lowered his stance, his stick a blur as he whirled it in his right hand. The champion squared his shoulders, and with another wild scream, he barreled forward. He slashed his stick at Zen's head and missed by inches. The momentum of the errant swing threw Toksu off balance for only a fraction of a second.

Zen moved in, and by the look in Toksu's eyes, the giant was not prepared for the boy's speed. He attacked the monstrous warrior's hands first. Toksu snarled, his fingers bloodied and unable to hold onto his weapon. The stick slipped from the brute's grip and fell to the canvas floor with a hollow *thunk*.

Zen followed up with another furious attack, striking Toksu several times in the head and chest in a flurry of blows. He moved with such speed that Enapay felt his mouth open in complete disbelief. He was about to lose his first bet in nearly ninety days. A whole season of victories, wiped away by the fury of a boy.

One final blow connected near Toksu's temple; the strike made a hollow thud against his tribesman's head. Toksu was still for a moment before crashing to the ground. The crowd quieted until the old man still minding Zen's belongings cried, "The boy wins!"

Their cheers surrounded Zen, but the boy did something peculiar. Instead of basking in the glory, he knelt down where Toksu lay in pain and clutched the ex-champion's muscular shoulder. Zen pulled him back up to his feet. Toksu's legs trembled as if they could give way at any moment, so Zen shifted the weight onto his own small frame.

Enapay motioned to Sike and Istas, who broke through the crowd to help drag the injured Toksu into a nearby tent. The audience kept applauding, and Enapay's own legs felt weak as he dragged his feet towards Zen.

"I've never seen anything like that," was all Enapay mustered.

Several members of the group of spectators stepped into the ring to give Zen a hearty pat on the back before returning to the commotion of the marketplace. Zen retrieved his things from the old man and handed Enapay the stick. He strapped on his belt and slung his canvas pack onto his back.

Without thinking, Enapay inspected the stick as if expecting it to show signs of enchantment. Any reasonable explanation for what he had witnessed just felt impossible. Any trace of ferocity on Zen's face melted away, and he looked harmless again. Enapay second guessed his faculties, and he wondered just what the hell he had witnessed. That was when the full gravity of his defeat sank in. Enapay fought the waves of nausea gurgling from his stomach. He didn't have the money to pay the boy.

"You agreed to pay me ten to one of the original wager if I defeated your champion. One thousand ibers."

"I don't have it here." Enapay's shoulders slumped. "It's not on me."

There was movement, and Sike came up from behind Zen. Enapay noticed Zen's right hand go to his holstered pistol. He had already underestimated the boy once, so he went with his instincts and shooed Sike away with a click of his tongue. Sike scurried back into their tent.

"Two things, Zen. First, I had no idea I was going to be waging a ten-to-one payout. Secondly, my friend has never lost. How could I have known that Toksu would have been crushed by someone by the likes of...you?"

"You have to be willing to lose if you are going to gamble," Zen said. He released his grip from his gun. "I am young, but hardly a child. I do expect payment. I would have honored our wager had I been defeated."

A storm of stupid ideas filled Enapay's head. He decided to pick the least stupid of them all. "I am Enapay of the Nabeho, Tribe of the West, and I can tell you are a man of honor. I am too most of the time, and I always pay my debts."

Zen gave him a look of doubt. No, this boy was not an idiot. He was smarter than all of the previous victims Enapay had swindled. The boy won, and Enapay hated losing.

"My money is back at my village," he continued. "What if I

take you there as my guest? The Nabeho will feed you well, give you a place to stay overnight, and you'll end up one thousand ibers richer."

Zen put his hand to his chin as if he considered the invitation.

"It is an honor to be a guest of the Nabeho. Not many outsiders ever receive such an offer." Enapay decided to appeal to the boy's arrogance once more. "Besides, I must show everyone the young warrior who soundly defeated the great Toksu in stick-war. Otherwise, no one would believe me."

"I am hungry." Zen rubbed his stomach. "I accept."

Enapay waved to Sike, whose head peered from the tent, before leading the two of them away from the marketplace and finding the narrow dirt road.

Enapay shook his head as they walked. "How do you move so fast? Toksu has never missed until today. You seemed to avoid his attack with such ease. You moved faster than I've ever seen anyone move."

"My people call it *Ishen*. In Standard language, it means *ferocity with intent*. I am able to alter my body's energy, focusing it," replied Zen.

Enapay stifled a laugh. "Alter and focus your body's energy? Now that sounds like something one of my Elders might talk about."

"*Ishen* is rare, even among the greatest warriors. My master said I inherently possessed the ability since birth, but my training has allowed me to control it and conjure it at will. Strength without effort."

"Sounds mystical," Enapay said, hoping his skepticism wasn't too obvious.

The dirt road led to a steep hill, and he heard Zen's stomach growl. Enapay still wasn't sure what he was going to do with the boy once they reached the village. He started to regret inviting him. Ten years had passed since he left the Nabeho, but his uncle did owe him six hundred ibers. He could shoot Zen in the back, but that wasn't Enapay's style.

"How far is your village?" Zen asked.

Enapay stopped mid-stride, his thoughts broken by the boy's inquiry. "It's about a hundred miles east of here."

"What?" Zen stopped. "That will take us almost three days." His hand grasped the grip of his sword.

"Relax!" Enapay held up his hands. "We will get there in under two hours."

"How is that possible?"

Enapay chuckled. "We're not going by foot."

He continued walking up the steep incline of earth and heard Zen's light footsteps behind him. When they reached the flat summit, Enapay was certain he caught Zen gasp.

Sitting in the middle of a wheat field was his airship.

Enapay pointed to his flying machine. "We're going by air."

SEVEN

STARING AT THE AIR TRANSPORT, Zen contemplated turning away and forgetting about his winnings. He hated flying. It had been seven years since he last took to the air. The day of his mother's death.

Nevertheless, Zen couldn't take his eyes away from the exotic craft. Steam rose from the exhaust at the rear of the ship. The wooden hull resembled the body of a large flotilla boat from back home, but everything else about its construction was strange and beautiful.

Two long metallic cylinders with propellers were connected to the hull by a spider's web of steel cables. The machine looked like a fire-breathing dragon made of metal. When he followed Enapay through a small swinging door onto the deck, Zen immediately noticed the brass controls up on the helm, reflecting what little sunlight remained.

Under his shirt, Zen felt his stone amulet pulse with heat. He placed his hand over the warmth, and he said a prayer to the spirits for their continued guidance.

Enapay, with his dark goggles covering his eyes, walked up the short stairway and worked the many levers and controls at the helm. The propellers groaned as they turned downwards and spun rapidly. Zen felt a creaking shift in the normal tilt of the wooden floor as the airship rose. The hull rattled, and the familiar agonizing sensation of leaving the earth crept into his core.

The propellers gathered strength, and when Enapay turned a smaller wheel built into the side of the wooden helm, the ship gently floated high up above the trees. Enapay's movements were automatic, and Zen felt a little more at ease from seeing the pilot's expertise. The propellers swiveled again, returning to their places at the front of the metal cylinders he assumed housed the gas ballonets. Enapay pushed a tall lever forward, and the airship went from hovering to gliding.

Zen held onto the metal railing and watched as the sun began its fall towards the horizon. He peeked over the hull's edge, surveying the unfamiliar landscape. Red mountains and miles of desert with sparse vegetation dominated the land. He felt the pilot's stare on his back, and his mistrust of the man returned. Zen couldn't bring himself to trust someone who wore a permanent smile, so he kept his right hand on the grip of his pistol.

"I assume you're a long way from home."

Enapay's voice cut through the constant humming of the propellers, and it made Zen jump.

"Where are you from?" Enapay asked.

Zen turned away from the railing to face him. "Nihon."

"What brings you here to Agrios?"

Several explanations almost escaped Zen's mouth, but he

reminded himself once again to keep his nobility a secret. It felt unnatural pretending to be someone else, and in his hesitation, he failed to find the right words. He had made the mistake of replying with the truth before, and it had drawn laughter from Zapitoni's pirates. Zen was reluctant to be the butt of jokes again.

"You must be looking for someone. Or something," Enapay added.

Zen tipped his head, just enough to let Enapay know he was correct.

"I'm well-traveled. Perhaps I can point you in the right direction. I've flown from one coast to the other, and I can navigate all the spaces in between." Enapay's tone conveyed sincerity laced with curiosity. "What are you looking for?"

"A sword."

It was almost a whisper, and Zen couldn't believe he actually said it. He wanted to take it back the moment his words escaped his lips.

"A sword?" Enapay scrunched his lips. "You're a treasure hunter. How magnificent. Now you're talking my language. What kind of sword?"

Zen took a long time in answering. There was no turning back now. "A special sword."

He fiddled with the strap pressed against his chest. The importance of his quest was a source of pride and embarrassment. The contradiction made no sense to him, and he kicked the wooden hull in disgust. Doubt had been his only companion during the long voyage across the Pacifica Ocean, and now it stalked him to Agrios.

"This is an untamed land, home to fleeing criminals, exiles, and eager pioneers from all over the world. If you're looking for a long lost sword, you've come to the right place."

Zen spun around and caught Enapay still showcasing his nonchalant grin. He waited for the pilot's ridicule to begin, and he already felt hot resentment burning his veins.

Enapay said, "Please, tell me more. I would like to be of help."

The pilot's response bewildered Zen, and he wondered if maybe he judged Enapay too harshly. Or perhaps the native feigned compassion in the hopes of drawing more information out of him. He went up the steps that led to the elevated helm. Zen sighed and willingly took the bait.

"My people believe Iberia's invasion of Xia is inevitable. If Xia falls, Nihon will be next. Xia is already weakened by a civil war. The sword will help unite them, so we can form a formidable alliance against Iberia."

"A treasure hunter with a purpose, searching for a special sword?" Enapay's right eyebrow arched.

"The Sky Blade," replied Zen. It felt foolish saying it aloud, but he continued anyway. "It is an object of high reverence to the Xian people. The one to possess it is the preordained ruler of Xia. The weapon is known to be enchanted with otherworldly powers."

Once again, he waited for Enapay to jeer at him. However, it never happened. This gave Zen enough courage to continue.

"With it, we can stop the civil war and unify the country. Together, with all of the powers of the Sun Nation as allies, we will have a chance against Iberian aggression."

Speaking of it made him feel naked. Zen regretted even answering. He turned away and looked back down at the thinning trees for answers. His lack of faith made him unworthy to find the mythical sword, even if it did exist.

"We have a similar story told by the Elders of our tribe," said Enapay. "In our version, the weapon is a golden spear."

Enapay's words offered no solace. In fact, it trivialized his quest. How many civilizations spoke of similar legends and myths? Maybe the Sky Blade was nothing but a bedtime story. He was so far away from Nihon, and returning home empty-handed was inconceivable. Zen would rather die than face such humiliation.

"The Iberian Empire is a growing threat here as well," Enapay said. "They've even managed to establish several metropolitan settlements along the Eastern Seaboard. The Wild Land tribes settled their differences in order to repel the Iberians."

The wind grew cooler, but it pushed the airship even faster towards its destination. Zen shivered. He was thankful Enapay had not belittled what he was sure sounded like a fairy tale, and Zen decided to change the subject.

"This is a remarkable craft. We have nothing like this at home. We use balloons for island hopping and observation, but nothing that can travel this fast."

Enapay pointed to the black towering machine sitting in the stern of the ship. The iron monster let out a constant growl. "The key is not the boiler, nor the advanced condenser I built with my own hands. The secret is the coal."

He pulled a small lever that seemed to lock the steering mechanism in place and walked over to a large wooden chest on the floor. From the way Enapay opened it, Zen guessed the contents were fragile. Inside was a mound of black coal, but upon closer inspection, the coal was infused with blue iridescent flecks. It illuminated the entire chest, and when Enapay grabbed a chunk with his hands, it seemed to glow.

"It's Iberian coal." Enapay held the rock as if it were a delicate flower. "They call it carbsidian."

Zen took the sample rock from him and noticed its warmth. "What exactly is it?"

"I worked for a great scientist and engineer on the Eastern Coast, right in the middle of the Iberian colony. When my tenure was over, I brought some of his new technology with me. The Iberian vehicles in the east travel at great speeds, yet need less combustible fuel. The secret is their carbsidian. I took two crates of it."

"You stole them?" Zen asked, speaking before he was able to choose his words with more care.

"Practically. I challenged an Iberian captain to a stick-war with Toksu. I wagered my airship, the captain wagered his stock of carbsidian. Toksu thrashed him."

Enapay laughed, and Zen couldn't help but follow.

"The problem was creating suitable components and mechanisms to burn the carbsidian correctly. The stuff creates such massive pressure in the boiler. Standard casing wouldn't work. My first dozen experiments didn't end well. I finally got it right."

Zen appreciated Enapay's talents, and the airship was most certainly a marvel. This was the kind of technology Nihon could use in a war with Iberia. Zen was not in the least bit mechanically inclined, and he admired the skill necessary to build such a machine.

"Carbsidian allows my ship to be the fastest and the most efficient flying machine in the world. Even faster than an Iberian Nao class warship." Enapay took the piece of blue coal from Zen. "A lot goes a long way. That one chest will last me two years at least."

"This carbsidian is mined in Iberia?" Zen asked. His amulet's heat grew, and its intensity caught him off guard.

"Not necessarily. They infuse standard coal with a blue rock called azullium. They re-manufacture it, and it's a process that must be complicated and expensive. I hear azullium is found throughout the Iberian Peninsula and is being mined along the eastern coast of Agrios. They say the blue rock might also be hidden under the mountains of Western Xia. Before I run out, I'll have to go back and sucker somebody else to give me their carbsidian."

With deliberate hands, Enapay placed the rock back into his trunk and closed the lid. "Makes you wonder what else those Iberians are working on, right?"

Zen nodded. "That is why I am here. I watched pictogram footage in which an Iberian soldier climbed into a massive suit of armor and suddenly gained the strength of a hundred men. They have created rapid firing guns that can cut down troops in mere seconds."

There was an uneasy shift in Enapay's eyes, and Zen felt the rush of blood fill his face.

"You do not believe me?" Zen asked in a low voice.

"Actually I do," Enapay began. "But..."

"You think I am an ignorant child, chasing after a dream." Zen wrapped his coat tighter around his body while he kept his eyes staring out into the distance. It was foolish to think Enapay or anyone else might believe him. "I can tell that you think I am a buffoon."

Enapay put a hand up in defense. "No, you're not a buffoon. Misguided maybe."

"It seems I keep running into faithless men like yourself," said Zen. "I have no choice but to believe. Maybe I am a buffoon after all."

Enapay looked as if he was going to speak, but he tightened his lips.

"I was taught to believe in Fate." Zen stood up, holding on-to a rope for balance. "That things reveal themselves in due time."

For a moment, Zen wondered if he was trying to talk himself into pushing aside his doubts. When his amulet pulsated against his flesh, he struggled to grasp the new found strength of his conviction and virtue.

Enapay shook his index finger. "Fate is when we construct meaning and order where there is chaos."

Zen couldn't resist any longer, and he pulled his glowing blue medallion from underneath his coat. He held it out while still around his neck. He watched Enapay's eyes grow wide as the amulet released its blue light in time with the rhythmic humming of the airship's engine.

"This is a special stone, enchanted by my master to assist me on my quest. It has been glowing like this ever since I have been in your airship." He held onto the stone, as if he was holding his resolve in his own hand. "It is a sign."

Enapay stepped forward and examined the necklace. "It looks similar to the shards of azullium fused with the Iberian carbsidian I have. Maybe your stone is reacting to it."

Without saying a word, Zen tucked his amulet back under his shirt. There was no use in trying to convince Enapay of the validity of his quest. More importantly, Zen still needed to convince himself. He wanted to change the subject again. Zen looked at Enapay's steering wheel in contemplation.

That was when he saw it. Zen rushed towards the helm. He couldn't take his eyes off of the intricate design etched into the wood of the steering wheel.

"What are you doing?" Enapay asked finally.

Zen stepped away. The veil of doubt and fear evaporated from his mind. "The carvings on your helm. I did not fully notice them until now."

Enapay's smile returned. "You like it? I hired a craftsman to carve this design for me to commemorate the dragonfly. I had him carve them into the wood, around the entire rim of the wheel."

"Why dragonflies?" Zen's heart hammered against his ribcage.

"My airship reminded me of a dragonfly. The propellers also make the same papery fluttering sound. You're on board the *Dragonfly*."

Zen hadn't moved. Surely he could make Enapay understand now. Without a word, he hurried to his backpack. He removed the rigid armor and held it up for Enapay to see. "This is my *nerigawa*."

Enapay shrugged as if he was lost. "That's your Origin word for chest armor, right?"

"The Kanze Clan symbol." He pointed to the center of the red breast piece. "This is the symbol of my clan, and it is now represented on my country's new banner."

Enapay grabbed a lantern from the floor, throwing light onto the armor. The pilot nearly dropped his light. His eyes came into focus on the crest embossed onto the red lacquered leather.

The dragonfly. It was the most sacred and profound emblem in Zen's family, and now for his whole nation.

Zen removed his coat and began to strap his *nerigawa* on his torso. Euphoria filled his heart, and his feet felt as light as air when he sauntered away from the helm to a small built-in bench near the stern of the ship. Wearing his armor brought him peace and solidified his conviction. When he plopped down on the hard wood, he let out a deep breath.

"It is Fate, Enapay. I am meant to be here, and I heed the signs because I have faith. Your lack of it changes nothing for me."

The Sky Blade was out there, somewhere in this untamed wild land. He would find it. Or die trying.

EIGHT

THUNDER RIPPED THROUGH THE SKY. It startled Zen, and Enapay veered the airship sharply to the left. The *Dragonfly* cruised at approximately a thousand feet in the air as it approached the Nabeho fortress. Even in the fading sunlight, Zen saw a wide river flowing north of the walls.

An imposing rampart surrounded the village, which looked more like an enclosed metropolis. In one corner of the compound, a tall castle-like structure dwarfed the tiny domed-shape homes scattered around it. At this western gate, a pair of bastions jutted out from the wall. This is where Zen saw a burst of flame and knew it was gunfire. Enapay must have seen it too, as his airship jerked before diving towards the ground. Zen held onto a rope. His stomach jumped with the sudden loss of altitude.

A wide dirt road led to the high wall, and Zen caught a wild commotion outside the iron gates. There was another flash of gunfire followed by a man's anguished scream.

"Raiders." Enapay maneuvered the speeding *Dragonfly* towards the gate. "They're trying to break into the village."

Despite the dimming light, Zen made out several large figures wearing overcoats and hats. There were maybe four or five of them forming a semi-circle around someone injured on the ground up against the closed gates. The menacing figures turned and looked up at them. They raised their weapons and fired at the airship.

The raiders' shots harmlessly cut through the air as the *Dragonfly* descended. Zen saw bodies scattered on the ground thirty feet below, which he concluded were fallen Nabeho guards. The bullets were getting closer to finding their marks, and Zen could wait no longer. He found his revolver and climbed to the starboard edge of the airship.

"What the hell are you doing? We're still too high." Enapay kept one hand on the steering wheel, but tried to grab Zen with the other.

Zen crouched low and gripped a rope for balance. He allowed the inner calm to settle in his body, and he beckoned *Ishen* to overtake him. His vision sharpened, and he welcomed the surging energy growing from within.

All four raiders stopped shooting and reloaded their weapons. After a deep breath, Zen let go of the rope and hurled himself into the air. He fanned his gun and unleashed three bullets as the ground swelled beneath him. His legs crashed onto the dusty ground. Zen's momentum carried him forward, so he tucked his body into a tight ball and tumbled towards the raiders.

Zen watched two raiders go limp before dropping to the ground, and that left another pair standing. They both drew their reloaded pistols, but Zen sprang up on one knee and fired first. Despite the sensation of the ground spinning, he struck both. One of them managed to pull his trigger before taking a bullet to the forehead, and Zen felt the shot tear through the air on his right. He got to his feet and went to the wounded Nabeho warrior who sat against the tall, iron gate.

The *Dragonfly* hovered above the ground. Distant gunfire rang out, but Zen couldn't discern where it came from. His head buzzed, and Zen felt *Ishen* dissipate. Thinning light clouded his vision, and he watched the dark forms of people inside the compound running towards him. Enapay landed the airship, and with his rifle in hands, he joined Zen at the gate.

The wounded brave whispered in his Origin tongue. Zen kept his face close to the young Nabeho. The brave's jacket was damp with blood, his breaths labored and shallow.

"We held them off, right?" the drifting warrior asked in the Standard language.

"You did," replied Enapay as he crouched down and touched the warrior's forehead.

The warrior let out one final breath before all the tension in his face and body released.

The heavy gate slid upwards, and more Nabeho approached from inside. They were all armed and breathing heavily when they surrounded the fortress entrance. The sounds of war still echoed from the distance, sounds Zen knew all too well. He realized that over two seasons had passed since his final battle with the Kaga Clan, and he thirsted for the thrill of war.

"More of them are at our east gate," one of them said to Enapay. The tribesman suffered from a still-fresh bullet wound on his left arm. "We have them pinned down there."

Enapay nodded. "We'll get back in the air and take them out."

The Nabeho warrior said something to Enapay in their native language, and Enapay responded likewise. Zen had no idea what they had said to each other, but from the looks on their faces, it didn't look like a pleasant exchange.

Enapay motioned for Zen to follow him to the *Dragonfly*. Zen stood over the dead Nabeho warrior and said a silent prayer before he followed Enapay to the airship.

The boiler roared and blew out blue smoke from the exhaust as the two propellers came to life. With a sudden whoosh from inside the metal cylinders, the airship lifted from the ground. Enapay stood behind the helm and grasped the levers and steering wheel to maneuver the *Dragonfly* back up into the air.

"That was incredibly stupid, Zen." Enapay pulled his goggles back over his eyes and wiped his mock frown away with his hand. "But amazing."

While Enapay steered the airship above the stone wall protecting the village, Zen went back to his knapsack to reload his guns. His body was full of tension and exhilaration. Whether he was fighting on Nihon soil or helping to protect a village another world away, it was all the same.

Enapay threw Zen a rifle. "This time, stay on board. Their bullets can't puncture the gas bags above our heads. Don't worry, the ballonets are encased in strong alloy metal for protection. Otherwise, one lead shot could bring us down."

Enapay steered the *Dragonfly* swiftly to the east entrance. The enormous iron gate seemed at least four times the height and width of the wall's west entrance. Two guard towers atop stone bastions blazed with gunfire downwards towards a large band of raiders fifty yards from the closed gate. Zen noticed the Nabeho rifle barrels protruding through the iron lattice of the gate, unleashing a curtain of bullets dropping several raiders at once. The invading bandits were out in the open, their vehicles the only cover from the Nabeho's bullets. They had nowhere to go, but showed no signs of actual surrender.

Zen counted ten cars in a semi-circle formation, each protecting the huddled, dark figures behind them. It became clear what the raiders' plan had been. They had mounted a large attack on the east entrance to lure the Nabeho defenses there. Once engaged, the pirates dispatched another assault force to the west to overtake the under-manned gate. The plan had almost worked, but the raiders didn't plan on a flying machine interrupting their invasion.

The *Dragonfly* swept behind the raiders' position without being spotted. Zen took hold of Enapay's rifle and pressed the butt of its stock up against his right shoulder. He leaned forward, using the railing for support. Despite the growing darkness, there was enough light for Zen to spot the raiders' hunched forms up against their cars. He lined up his right eye with the rifle's brass scope and found his target.

Zen pulled the trigger, and he knew his bullet struck a cloaked raider square in the back. The man's body jerked before falling face-down onto dirt. His comrades spun around and scampered on their hands and knees.

He bolted the rifle, ejecting the spent shell, and shot again. His bullet took out another pirate. The others scurried and returned fire while trying to get underneath their vehicles for cover. A deafening explosion, and the blooming fireball that followed, stopped the barrage of gunfire from both sides. It looked as if one of the raiders hurled a grenade at the Nabeho wall, but it fell short by about ten feet.

"They have dynamite." Enapay pointed at the raiders before taking the airship several feet closer to their position. "They're going to try again."

Zen put his eye back to the scope, spotting one of the raiders underneath his roadster by catching the light of the ignition of another stick of explosives. The sparkling fuse coming from the bomb was unmistakable, and he bolted the rifle while he watched the pirate leave the safety of his cover. A bead of sweat ran from Zen's scalp down his forehead and tickled the side of his nose, but he kept his weapon steady.

The man stood up and his arm cocked when Zen punched a bullet through his chest. Before collapsing, the bandit lost his grip on the explosive and dropped the lit dynamite onto the ground. The raiders rushed to get away from their fallen comrade. A brilliant flash burst from underneath one of the vehicles.

The rear end of the roadster lifted up into the air as the ear-piercing explosion lashed out with dazzling ferocity. A rush of intense heat buffeted Zen's face, and he closed his eyes to avoid being blinded from the blast. A large mushroom of fire floated upwards, igniting the once dark desert sky. Even Zen was surprised by the violence of the eruption.

Two surviving raiders threw down their weapons and thrust their hands up in surrender. Zen expelled the empty cartridge and kept his rifle trained on them. With a loud clanging of metal, the gate rose until it disappeared up into the wall. A small squad of armed Nabeho warriors subdued the two raiders and dragged them inside the fortress.

Enapay took the *Dragonfly* over the towering walls into the village. The eastern side of the settlement was dotted with more small circular homes, a few stone buildings scattered up throughout. Zen noticed every structure faced eastwards.

The airship came to a clearing near the corner of the compound. The craft's propellers slid into a horizontal position, and Zen perceived a hissing sound coming from the two long cylinders above his head as the ship lost altitude. The airship landed with a jostle and was greeted by jubilant cheers and war cries. Enapay pulled his goggles down and let them hang around his neck. He seemed apprehensive. His feet shifted back and forth underneath him.

They exited the *Dragonfly* and found themselves surrounded by the tribesmen. They reached out to Enapay and took turns grasping his forearm in some sort of tribal greeting. Zen sensed their curiosity when their eyes turned to him, but he also felt their gratitude.

An older Nabeho stepped from the crowd, his manner majestic and deliberate. He wore the same brownish jacket and pants as the others did, but his hair was gray and thinning. The high cheekbones and sharp angles of his face resembled a statue chiseled from marble, and when he spoke, the crowd obediently fell silent.

The elder greeted Enapay with their tribal arm shake and what seemed to be a few kind words of thanks in their Origin tongue. "We are grateful to you." The smiling leader turned to Zen. "And your friend."

"You are most welcome, Chief." Enapay stepped aside. "This is Zenjiro, a traveler from Nihon." He turned to Zen and whispered, "He is Chief Ohitekah."

Ohitekah approached Zen with his arm outstretched. The chief took a firm hold of Zen's forearm. "Zenjiro of Nihon, the people of the Nabeho thank you for your bravery."

Another warrior made his way through the crowd, his shaking finger pointed at Zen. "I watched him soar from Enapay's cloud-hugger, destroying the raiders in a flurry of bullets. He moves like a mongoose."

Zen recognized the man from the fresh bullet wound on his left arm. He had been the first to greet them after securing the western gate. The brave continued to re-tell the story to his people in Nabehon, which Zen couldn't even begin to decipher. Any sign of tension the tribesman exhibited earlier with Enapay disappeared, and he even shook the pilot's arm. The crowd's clamoring grew louder when the man finished his story. Chief Ohitekah studied Zen for a moment before an amused smile danced on his wrinkled face.

"It is easy to see how one would underestimate you," Ohitekah said. "Zenjiro, you've traveled a long way. You must be tired and hungry. You are our guest tonight and for as many nights as you wish."

Enapay's grin couldn't have stretched any bigger. "You should see the boy with a stick. I have a great story to tell."

Ohitekah said with a tinge of regret, "It has been a long time, Enapay. Welcome back."

The chief made a proclamation to the crowd is his native tongue. For Zen's sake, he repeated his words in Standard. "We will go to the Spirit Hall where I will hear your stories." Ohitekah turned to the warriors holding the two prisoners. The raiders wore long black dusters, their rough faces partially covered by grime and soot. "Take them to the pit. We will question them in the morning."

Zen noticed the men, women, and children in the crowd staring at him. They appeared fascinated, at the very least curious. All of the children wore their dark hair long as the adults did, and many of the women were armed with rifles. Zen felt a little embarrassed by their scrutiny, but he was eager to learn more about them too.

"Tonight, Zenjiro, you are one of us," Chief Ohitekah said, but addressing the entire congregation. "Tonight and forever."

Enapay leaned over and whispered, "This is my tribe's greatest honor. I've never seen the chief adopt a foreigner, and that practically makes us brothers."

Zen's face warmed with pride. "It is my honor.

NINE

THE SPIRIT HALL, BUILT FROM red stone in the center of the village, towered over the surrounding stocky homes. Enapay explained that the circular structure was their place of worship where many tribal ceremonies took place, and that all Nabeho buildings faced due east to greet the arrival of the sun with each new day.

When they entered through iron doors, Zen noticed the low ceiling and a faint but distinct smell of incense permeated the common area. They opened a set of double doors leading to a well-lit chamber. The Spirit Hall was circular like the building itself, and cavernous. Zen estimated it was nearly the size of the Grand Chamber at the royal palace back home.

Opposite the entrance stood a large altar made of the same red stone, the facade decorated with various banners. In the center of the chamber, a monstrous circular pit containing a blazing bonfire illuminated the entire area. Long tables and chairs filled the rest of the hall.

A throng of Nabeho followed Zen's party through the village, but the guards didn't allow most of them in. Chief Ohitekah led the selected few to the largest table in the chamber directly in front of the fire pit. Zen noticed that other than himself and Enapay, they all had gray hair. Ohitekah sat down at the head of the table and signaled the rest of them to take their assigned seats. Zen sat adjacent to the chief with Enapay taking a seat across from Zen.

"These raiders have attacked us several times this season. We've managed to easily defend ourselves up until tonight." Ohitekah signaled to someone near the doors. "Their attempts have become bolder as of late, and their numbers have increased with each attempt."

The doors opened, and several men and women carrying large platters of food entered the Spirit Hall. They placed a heavy bowl of some kind of stew in front of Zen, and his stomach churned with hungry anticipation. Without a word, they left the food on the table and exited. Ohitekah was the first to eat while the other Elders refrained before taking their first bites.

"Who are these raiders?" Zen gulped down his first spoonful. Its warmth ran down his throat and filled his empty belly.

"We at first believed they were a band of nomads. There has been a semblance of organization and planning with their attacks recently," Ohitekah said. "I believe that they are part of a new tribe consisting of outsiders."

Zen emptied his bowl, and someone from behind immediately replaced it with a full one. "This is a strange land to me, many things are difficult to understand. However, some things are the same everywhere. There will always be those who crave what you have and will kill you for it."

Chief Ohitekah nodded. "Very true. I have grossly underestimated the raiders, but I will remedy that soon. Tomorrow morning, we will question our prisoners and locate their dwelling. We will end their threats immediately. Otherwise, we will become prisoners in our own village, afraid to leave the safety of our walls."

Enapay remained quiet for a while, and Zen had forgotten about him until he spoke. "Luckily we came when we did. The raiders were about to breach the western gate when we arrived."

Ohitekah's wrinkled face flashed annoyance. "Enapay, you know the Nabeho do not believe in luck." The chief turned to Zen. "We believe all things have a purpose, a reason."

Zen said, "My people practice the same belief. It is taught to all the children of Nihon." In his periphery, he noticed Enapay squirm. "Fate has brought me here."

The group of ten Elders nodded and muttered in agreement as they ate.

"You see, I told you they would love you," Enapay remarked.

Ohitekah tapped Zen on the back. "Which brings us to our question: how did you and Enapay meet? Why have you come all the way here to the Wild Land from Nihon?"

The Elders waited for their guest to tell them his story. While Zen spoke about the union of all the major clans of Nihon, the Sky Blade, and the Iberian Empire, they continued their meal and listened with sincere ears and open minds.

Zen might have been a world away from Nihon, but he felt at home.

A FAMILY IN MOURNING CARRIED the body of a fallen warrior into their wooden home. Enapay shut his eyes and shook his head when the guards closed the door to the Spirit Hall behind them. He motioned to Zen to continue their stroll through the village square. The sky was littered with shimmering stars, and a cooling wind swept within the Nabeho walls.

"Seven. We lost seven braves tonight," Enapay said in a soft voice.

"To die in battle is the greatest honor for my people," Zen said. "There is no death. Just transition to the next world."

"The Nabeho have a similar belief." Enapay shrugged his shoulders. "Me personally, I enjoy my life in this world too much to think about the next one."

Zen asked, "Why do you go against your own people's beliefs? You are surrounded by all of this. Yet you do not believe as they do."

"I've ventured outside of this village quite a bit in the last ten years," replied Enapay. "I decided to see things from different points of view."

It made no sense to Zen why anyone would rebel against such enlightenment as that of the Nabeho. "I still do not understand." He was going to argue with Enapay more, but he yawned instead.

"You look exhausted." Enapay took him to one of the octagonal dwellings. "This is my uncle's. He and his family now live on the other side of the village. It's not much, and it's drafty compared to the newer hogans built with stone. As for me, I'm accustomed to sleeping on my ship."

Zen recalled that the *Dragonfly* housed a small cabin. It was large enough to contain a cot and a nightstand maybe. It made no sense as to why Enapay insisted on sleeping in his vessel.

"Don't worry. I will pay you in the morning," Enapay said.

Zen had forgotten about the wager back in Porticus City. Much had happened since this afternoon, and he wondered if he could sleep without the gentle rolling of the ocean.

"You should listen to your people more often. They are wise," Zen said before yawning again.

Before Zen could open the door, Enapay placed his hand on it. "When I was younger, we were at war with the Ndee tribe. My father was a great warrior, and he was killed in battle. When my mother died, my sister raised me. Later, she too was killed in battle. For what? Honor? When I was old enough, I left the village to find my own answers."

"Did you find them?" Zen asked. He was pushing Enapay, but in many ways the man was asking for it.

"I discovered a lot about myself, that I had a talent for building things," Enapay said. "A master inventor took me in as his apprentice, and for a few years, I thought I couldn't be happier. Then one day, it was all taken from me. It seems the only one I can rely on in this world is me."

"That is a lonely way to live," Zen said.

Enapay's face softened. "It is. I still love my people, but I reject their beliefs and teachings." He slid his hand away from the door.

Zen pulled it open, but stopped short of crossing the threshold. "Why did you return? Why did you make your way back to the Nabeho?"

Enapay hesitated, blankly looking Zen in the eyes. "Because I lost a wager to a boy warrior, and my uncle owed me money."

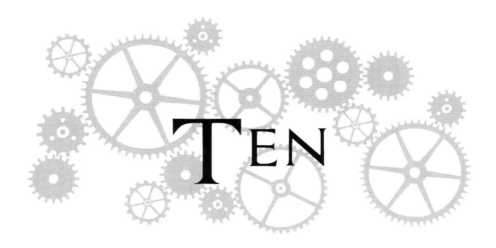

TEN

A FORTIFIED CITADEL OF RED stone overlooked the river and dominated the southwestern corner of the Nabeho fortress. Chief Ohitekah had sent a messenger requesting Zen and Enapay to join him on the training grounds in the morning. The chief likely wanted to share strategies with Zen, who was happy to oblige.

Zen was relieved to talk of war tactics after the somber start to the day. At sunrise, he and Enapay had attended a ceremony for the seven braves killed in the previous night's raid. Chief Ohitekah allowed Zen to witness their sacred rite. Quite a distance away from the western gate of their fortress, they paraded over the river's narrow bridge and came to a clearing where they placed their dead on high platforms and sang their tribal songs. The lyrics were in their Origin language, but their grief needed no translation.

Later, Enapay's demeanor remained dark. No smiling or jokes; he was silent as the two ate eggs and bread under a

86

small pavilion outside.

When they reached the citadel, Zen noticed the warriors weren't training. Instead, they stood clustered in silence. He saw abrupt movement on the other side of the crowd, and Zen and Enapay stepped through the assembly to make their way to the front.

A raider, stripped to only his dusty pants, hung upside down by his ankles. Thick rope held him there, attached to a wooden scaffold. The pirate's sunburned and scar-covered skin was fully exposed to all the Nabeho spectators. His bald head gleamed under the morning light. His arms dangled straight down, his fingertips barely touching the dirt.

A Nabeho warrior stood behind the prisoner, readying a type of wooden club. Enapay identified the warrior as Itan, the tribe's military leader.

"I know him. He's our war chief. He used to bully me when we were children," Enapay whispered. "Itan will beat the truth out of this man."

Itan was tall and dark like his fellow tribesmen. His sharp, handsome features so closely resembled the chief's, he could easily be their leader's son. Itan stood motionless; the wind swirled in the courtyard and threw a cloud of dust up into the air.

"What is the location of your camp?" Itan asked in a deep, commanding voice.

The prisoner gasped. His back and torso were already bleeding. He gritted his teeth and refused to answer. Zen held his breath. He knew what was to follow the raider's silence.

Itan drew back the club, and Zen saw the metal tacks on the flat edge of the weapon, like jagged dragon teeth. When the brave smashed it against the prisoner's back, the man unleashed an agonizing scream. Itan circled around the raider. He bent low and let the prisoner see his own blood dripping from the weapon.

"What is the location of your camp?" Itan tapped the prisoner's groin, letting one of the metal spikes catch on the fabric of his pants. "You will answer me."

The raider's body shook, and Zen thought he heard the man sob.

"Our camp is twenty miles east," the prisoner said between gasps. "In a town we've named Cheng City."

Itan looked puzzled. "Twenty miles east is a settlement of the Oraibi Tribe. Are you lying to me?" He brought the club back to the prisoner's groin. "How can this be? Tell me the truth."

"I am telling you the truth. We battled the Oraibi and overtook the town." The raider coughed and spat blood. "This is the truth. I swear it."

"I believe you," Itan said in a voice that mocked mercy. He swung his bloodied weapon in the air, taking practice swings. "How many do you number?"

The prisoner hesitated, and it was all Itan needed. He swung the club downwards. It crushed the man's upside down torso. The pirate wailed, as if his tortured body tried to release the pain through his open mouth. Itan let the club linger against the man's skin. Enapay let a miniscule gasp escape his mouth.

"How many?" Itan asked again.

"We number five or six hundred." The captive tried to catch his breath. "Maybe more. Our leader has several lieutenants out recruiting members."

Itan pulled his arm back to strike the raider again but let his club fall to the ground. The war general signaled for his men to take the prisoner down. They cut the ropes, and the raider tumbled headfirst to the ground. Coarse dirt stuck to the raider's wounds. Chief Ohitekah broke through the crowd from the rear and approached his prisoner.

The chief gave his verdict in his Origin speak, which Enapay translated for Zen. He had ordered the medicine men to tend to the raider's injures, and then allow him and the other prisoner to leave the village.

Ohitekah bent down and raised the prisoner by his chin. "You give your chief this message: the Nabeho will not be defeated as easily as the Oraibi. Five hundred, or five thousand of you will never conquer us."

The crowd dispersed, and the warriors returned to their training with spears. Ohitekah and Itan turned to make their way to a small building, but before entering, the chief signaled for Zen and Enapay to join them inside the war room.

Two braves carried the prisoner. They dragged his rag-doll body past them. Zen put a hand up and approached. He crouched down and leaned in close to the pirate's ear.

"You said you renamed the settlement Cheng City. Is your leader from Xia?" Zen whispered.

The captive was about to pass out. "Yes. Exiled."

He was going to say more, but he lost consciousness.

Zen stepped aside, allowing them to carry the raider away.

"Chief Ohitekah is waiting in the war-room," Enapay said. He took one final glimpse at the unconscious prisoner being swept around the corner. "What did he say?"

"Now I know why Fate has brought me here," Zen answered.

THE FOUR OF THEM SAT in the war room, a small chamber inside the citadel. An oblong wooden table that sat eight was placed in the center, and various antique weapons hung on the walls. Zen understood this was where the chief often consulted with his military leadership. When he settled in his wooden seat, he noticed Enapay's hands fidgeting on the table.

"Our captive said the raiders have named their new camp Cheng City," said Ohitekah. "I assume their leader is an out lander."

Zen nodded. "You are correct, Chief. The prisoner confirmed that his commander is from Xia, my neighbors across the sea. If Cheng is in exile, it defies their traditions, as they execute war criminals."

"Cheng commands five to six hundred men. Should we believe that?" Itan asked the chief.

"If it's true, the raiders' numbers are too great for us to overcome if we take the offensive," Ohitekah said with a frown. "Why have they not brought such a force against us yet? Why attack us with these small war parties?"

"It is a Xian tactic," Zen answered. "He is testing your defenses, gathering information and seeking patterns within your strategies. Learning your strengths and identifying your vulnerabilities. The Xians tend to be methodical."

Itan hammered his fist on the table and cursed in his native speech. "We must strike before they launch a full-scale assault on us." Fury flared from his dark eyes. "If they are indeed six hundred strong, they might be able to breach our defenses. We should dispatch a war party at once."

"We can't," Ohitekah rumbled. "To defeat that many raiders would take every brave we had. Our warriors are not versed in offensive tactics, nor do we have the means of transport. Our strength is defending our walls. That is our way."

Zen had studied Xian military strategy during his frequent visits to his western neighbor. Regardless, there wasn't enough time to train the Nabeho. He'd need at least an entire season, and the chief conceded that they lacked the means to transport their warriors twenty miles away. The only vehicles Zen saw in the fortress were dozens of roadsters and a few small steam wagons.

"My initial reaction would be to strike them first," said Zen. "But these walls have protected the Nabeho for this long. Why should that change now?"

Itan and Ohitekah gave each other a quick look of agreement.

"Zenjiro, the Nabeho people thank you again. Your expertise is appreciated." He glanced at Enapay and winked. "I have decided to pay Enapay's debt to you as a gift."

Enapay's eyes grew large. "Chief..."

"I insist." Ohitekah's deep voice brimmed with authority. "It is the least we can do. Besides, Enapay's uncle does not have the means to pay. Looks like the gambling disease runs in the family."

Enapay rubbed the back of his neck. "Yes, but my gambling brought the boy here."

Without thinking, Zen stood and bowed. "Thank you."

Ohitekah looked like he was going to return the gesture, but he remained seated.

"I do not intend to leave yet." Zen sat back down. "You are in need of gathering more information on your enemy. I am well versed in Xian tactics, and I would like to assist Itan and your warriors prepare."

Ohitekah got up from his chair. "You honor us. I am at a loss for words. I welcome any assistance you can provide us."

The chief put a hand on Enapay's shoulder. "I trust you will remain with us during this campaign as well. No matter how long and far you've traveled, this will always be your home." Ohitekah smiled. "The cloud-hugger you've built is most impressive."

"Of course I will stay." Enapay turned to Zen. "What did I tell you? I always pay my debts."

Zen caught Itan sigh and fold his arms.

Enapay's forehead wrinkled. "I can modify the *Dragonfly* to be fitted with additional armaments. Commanding the sky will prove to be a useful means of driving these barbarians back."

"We have much work to do," said Itan. "I will send scouts to summon all of our Nabeho warriors outside these walls and seek surviving Oraibi warriors. We will prepare for another invasion."

"We will refortify our defenses," added Ohitekah. "When Cheng and his raiders come to take what is ours, we will decimate their army."

ELEVEN

CHENG SAT OUTSIDE, SHIRTLESS. EVEN after three years of living in Agrios, his morning ritual always began with meditation and exercises. As a military commander of the Jin Faction in Xia, he had followed a strict regimen every day. He was now a free man, and yet he stuck to his rituals. Discipline and his beard were all he had from his old life.

Still immersed in serenity with eyes closed, he knew his lieutenant approached the tent. Even old Igor, who usually feared nothing, was blindly obedient to Cheng.

With his concentration now broken, Cheng sighed. Igor waited silently a few feet in front of him. He let his Russiyan lieutenant wallow in apprehension for a moment. The man was a giant, standing nearly seven feet tall, and the men feared him. He cast a large shadow that blocked out the morning sun.

"What is it?" Cheng finally said.

Igor stepped forward. "I executed the two disgraced men as

ordered. Walker died in agony, and I made sure a nice-sized crowd witnessed it. With Khan, the natives already tortured the hell out of him, so I killed him quickly."

Cheng opened his eyes and caught Igor staring at the tribal markings on his body. "Thank you." With one swift motion, he jumped to his feet. "Did they have anything interesting to share before they died?"

"Yes, Commander." Igor averted his eyes from Cheng's military tattoos. "Our men nearly gained entrance to their fortress. The Nabeho concentrated their defenses on the smaller western gate when we attacked."

"Nearly?" Cheng grabbed a white shirt and pulled it over his head.

"An airship came out of nowhere and took out our men." Igor winced, his gray beard twitching. "Our men at the main entrance never got a chance to use the dynamite."

"Airship? The Nabeho have no knowledge of aeronautics." Cheng hated surprises. He had done his due diligence, and he was sure no native tribes in Agrios possessed that kind of technology. The Nabeho instead had their cursed wall. It protected their treasury, rumored to house a chamber full of gold.

Igor fiddled with the leather whip hanging from his belt. Never a good sign. "There's more, Commander."

Cheng gave another exaggerated sigh. He crossed his arms and prepared for more bad news to dribble from the Russiyan's mouth.

"It was a foreigner who rode in on the airship and killed our men. They said he was a warrior with no equal." Igor shrugged his shoulders. "Maybe it's all crazy talk. Their account sounds unlikely."

"Did either of them give you a description of this man?"

Cheng asked. He was intrigued and infuriated. An airship. A foreign soldier. These were new factors and called for a re-examination of his original strategies.

Igor blinked for a moment. "Yes sir. They both said he was young. Black hair worn up like a girl. Tan skin, eyes like slant-ed slits. They were sure he was from the Orient. He wore red armor with a dragonfly on it."

The foreigner had to be from Nihon. Cheng had trained with several Nihonese soldiers twenty years ago in Koreya. The nobles wore their long hair up in a top knot, which made their men look like ladies. What was a *samurai* warrior doing in Agrios? Cheng's original plan was to launch a full-scale at-tack on the Nabeho in seven days. His newly smuggled Iberi-an weapons had just arrived two days ago. The new cannons were the key to destroying the Nabeho wall, and the auto guns were critical since he estimated that his men were out-numbered two-to-one by the natives. But his men needed more training.

Cheng had purchased the cargo at a bloated price from a snake of a man named Geller. Despite paying far too much for secondhand weapons, everything had been progressing smoothly until now.

In the distance, another one of his men escorted a strug-gling prisoner with long auburn hair. As they approached, it became clear that the captive was a woman. In Xia, women adhered to a strict social code. They strove to perform their duties as both wife and mother, and nothing more. Agrios was not Xia. Here, women didn't know their place.

Despite having a pistol aimed at the back of her head, the woman's pale face radiated defiance. She wore a dusty white shirt and brown pants, and her black leather boots looked expensive. Cheng was intrigued by this beautiful woman, and already his mind was turning over all the ways he could use such a creature for his enjoyment.

Jaarg, just one of many criminals Cheng had liberated from prison, took advantage of his long arms. With his free hand, he grabbed the woman's hair and yanked hard.

"Commander, she attacked our men in the tavern." Jaarg threw the female forward and shoved her down to her knees.

The woman was rough looking, but still naturally attractive. She refused to remain on the ground and sprang to her feet, drawing a small laugh from Cheng. Jaarg thrust a hand towards her shoulder, but she deflected it with a swing of her elbow. Igor drew his revolver when she dusted her pants off.

"Who are you?" Cheng asked.

"I was looking for a meal and something to drink, so I stopped in your town," she answered him directly. "I went inside your tavern and your men started making trouble."

The woman's eyes held steady, and Cheng knew she spoke the truth.

Jaarg tossed Cheng a leather two-gun holster rig. The guns' handles were made of pearl and specially manufactured for small hands.

"She killed three of our men, Commander," said Jaarg.

Cheng kept his composure. His hands gripped the belt so tightly that the leather creaked. "You did not answer my question. Who are you?"

The woman's face softened. "Neva. I've traveled from Europa on an important mission. I didn't come here looking to start a quarrel. I wanted to buy food."

Cheng gazed at her exquisite revolvers. She had taken down three of his men, which wasn't an easy feat. Many possibilities ran through his mind. Gruesome possibilities. This could be an opportunity to raise his men's spirits.

"What is your important mission?" Cheng inquired, removing one of her guns from her holster and twirling it.

Neva's eyes fixed on her twirling sidearm. "I'm searching for my son, Marcel. My husband sold him to a merchant."

Cheng's eyes widened. "The boy's father sold him?" This little diversion was turning out to be entertaining.

"He wasn't my boy's father. My son's father died three years ago. My second husband sold him to a merchant named Geller. I've been tracking Geller's caravan westward, across all of Agrios."

"Geller?" Cheng kept his face like stone.

Neva's thin brows furrowed. "Why? You know him?"

Cheng maintained an even face. "No."

"If you're harboring him here, you will be sorry," Neva said, her words dripping of venom.

The woman seemed brave. A warrior, despite her gender.

"What of your husband?" Cheng asked, changing the subject. "The man who sold your son. What became of him?"

The defiance flashed again from her emerald eyes. "I killed the bastard."

Cheng laughed, and Jaarg and Igor followed their commander's lead. This woman bore the same hot temper all of Cheng's men harbored in their stone hearts. She was perfect for what he had in mind.

"Let me kill her now," Jaarg pleaded.

Cheng handed Igor her holstered guns and paced in front of Neva. His men needed a diversion. Morale was something to be forged and nurtured, but always balanced with the swift hand of fear. The recent defeat by the Nabeho might allow doubt to creep into his men's minds, as they could never comprehend the delicate strategies involved in learning about your enemy. Nevertheless, it was time for a little fun.

"Ms. Neva, your quest is an honorable one," Cheng began. "The bond between mother and child is one of the strongest forces of nature. In Xia, mothers are revered. Honored. Even worshiped."

Neva managed to smile as if she concluded Cheng was the only sane human in this town. Compared to the men he surrounded himself with, he was.

"However, you did kill three of my men. My soldiers are of high quality. Each serves an important purpose. My purpose. This is my town, and it is not welcome to the public. You are trespassing, and you took three of my lives."

Cheng watched the hope drop from her face. It gave him pleasure. "Jaarg wants to kill you. I am inclined to let him do it."

"No! My son, Marcel, is only nine years old. Just let me go." Neva's eyes fell on her guns, now holstered and resting on Igor's right shoulder. "I'm unarmed. Only cowards kill those who cannot defend themselves."

Jaarg threw his head back in exaggerated laughter, but Neva elbowed him in the chin. As he reeled backwards, she took hold of his pistol. The gun went off, and Cheng hit the ground as the bullet whizzed over his head and ruined the table inside his tent.

Neva managed to wrestle the revolver away from Jaarg, who sprawled on the ground with blood pooling in the left corner of his mouth. When she raised the weapon, Igor snapped his whip against her right hand. She screamed and dropped the gun. Jaarg's long arm reached up and yanked on her hair, pulling her backwards and forcing her to the ground. He punched her in the face before he picked up his pistol and returned to his feet.

Cheng dusted himself off as he got up from the ground, a little irritated, but all the same, amused. Before Jaarg could do any more damage with his cocked right boot, Cheng lunged forward and grabbed him by the arm. Jaarg's face showed annoyance, but he backed off when Cheng shook his head.

Neva swept her extended left leg and brought Jaarg back to the ground with a harsh thud. She pounced and let fly a sharp elbow. The fierce woman struck him in the diaphragm. A low groan oozed from Jaarg's chapped lips.

Igor snapped his whip dangerously close to Neva's face. She stepped away from Jaarg who remained gasping for breath.

"You and Jaarg will duel. Tomorrow. I would do it today, but I have important business to attend to," Cheng said. "Tomorrow when the sun rises, you and Jaarg will put your lives in Fate's hands. If it is your destiny, Ms. Neva, you will strike down my man. If you do so, I will allow you to leave unharmed. If Jaarg wins, your son will grow up with only the memory of his mother's face."

Jaarg got up, his tall frame looming behind the woman. Before Cheng could command him to stand down, he punched her in the back. Neva's head snapped back, and she fell to her knees. She was about to retaliate, but Cheng moved in quickly. His boot pressed her face into the dirt, and he pushed it harder until she finally raised both of her hands.

"I like the fight in you," Cheng said. He released his foot from her face.

Neva's left cheek was already turning violet when she

stood up. "As much as I'd love to kill your friend, I'll be dead by nightfall in a town surrounded by bastards like you."

Cheng shut his eyes and exhaled, allowing the insult to dissipate in the hot wind swirling around him. Her mouth was filled with such filth. Tomorrow, Jaarg would shoot it off.

"Until then, I will guarantee your safety," Cheng added. "Igor will ensure that no harm will come to you."

Igor nodded, a hint of confusion in his eyes as he gathered the length of his whip back into a loop.

"I will return your guns when the time is right." Cheng reached over and took her belt and pistols from Igor's shoulder. "I do have one final question for you, Ms. Neva."

Her face hardened like steel, her demeanor ice cold. "What?"

"Are you fast?" Cheng gripped the pearl handle of one of her revolvers.

Neva answered in an even voice, "Yes."

Cheng gave her one final look before turning away. "For your son's sake, you had better be."

TWELVE

Enapay had spent the last two days working on the *Dragon-fly*. From afar, Zen noticed hot glowing embers spitting from the hull of the airship and assumed Enapay was busy welding something. The smell of burning carried on the breeze.

Zen, having finished discussing potential Xian attack strategies with Chief Ohitekah and Itan, strolled towards the village's eastern entrance. Typical Xian tactics usually began with heavy artillery bombardment to soften defenses. According to the Nabeho, the raiders hadn't displayed such weapons. Yet.

Itan disagreed initially when Zen suggested they dig a large trench inside both the eastern and western gates. He declared the Nabeho walls invincible and trenches unnecessary. Zen countered that nothing was impregnable, and should the enemy make it through or over the walls, the layout of the village provided no effective protection for the Nabeho to make a defensive stand. The citadel was not large enough to house all of the people, and it was the only fortified structure in the entire village.

There were too many unknowns regarding the raiders' capabilities for Zen's liking. He needed to scout the enemy and see for himself what Cheng and his men were planning. He also had to satisfy his curiosity about the man from Xia.

Enapay held a welding torch in one hand and a rectangular black piece of glass with a handle in the other. When he turned to see Zen, he extinguished the torch. Zen gave the airship a long once-over, admiring Enapay's handiwork.

He'd installed four adjustable metal plates along the hull, each with a cutout port large enough to slide a barrel of a rifle through. At both the bow and stern, Enapay installed small swivel cannons.

"The *Dragonfly* looks ready for war." Zen stepped through the ship's open door.

Enapay straightened his back and inspected his workmanship. "The new weapons do add weight, so I made adjustments to the boiler and engine. Cranked up the output. The *Dragonfly* should be even faster now. I'll teach those raiders to mess with my home."

Zen wondered if he'd ever see Nihon again. If he did, would his homeland feel different after having been away for so long? He felt every single mile separating him from home, and it hurt. He paused before asking, "What is it like, returning home after such a long absence?"

"Nothing has changed," Enapay said, fiddling with the dark goggles hanging loosely around his neck. "My people treat me as if I never left. We are a forgiving people. They know all about my lack of their beliefs, my gambling, and my issues with taking things that don't belong to me."

Zen smiled. "Stealing."

"Yes. The Nabeho still accept me. It feels good being here. I'm the one that's changed, and maybe I see my people from a new perspective."

Zen put his hand to his chin, comforted by Enapay's reply.

"It looks like I picked the perfect time to return," Enapay continued. "Something tells me this Cheng guy and his raiders are not ordinary thieves looking to do a little looting."

"It is not by accident you are here when your people need you most. Just as it is not by accident you and I met." Zen became aware of the amulet under his shirt vibrating and pulsating with warm energy.

Enapay rolled his eyes. "Look, the whole *Dragonfly* thing is a coincidence. Let's not argue about it anymore. I'm here because as the chief said, this is still my home. I will do anything to defend it. I tried staying away, but my people need me now."

"Yes they do. I need your help as well," Zen said.

"Help with what?" Enapay dropped his welding instrument into a small wooden tool box. "Why do I get the feeling I'm not going to like what you're about to ask?"

"Tonight, you will take me to Cheng City."

Enapay shook his head, but a wry smile spread across his grease-covered face. "Why does it seem like my whole world has turned completely upside down since the moment I met you?"

Zen replied, "It is Fate."

THE *DRAGONFLY* CRUISED EASTWARD TOWARDS what had once been the Oraibi village. Zen watched hot bluish smoke pour from the rear exhaust stacks of the airship. The rhythmic chugging of the engine made it easy to doze off. Toksu stood silently on the starboard side of the ship next to Zen.

More than two dozen Nabeho warriors previously living outside the tribe's walls had returned to the village in the last two days. Chief Ohitekah expected more than a hundred tribesmen to come home soon, bringing their warrior count to twelve hundred. Toksu was one of the first to rejoin his tribesmen in defense of his home.

Enapay's friend wore two-day-old bruises around his eye and left cheek, and Zen had felt uneasy during their reunion before leaving the village. Toksu was sure to hold a grudge against him. Despite his intimidating aura, Toksu proved to be a thoughtful and humble man. Not once did he display any lingering animosity towards Zen. In fact, he had thanked Zen for assisting in the defense of his village. When Enapay told him of their new mission, Toksu eagerly volunteered to accompany them into the air.

"So, what's the plan?" Enapay kept both hands firmly on the large steering wheel.

"You will drop me off two miles from the city," replied Zen. "Alone, I will travel the rest of the way by foot. If I do not return by the time the sun rises, you will return to your village."

Enapay shook his head in protest and slid his goggles up. "I'll do no such thing. Toksu will go with you to make sure you get out of there alive."

Toksu came forward. "Yes. I agree."

"It is best I go alone. Despite my youth, I have done this before." Zen waited for an argument which never came.

He was accustomed to having these debates with his father and Takeo. No matter how many victories he achieved on the battlefield, he constantly had to prove himself.

"I will return when I have gathered the valuable information we need," Zen continued. "Do not worry, I will return before sunrise."

"Why are you doing this?" Toksu asked. "You are not Nabeho. Why risk your life in this way?"

Zen checked to make sure both of his revolvers were fully loaded. "Chief Ohitekah bestowed upon me the honor of being an honorary member of your tribe. Enapay said that makes us brothers."

The stone around his neck glowed brightly. Zen caught Enapay and Toksu staring at it. He welcomed the warmth it emanated before pushing it behind his leather *nerigawa*.

"It is a sign I am on the righteous path. My deeds will lead me to complete my own quest." Zen tapped his armor where his stone lay underneath. "I am risking my life to help save your people because I am supposed to."

ENAPAY LANDED THE *DRAGONFLY* CAREFULLY in a small forest west of Cheng City. He watched Zen vault over the brass railing and onto the thick grass below. Soon, the boy disappeared into the black woods where he would have to make his way up to the top of the plateau. Toksu paced along the deck, gripping his rifle with both hands.

"I don't like this," Toksu said, his agitation showing on his tightly curled lips.

"Do you remember what he did to your face a couple of days ago? He's young, but he can take care of himself," said Enapay, trying to ignore the pang of regret for putting Zen's life in danger for the Nabeho. "I saw him cut down four raiders last night...all by himself."

Toksu looked unconvinced, and Enapay shared his sentiment. Whipping Toksu in stick-war was amazing. Taking out a handful of pirates single-handedly was extraordinary. However, going into a town full of raiders seemed like too much danger, even for Zen.

Toksu checked his rifle for the eighth time since landing. "Okay, Zen is a deadly warrior, but I still don't like it."

Enapay tugged at his goggles around his neck. "I don't like it either."

Zen looked to be maybe seventeen years old. But the young soldier was like no other Enapay had ever seen. His scientific mind took over, organizing his scattered thoughts and observations. Zen was fearless. Reckless. Humble at times, but arrogant all the same. That thing he did, *Ishen* he called it...how could that be explained? After witnessing Zen's fighting prowess twice now, Enapay believed Zen indeed could make his body enter such an altered state. In battle, his childish countenance was replaced with something cold and menacing.

The body and mind held such secrets, still beyond science's grasp. There was nothing mystical about Zen's *Ishen*. Rare? Certainly. Magical? Not a chance. Zen was a maestro of killing. But tonight's mission didn't seem right. Zen was formidable, but not invincible. Zen's blind faith in Fate was to be his undoing.

"I think I should follow, only to make sure all goes well. He won't even know I'm watching over him." Toksu checked his rifle again and buttoned up his thin hide jacket.

Enapay shrugged his shoulders in halfhearted resignation. "If you feel that strongly about it, I'm not going to argue. You should do what you think is right, of course."

Toksu's eyebrows rose. Without saying a word, he exited the helm area and stepped onto the main deck. He hopped over the edge of the airship and landed on the soft earth with a thud. Enapay watched the giant follow Zen's trail through the woods towards the village.

Enapay's fingers traced the dragonfly carvings on his steering wheel. Instinct screamed that something bad was going to happen. He trusted his gut feelings, but his face frowned at how easily Zen placed his life in Fate's hands.

Fate. Destiny. There was no such thing.

THIRTEEN

Twenty days ago...

THEY SHOULD HAVE RETURNED FROM their hunting trip by now. The other boys at school hunted often, and it seemed like a good idea for Marcel to do typical activities for a change. Marcel spent his days and nights reading books on all subject matters, his mind absorbing even the most complex of concepts.

Neva was always overly protective of her son, but she longed for Marcel to have a normal life. According to Pierce, boys his age went hunting. Her instincts had made her suspicious since Pierce so outwardly detested her son.

To her new husband, Neva was nothing more than another achievement, an object to put on display. Pierce was proud to proclaim himself the only man able to tame the warrior widow. She knew this from the beginning, and although she felt like a street whore for accepting his proposal, she did it for Marcel.

Neva's motivations weren't any nobler, she supposed. She and her son lived on a farm after the death of Marcel's father. When her first husband fell ill, that's when their financial problems began. When he died, their farm slowly followed him. Neva had been desperate.

Her sole reason for living was to provide for her boy, and Pierce's family fortune did just that. Neva was able to buy the finest clothes for Marcel, send him to the most exclusive school in Parisii. Recently, Pierce grew to be more accepting of the child that was not his own. Still, Neva did not fully trust him. Despite her doubts, she consented to their hunting trip.

Dusk was rapidly approaching.

Alone in the house, waiting for Pierce and Marcel to return from their hunt, her impatience grew into blind terror. She rifled through Pierce's belongings, ransacking their bedroom and his study. She found nothing, and she felt like such a fool for doubting Pierce's fatherly intentions.

Her eyes scanned the desk in the den and found a tiny drawer she'd never noticed before. It was shallow, as if it was meant to only hold documents. The drawer was locked, but she forced it open with a knife. She hoped to find something innocuous like romantic correspondence from another woman, or maybe proof of Pierce's other crooked dealings.

Instead, she found letters from a well-known criminal named Geller. Neva learned the foreigner was more than willing to pay a large fee to take Marcel away permanently. Pierce's plan was to meet with Geller's men outside of town to make the exchange. One of Geller's written replies said something about taking Marcel across the ocean to Agrios, where the child would be treated like royalty.

She was about to go after them when Pierce returned home

alone. He acted frantic. Dirt smeared his thin face, spittle foamed from his mouth, and the look of absolute horror filled his eyes.

He began to spin a tale about being ambushed during the hunt and how a pair of common thugs abducted Marcel. Neva found his performance wanting, and she drew her pistol.

Neva shot him in the kneecap. She questioned him, and for once, Pierce answered her truthfully. He believed Geller intended to sell Marcel off to slave traders in Agrios. Without hesitation, Neva put a bullet through Pierce's head and tracked Geller to The Wild Land. She had to get to Marcel.

NEVA SLUMPED TO THE DIRTY floor of her cell. Only iron bars separated her from the criminals infesting this sorry excuse for a town. If only she had kept going, ignored her empty stomach even for a few more miles, she'd still be on the road tracking her son instead of waiting in a grimy cell to die. Before locking her up, they gave her a tin plate filled to the rim with cold gruel. Despite her belly's protests, she refused to eat. She wanted water, but no one brought it for her. Frustration grew into depression.

Cheng had promised to let her go if she defeated his man in the morning, but she doubted anyone around here kept their word. Her hands covered her face, overcome with grief and a sinking feeling of failure.

Neva found her mind drifting. She imagined the horrors her nine year-old was surely suffering at the hands of Geller. He possessed a nefarious reputation, and she couldn't presume her son would be spared from abuse. Geller was a perverted crook, and every blow that struck her boy might as well have come from her own hand. However, she found a speck of comfort in knowing Marcel's life would be preserved, as he wouldn't dare kill his precious merchandise.

Neva grasped the metal bars with both hands and rattled them violently as the tears poured from her eyes. In her delirium, she expected the bars to shatter, but they refused to give way. She tested every iron rod with a ferocious shake. She cursed Cheng, Pierce, and Geller. She cursed herself the most. Her life was a montage of poor decisions, and in the end her son was paying the price.

Anguished sobs escaped her lips, and she lost control. With her hands still clasping the iron poles, she kicked the bars of her prison. Her boots smashed into the solid metal, her death knell ringing with each clash, coursing through her body, burrowing into her soul.

Escape was impossible.

A shadow of movement outside the bars shook her free from her useless frenzy. Although she was imprisoned, she was vulnerable to anyone wanting to kill her from the outside.

The town grew dark with night. Neva forgot she was practically out in the open. She caught distant laughter and yelling from the center of town, but her cell sat in a lonely corner of the village. It would only take one drunken jackass wandering over to the jail with a pistol to end it all. Her cell was empty of any furniture she might use as cover.

Neva huddled in a corner, trying to make herself as small as possible. With each footstep she heard, she lost herself more and more to panic. She held her breath, hoping the intruder would just shoot her instead of opening the cell door. Neva imagined a small gang of them wanting to get at her.

"You're one lucky girl," a rough voice cut through the dark.

A man stepped forward, a rifle shouldered up against his jacket. It was too dark to make out his face, but she spotted his whiskers.

"Who are you?" Neva asked.

"Commander Cheng sent me here to guard you overnight. Several of the fellas might have unsavory plans for you, but the Commander put an end to that right away. We're all criminals and outlaws here, but Commander Cheng does have honor."

Neva couldn't stop her body from shaking. "How chivalrous of him."

The guard pulled up a chair and sat directly in front of the cell, but he remained out of her reach. He tapped the barrel of his rifle on the iron. "You're the entertainment for tomorrow. If the Commander allows the guys to get a hold of you before then, there goes our contest in the morning. This is the first time we get to watch Jaarg kill a woman."

"You sure know how to make a lady feel special." She felt her face get hot, and she rushed to her feet. "Please, let me go. I'm begging you."

The guard turned around, and Neva recognized the pirate. He was the tall one with the whip.

"Why don't you shut your mouth and sleep?" he said.

Neva pounced forward, her right hand launching between the iron bars. The guard jumped back, her fingernails barely missing his bearded face. It was dark, but she still caught the man's sick grin. She pushed forward, her face pressed up against the bars.

"Go to hell!" She reached out again with steely claws and

let out an inhuman shriek as she just fell short of reaching him. She ignored the burning pain from the reopened wound on her hand. "You will burn for this!"

The man kept his distance. He pulled his hat low and sat in his chair. "Eventually, little lady. Eventually."

"Please. I'm begging." Neva's convulsions returned, and she felt like a miserable coward showing the enemy such weakness. She was beyond upholding her honor. "Let's cut a deal. How long has it been since you've been with a woman?"

The pirate remained seated. "What are you offering?"

She swallowed hard. "Do what you will with me. I won't fight you. When you're done, allow me to escape. I don't know what else to do. My baby is out there, and I have to get to him. I'm willing to do anything."

Neva dropped to the floor, the explosion of rage giving way to cascading waves of guilt. "Please. Take me. Have a shred of humanity. My son will think I've abandoned him."

The man's eyes were invisible in the darkness, but she knew he was staring at her. She began to unbutton her shirt with trembling hands, but he struck the bars with his rifle.

"Stop it," he said in almost a growl.

There was no way out of this. She would die here, at the hands of dirty criminals. She had been close to catching Geller, but now he might as well have taken Marcel to the moon. Her son would forever believe she had given up on him, and her insides felt as if they were being eaten alive.

"Just kill me now," she whispered with quivering lips. "If you won't let me go, then kill me."

"Tomorrow," the man replied. "Your time will come tomorrow."

Neva's body lay limp against the wall. Any spark of fight

doused by her tears. "I'm so sorry, Marcel." Her neck failed to hold her head up. "I tried."

AS HE CLIMBED A TREE to get a better view of the town's layout, Zen heard the loud drunken commotion. Most of the buildings displayed the flickering lights of lanterns, but there seemed to be little or no signs of life outside the cluster of raiders in the town square.

He pulled Enapay's spyglass from his belt for a better look. Sure enough, many of the raiders gathered around a raging bonfire in the center of town.

To the west, he spotted a building standing apart from the others. The village was comprised mostly of simple architecture with structures of wood and stone. This one seemed to be a palace among the shacks. It stood four stories, and its roof line was a series of jagged crenellations. Zen assumed it was Cheng's chosen dwelling.

After several more minutes of surveillance from afar, he put away his spyglass and decided it was time for a closer look. He swept eastward, away from Cheng's castle and the drunken pirates in the town square. Zen took quick but silent steps, and he drew his pistol as he approached the back of a stone building. The windows were dark, and no sounds came from inside.

Zen slid along the wall and turned the corner slowly only after chancing a quick peek with one eye. He waited a few seconds before continuing towards the front of the building. He looked left and right before finding the handle to a large sliding door and opening it. Zen grabbed an old lantern hanging on a wooden beam. He used its dying light to see. Other than old tools and empty crates, the building looked innocuous. The next two buildings he infiltrated were similarly void of anything significant. The raiders had cleared out both structures, presumably taking anything of any value after they drove the Oraibi tribe from their own village.

The fourth building he approached was wood and painted red. He found its entrance. With a quiet pull of the door, he led with his revolver and slipped inside.

It was a large supply room filled with grains and farming tools. Taking up most of the area were long, bulky crates from wall to wall. He inspected the entire building and counted twenty of these crates. Holding the lantern closer to them, he recognized the symbol stamped on the lids. It was a dragon's winged silhouette. A *culebre*. The Iberian Empire's royal symbol.

Zen searched for anything he could use to pry open one of the containers. He found a crowbar nearby and used it to remove the lid. Zen held the lantern over the crate's contents. The black metal of a cannon reflected the light back at him, cold as a grave and smooth to the touch.

Zen's mind raced to form a plan. It might be possible to sabotage the cannons. He scanned the walls, searching for anything he might use. As he moved to take a step towards the farm tools, the loud thunderbolt of gunfire destroyed the silence from the street outside.

A gruff voice yelled, "I'm talking to you, Nabeho spy. Come out right now, or I will put a bullet through your partner's head!"

Zen felt cold beads of sweat form on his forehead. Enapay

or Toksu had been captured.

"If you don't come out in three seconds, I will pull the trigger. I swear it," the man from outside called out.

Zen glanced at the Iberian cannon still in its crate. Zen let out a shaky breath and exited the red storage building. He walked out into the dirt street and saw the torches and gas lanterns that cast new light on this end of town.

"I surrender." Zen put his arms up. It was the first time his lips had uttered those words, and it was as painful as swallowing glass.

In the distance, Zen watched a familiar hulking figure walk towards him. Toksu's nearly bald head hung low, and he was flanked on both sides by several armed raiders. The bandits and raiders all wore gray dusters and flashed menacing looks on their ugly, dirty faces.

Toksu approached slowly, averting his eyes downwards and sighing. Behind him was the man Zen knew was their leader, Cheng.

"He's not Nabeho," one of the raiders said, pointing a rifle at Zen.

Cheng nodded. "No, you are not, are you?" He pushed Toksu forward under the light of the street lamp. "You are the one from Nihon we have all been talking about."

"I'm sorry." Toksu took his place next to Zen.

Cheng was stocky, solid. He held a pistol, but he also had a Xian straight sword on his belt. He wore a long dark beard, his hair equally wild. Cheng's sharp eyes narrowed as he stepped forward, keeping his gun pointed at Zen's face.

"You are this so-called Dragonfly-man they described," Cheng said, an amused smile cracking from underneath his beard. "What is your name?"

"Zenjiro."

Six raiders surrounded him, but he felt the stares of dozens more hidden in the darkness. Even if he could harness *Ishen*, he wouldn't stand a chance. Too many guns were pointed at him.

Cheng paused. "So how are things on the islands? Still killing each other I suppose?"

Zen felt the heat of anger, but let it subside. "Nihon is unified now, unlike Xia. While the Jin and Sui factions continue to bicker, the Iberian Empire builds its forces only miles from your western border."

"*My* western border? Listen boy, I am an outlaw. Exiled by my own people. I was a distinguished officer in the Jin army, and they discarded me like trash. I could have been king. No, I could have been a living god to those fools!"

Judging from the wicked look in Cheng's eyes and referring himself as a living god, the man had to be insane. Drunk with delusion. But it made no sense how he ended up in Agrios. Xians always executed their traitors.

"This is my city now. I killed the Oraibi natives, and the Nabeho fortress is next." Cheng holstered his revolver. "Why, Zenjiro, are you here? Why are you helping the Nabeho?"

Zen had to think quickly. "I am the same as you. Banished by my people. So I came to Agrios to seek fortune. The Nabeho hired me to help them protect their village."

It was a convincing lie, he thought.

Cheng leaned forward. "How much are they paying you?"

"Ten thousand ibers once I help them defeat you," Zen replied.

Zen couldn't tell if Cheng was buying this. The criminal, in his insanity, was impossible to read.

"That is all?" Cheng laughed, and his men did likewise. "My men told me of your fighting skills, said you took out four of my soldiers all by yourself. Zenjiro from Nihon, surely you are worth more than that."

More wild laughter came from beyond the edge of the light, but Cheng's expression hardened.

Zen's neck tightened with each hyena cackle.

"You are a terrible liar, Zenjiro." Cheng stood with his arms crossed. "You were not banished by your people. I know of Nihon and your ways. The Nihonese value honor above all else; your warriors are some of the bravest in all the world. You wear the clan emblem of a noble warrior. Dishonored warriors meet death by their own swords in order to preserve honor. *Seppuku*. Right?"

Zen took a deep breath. His body prepared for action. If they were going to kill him, he was going to go out fighting.

"Remove his weapons," Cheng ordered as he drew his own pistol and pressed it against Toksu's damp forehead. All the fight drained from Zen's body.

Two raiders stepped forward and held him with dirty hands while another removed his belt, pistols and sword still attached, before scurrying away. Toksu's face twisted in anguish, as if preparing for death.

Cheng motioned to one of his men to come forward. "Take as many men as you need to do a three mile sweep of the area." He glowered at Zen. "By chance, did you two get here by airship? I hope you did."

He turned to another raider. "Check the storage building and make sure our weapons weren't tampered with."

The sun would rise in another couple of hours. Enapay was supposed to leave if Zen hadn't returned by dawn, but it was obvious he was no longer sticking to the original plan. He assumed Enapay had told Toksu to follow him, and Cheng's men would eventually find the *Dragonfly* in the forest during their search.

"Since the Nabeho favor torturing their captives so much, maybe I should return the favor. I still have questions, Zenjiro. Questions you refuse to answer truthfully."

Cheng turned around to address his pirates. "Tomorrow will be a busy day for us. After our contest in the morning, we will interrogate our prisoners."

Cheng holstered his sidearm. In one swift motion, he unsheathed Zen's sword and spun around with astonishing speed. Zen ducked, feeling the breeze of the steel cut through the air above his ear. Toksu hadn't moved, despite the blade coming dangerously close to his left arm.

"You are fast," said Cheng with a smile. His eyes steadied on Zen's chest, staring at the Kanze emblem embossed on his armor. "How appropriate, since they said you move like a dragonfly."

Zen straightened himself. "I have never been defeated in battle."

Cheng examined Zen's *katana*. "Such a boastful one. Tomorrow, you will learn what real pain is like." He glared at Toksu. "You too, giant."

He held the *katana* up, letting the sparse lantern light reflect off of the steel. Zen fought the urge to spring forward and get his sword back. In Nihon, it was sacrilegious to covet another man's sacred weapon.

"Is it true they say a warrior's soul is forged in his steel?" Cheng asked, still admiring the *katana*.

Zen remained silent. Cheng looked as if he was going to

swing once again, but he slid the sword back into its scabbard instead.

"You Nihonese are such romantics," Cheng said.

More than another dozen armed pirates came out of the shadows and ambled into the street. They surrounded Zen and Toksu with their rifles.

"Put them in the prison with the woman." Cheng gave them an icy glare before stepping back into the darkness. "We have a busy morning ahead of us."

FOURTEEN

EMPEROR HIDEAKI WAITED FOR THE arrival of the Xian ambassador in his study. He sat behind his desk, but he was in no mood to work today. He wondered where Zen was and what he was doing. He would have reached Agrios by now, and Hideaki implored the spirits to keep his son safe.

A knock came at his doors, and the royal guard swung them open and allowed the Sui faction's emissary to enter the chamber. Li Zang had an athletic build but possessed the face of a courtly scholar. His simple blue and white robe flowed down to his feet, while his tall triangular hat gave him an extra five inches in height. Li's round spectacles reflected the morning light coming through the large windows behind him.

"It is with great honor I come to you as a representative of Xia," Li said in fluent Nihonese. "We received the news of Nihon's unification with wondrous applause, and we hope to continue our strong friendship." Li bent his head low.

The ambassador's use of the Nihonese language was flawless, and Hideaki was both pleased and impressed.

"I hope your journey was a comfortable one," said Hideaki in Standard before taking his seat.

Li raised his face and took his seat. "Yes. Your hospitality is without equal."

Hideaki grew tired of diplomatic pleasantries. "It is of profound importance that our two great countries come together during this time of global strife and uncertainty. As your two ruling factions continue to devour lives and resources in your protracted civil war, there are threats looming outside of the Sun Nation. Iberia will soon be marching into Western Xia."

Li lowered his head, his face solemn and serious. "Supreme Chancellor Song is aware of the gathering forces at our western border. However, we are locked in a stalemate with the Jin as to which ruler is the rightful heir to the throne."

"I can appreciate your situation," said Hideaki. "However, if Xia continues down this path, neither Chancellor Zhi nor Chancellor Song will have a country left to rule. The Iberian Empire's victory over your Russiyan neighbors is complete. No one could have predicted such a swift victory, but they have been employing new technology far more advanced than what Xia or Nihon currently possess."

"Yes, refugees from Russiya crossing our northern border have described such weapons." Li's face tightened. "Xia's land is rich in resources and manpower, both of which Iberia craves."

Hideaki said, "The Sun Nation Alliance must rise again. I have worked steadfastly with the rulers of the other Eastern Powers. In fact, Australasia and other countries of Oceania have ratified their acceptance into the Nihon Dominion."

Li's eyes widened. The recent Nihon expansion must have

been news to him.

"If Xia fails to heed the warning signs, your country will fall. Your division makes you vulnerable, and Iberia will unleash its monstrous exomechias into Xia like hungry steel demons. When they are through with you, they will set their sights on Nihon."

"I assure you, Xia is well aware..."

Hideaki slammed his fist upon his desk, rattling his stack of books. "Koreya has long declared its independence from you, and your own chancellor surrendered that territory without even a feeble attempt to squash their rebellion. What of Hindia's uprising in the South? Your grasp on that long-held territory has slipped from your hands. Iberia knows of this too, and sees it as further evidence of your growing instability."

Li began to speak, but Hideaki cut him off. "Hindia has chosen its own ruler. After expelling your weak military contingent and governor from their country, General Basu is on his way here to discuss an alliance. Nihon has secured two military bases on the Koreyan Peninsula." Hideaki paused, allowing Li to collect himself. "Supreme Chancellor Song has a choice."

Once Li's mouth moved to speak; however, he remained silent.

"He can continue his pointless war, further eroding what is left of both the Jin and the Sui armies. My forces will swoop down upon the Eastern Sui like a hawk, displacing your chancellor and appointing my own viceroy to rule over your provinces."

Li's hands shook like cherry blossoms in the wind.

"Or, Song can come to his senses and submit to Nihon rule

and join our growing dominion. We will offer our greatest military leaders and industrial backbone to your people. We have been developing our own new weapons. Once you join us, the Jin will follow. Xia will be whole once again."

"Under Nihon rule," Li muttered.

"Xian leadership is weak," Hideaki said, allowing a trace of his rancor to linger in his voice. "You have massive armies, but they are comprised of ill-trained men with obsolete weapons, and they are led by equally useless generals. To make matters worse, your civil war has demoralized both factions. With Nihon leadership, discipline, and industry, your people will be able to stand up against the Iberians."

"I do not know how willing Xia is to become a puppet state of Nihon." Li finally brought his eyes up to Hideaki. "We already conceded the Koreyan peninsula to your kingdom just one year ago. Chancellor Song will not easily give his half of Xia to you."

"Chancellor Song will remain in power, ruling over the East as my representative. He will maintain his lands and his authority under the Nihon banner. The alternative is not as generous." Hideaki motioned for Takeo to approach.

Li jerked his head to the right, as if he failed to notice Shogun Takeo standing in the far corner of the chamber all this time. Takeo moved to the emperor's side and gave a quick bow before handing Hideaki a large scroll. The shogun remained still, his sharp eyes falling on the Xian politician.

"Take this to Song," Hideaki said as he held the scroll out for Li to take. "All of my conditions are written, including the taxes and other tributes the Eastern Sui provinces must provide to the Nihon Empire. It is lenient and allows for much freedom for your people. Our rule will not be oppressive.

Stern, but beneficial for both our countries."

"Understood, Your Excellency," Li said.

"Time is of the essence," said Hideaki. "Chancellor Song will have five days to concede to my terms. There will be no negotiations. If he fails to sign these documents in five days, Song will find my forces marching towards Beiping."

Li's mouth drew open in protest. "Five days? There is much to review."

Hideaki knew this would be Li's reaction to the deadline. "I will not give Chancellor Song the opportunity to recall the bulk of his forces back to the capital. Five days, or Nihon will rain down upon Beiping and unseat him. That is final."

Takeo once again left the corner and stood next to Li's seat. The ambassador looked up at the shogun for a long moment before standing and bowing his head to Hideaki.

"Talk some sense into Song," Hideaki said. "Make him see the light in what I have said. If he values his crown and his legacy, he will join me."

Without a word, Li brought the scroll to his chest and exited the study. Takeo escorted him to the doors, allowing the royal guard to take the ambassador back to his ship.

"Takeo, share with me your thoughts," Hideaki inquired.

"I think Li will convey the gravity of the matter to his ruler, and persuade him to forgo further bloodshed," Takeo replied as he sat in the empty chair across from the king.

Hideaki hoped Chancellor Song wouldn't call his bluff. Nihon was not prepared for any such invasion of the Sui territories. Takeo was the most effective military leader in the country, but he could not work miracles. He would need more time before undergoing such an operation.

"Chancellor Song is intelligent," continued Takeo. "As you

said, they have left their capital vulnerable by battling the Jins out west. There is too much at risk for him to reject your treaty."

Hideaki said, "I agree." He looked up at his map and his eyes followed the drawn outline of the Koreyan peninsula. "How are things progressing in Koreya?"

"Things are ahead of schedule," replied Takeo. "Dr. Sanu has recently completed her first round of experiments. I am personally taking a steamship across the strait to see for myself."

The emperor sighed despite the shogun's good news. Takeo stood up and bowed, preparing to take his leave. For a heartbeat, Hideaki pushed his work from his mind.

"I miss my son," Hideaki confessed. "I hope he is doing well."

Takeo stopped. His hand grasped one of the doors' iron handles. "Zen is resourceful. I am confident he is having a wonderful adventure." Before opening the doors, he added, "That is what we must keep telling ourselves."

With that, Shogun Takeo Yoneda was gone.

IT WAS GOING TO BE a full day of more diplomatic appointments, but Hideaki decided to retire to his private chambers for a brief rest. He longed for sleep, but knew it was worthless to try. He stood on the balcony, overlooking his capital city of Tokei. The mountain air was cool and soothed his lungs.

Far out in the distance, he watched a slow moving airship hover near the industrial smokestacks along the outskirts of the city. The factories ran constantly now, building his new battle transports.

Master Kyta entered the chamber and shuffled towards the balcony. She walked slowly, and her frail body leaned heavily on her staff when she joined Hideaki. Kyta scanned the bustling city below, smiling.

"It is a beautiful sight," Kyta said finally. "Taking a much needed respite?"

Hideaki kept his eyes shut. "Yes. My meeting with the Xian ambassador sapped my strength. I have a long day ahead of me."

"What troubles you?" Kyta's pale hand touched his shoulder. "Is it Zen?"

Hideaki shut his eyes once again. "I am tired."

Kyta wasn't fooled. "We knew we were going to have to take drastic measures to protect our sovereignty. It is not enough to establish the Sun Nation once again. To the Iberian Empire, we are nothing more than a pesky mosquito to be slapped aside."

"I know," Hideaki said.

Kyta nodded. "It is best Zen remains absent during these difficult times."

Hideaki agreed with her, but secretly, he hoped the spirit of his dead wife didn't curse him should something happen to their son.

"This is the only way," Kyta said, taking Hideaki's arm and leading him back to his chamber. "If we are to have a chance against the Iberians' horrible instruments, we must do what is necessary."

Slipping from Kyta's grip, he leaned against a tall post on his bed, and for one fleeting second, he caught a flash of his wife's face on the pillow. He closed his eyes, and pushed the vision away. When he opened them, the image was gone.

"Horrible instruments indeed. Like the Shadows?" Hideaki both admired and distrusted his clandestine army.

The Shadows were brutal, able to perform the nefarious work even the most loyal soldier couldn't stomach. The Shadow Army was not much of an army, as only five of them remained loyal to Hideaki. There were others, living in the remote Qomolangma Mountains of southern Xia. His hope was to one day bring the rest of them under his command. They would be a formidable resource at his disposal.

As things currently stood, their allegiance was never clear, and his alliance with the Shadows constantly stood on shaky ground. Hideaki rewarded the few faithful generously, and they made themselves available for these secret missions. He paid tribute to them in the form of food and money, just to remain in their chief's good graces. Kai was the only one he truly trusted, however.

That was why he had given his most loyal Shadow a separate and vital mission. Kai was sent to the continent south of Agrios two days after Zen left home.

After Zen's successes on the battlefield, Hideaki had considered reassigning his son to the Shadows. He could have persuaded Kai to train him. The boy was a born killer, but he was also such an innocent. He lived and breathed the *samurai* code. Zen could not do the work of a Shadow no matter how intense his training had been.

Hideaki had sent two pairs of Shadows to Xia. Two Shadows were hired to abduct Chancellor Zhi's wife and four children in order to coerce him into signing Nihon's treaty. They would be killed if the chancellor refused. The other two Shadows had gone to the Eastern Sui to hold Chancellor Song's family hostage likewise. Zen would never be able to do such things. His son was not meant to be a Shadow.

Kyta pointed a bony finger in his face, breaking the spell. "I can see your mind is full of grievous thoughts. Do not second guess utilizing the Shadows. They are a valuable asset."

Hideaki chuckled dryly. "Kai left Nihon with a lot of my gold on board his ship."

"True," said Kyta. "He represents the best in them. Kai is a single-minded machine obsessed with completing his task at whatever the cost. You need not worry about him. He can be trusted."

FIFTEEN

NEVA WAS RELIEVED TO HAVE company inside her jail cell during the night. A young foreigner and a mammoth of a native were thrown in with her about an hour before sunrise. Even in her despair, she couldn't help but notice what a stark contrast her fellow captives were to each other. They were as opposite as two people could be.

The one called Toksu was a giant, with his head mostly shaved except for the wedge of black hair on top and the sideburns connecting to his beard. By the thinnest streaks of emerging light, his dark skin glistened in the gloom of their prison.

Zen looked young and fragile. His black hair was neatly tied up at the top of his head. He wore bright red chest armor with an embossed golden dragonfly in its center, but there was something distinctive about him. Neva had been around nobility before, and there was an air of aristocracy to his mannerisms. How had these two very different people become friends?

Zen gave a colorful story of how they met, and Toksu pointed to the bruises the boy had given him in their contest. She wondered if her cell mates were trying to play a joke on her. After laughing, she allowed herself to cry.

A hint of sunlight painted the cloudy sky, and her already desperate situation now looked even bleaker. Zen seemed genuinely sympathetic to her struggles. He and Toksu listened in silence as she told her story. Talking about it was painful, and the regret stabbed her straight in the heart all over again. They sat in silence until she'd concluded her tale, and both watched her cry until she collected herself. Neva's tongue felt swollen, and the dizzy spells came more frequently. She wondered if it was from Jaarg's blow to the back of her head or the lack of food and water for two days that brought on this weakness.

"Cheng is cruel," Zen said, shaking his head. "Only one so vile would do this to a woman."

Neva jerked her head towards the boy, pulling herself out of her dizzy spell. "A woman?"

Zen looked perplexed.

Toksu laughed and shook his head. "Forgive the boy. Where he's from, perhaps women are not allowed to carry a weapon."

"I apologize," Zen said to her. "Toksu is correct. In Nihon, women are held in high esteem, but are not allowed on the battlefield. Women assume other vital roles in our society. In fact, my greatest teacher and my father's most trusted adviser is a woman."

Neva accepted the boy's sincerity. "In my country, women fight alongside the men. I served in the military as a master pistoleer. I fought against the Iberian Empire in the Francian Rebellion until our politicians decided to surrender our independence. I led a battalion until I chose to retire."

Toksu stood up and stretched his legs. He gripped the iron bars while looking out into the dim, gloomy street. "I hope Enapay is able to avoid getting himself killed."

"Who's Enapay?" Neva asked.

"He's my tribesman. He's the one who transported us here from my village in his cloud-hugger." Toksu gave the bars a useless rattle.

"Cloud-hugger?" Neva shrugged her shoulders.

Toksu pointed to the sky with his eyes. "Airship."

Zen picked up a stone and threw it against the wall. "I told him to leave if I failed to return by sunrise. Let us hope he followed that part of the plan. I do not think he would endure torture very well."

Zen got to his feet and began to pace on what little floor they had. "We must figure out a way out of this. I have information vital to the Nabeho. Cheng has a warehouse full of Iberian cannons. He is sure to use them to destroy the fortress wall."

"If you have any ideas, I'd like to hear them," Neva said, exasperated. She had run a million schemes through her mind since her capture, and they all ended with her death. "Even if I kill Cheng's man, there's no way he'll let me leave this town alive. Criminals aren't known for keeping their promises."

"I will think of something." Zen sat down and closed his eyes. "I must stop all of this nervous energy. Allow my mind to work quietly."

Neva looked at Toksu and shrugged. "What are we supposed to do while you're meditating in the corner?"

The boy opened his eyes and spoke with the authority of a commanding officer. "You must do the same. Prepare yourself for battle, as you did when you were a soldier. You must survive for the sake of finding your son."

Zen was right. She had earlier accepted defeat and assumed all was lost. At the very least, she needed to make sure she gave herself the chance to escape this town with her life. That meant killing Jaarg.

"I lost my mother when I was a child," Zen added, his tone softening. "I understand the importance of your quest."

Neva met his brown eyes, and she couldn't deny the wisdom of Zen's words. She did not want to leave her own son alone in this world.

"Besides," Zen said, "my plan will likely rely on your survival. You must win your contest. Stay alive for your son."

Neva caught a reassuring smile on the boy's face before he returned to his meditation. Toksu gazed out at nothing through the metal bars. She looked at Zen for a moment, appreciating his cool demeanor. With controlled deep breaths, she worked to contain her despondence and focus on only one thing: defeating Jaarg.

If killing the raider gave her even a slight chance of escaping with her life to continue her search for Marcel, then she had to fight through her guilt and anguish at all costs.

TWO RAIDERS CAME FOR NEVA in the morning. They snickered like they shared some sick secret, and their smiles revealed yellow and rotten teeth. One of them tried grabbing her arm, but she slid to her left and punched him square in the jaw. The other guard drew his weapon, and Neva threw her hands into the air and let them snatch her out of the cell.

Zen tried to come up with a resemblance of a plan before sunrise, but nothing solid had come to mind. He would keep his eyes open for any opportunity to escape.

Neva was led towards the main square while another round of pirates came for Zen and Toksu. The raiders tied their arms with rough, thick rope before escorting them out. Feeling helpless was new to Zen, and he was disgusted with himself.

Neva swiveled her head briefly, and she wore a quiet and cold look on her face. There was no sign of fear in her eyes, which was reassuring. Zen and Toksu followed with their arms bound behind their backs.

Cheng wore a dark brown coat, his scraggly hair going past his shoulders. He held a large rock in his hands when he met them in the town square. The raiders watched from along the edges of the dirt street. They were all filthy, armed with rifles and pistols, and hundreds more were perched on top of the buildings. They flashed hungry jackal eyes and wore sick smirks on their faces. Zen estimated at least three hundred men surrounded them in the main square.

Two guards led Zen and Toksu to a saloon, allowing them to stand on the front steps to watch the duel. Cheng waited patiently between Neva and Jaarg in the center of the otherwise empty street. Jaarg looked like a humanoid spider with dirty hair and long limbs. He looked as sinister as Cheng. His beady eyes locked onto Neva and he licked his lips, as if to savor a meal he was about to enjoy. A smile meandered across his sun-dried face as he blew Neva a kiss.

"The rules are simple. You and Jaarg will face off at opposite ends of the street, each taking twenty paces away from each other." Cheng slightly lifted the heavy rock in his hands. "When I drop this, that is your signal to begin. Either of you fire your weapon before the signal, I will kill you where you stand. Is this clear?"

Both nodded.

Neva kept her eyes trained on Jaarg. "Where are my guns?"

"Igor has them at your end," Cheng replied.

"How do I know you didn't sabotage them?"

Cheng let out a hollow laugh. "When you check your pistols, you will see I did not tamper with them in any way."

"If you say so."

"That was my best friend you killed in the tavern," Jaarg barked. "I'm going to put a bullet in that pretty face of yours."

Neva's expression remained unchanged. She was calm, perhaps experiencing her own version of *Ishen*. Strength without effort. It was a good sign.

"Take your places," Cheng ordered.

Toksu's face wrinkled while he watched Neva saunter to the other side of the street. She took her belt and holsters from a long haired man nearly as large as Toksu himself.

One by one, the pirates cheered and yelled foreign obscenities to the woman. Jaarg, still smiling, looked up at his comrades and their cheers grew into roars.

All of this was strange to Zen. In Nihon, duels were in keeping with the old ways of the blade. The rituals performed prior to a duel conveyed the mutual respect buried beneath the hate between two opponents. To kill with a bullet from forty paces lacked honor.

He was in Agrios. There was no honor here.

135

Neva strapped her belt on and checked her pistols before facing her enemy. Without blinking, she pulled her long hair away from her face.

Jaarg was already at his station sixty yards away. He threw aside his long coat, revealing his guns and a sheathed dagger attached to a bandolier strapped to his chest. The raiders' yelling subsided, replaced by murmurs and chuckles.

Zen lowered his head and he said a prayer for Neva. *May her ancestors cast their strength her way.* She was going to need it. Something looked wrong. Despite the admirable focus in her eyes, she looked as if the effort to fasten her gun belt had sapped her energy.

THE SUN'S LIGHT GREW BRIGHTER in the distance, casting a play of shadows in the square. Neva noticed the raiders watching her with lean and hungry looks.

Cheng took his place off to the side and lifted the rock up with both hands. "This is a fight to the death, where only the righteous is left standing."

Neva glared at Jaarg. He bounced on his toes, as if he might charge. From this range she could put a bullet through his heart, but only if he remained still. To hit a moving target was difficult, and she didn't want to waste her bullets unless she was sure to hit him. Neva reached down, pinched a bit of dirt, and released it into the air. There was a strong wind coming from the west.

She was beyond thirsty, and she hoped she didn't pass out in the middle of the fight. She considered Zen's words. *You must survive for the sake of finding your son.* With one more deep sigh, Neva expelled the fog that clouded her mind.

Cheng hurled the stone, and it seemed frozen in the air. Neva's right hand bolted to her side but stopped short of touching the pearl handle. She held her breath and watched the black rock finally slam into the dirt road with a thud.

Neva drew her revolver and cocked back the hammer. She steadied her aim. Jaarg let out a barbaric roar as he bolted forwards. His long legs kicked up clouds of dirt as he ran wildly like a madman blasting from both pistols. Neva fired. The swirling wind blew the acrid gun smoke into her face, and she held her breath. She felt no pain, so she assumed Jaarg had missed. He continued his mad dash. She cursed for missing him with her first bullet.

Jaarg's movements were disjointed and crude, making him difficult to hit. Her heart raced, but she fought to keep from panicking. She rarely missed with her pistol, but she couldn't afford another mistake.

Pausing to steady his own aim, Jaarg brought up his left gun and fired. A hot razor cutting through Neva's right thigh nearly brought her to her knees. Ignoring the pain radiating from her leg, she willed her body to steady itself and drew a bead on her target. She squeezed off another round.

Jaarg screamed and clutched at his left shoulder. He stumbled forward and dropped to one knee, whipping his right arm up and pulling the trigger. It was a wild shot, and it nearly killed a spectator.

Jaarg winced and struggled for breath. He cocked his revolver once more.

Neva closed the distance with quick and light footsteps, stopping only to aim and fire before Jaarg could do the same.

His lean body arched backwards and his arms lost their tension. He stared blankly into the sky, his mouth agape as he collapsed flat on his back. Neva holstered her pistols and did her best to keep from fainting. She checked her leg to assess the damage from Jaarg's bullet. Her torn pants were wet with blood, and she felt the warmth running down into her boot.

The raiders remained silent. Their eyes were fixed on Jaarg still on the ground, his legs twisting in the dirt. Her lungs burned, and now, terror consumed her. Cheng was sure to kill her now, and she would never see her son again.

THE RAIDERS STIRRED. ZEN AND Toksu exchanged quick looks of astonishment. The men all around them were frozen, as if they couldn't believe what had just happened. Cheng closed his eyes for a long moment, and he leaned his head back in disbelief. Zen felt a heavy dread in the air, and their opportunity for escape was approaching.

Neva jogged towards Jaarg's quivering body. He jerked and convulsed, and Zen noticed the splotch of red blood spreading over the man's chest. Cheng's men got to their feet, their faces pale.

Neva's right leg was bleeding. She panted and looked as if she was about to fall over, but her weapon remained steady.

Cheng stepped forward, exasperation in his dark eyes. This duel was supposed to be entertainment, and Zen doubted any of them were entertained. Zen knew the dynamics of leadership, and this display was going to be demoralizing for Cheng.

Neva aimed her revolver at Jaarg's head. She turned to Cheng for a moment, as if seeking his approval. Jaarg's mouth opened wide. Blood bubbled from his lips. Cheng nodded, and Neva put the raider out of his misery.

Everyone around Zen froze, and this was the time to act. He was about to tap Toksu with his foot when a low chugging sound filled the air. Even when the earth-jolting explosions from the far eastern side of the village shook the ground, it took longer than it should have for the raiders to react. Finally the pirates snapped out of their trances and scattered towards the blasts. Large plumes of smoke and fire mushroomed at the far end of town. Cheng reached for his belt and tore his own weapon free. When he whirled around towards Neva, she was gone. Hopefully, she was safe.

Hundreds of armed raiders poured into the street in panic, and Zen and Toksu took advantage of the confusion. Toksu slammed one of the guards against the tavern walls, knocking him out. Zen launched a spinning rear kick, crashing his boot against the other guard's groin. With his hands bound, it was an ugly but effective maneuver, and the raider curled into a ball on the ground. Zen and Toksu kept their heads low and ran away from the explosions. Zen caught a glimpse of Cheng being swallowed by a swarm of his own men; a wave of dusty raiders ran towards the fires.

Zen fought to keep his balance, considering both hands were tied behind him. Toksu nearly tripped over a rock, but he was able to stay on his feet. They found themselves in the deserted section of the village. More explosions sounded from across town, and Zen could hear the distant cries of Cheng's soldiers. They took cover behind a small shack, almost barreling directly into Neva.

"Perfect timing," Neva said, pointing to the faraway explosions. "Was all of that part of your plan? If so, I'm impressed."

Zen shook his head and showed her his bound hands.

She unsheathed a small knife from her belt and cut them free. Zen rubbed his hands together to recirculate the blood into them. Neva was right; the explosions had come at the perfect time. Zen lifted his head as he recognized a familiar faraway sound. From their left, he watched the *Dragonfly* swoop in low before hovering twenty feet above them.

Enapay stood at the wheel, his eyes hidden behind his aviator goggles. He left the helm to throw down a rope ladder. "Thought I'd left you, hmm?"

Neva was extremely weak, and Toksu had to practically carry her up the ladder. Zen followed up the coarse rope and wooden planks.

Zen noticed two Nabeho warriors helping them once they reached the top of the ladder. When they were all on board, Enapay maneuvered the *Dragonfly* up and away from the town. Zen's breath caught in his throat, and he took hold of the brass railing when Enapay pushed one of his levers, increasing the speed of his airship.

Zen heard rifles in the distance and caught sight of a small group of raiders below aiming at them. The *Dragonfly* soared safely out of range, and the others joined him in watching the fires raging inside of Cheng City.

SIXTEEN

"HOW DID YOU DO THAT?" Zen asked as he made his way up to the helm.

Enapay kept the airship's steering wheel steady as he replied, "When I was out East, I worked with this funny Celt. He happened to be the best pyrothermologist in the world. He created new forms of dynamite and other fun things that go *boom*. I had a small box of his fist-sized bombs. A mere spark will ignite the chemical inside each glass ball, strong enough to blast through granite."

"He gave them to you?" Zen suspected otherwise.

Enapay's eyes gave away the truth. "The Celt was as unstable as the bombs. I did the world a favor."

Despite being stolen, Zen was relieved Enapay had them. He doubted that they could have escaped without the diversion. Maybe he and Toksu might have gotten away, but Cheng would have put a bullet through Neva's head.

Toksu led the others up to the helm deck. He looked down

at a small wooden chest on the floor near his feet. "Did you use all of your bombs on the raiders?"

Enapay replied, "No. I have one left. Don't worry, I padded the box with straw."

"I was worried Cheng's men were going to find you after our capture," Zen said. "They knew about your airship and even searched for you."

"It must have been my lucky day," Enapay said. "I managed to fall asleep sometime after Toksu ran after you. A gunshot in the middle of the night woke me up, so I took to the air. I hoped you two would manage to stay alive long enough for a rescue. I flew back to the village to pick up reinforcements, and Ahak and Sike here are expert scouts. They went into the town to find out what had happened to you two."

The shorter of the two warriors looked familiar, although his name escaped Zen's memory. The brave turned to Zen and said, "We saw you and Toksu bound and being taken from a prison, but you were too well guarded for us to help. We returned to Enapay's cloud-hugger to devise a plan."

Enapay added, "When we approached the town, we noticed all of the raiders were concentrated in the main square." He pointed to the wooden chest near Toksu's feet. "We decided to give you the opportunity to get away."

Zen placed a hand on Enapay's shoulder. "I am grateful."

"We have valuable information for Chief Ohitekah," said Toksu. "Cheng has gotten his hands on Iberian cannons. Zen saw an entire storage building full."

"So that's how he was planning to break through our walls," Enapay said. "You said the cannons were kept in a storage building?"

Zen nodded.

"Was the building on the eastern edge of the village? The building was long. Its exterior walls were painted red?" Enapay's thick brows danced.

"Yes."

Enapay pulled one corner of his mouth up into a wry grin. "We blew that up!"

"Cheng will be seeking revenge for this humiliation," Toksu said. "We must prepare for his entire army this time."

Neva waved her hand in front of Enapay's face. "I'm sorry to break up your war strategy meeting, and I do appreciate the ride, but I need out. I was tracking my son's captors westward, and I have to get back on the trail before it gets cold."

The taller Nabeho warrior stepped forward. "We saw you duel. Impressive."

She ignored the compliment and poked a finger into Enapay's chest. "You need to land this thing *now*."

Enapay glared at her finger. "The raiders will give chase in their vehicles, and it would be cruel of me to land and just practically hand you over." He slid his dark goggles up to look her square in the eyes. "Our village is not far from here, and it's protected by an impenetrable wall. Let's make sure the way is clear before you get back on the road."

Toksu agreed with a grunt.

"You are injured." Zen pointed to the dried blood on her right leg.

Neva shrugged her shoulders. "I'll live." She closed her eyes, clinging to the brass railing. "Now let me out of here!" she screamed at Enapay.

"I'm not going to be responsible for your death," he replied.

Zen took a step to get between them, but Neva's knees gave out. Before she fainted, she managed to throw a tight fist that connected with Enapay's temple with a smack. The pilot kept his hands on the steering wheel, but his sideways staggering made the *Dragonfly* jerk to the left before he regained control.

Neva tumbled onto the floor face down, her arms and legs sprawled out like a dead spider. Enapay rubbed his head and stared at her for a long time before saying, "I can't believe she punched me. Ungrateful wench."

"She is weak." Zen reached down to feel her pulse throbbing against her neck. "When she awakens, do you have water for her?"

Enapay looked as if he was going to spit. "I guess."

Toksu motioned to the two tribesmen. "This is Ahak and Sike," he said to Zen.

Zen noted Ahak was the taller one, and he finally recognized Sike from Porticus City. They greeted him with their traditional arm shakes.

"Where did you find her?" Enapay said, glancing at the unconscious woman.

"It is a long story," Zen replied. "Neva is a warrior from Francia, and she seeks her abducted son."

Zen felt his amulet coming to life, pulsing with rhythmic warmth that caught his attention. He assumed it had to do with the woman. Maybe Neva was here for a reason, and it would be only a matter of time until that reason would reveal itself.

Enapay said, "I've spent a little time in Francia. My mentor hailed from there, and I accompanied him to Parisii when he visited during their Rebellion."

"Your mentor?" Zen asked.

"He was a great engineer and inventor. Lionel DePaul." Enapay pulled his goggles down to cover his eyes. "I studied under him for ten years. He brought many of his designs to Francia in hopes of aiding the Rebellion against the occupation."

Zen said, "DePaul sounds like an important man."

Enapay gave a slight nod. "DePaul fled his homeland and settled in Agrios. He owned a workshop in Haven City, on the Eastern Seaboard. The Iberian Empire's foothold was expanding quickly throughout the northeast. I worked for him for ten years. One day when I came to the workshop, he was gone. His blueprints and works were missing too. That was a year ago."

"This man is the one who inspired you to build the *Dragonfly*?" Zen asked.

"He did more than inspire me. The *Dragonfly* is based on DePaul's design. In Agrios, he stopped creating weapons. Some workers built mechanical prosthetics for injured soldiers, while others built new forms of transportation. In order to construct this airship, I recreated his blueprints from memory. I worked in other shops and utilized other creative methods to scrounge up enough parts to build her."

Toksu rested his giant paw on Enapay's shoulder. "I'm glad you built this cloud-hugger. Otherwise, Cheng would have tortured and killed us."

Zen's hand reached down and grasped for a belt that was not there. He let out an exasperated sigh and felt warm blood flush his face.

"What's wrong?" Enapay asked with a trace of a grimace.

"Cheng has my sidearms and family sword." Zen kicked the side of the wooden hull. "They are irreplaceable."

Enapay shrugged his shoulders. "So is your life. At least you have that."

PUNGENT BLACK SMOKE STUNG CHENG'S eyes. His blood was as hot as the blazing-red embers crackling inside what remained of his storage building. The structure's charred skeleton mocked him. Out of the twenty Iberian Thunderbolt cannons he purchased from Geller, the initial report suggested only three were left intact.

Igor surveyed the damage and approached Cheng with considerable caution. His long face was smoke-blackened, which gave him a ghastly and pitiful expression. Igor didn't dare make eye contact when he finally spoke.

"Commander, two other storage rooms were burned to the ground. One empty bunkhouse is a complete loss, another one has smoke damage." Igor paused. "Total losses are ten crates of auto rifles, twenty crates of ammunition, a third of a season's worth of provisions, and two roadsters."

Cheng's jaw tightened; he felt the tension radiating to his forehead. "And...?"

Igor kept his eyes downwards. "Seventeen Thunderbolt cannons lost, along with ten crates of artillery shells." The lieutenant shrugged his wide shoulders. "We did find half a crate of auto guns, forty clips, and empty drum magazines."

Although Igor was a mountain of a man, he looked like a child about to cry.

"If you were the Nabeho, what would you be expecting?" asked Cheng, rubbing his temples.

"Commander?"

Cheng took a deep breath and relaxed his jaw muscles. "If you were the Nabeho, what kind of response would you anticipate coming your way after all of this?"

Igor looked up into the sky, as if searching for an answer written in the clouds. "I would expect retaliation."

"Exactly. Full scale attack. Preparing for such an invasion would take me several days. Several bands of my men are still out in the Plains. It would take time to gather our resources."

"Commander?" Igor looked uneasy, and that's how Cheng liked it.

Cheng crouched to grab a burned piece of lumber. "How can I smash the Nabeho wall now?" He kicked a pile of smoking ashes, using all of his strength to keep his composure. "This whole thing has been most embarrassing. Morale is low."

Igor backed away.

"I underestimated that woman," Cheng continued. "And that Nabeho airship. Again, I lacked foresight." He hurled the charred wood into a burning pile of rubble. "The worst thing I can do now is to be predictable. Especially if the Nabeho are being advised by the boy from Nihon."

"Yes, Commander," said Igor with tight lips.

"How many men do we have here in Cheng City right now?"

Igor again looked up to the sky. "More than half of our total forces. About three hundred and fifty, Commander."

"How many vehicles do we have?" Cheng asked him.

"We have thirty-one, including the vehicle the woman left behind. That makes it five roadsters and the rest are Iberian steam locomobiles. We also have about fifteen cab cars for the transport of men and supplies." Igor stopped fidgeting. "Why, Commander?

This was setback upon setback. Instead of panic, Cheng felt liberated. He had relied on Xian military strategy since coming to Agrios, and it served him well. Now was the time to cast aside the last remnant of his heritage once and for all.

"Surprise will be my ally. We will strike tomorrow at dawn. The Nabeho will assume that I will take the time necessary to gather and prepare for a full invasion. Instead, we will strip two of the Iberian locomobiles of their metal armor and transfer them to one transport. We will build a battering ram on wheels and steamroll right through their iron gate. That is how we will breach their walls. Then we will flood their streets and kill every Nabeho we see."

Igor shrugged. "The men inside that ramming vehicle will surely be killed. It is suicide, Commander. Our men are brave, and in fact most are crazy, but none of them have a death wish."

"Lead by example," Cheng whispered. "I am sure many of our men are questioning my leadership. I will pilot the locomobile and lead the attack."

"Commander, I strongly recommend against this. Ramming through those gates means sure death," said Igor.

"If I lead the charge, our men will follow," Cheng said.

"You might not even get to their gate. They will know you're coming within several miles before reaching their walls," Igor said with more persistence than he normally showed Cheng. "They have an airship. And bombs."

Cheng looked Igor in the eyes. "Then you must make sure to add enough additional armor to my transport to withstand the rain of Nabeho bullets. Or anything else they may drop from the air."

"Yes, Commander."

An idea popped into Cheng's once-throbbing head. "Do you have the boy's weapons? His *katana*?"

"I do, Commander."

"Bring them to my quarters when you are done with my locomobile."

Cheng felt eager, almost giddy. However, Igor stood perfectly still, his deep-set eyes full of doubt.

"I have been humiliated in front of my own men," said Cheng. "I will regain my honor by striking the first blow upon the Nabeho. Better to die with my honor than to live a coward."

SEVENTEEN

THE BREEZE HIGH ABOVE THE ground made Neva shiver. The *Dragonfly* began its descent, and she immediately noticed the wall surrounding the Nabeho city, visible even from afar. When Enapay turned a smaller wheel forward on the right side of the helm, she felt the airship's nose lower. She held onto the railing tightly and willed her quivering stomach to settle. Enapay took hold of a glowing lantern and hung it on a post near his head. The lantern had small, vertical metal slats on its brass casing, and Enapay turned a small knob on top to open and close the shutters in rapid patterns.

Somewhere along the wall, a light flickered from a tall tower in reply. With expert maneuvers, Enapay guided the airship over the wall and towards a clearing. The village was made up of small, round homes, and in the center, a domed building made of stone got Neva's attention.

Neva was nervous about meeting more of the Nabeho people, as she had been told to be wary of these savages. She looked at Toksu, and his appearance embodied the monstrous and fierce native stereotype. The giant, however, had shown sincerity and intelligence in the little time she'd spent with him. She hoped the rest of his people were like him.

"I know all you want to do is to search for your son, but this is for the best," Enapay said, his dark eyes sympathetic. "As soon as we can be sure you're able to avoid the raiders, you can continue your hunt."

Neva's stomach growled out of anger and because it had been two days without a proper meal. "Sorry for punching you, but I don't know how I'm going to track them now. My car is still back at the Oraibi village, along with all of my other belongings."

"We will provide you with whatever we have to assist you," Toksu said. "Including a vehicle."

Neva felt her belly flutter again when Enapay landed the airship. The two propellers at the front of the metal cylinders above them changed angles, becoming horizontal. Enapay was busy at the controls, bringing the craft lower until it finally landed perfectly within the walls with a soft thud onto the dirt.

"I'm thankful for all your kindness, although I'm wondering why people would assist a complete stranger," Neva said.

Toksu said, "The bond between mother and child is sacred to our people."

She allowed herself to smile.

It was hard to trust again. She studied Zen, still wondering what the foreign youngster was doing with the Nabeho. He caught her stare and opened the airship's door.

"I hope you are hungry," Zen whispered to her. "The Nabeho way also includes feeding you until you swear you shall never eat again."

A small group of natives holding gas lanterns approached the airship. The man leading them looked like their chief. The others were careful to not step past him, and despite his obvious old age, the leader looked strong.

While exiting the *Dragonfly*, she heard her stomach rumble again.

The Zen and his companions stepped off the airship, and Enapay led the introductions. "This is Chief Ohitekah, leader of the three Nabeho bands in his village," he said to her.

Neva was unsure how to greet the chief, so she simply bowed her head. Ohitekah returned the gesture.

"Chief, this is Neva. She comes from across the Atlantica Sea, from Francia," Enapay continued.

Ohitekah smiled, his once stone face cracking with friendly lines. "I welcome you, Neva of Francia." He nodded a greeting towards Zen. "It seems Enapay is making it a habit of bringing foreign visitors to our village. When he returned before sunrise to collect Sike and Ahak, we knew something had gone wrong with your mission."

Zen stepped forward and bowed before speaking. "Toksu and I were captured. Luckily, Enapay and his reinforcements came back to rescue us." Zen looked profoundly serious when he addressed Ohitekah, which she found funny. Zen seemed out of place, yet the others regarded him as if he were royalty. The young man intrigued her.

"I have vital information concerning the raiders we need to discuss immediately," Zen said, a trace of impatience in his tone.

Ohitekah nodded slowly before addressing Neva. "I do hope you have a good story to tell us as we sit to eat our morning meal."

She touched her hollow belly. "If you provide the food, I will provide the story."

"Then we'll eat at once," Ohitekah said to the entire group. "We have much to talk about, it seems."

THE SPIRIT ROOM WAS ILLUMINATED by various lamps on the walls and the circular bonfire raging in the center. The head table was full of cooked meats, breads, and vegetables. Zen noticed this morning's feast looked just as elaborate as their evening meal and felt immediately famished at the sight of it.

Neva managed to tell her story in between the three loaded plates of pork and exotic vegetables she consumed, each in a matter of minutes. Chief Ohitekah and a dozen Elders remained attentive and conveyed their sorrow as Neva described her tragedies.

She spoke of her true love's untimely death and how she married a scoundrel for his money. Her voice trembled when she recounted how she learned of her new husband's betrayal, and that the man called Geller had taken her son across the ocean.

The chief's wife, sitting at her husband's side, was especially sensitive to Neva's plight. She even got up from her seat to embrace their guest. Neva accepted the gesture with reluctant eyes. Zen's urgency concerning the Iberian cannons evaporated as he listened to Neva recount her struggles in Francia. She had proven to be a capable warrior, but Zen was reminded of his own mother when Neva described her emotions at having her son taken. His own mother's strength may have been silent, but it was firm. Neva was similarly indomitable.

Her tale turned to Agrios and having been imprisoned by Cheng. The Elders in the Spirit Room cheered with enthusiasm as she described her showdown with Jaarg. She went into every detail leading up to putting that final bullet through Cheng's champion, and it was easy to see the warrior's pride in her eyes while she boasted of her victory.

The chief assured her that the Nabeho would help. Neva's eyes welled up with tears, and she continued eating in silence.

"What did you learn at the Oraibi village?" Ohitekah asked Zen directly.

"Cheng is a disgraced Xian military leader," Zen replied. "I saw about three hundred men in the town."

Ohitekah's eyebrows arched. "Maybe the rest of his forces are spread out elsewhere?"

Zen nodded. "Perhaps. I discovered Cheng was in possession of twenty Iberian cannons. They were hidden in a storage building."

"Which I blew up," Enapay added before he took a hearty bite from a loaf of buttered bread.

"Blew up?" Ohitekah's worried face melted away. He gave Enapay a quick slap on the back. "You destroyed their weapons?"

"He did," Zen answered for him. "However, we cannot be sure it was their only armory."

Itan had been silent all morning, but the bold military leader finally spoke up. "Zenjiro is right. We can't assume all of Cheng's weapons were destroyed. He might have more stored elsewhere. Or he can get replacements."

Ohitekah was silent for a moment before asking Zen, "What

do you believe will be Cheng's next move?"

Zen put down his spoon. "My initial thought is that he will assemble his entire army. If only half of his forces are local, it could take days to complete. If he does have any functioning cannons left, he will use them. If not, he will employ his ground forces to volley other types of explosives over your wall."

"Without artillery, his offensive would be foolish," Ohitekah said with a smirk. "Even if they were to approach in vehicles, they would have to get close enough to launch their explosives at us, leaving them vulnerable to our defensive gunfire from our towers and wall."

Neva stopped eating and spoke up. "Cheng is crazy. If attacking your fortress without heavy artillery is suicide, I would say Cheng is mad enough to do it."

Ohitekah thought for a moment. "Zenjiro, what do you think?"

Zen mulled over Neva's insight. "Cheng has followed Xian strategy thus far, and logic tells me he will continue to do so. But Neva is right. He is, without a doubt, insane."

"Is he bold enough to blindly attack my walls without the cannons?" Ohitekah asked.

Neva looked at the chief's wife at the head of the table across from her. "Yes. My victory disgraced him. Cheng is coming soon."

Ohitekah turned to Toksu. "What do you believe?"

Toksu replied, "I believe he would lead his men to certain death to appease his ego and thirst for blood."

Battle strategy and Zen's gut feeling were at odds; it was difficult to predict the actions of a madman. "Cheng is capable of acting irrationally. Neva did dishonor him in front of his men. We should prepare for the worst."

Ohitekah got up from his chair, and his voice filled up the entire Spirit Hall. "We will fortify our defenses immediately. If Cheng does decide to attack, he and his men will meet certain death."

The entire chamber erupted in a war cry, and Zen watched the chief's wife discreetly escort Neva out.

NIGHT WAS ABOUT TO GIVE way to morning.

Chief Ohitekah's wife, Winona, arranged to help Neva gather the supplies she needed. She also brought a healer to properly care for her thigh wound. Toksu secured an old recumbent roadster for her. Neva appreciated the Nabeho for supplying water and coal to last her several hundred miles before needing more fuel. Enapay handed her a map of central and southern Agrios.

Neva's belly was full, and her strength had returned. Her muscles were soothed by the hot bath she'd taken the night before. The new billowy white shirt and tan leggings Winona gave her were clean and comfortable. She wore her brown jacket to protect her from the wind, and she was eager to get going.

Enapay, Toksu, and Zen stood next to Neva's roadster when she got to the main gates. Thousands of Nabeho warriors bustled all around them, readying their fortress for invasion. The humid air was filled with a familiar mix of anxiety and fervor. The sun's light would be creeping into in the sky in a couple of hours, and she wanted to leave before dawn.

"You know where to begin?" Enapay asked while he checked her roadster's main boiler one final time.

Neva held up her new map. She noticed this was a more recent version than the one she left with the raiders. New roads crisscrossed through Agrios, and they gave her more alternatives than she originally thought.

"I will backtrack east for a little bit, but head south. I have a hunch Geller's caravan might be heading for the southern border crossing over into Mexihco."

Toksu gave her a solemn look. "Be careful."

"I will be." Neva climbed into her vehicle. The old car was built for speed and lay close to the ground, but it looked sturdy enough.

"I can take one more scouting flight if you want, just to make sure the way is safe," Enapay offered.

He'd taken the *Dragonfly* up twice already in the last three hours, surveilling the way ahead, for which Neva was thankful. She secretly wanted to ask for Enapay's help again, as the *Dragonfly* could cover more ground than the steam car, but she understood his duty to protect his village was his priority.

The engine started with a few sputters but grew into a full roar seconds later. She eased up on the regulator and allowed the engine to idle. The small smokestack in the rear rhythmically blew small clouds of steam.

"I pray for your victory as you continue your quest," Zen said, raising his voice above the engine.

The foreign boy remained as much of a mystery to Neva now as when she had first met him; it was a pity she wouldn't get the opportunity to know him better. "I hope the same for you."

She admitted there was a sliver of desire to stay and help

the Nabeho. It was the old soldier in her longing for battle. But Marcel needed her, and the trail was getting colder with each passing minute.

One of the Nabeho guards signaled for the main gates to open. The interior steel portcullis slid upwards with a heavy clanking of metal chains, and the exterior gate drew open.

With one final wave of her hand, Neva stepped on the throttle pedal and powered her roadster through the open gates and outside the safety of the natives' wall.

EIGHTEEN

ZEN HELD HIS *NERIGAWA* UP to the lantern and stared at the golden dragonfly emblem. He prayed silently to his ancestors before putting the armor back on the wooden table. He considered taking a nap since the small hogan had no windows to let the morning's early light in. A soft knock at the door made him jump. Zen opened it and let Enapay in.

Enapay pulled a wooden chair up to the table and sat down. "I know this place is small, but it's better than a prison cell."

"Yes. Much better. How are the preparations coming along?"

"The chief has tripled the number of guards on the village walls," Enapay replied. "My body wants to sleep, but I keep finding more work to be done."

Zen's own eyelids felt heavy. "My body yearns for sleep as well. I think I might give in for once," he said. "You should do the same."

The blue stone around Zen's neck emitted no light or heat since he had escaped from the raiders. Zen had wondered if it glowed because of Neva, but she was long gone now. He felt lost and spiritually off course. His body was weary, and his strength and faith both wavered. It took effort to maintain piety.

Enapay broke the silence. "Listen, you don't have to do this. This isn't your fight. You've already stuck your neck out more than once for my people."

The need for sleep was overwhelming. "I am here for a reason," Zen said more to himself than to Enapay. "Ohitekah made me a member of your tribe, remember? We are practically brothers." He smiled, which became a yawn. "After we defeat the raiders, I will get my weapons back. I cannot lose my sword."

"It's that important to you?"

Zen nodded. "To my people, the sword is the embodiment of the soul." His eyes blinked with fatigue. "Like the sacred spear that hangs in your War Room."

Enapay stood up. "Get some rest. I doubt Cheng will attack in broad daylight. I might go back up one more time in the *Dragonfly*."

Without another word, Enapay left the one-room cabin and shut the door. Zen turned down the lantern's light on the table and finally allowed his body to swim in the sea of sleep.

CHENG LEFT HIS PALACE WEARING what remained of his old Xian armor. The leather chest piece and thick faded gauntlets and greaves seemed molded to his body, and he wallowed in the feeling of invincibility he felt while wearing them. When he swaggered out into his town's main square, he felt reborn.

The modified locomobile sat idling; Igor stood proudly next to the hulking vehicle. Cheng pursed his lips as he inspected the new plating fastened onto the exterior, which gave the transport an ominous and imposing presence. The vehicle seemed to be heavy and solid enough to smash open the Nabeho's gates. The angry iron bull blew smoke from its two rear chimneys.

"Excellent work."

Cheng walked around to the front of the transport where Igor had added two thick metal plates to serve as a menacing wedge. The best part, however, was how the boy's *katana* jutted straight out from the deadly nose of the transport, welded to the metal exactly as he requested.

"I do hope he sees this," Cheng whispered. "It will be the ultimate insult."

Igor smiled, satisfied with himself. "We've loaded all our supplies and men on the other transports. They stand ready to follow you."

NEVA'S ROADSTER CHUGGED WITH STEADY rhythm. Although her body demanded sleep, she denied it. She had lost precious time. Every time she felt herself dozing off, she would imagine her terrified son calling out to her. She intended not only to save her boy, but she swore to the fading stars in the sky that she would put a bullet through Geller's head.

With only a hint of orange light from above, the dusty highway seemed like a dream. Something far in the distance broke her trance. She eased up on the throttle until her roadster slowed to a crawl.

Neva squinted her eyes to focus her vision. She wondered if she was delusional from exhaustion. Something metallic was moving towards her and kicking up clouds of dust in its wake. It was little more than a speck, but she couldn't help feeling something bad was heading her way. She pulled a red lever and killed her engine.

The warm wind blew eastward. Neva closed her eyes. She hoped her hearing would somehow become more acute with the lack of sight. At first it sounded like the thunder of an approaching storm, but the rumbling was too constant and mechanical.

Neva got out of the car. She watched the tiny object grow on the horizon. The dark foreboding creeping through her made her shiver, and now she was sure of what she was seeing and hearing. She jumped back into her roadster and revved the steam engine.

With a slight grunt, she turned the steering wheel hard right, bringing her vehicle around and streaming west.

Back to the Nabeho village.

THE LAST BELL ZEN REMEMBERED hearing was during a funeral for his fellow Kanze soldiers. It was a glorious and somber ceremony. His clansmen had died good deaths on the battlefield, thus bringing glory and honor to their families. The monks had been gently ringing brass bells as they sang their traditional songs.

The bell clanging violently from outside his hogan reverberated in his head and yanked him from sleep's heavy arms. When he jumped to his feet and hesitated for a moment, he wondered if he was still at his comrades' funeral. The panicked shouts that followed snapped him fully awake, and he knew it was time.

There was an ancient Nihon ritual always performed when a warrior methodically put on his armor in preparation for battle. This wasn't the time for such formalities. He threw on his *nerigawa*, tying the chords connecting the rigid breast and back pieces firmly against his body. In a controlled rush, he slid on his boots and gauntlets. Without thinking, he reached for his sword, but instead found the plain leather belt Enapay had given him.

When he swung open the door, he watched the Nabeho warriors, men and women, rush to take their positions with weapons in hand. A young brave inside one of the tall towers within the fortress yanked a long rope with all of his might, rocking the massive bell back and forth with a violent clangor. All the homes shut and locked their doors and shutters. Weaponless, Zen sprinted towards the main gates.

The interior gate was guarded by no less than thirty men, and Zen saw the entire wall lined with armed warriors. He ran around the deep trench the Nabeho had dug earlier and climbed up a steep wooden stairway to the parapet. He hurried across the narrow walkway to one of the towers adjacent to the main gates. Chief Ohitekah and Itan were already inside, surrounded by their fellow warriors. They watched the *Dragonfly* in the distance.

"Enapay signaled that the raiders are coming." Itan readied his rifle. "Everyone is in position."

The *Dragonfly* sped towards them, and something below it caught Zen's eyes. He strained to see it at first, but the steam flowing from the rear stack of the car left no doubt that it was Neva's roadster.

It seemed to take hours, but the airship came within shouting distance before slowing down. Enapay carefully guided the hovering *Dragonfly* right alongside the tower.

"Neva must have seen the raiders on the highway," Enapay said over the whirring of his propellers. "When I was doing a quick patrol, I thought maybe hidden raiders were shooting at me. Hell, it was Neva trying to get my attention." He turned to Zen. "You coming on board?"

Zen climbed to the ledge of the tower, grabbed onto the lip of the roof with one hand, and reached down towards where his holster should have been with the other. Chief Ohitekah came forward and handed Zen his own spear. The wooden weapon was light, but the jagged steel blade looked menacing.

Ohitekah stepped away after Zen took a firm hold of the weapon. "Ahak, Sike, and Lena will ride Enapay's cloud-hugger as well."

Zen recognized the two approaching male braves, but he hesitated when he saw Lena. She slung her rifle over her shoulder and cast a scowl in Zen's direction. The four of them leaped from the tower and landed in the *Dragonfly*.

Itan raised his gun high. "Rain death upon those dogs!"

Enapay nodded. "We will."

The chief looked down, and Zen followed his gaze to see Neva's roadster reach the entrance. "Open the gates!" Ohitekah commanded.

The clanking of chains followed as the exterior and interior gates slid upwards. Neva looked up at the airship before driving the vehicle into the safety of the Nabeho stronghold. The heavy iron gates crashed closed once more. Enapay pulled his goggles over his eyes and thrust the *Dragonfly* higher up into the air. Zen clutched onto the railing with one hand and grabbed his belly with the other. His stomach felt as if it was in his throat. Enapay let out a war cry and spun the ship's wooden steering wheel. He commanded the airship to roll right and tumble away from the fortress.

When the *Dragonfly* leveled out, Zen and the others took their positions behind its four protected gunner stations. The braves slid their rifles through the slits in the metal shields, but Zen had only the chief's spear.

"Here." Enapay tossed Zen his rifle. "You seemed to shoot pretty well with this before."

Zen smiled as he held the gun in his hands. The airship picked up speed. Far out in the distance in front of him, he watched the whirlwind of desert sand being kicked up from Cheng's speeding army.

"I still have one of those bombs left," Enapay shouted over the din of the airship's propellers. "We'll save it for when the time is right."

The *Dragonfly* soared over the highway; Zen eyed the enemy barreling down the dirt road in a column formation. The lead vehicle looked bizarre. It was misshapen, as if it had swallowed another locomobile. It was anything but graceful, and it was a wonder the bulky iron monster was able to travel at such great speed. Behind it, a tightly-knit swarm of menacing vehicles followed.

"There's something up ahead, but I can't tell what it is,"

Enapay squawked.

Zen left his station and grabbed the spyglass lying on the control panel near the steering column. Squinting through the small telescope, he saw that it was indeed a steam locomobile. Two rear smokestacks spit black smoke as it approached. The monstrous nose of the vehicle was heavily fortified with additional plates of armor. Two giant iron plates were joined to form a v-shaped wedge at the front of the vehicle. But what made Zen nearly drop the spyglass was the sight of his *katana* attached to the front of the locomobile.

"What do you see?" Enapay asked.

Taking a deep breath, Zen put the spyglass down. "It is Cheng in an armored locomobile. As an insult, he has fastened my sword to the front of it." Zen's teeth clenched. "He is mocking me."

Enapay reached over for the telescope to take a look himself. His mouth fell open as he stared into the lens. "He's crazy. You don't think he..."

"Cheng is planning to strike your wall head-on," Zen said. "He will drive that thing straight through your gates. We must intercept him before that happens."

Enapay slapped his steering wheel with both hands. "The man is insane!"

Zen's mouth went dry as he asked, "Where is your explosive?"

So it has come to this.

The lives he'd taken. The battles he'd won and lost. The

things he'd achieved. Now on foreign soil, surrounded by filthy criminals, he was about to commit suicide by catapulting himself into a wall.

His armored locomobile shook as he led his raiders on a collision course with the Nabeho gates. This was the end, and he felt the ache of regret consume him. This was not how he wanted to die, and he couldn't help but wallow in the memories of his past.

Cheng admitted to himself that he hadn't entered the military out of patriotism. It was the power. Cheng knew his insatiable thirst for power was what drove him to excellence and allowed him to carry out the orders no other man was willing to perform. But his commanding officers had seen this as a weakness.

During Cheng's tenure as a Jin officer, he never gave the politics of the civil war any thought. He'd decided to widen the campaign while leading a vital operation. He targeted civilians in small villages near the enemy outpost. They were, after all, guilty of conspiring with the enemy and providing refuge for the Sui. He ordered his men to kill them all and set fire to their homes. A few of his soldiers refused and were executed for their insubordination.

His battalion completely disrupted the flow of supplies to the Sui out west, and the Jins took advantage by securing five consecutive victories thereafter. Word of Cheng's achievements spread, as did the tactics he employed. Soon, he enjoyed a greater following than his own generals, and they conspired to capture him and bring him in front of a military tribunal.

Jin leadership might have called for Cheng's execution, but to many within the faction, Cheng was a hero. Banishment was the compromise. At first, he insisted on death to preserve his honor. However, he eventually realized that exile left the door open to new possibilities.

Despite his victories over the native Agriosian tribes, it all felt empty. However, today he would greet the death he should have received back home.

Cheng scanned the fortified cabin, which was to be his tomb. His eyes caught something that gave him pause. Anchored to the rear wall directly behind him hung a makeshift harness made from thick rope. He hadn't noticed this when he first climbed in. He smiled, admitting that his lieutenant just might deserve more credit than he gave him. Maybe with Igor's handiwork, he might just pull through. In the distance, Cheng saw the faint outline of the Nabeho wall. The airship closed in from above. He chuckled to himself and hoped that the boy from Nihon saw the *katana* attached to the front of his locomobile.

Zenjiro's boasting echoed in Cheng's mind while he strapped himself into the rope harness. Perhaps if he did withstand the impact, he would have the opportunity to ram whatever remained of the *katana* through the little weasel's guts. If he could find the woman that killed Jaarg, he'd get the satisfaction of killing her too.

Cheng finished tightening the knots securing him against the rear wall. He took deep breaths and filled his lungs with desert morning air. Cheng was ready to die, but not before taking as many as he could with him. He wished destiny would grant him the chance to kill the boy and the woman.

Fate owed him that much.

NINETEEN

WINONA MET NEVA ONCE SHE was inside the Nabeho fortress. Neva parked the roadster off to one side before getting out of it. Surrounded by guards, Winona put her arms around Neva and led her away from the gates in haste.

"You must come with me, we have several shelters in the village citadel," Winona said.

Neva shrugged her off. "I will stay here and fight."

The chief's wife put her hands to her hips and turned her face up towards the wall, but she didn't argue. "Toksu is there. You can take a position near him."

Neva bolted towards the steep walkway leading up the wall. She jogged her way down the narrow and crowded terrace until she found the hulking warrior leaning forward against the stone merlon. Hundreds of anxious warriors lined the walls, waiting for the enemy's arrival.

Toksu held a rifle in both hands while he kept a backup near his right boot. Even when Neva came right up to him, he didn't move.

"I guess you didn't make it too far," Toksu said, still looking out.

Neva checked both of her revolvers. "No. Maybe ten miles."

She squinted her eyes and sought to find what the warriors were watching. In the emerging daylight, she recognized the small dot in the sky that was the *Dragonfly* heading towards the approaching swirl of dust on the highway. From her estimation, Cheng and his men were less than five miles away.

"Are you sure you want to do this?" Toksu watched her inspect her pistols.

"I suspect Cheng is wanting to even the score. I might as well give him the opportunity before I kill him."

Toksu smirked and squinted at the scene in front of them. "He won't even reach us. Enapay still has one of those glass bombs on board his cloud-hugger."

"Then this should be a quick battle." Neva imitated Toksu, leaning forward against the wall. "As soon as the Nabeho clear the highway of these bastards, I'll be on my way. So I'm doing myself a favor."

"Just don't die. Your son needs you."

Neva holstered both pistols and smirked. "Don't worry about me, savage."

ENAPAY NAVIGATED THE *DRAGONFLY* INTO position about one hundred feet above and to the right of Cheng's armored loco-mobile. A curtain of gunfire spewed from the raider caravan, and Zen and the others got low. Ahak and Sike returned fire with their rifles protruding through the slots in their turret shields. Lena crouched near Zen and readied her own weapon.

"I must ask," she yelled over the blasts of gunfire. "Did you actually defeat Toksu in stick-war?"

Zen peeked his head over the edge, making sure they were still following Cheng's powering locomobile. "Yes."

He held the glass bomb in his hand firmly, but carefully. He recalled Enapay saying the chemical inside of it was extremely volatile. He glanced up at the young woman still scrutinizing him.

Lena shook her head and crawled back to her station to return fire. "Unbelievable," she said after bolting her rifle.

Enapay let out a squeaky yelp as bullets zipped by him. With steady hands, he kept the *Dragonfly* close enough for Zen to have a better chance of hitting Cheng's locomobile with his final bomb.

"This is as good as it's going to get, Zen."

At the same exact moment Zen pulled himself up to throw, Cheng's arm shot through a small opening in the side of his vehicle's cabin, gun in hand. The raider fired his pistol, and incredibly, two of the bullets came precariously close to hitting the *Dragonfly's* hull. One zinged over Enapay's head.

The *Dragonfly* nearly careened out of control when Enapay dropped to the floor. His hand pulled on the helm and forced the airship to bank hard to the right. The other four lost their balance and stumbled to the deck. Zen managed to keep his grip on the railing and the bomb. Lena tumbled and slammed into him with a crash.

Zen caught her with his body, the weight of her impact punching the air out of his lungs. Lena pulled herself up, flashing him an apologetic look.

"Sorry!" Enapay brought the *Dragonfly* level.

Zen forced his lungs to expand and looked up towards the airship's bow. They were now only minutes from reaching the Nabeho village. He turned to Enapay who gave him an abrupt and frantic hand signal. It was time for Zen to throw the bomb.

The other three warriors unleashed a barrage of their own and provided cover fire for Zen. He left the safety of the iron shield long enough to aim and hurl the explosive at Cheng's vehicle.

The wind took hold of the glass sphere and blew it wildly off course. Zen held his breath and watched the initial bright flash consume the rear of Cheng's locomobile. The violent shock wave of the blast blew Zen's hair loose from its knot. He shut his eyes and hit the floor, praying he hadn't gone blind. The fiery eruption rocked the airship, and Zen felt the *Dragonfly* veer sharply to the right as the full force of the explosion filled the air.

With his sight still fuzzy, Zen peered over the airship's rails. He prayed he'd been successful. Once the smoke cleared, what he saw astounded him.

The bomb failed to strike the locomobile's cockpit, but instead blew off a piece of the rear. Cheng's transport continued its course, blazing like a comet. The back end spewed streaking flames, but the engine was protected by the cockpit's armor and still thundered on. Zen couldn't see Cheng inside the well-armored cabin, but he imagined the Xian smiling.

"I was never good with those things." Zen slumped against the side of the hull. He wiped the long black strands from his face in disgust. "I am sorry."

Enapay kept in pursuit, but at a higher altitude. "Now what?"

Zen struggled upright to steal another look at what remained of Cheng's monstrosity below. "He is hiding behind the iron plates. We cannot get a clear shot at him. We are out of bombs and out of time."

The stone wall loomed before them as Enapay sped the *Dragonfly* to beat the raiders to the fortress. Zen noted the Nabeho warriors in their defensive positions lined up on top of the wall and crammed inside both main towers flanking the main gate. He had failed them all, and now the *Dragonfly* had seconds to warn them.

"Get out of there!" Enapay waved his arms wildly at the Nabeho on the wall. "Get out now!"

The *Dragonfly* streaked above the warriors' heads and rushed towards the center of the village before circling back around. Thankfully, the braves heard Enapay's warning. They scattered and pushed each other away from the fortress' main entrance.

Cheng's fiery locomobile rumbled towards them. Zen's throat was dry and his hands clutched the edge of the airship's hull when Cheng smashed headfirst into the tall iron gates, blanketing the whole front of the fortress in fire and smoke.

The sound of metal smashing metal filled the air, followed by a violent outburst that rattled the *Dragonfly* for several seconds. It was as if the land had ripped open. The sharp blast gave way to a growing rumble. Zen swore he heard two explosions, and through the thick fog, he could hear the terrified cries of the Nabeho coming from below.

The dark cloud billowing from the Nabeho wall expanded

overhead. Zen grasped Enapay's shoulder. His mouth tasted of blood, and his head still pounded. It took him a moment to say, "We need to get down there."

Enapay nodded reluctantly. "Okay."

With the turn of a smaller wheel on the side of the helm, the *Dragonfly* lost altitude. Shards of stone and slag iron fell from the sky; the locomobile was twisted metal trapped in a maelstrom of earth and fire. As the *Dragonfly* drew closer, Zen watched a second transport smash head-first into the wall to the right of the gate.

The rest of the raiders poured from their now-stopped vehicles towards the fortress, forming a loose charging column towards the open gash in the Nabeho defenses. Cheng's ruined vehicle was lodged where the main gate had stood. The transport's heavy armor blossomed like an iron flower, and it made the damaged gates impassable. The second locomobile had punched straight through the fortress' barrier, creating a wider opening in the stone rampart.

Enapay plunged the *Dragonfly* towards the damaged front gates. Zen heard the Nabeho fire their weapons at the invaders, keeping the raiders at bay. The smoke thinned, and Zen caught sight of Cheng crawling out of his vehicle's crumpled cabin.

Cheng looked mostly unhurt, and he took refuge behind what was left of his locomobile. Lena raised her rifle, but Zen grabbed the barrel and shoved her weapon aside.

"Cheng is mine." Zen found Chief Ohitekah's spear on the floor and tore Lena's pistol from her holster.

Enapay brought the *Dragonfly* above the burning wreckage, and Zen threw him one final look of assurance before jumping overboard. Zen landed hard on the dusty earth. His momentum carried him forward, and he tucked his body and rolled until he dug his boots into the ground. Zen crouched on one knee and waited for the world to stop spinning.

Zen straightened himself and prayed. *I have no life. I have no death.*

Cheng emerged from his cover with his gun raised; his white teeth gritted as he squeezed the trigger. Still dizzy, Zen flung his body behind the wrecked vehicle; its smokestack belched the last of its wet steam. He waited for Cheng's gun blast, but only the click of an empty chamber came.

Zen took a hold of Lena's revolver and spun away from the smoldering wreckage.

"Out of bullets." Cheng drew his Xian sword from behind his back. His narrow eyes glared at the barrel of Zen's pistol. "Face me like a real *samurai.*"

The sounds of war surrounded them, and the deafening thunder of gunfire echoed from behind the wall. Zen looked to his left and watched clusters of Cheng's raiders attempt to pass through the large crater in the wall, only to be mowed down by Nabeho bullets.

Zen's muscles tensed. He let the boiling fury burn itself out. His finger lingered on the trigger, but he beckoned a glacial calm into his body.

"Put the gun away, boy." Cheng raised his sword. His hand tore the damaged armor from his chest. "Let us do what we do best."

Zen threw the gun aside. He was still a nobleman of Nihon, and he would fight with honor even in the presence of the honor-less.

Cheng twirled his one-handed blade in swift circles, coming to a low fighting stance with the sword pointed at Zen. "Big mistake."

The Nabeho spear was lighter than the naginanta blades Zen had used back home. However, the wooden shaft felt solid as he swung the spear in large menacing circles in order to gain a sense of the weapon's balance. The long steel spearhead gleamed as he held it horizontally and level with Cheng's heart.

Zen felt his breathing and heart rate slow as the familiar energy of *Ishen* filled his insides. His entire body felt energized, his mind sharp.

Cheng lunged forward. His double-edged blade darted forward like a serpent's tongue and clashed against the metal of Zen's spinning spear. Without hesitation, Cheng wheeled his weapon in rapid circles towards Zen's head. His movements were fluid as if his wrist were made of silk.

Zen easily parried all of Cheng's lightning-quick attacks. His mind was calculating and empty; his body moved without effort or thought. The Nabeho spear was a blur when it met the Xian steel with a high pitched song.

Cheng backed off. He breathed heavily as he solidified his balance.

"You are good." Cheng maintained a safe distance while his chest heaved. His face was smeared with sweat and soot. "Who are you really?"

Zen remained still, his spear ready for another attack. "I am Zenjiro of the Kanze."

It felt right to tell him who was about to plunge his soul into the next life.

Zen swept his weapon in a circular motion, giving the razor-sharp spearhead momentum before arcing towards Cheng's midsection.

Cheng was a brute, but his movements were graceful and smooth. He maneuvered his body below the long slash of Zen's spear and rushed forward to counter. Zen brought the spearhead upwards, and the butt end of the shaft circled forward and crashed into Cheng's chin with a hollow crack.

Cheng groaned and slithered backwards. He tripped over a piece of metal debris embedded in the dirt. His arms waved wildly, but he managed to steady himself. Drops of red from his mouth dribbled down into his black beard, and rage flowed with it. Cheng spun his sword once again before unleashing a series of rapid attacks with new ferocity.

The blows were powerful, and Zen wheeled backwards as his spear vibrated and sparked with each strike. Despite his heightened senses and reflexes, Zen still wasn't fast enough. Did the Xian also possess the power to conjure *Ishen*? Cheng's blade was a typhoon, and searing pain in Zen's right leg forced him to retreat.

The warmth of blood flowed from his thigh to his boot, and Zen gave himself only a split second to glimpse at his burning wound. His knees buckled, but Zen fought the urge to crumble. He kept his spear pointed forward to weather another Xian storm.

Being in the state of *Ishen* made his senses sharp, but so too was his mind honed. Despite the sparks of fireworks alighting from his fresh wound, his acute willpower pushed it aside. The energy within him surged again, forcing the pain to be just a memory.

"You are more than good." Cheng's eyes flashed downward at the gash weeping blood through Zen's torn pants. "You are the best I have ever faced. It is as much an honor to kill you as it is to die by my hand."

Zen took deep controlled breaths; the point of his weapon followed Cheng who circled him in quiet, yet deliberate, footsteps. Raiders continued to fall around them, but he and Cheng may as well have been invisible to the rest of the battle. Zen was content with allowing the fighting to remain in the background, but he caught a glimpse of the Nabeho watching him from above.

Cheng stopped his stalking and raised his sword. He burst forward at Zen with a flurry of stabs and slashes. Zen anticipated each attack and responded without conscious effort. He was water, ebbing and flowing with the motion of his enemy's steel. Cheng's rhythm was steady, but Zen noticed the Xian's breath labored to keep up. Zen found that each new strike became slower and weaker. Cheng back-pedaled, but Zen would not give him the luxury of catching his breath. Zen thrust his spear in several rapid jabs, piercing Cheng's left shoulder twice.

The Xian let out a hideous shriek and circled his sword to block the oncoming assault, but he couldn't match Zen's resolve. Overpowered, Cheng couldn't stop Zen's blade from plunging deep into his abdomen. A muffled gasp escaped the Xian's lips before using his sword's hilt to slide Zen's spear from his open gut.

In desperation, Cheng brought his blade up and released a vicious final blow downwards at the crown of Zen's head. Zen was taken by surprise as he side-stepped the Xian sword. He severed Cheng's right hand for good measure.

Cheng fell to his knees and pressed his bloody right arm against his chest. His mouth drew open in a silent cry, full of venom and hot fury.

Zen brought his spear's blade high. He looked down at the

Xian whose eyes still flashed madness.

"You have fought bravely," Zen whispered. His body coiled. *Ishen* was beginning to fade, and the blazing pain in his right thigh returned. "This is an honorable death."

Cheng mumbled a curse in his Origin tongue. Blood gushed from his open mouth, and his eyes remained full of hate.

Zen let his blade fly.

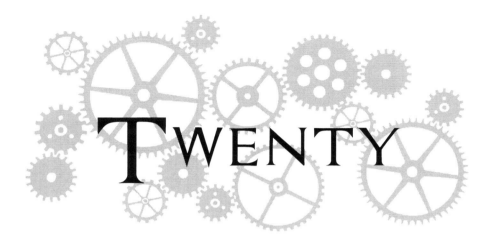

TWENTY

THE CRUMBLING BREACH IN THE Nabeho wall allowed a column of six or seven raiders wide to get inside the fortress. The braves assembled in the courtyard and formed their own defensive formation. From above, Neva watched the Nabeho obliterate the rushing pirates.

All around her, warriors on the walls fired a rain of bullets and mowed down the raiders' advance. This had been an ill-planned attack, and the Nabeho made them pay dearly for it.

Neva and Toksu had abandoned their original post when the two locomobiles slammed into the wall, and they now found themselves sniping from one of the east gate towers. They met Chief Ohitekah and Itan there, and Toksu volunteered to take the chief to the citadel when the fighting at the breach intensified.

An unusual sound carried above the discord of rifle fire, a quick metallic rapping noise. Neva found it disturbing, and her eyes roamed the battlefield below until she found the source.

A squad of raiders carried strange looking rifles that fired at an unbelievable rate. Neva recalled hearing about early proto-types of such guns during the rebellion against the Iberians, but she had never seen them in action until now.

The raiders with the auto guns pushed their advance; the column marched through the breach with renewed vigor. From the tower, Neva took several invaders out with careful aim, but as each raider fell, a new one snatched up the power-ful rifle and continued the attack.

The *Dragonfly* soared overhead, and it made several passes at the raiders. They pointed their auto guns at the airship, spraying bullets with such deadly speed that accuracy meant little.

Neva blanched at the sight of sparks lighting up the craft, and its flight became erratic. Even from a mile away she could see it sway and rock. Black vapor from its engine left a long, dark trail, and its wings flapped like a wounded bird. The raiders continued to follow it with their auto gun fire as the *Dragonfly* dropped from the sky.

The heavily armed raiders from the rear pushed the invad-ing column forward, and the momentum of the battle quickly shifted. Itan snatched a flare pistol from a hook and fired a dazzling red streak that blossomed into a crimson fireball in the morning sky.

The Nabeho warriors on the ground pulled back, leaving the courtyard and retreating towards the center of the village. There, she estimated at least three hundred Nabeho braves stationed inside the trench fired on the raiders that poured in-to the fortress.

She turned her attention back to the airship as it spiraled

downwards. Neva wanted to close her eyes, but she forced herself to watch. The *Dragonfly* pulled its nose up just before impact.

The craft almost seemed to take flight again after bouncing off the ground, but it came back down and slid across the sand instead. After skidding for several hundred feet, the *Dragonfly* finally came to a halt.

Neva looked down and noticed a handful of the raiders armed with auto guns break away from the invading column to finish off the *Dragonfly's* survivors. Her head throbbed in alarm, and she descended the ladder in haste.

THE ENGINE SPUTTERED, AND THICK smoke made Enapay's eyes water and his throat close up. He grabbed onto the side of the *Dragonfly's* hull and pulled himself up and over until he crashed to the desert floor. His vision spun and his jaw hurt, but he forced himself up to check on the others.

"Everyone okay?" Enapay called out before choking on the black cloud spewing from what was left of his airship. He kept his goggles on to protect his eyes from the harsh smoke.

He heard shuffling against the hull, and a weak voice finally replied, "I'm alive." It was Lena's, though he couldn't see her through the fumes.

"I am too," grunted another voice from the stern.

"Who's that?" Enapay could barely discern his own hand in front of him. Billowing smoke swirled all around him, and it was like night had fallen. He tried waving the blackness away.

"It's Sike. I found Lena. I think her leg is broken."

That left one more.

"Ahak, where are you?" Enapay walked towards the bow of his airship. "Are you all right?"

A breeze blew the smoke away for a moment, long enough for Enapay to see Sike helping Lena out of the *Dragonfly*. He pushed his goggles up to his forehead to get a better look. The girl hobbled on one leg, and Sike had a nasty cut on his forehead. Other than that, they looked relatively healthy for having tumbled from the sky. There was no sign of Ahak

His mind came to a ghastly conclusion, but he couldn't allow himself to finish the thought. The wind died, and another wall of black smog enveloped him. Enapay covered his mouth and took several steps away from the wreckage. He scanned the desert. From afar, he saw movement, and it filled him with hope.

"Ahak?" Enapay called out.

Lena and Sike hobbled over and stood next to him. They waited for Ahak to emerge. Enapay heard a fierce staccato sound, and several flashes cut through the gloom. In his periphery, he saw Lena double over and sink to the ground. Sike and Enapay locked eyes for a fraction of a second before they both scurried back over the airship's hull and got low.

Sike crawled on his belly to a rifle and dumped a bag of bullets onto the floor. With trembling hands, he clumsily loaded the weapon. Enapay drew his pistol, but he didn't dare move as the torrent of gunfire went right over his head.

Stupid auto guns. The raiders had smuggled them from Iberia for sure.

He heard the sound of another vehicle approaching, and his heart sank. If a whole carload of raiders with those rapid-fire guns were coming, he and Sike were done for. Enapay looked down to check his revolver, and the sight of his own blood made him gasp.

The bottom of his jacket and his left thigh were covered in blood. There was no pain, so Enapay thought he might be in shock. His hands shook. He debated whether he should sit there and wait to die or peel away his jacket and shirt to inspect the damage. Sike remained face down, afraid to move.

"Now what do we do?" the young brave whispered.

Maybe this was the right time to become spiritual. Why not? It worked for Zen. The sudden desire for a cold ale made his mouth go dry. He decided to hedge his bets and pray to the Wind and Sun gods for protection, or at least a quick and painless death. The worst that could happen was that no supernatural force would get him out of this. Maybe it was a day for miracles.

Enapay had made so many damn mistakes in his life, so he whispered a quiet apology for all he'd done. He always planned on eventually going straight, and a big part of him had thought that coming back home would help.

With every blast, his body involuntarily jerked. There was no escape this time. This was not how he'd imagined his death, and his reverence melted into regret.

Another burst rang through the air, and Enapay shut his eyes to wait for the inevitable. When the sound of gunfire suddenly went silent, he wondered if he was dead. The volcanic heat searing his side and leg let him know that he yet lived.

"Enapay?" a voice cut through the thick smoke.

Sike pushed his body upwards cautiously, leading with his rifle.

"Is your crew all right?" the voice came again.

Enapay blinked. He didn't recognize the voice. He shook his head in the hope of rattling some memory into place. It sounded like a woman.

The voice emitted a muffled cry as the thumping of footsteps came closer. Enapay took an unsteady breath, assuming the woman must have discovered Lena's body lying next to the *Dragonfly*.

"Sike and I are here, inside the ship. I've been shot." Sharp, stabbing pain stole his breath. "At least twice, but I'm too scared to look."

Neva climbed aboard. She greeted Sike before coming to Enapay with a worried look on her face. "Where are you hit?"

"I know my left leg for sure," Enapay replied. "I don't know. Maybe somewhere on my left side too."

The pain took an opportunity to reassure Enapay of his diagnosis. He'd taken two bullets. One buried itself in his thigh, and the other ripped through his left side. Neva bit her lower lip while inspecting his wounds.

"You're lucky," she said.

Enapay laughed, but laughter turned to pained coughs abruptly as another wave of agony took hold. "You call this lucky?" His noticed Neva was bleeding from the left arm. "You're hit too."

"Those raiders might have been armed with auto guns, but they had horrible aim." She pulled back Enapay's jacket. "You'll live. The bullets grazed you. The girl isn't so fortunate."

"I had four braves with me," Enapay said weakly. "Ahak must have fallen out."

Sike's stocky figure loomed over Lena's body, his eyes wet with tears. "Who's going to tell Toksu his niece is dead?"

Neva put her palm to her mouth. "She was Toksu's niece?"

Enapay lay still, even breathing hurt. "I will. She was my responsibility."

"I saw what happened. Once the raiders used their auto guns, you didn't stand a chance," Neva said as she touched his hand.

Imagining the raiders cutting down his people with their rapid fire weapons filled Enapay with dread. It was sure to be a slaughter. He didn't want to know, but he forced himself to ask, "How are our defenses holding?"

"Several of Cheng's men got their hands on auto rifles and pushed their column past the wall," she explained. "Your ground force pulled back into a trench. The raiders had nowhere to hide in the open square, and their bodies were beginning to pile up."

He wasn't sure how much damage the *Dragonfly* had sustained from those cursed weapons, but he knew it would take more than tinkering to get her off the ground again. With a grunt and Neva's help, he stood to inspect the airship.

The armored cylinders encasing the hydrogen-lifting ballonets had done their job, but more than two dozen bullets penetrated the hull and struck the engine and boiler. The rudder had flown off when they crash-landed. Its crumpled wings were beyond repair.

Enapay spat. "Look what they did. The *Dragonfly* is a wreck."

Neva playfully slapped Enapay's chin. "You don't look so great either, savage."

ZEN RIPPED THE SHIRT FROM a dead raider. He tore off a long strip of cloth and tied it tightly around his leg. The open wound throbbed and bled as he took cover behind Cheng's wrecked transport. He watched the *Dragonfly* crash into the open desert. His first instinct was to help Enapay and the others, but when he heard more of the auto guns opening fire nearby, Zen turned towards the fortress instead.

His hands searched the ground until he finally found the pistol he'd discarded. Cheng's blood drenched the metal blade of his spear, so Zen gave the weapon an abrupt swipe towards the ground to clean it. Carrying a weapon in each hand, he peered over the wreckage of the two locomobiles.

Zen noticed the raiders' abandoned vehicles. They were scattered in a haphazard line fifty yards away. A quick plan formed in his mind, and he hoped to have the strength to carry it out before he lost too much blood.

Ignoring the stabbing pain in his right leg, Zen ran unnoticed to the unguarded vehicles. He picked an empty and idling locomobile. He unhitched the passenger car, jumped into the cab, and with a push of the red lever, released the brakes. Zen pushed the throttle lever, and the vehicle surged forward. Fresh steam blew from the rear smokestacks, and the pistons gained momentum. He maneuvered around the other vehicles until he spotted his target.

The raiders' formation was barely a column at all, and because the breach in the Nabeho wall was so narrow, they were in more of a haphazard wedge.

When Zen put the locomobile in full throttle, the raiders at the rear of the formation finally noticed him coming right for them. They brought their auto guns level and fired a storm of bullets, but the cab's armor protected Zen. He continued to close in. His heart rate accelerated, keeping time with the tireless chugging of the locomobile's pistons. He was going at top speed, and while a handful of the raiders managed to dive out of his way, for the others, it was too late.

Their grimy faces twisted in sheer terror as Zen drove the bull-nose front of the vehicle into the helpless raiders. One pirate crashed into the cracked windshield with his head, his face jagged with horror seconds before smashing into the glass. Bodies bounced off the iron plates, flailing like rag dolls as their bones shattered. They cried out after being thrown into the air and crushed by the locomobile's merciless steel wheels.

The Nabeho wall loomed inches to his right until Zen pulled the steering wheel sharply to the left and hit the brakes. The vehicle protested with a metal-on-metal screech and nearly rolled over before Zen regained control.

He pushed the throttle again, mercilessly striking several more raiders with his front end. Zen struggled to see through the spider-webbed cracks covering the windshield.

Zen turned hard left again, bringing it around for another run, but the pirates' formation had already completely collapsed. At least two dozen raiders abandoned their positions and retreated. They scrambled into the remaining cars and sped away. Zen killed the engine and took the first breaths he'd taken since getting behind the steering wheel. He took deep gulps of air, fighting off the siren's song for sleep. He'd lost a lot of blood, and he knew he was in danger of blacking out.

A handful of Nabeho warriors cautiously emerged from the breach in the wall. They watched the last of the raiders jump into a locomobile and flee. The braves threw their arms up into the air and screamed their celebratory war cries. Itan was among the growing group of warriors cheering, and the general spotted Zen.

Zen's leg was on fire, and he felt lightheaded. He climbed out of the cabin against his body's pleas to stay still. Itan wore a concerned look on his sweaty face as he ran to assist him.

Itan held him up by his shoulders. "You are extraordinary."

Zen was about to give thanks, but his tongue was like baked leather.

The ruined bodies of the raiders lay scattered all around them, and Zen allowed himself to take in the victory. For one fleeting moment, he felt like he was back home. His *nerigawa* was covered in dust and blood. Takeo would have gotten a chuckle out of that.

The surviving raiders had left behind most of their locomobiles and empty cargo cars. Itan barked an order to his men, and the front gates opened. Nabeho braves stepped out to inspect the damage and casualties. Some of them picked up the auto guns the pirates had abandoned and put them in a small pile one by one. The others climbed on top of the vehicles and danced.

With Itan's help, Zen took slow steps toward a large group of jubilant warriors. With a wide smile, he let himself become enveloped by the Nabeho war cries and arm shakes. But all he could think of was the fallen *Dragonfly*.

Twenty One

THE LONG CARAVAN OF ARMED roadsters, locomobiles, and their train cars lumbered south along the unmarked barren highway. The desert was a still and desolate wasteland that made Geller nervous. His private train was out in the open, and he didn't like to be vulnerable. He had a line of five swift roadsters mounted with .30 caliber, water-cooled auto guns on each flank of his cavalcade, yet they failed to help him feel safe.

His guarded cargo consisted of many valuables. After leaving Europa and crossing the Atlantica Sea, he acquired stores of Iberian weapons and a fleet of Iberian vehicles, which he sold at a three hundred percent profit to an army of pirates out west.

He had purchased a dozen adolescent boys from a poor orphanage at the southern border of Agrios. Most of them were possessed of a unique orphan fury, and they would make excellent gladiators. Public fights to the death were a favorite sport in the coastal Azincayan towns. His most prized possession, however, was kept right beside him.

The boy sat quietly, pouring over the engineering manuals and books Geller had given him. Marcel Bouvier was oblivious to the outside world, and he only looked up when he needed to eat or relieve himself.

Geller's own father was an inventor, so he had a sincere appreciation for the engineering arts. That idiot Pierce had no idea what his stepson was capable of. The child's stepfather came from a wealthy family, and their money came from trades no cleaner than Geller's. From narcotics to extortion, Pierce inherited a small empire. The rebellion against Iberia only made it easier for his family to flourish while the rest of Francia plunged into poverty.

Up until the end of the winter season, Geller had little contact with Pierce and his company. When Geller found himself having to work with the spoiled brat in order to smuggle Iberian weapons out of Francia, the two had a life-altering conversation after finalizing the terms of their contract.

Forty days ago...

PIERCE BREACHED PROPER ETIQUETTE, DISCUSSING private personal matters during a business meeting. Geller sat in Pierce's study and glanced at the painted family portrait hanging over the fireplace. Marcel wore the face of a complacent and soft-spoken child. Harmless.

"He looks innocent. Your wife is absolutely stunning," Geller said.

"Sure," responded Pierce with a wave of his hand. "Marcel is well behaved. My wife, though difficult to tame at first, has finally learned her place and is obedient without question."

Geller took a sip of his whiskey. "Sounds like everything is perfect. What is the problem?" He was growing bored, but abruptly walking out would be counterproductive.

"I need an heir," Pierce muttered. "It has been almost two years, and Neva has failed to give me a son. My surgeon is at a loss, she is perfectly healthy. There's a part of me that believes her body refuses to carry my child."

Geller wondered if the man was insane or just stupid. "You have adopted her son as your own. There's your heir."

Pierce stood up and began to pace. "He's not mine, not really. It's not the same. Besides, the boy is strange. Marcel would rather read than play. He only speaks to his mother, the rest of the time he's mute. Hardly worthy of running my company. And divorce is forbidden under Iberian law."

Geller looked at a framed photograph of the boy on Pierce's desk. Marcel looked to be eight or nine years old, his body long sticks glued together. "I see your point."

Pierce was coming to a slow simmering anger. "I can't even stand looking at the boy. Fathered by an idiot inventor who couldn't make a dime to save his life."

Geller's curiosity piqued. "Who, may I ask, is the boy's father? I have a keen interest in keeping up with the invention industry."

Pierce stopped his pacing. "His name was Bouvier. The child is named after his father."

Geller nearly choked on his own tongue. It took him a few moments to collect himself. Pierce was absolutely ignorant, and Geller worked to control his excitement.

"I know this man," said Geller nonchalantly. "He was a tinkerer of some sort, I believe. A failed hack that decided to try his hand in growing animal feed."

That was a lie, but Pierce was as observant as a scarecrow. Geller's mind was awash with new ideas, the kind that lined his pockets richly.

"Do you have any idea why Bouvier abandoned his work and became a farmer before he died?" Geller asked. "Such a mystery. Who knows what astounding inventions died with him?" He bit his lower lip, wondering if he'd said too much.

Pierce shrugged. "Neva never speaks of him."

"May I offer a suggestion?" Geller asked him.

Pierce took a deep breath. "Yes. Please do."

"Let me take the boy."

Pierce stepped away as if he had been struck. "I'm sorry?"

"Let me take the boy off of your hands. Problem solved." Geller stood up and joined Pierce in his pacing. "Figure out a way for the two of you to be alone, far from your estate. A father and son hunting trip. Child abductions have been known to occur out in the wild."

"I don't know." Pierce shook his head. "Marcel and his mother are close. She would go mad. Her time on the battlefield has made her a little unstable. Neva was an officer in the Francian Rebellion. Did I ever tell you that?"

Geller smiled. Pierce was negotiating. "No, I did not know that about your wife." He turned again to the family portrait. Neva looked every bit a woman. Her hair was auburn, her face immaculate. "She's the most beautiful soldier I have ever seen."

"If she were to lose her beloved son, who knows what

would become of her." A crease formed between Pierce's brows.

"That would be a tragedy. She might do something. . . irrational." Geller put his glass down.

"The boy is bookish, but he's well behaved. He's not a nuisance." Pierce sat back down behind his desk. Still negotiating. "Still, I would consider it if the offer was worthwhile. On my end, I would be losing a potential heir. I would have to deal with my wife, who might be driven to suicide, as you yourself suggest."

"Suicide? I never said suicide." Geller was playing with him.

Pierce swallowed. "I told you she was already emotionally fragile. If her son was abducted, she would do something drastic. Suicide is very drastic."

"The most drastic there is."

"I don't know," Pierce said.

"Consider my offer." Geller would not be baited. "I would take him to Agrios. Maybe sell him to a factory, an engineer, or inventor's workshop. The boy is clearly intelligent. His literacy will be a premium in the Wild Land. Hell, you will be doing the boy a favor."

Pierce's eyes shifted back and forth. "I wouldn't want him to be laboring in the fields or a grungy factory. No one would want the scrawny mouse for that kind of work anyway."

The seed was planted.

"I will be crossing the Channel tonight, staying in a small town on the Albion Isle," Geller said. "I plan on procuring additional cargo and securing my passage to Agrios from there. You have ten days. I shall dispatch my couriers shortly with the details of my offer."

Pierce stood and started pacing again.

Geller offered his hand. "We can correspond on the matter until we come to a mutually beneficial agreement. Agreed?"

Pierce took his hand, and a sly grin cracked on his face.

GELLER WORKED BEHIND HIS MAKESHIFT desk in his spacious car hitched to the lead locomobile. He paused to stare at Marcel. Two hundred thousand ibers was such a small price to pay for such a child. He had watched the boy devour volumes of books that even the most educated scholars would struggle with.

A knock at the car door brought Geller out of his day-dreaming. One of his bodyguards entered, steadying himself as he hopped into the moving car and shut the door behind him. The man was a brutal mercenary. Even his name was brutal: Kamau. Geller made sure all of his employees were properly dressed. The fine long gray coat, ruffled business shirt, and black slacks neatly tucked in his shiny boots made the man look more like a gentleman than a trained killer.

Kamau was of average height, slightly taller than Geller, and his body was like chiseled black granite. The man looked terrifying, even dressed in finery, but that was exactly why Geller hired him.

"Sir, we are nearing the Mexihcan border." Kamau's dark skin glistened with sweat in the desert heat. "We are making excellent time."

Geller leafed through his paperwork, searching for a map. "How far can we travel until we need to stop for fuel and supplies?"

Kamau crossed his muscular arms in thought. "We have enough fuel to get us to the southern tip of Mexihco. That's about forty hours, nonstop, at full speed."

"Let's stop once we reach Mexihco City. We can resupply there for the voyage south. I have a contact I need to meet with anyway." Geller turned to Marcel who was lost in a book about clockworks. "We can stretch our legs then."

Kamau bowed. "Very good sir."

Geller stared at Kamau's dark wet face. "Please change into more comfortable clothing. In fact, tell all the men to change. The heat is merciless down here."

With an obedient nod, Kamau left through the door again. Geller looked out the window and stared at the sandy void. The landscape was empty except for those awful prickly plants on the side of the desolate highway. He allowed his mind to drift again, dreaming of life on his own paradise island in faraway Oceania.

"All thanks to you, Marcel," Geller said out loud.

Marcel did not look up.

Geller rested his chin in his hand. "All thanks to you."

Twenty Two

ZEN SPENT MOST OF THE next day in the closest thing the Nabeho had to a hospital. While the village only had two healers, and there were three citizens with extensive outside surgical training, together they effectively combined ancient techniques with modern methods to help heal the wounded.

After one of them stitched the gash on Zen's right leg, they applied a poultice of crushed petals from a yellow plant as an antiseptic. A nurse bandaged it tightly and warned him to not do anything strenuous the next couple of days.

As Zen lay on a small cot made of wood and canvas, Neva made short but frequent visits and kept him updated with all of the happenings around the village. Several crews had moved the fallen raiders to a mass grave outside of the walls. She guessed there were over two hundred dead.

Neva's wounds were trivial, and she assisted the surgeons in tending to the wounded. Zen could feel the tension grow within Neva with every passing hour, but he suspected the soldier in her wouldn't let her leave as long as the tribe could use her help. One moment it would look as if she were going to depart for good, but then someone would ask for her assistance. She couldn't say no.

Zen learned that a handful of injured raiders were captured and put in the underground jail known as The Pit, which was located directly below the citadel. The Nabeho had lost twenty-two men and women in the defense of their village, and Chief Ohitekah estimated it would take at least thirty days to repair their wall and heavy iron gates.

Enapay was nowhere to be seen, but Neva assured Zen that the pilot's wounds were superficial. After a healer tended to him, Enapay became engrossed with hauling his airship back to the fortress. From what Neva said, it sounded like the *Dragonfly* was completely beyond repair.

Neva was sure Enapay felt personally responsible for Lena and Ahak's deaths. Ahak's body had been recovered. He had fallen out of the airship after the raiders assaulted the *Dragonfly* with their auto guns. Enapay blamed himself, and Neva said it was best to leave him for now.

In the afternoon, the tribe held a ceremony for their dead outside the Spirit Hall. Zen felt well enough to accompany Neva as guests to their most sacred ritual. The twenty-two bodies were carried out and lifted onto an elevated platform. Nearly all the attendees wept. The cries were replaced with their shaman who led them into singing their ancient chants.

Toksu looked especially devastated, and he remained clustered around his immediate family members throughout the ceremony. Neva informed Zen that Lena, who was shot by the raiders, was Toksu's niece.

Later, Itan pulled Zen aside to speak with him in private. During the battle, he had witnessed Zen's fight with Cheng. Itan praised him for his spirit and his courage, and that he and Chief Ohitekah truly believed that fate had brought Zen to their village to help save the Nabeho.

Zen felt honored, yet depressed. His family sword was sure to have been destroyed by Cheng's locomobile. His lost heirloom reminded him of his original quest, and he hoped to receive a sign as to what he should do next.

Neva joined him in silence, wandering towards the damaged eastern gates of the fortress. That's where they found Enapay. The pilot stood motionless with his hands on his hips, tugging at the goggles around his neck. What remained of the airship lay in a mutilated heap at his feet.

Zen noticed his amulet's hot pulse when he approached and stood next to the wreckage. Was this the sign he was looking for? He wondered what it meant, but he decided to put it out of his mind for the time being.

"Sorry about your airship." Neva patted Enapay's back.

Without looking up, Enapay replied with a low grunt.

She stared at the wrecked airship in silence for a long time before saying, "You know, I was going to ask you for your help in tracking my son. I thought I could make up for lost time if I took to the air. So much for that."

Enapay finally turned to her. "Thank you for saving my life. Those raiders were going to fill me up with lead." He managed a weak smile. "I would have helped you find your son."

Zen said, "Iberian machine guns. Iberian cannons. How did Cheng get his hands on these arms?"

"Lots of smuggling going on in the East," Enapay replied. "People steal from each other, and it's not uncommon for highly sought-after contraband to change hands several times. These days, you'd better have a small brigade to protect you if you're going to be lugging artillery and auto guns all over Agrios."

Neva kicked dirt. "Geller had to be their source. He has his own private army and the resources to smuggle these kinds of weapons. He must have met with Cheng to complete the sale just before they captured me."

Enapay climbed into the demolished hull of the *Dragonfly*. He examined the boiler and components attached to it. "I think I can salvage some of this. I have the necessary tools, but not the proper replacement parts needed to put her back together." He gave Neva an apologetic look. "I'm sorry."

"Those steam locomobile the raiders left, are those of Iberian origin as well?" Zen asked.

"I think so," Neva replied.

Enapay raised both arms in exultation, nearly doing a clumsy dance until he winced from his wounds. "Zen, I know exactly what you're thinking. Those locomobiles run on carbsidian, exactly like the *Dragonfly*."

Neva looked lost. "Carbsidian?"

Zen remembered the carbsidian rocks the *Dragonfly* burned for power. "It is a fuel source. A modified coal," he said to her.

Seeing Neva's failure to understand, Enapay explained, "The Iberians have been infusing standard coal with another type of ore for a couple of years now. It allows their vehicles to have increased power and sufficiency. I flew all over Agrios for four full seasons, and used maybe only a quarter of all the carbsidian I stored in a small chest."

Neva's eyes grew. "So I'll be able to travel faster without needing to stop for refueling as often. I might be able to catch up to Geller and my son in one of those locomobiles."

Enapay's grin returned. "We just might."

"We?" Neva looked surprised and relieved. "You will help me?"

The amulet was fiercely radiating now, almost burning Zen's chest.

Enapay bent his lanky body to look her in the eyes. "Like I said, I owe you my life. I might not have the *Dragonfly*, but the least I can do is help you get your son back."

Neva's tears rolled down her cheek. "You too?" she asked, putting an arm around Zen.

The hot stone power penetrated his flesh, demanding his acknowledgment. Ever since he had met Neva, he knew their destinies were somehow intertwined. At first, he thought maybe it was because she was a mother, desperate to rescue her son. In many ways, she reminded him of his own mother, but now he was sure of one thing, he was meant to go with Neva on her quest.

"I was going to ask you first, Zen," said Enapay. "I didn't want to speak for you."

"I could use your help." Neva's arm tightened around his shoulders.

Zen clutched at his radiant amulet, which the other two finally noticed. "When do we leave?"

IT WAS EVENING, ONLY A whisper of sunlight traced the far end of the horizon. Zen was alone on the Nabeho wall open parapet, and he watched the transition from day into night. Waiting meant more scattered thinking. Before he got too homesick, the sound of muffled voices kept him from wallowing in his depression.

Down below, Zen watched a long line of natives enter what was once the east gate. The visitors walked through the twisted metal slowly and greeted the Nabeho when they entered. This tribe looked similar to the Nabeho. Their skin was bronze, their clothing the color of earth. The men wore their dark hair long and wild. They represented the Oraibi Tribe who had come to express their gratitude to the Nabeho. Zen watched the Oraibi contingents gather in the open courtyard. Itan brought them to the deep trench Zen had suggested they dig, which proved to be an effective defense against the raiders who breached their damaged wall. It sounded like Itan was retelling the battle against Cheng's army, and the Oraibi applauded at the end.

Zen noticed the large group was led by Chief Ohitekah who steered them towards the center of the city, in the direction of the Spirit Hall. Below, his eyes caught someone stirring, waving long arms trying to get his attention. It was dark, but when the figure lifted a lantern, Zen saw Toksu motioning for him to come down from the wall.

Zen walked down the stone steps and noticed Toksu concealing something behind his back. Although it had been a difficult day of mourning for the giant, the warrior wore a gentle grin on his face.

"I have something of yours," Toksu said, his smile growing. The giant brought his arm around, and his bear claw of a hand revealed his gift. It was his pistols, both in their holsters attached to the belt.

Zen took them, and after a quick examination, he concluded

they were in perfect condition. After closing the cylinder of one of his guns, Zen exhaled with relief. These were not the irreplaceable relic his family sword had been, but to feel their familiar steely weight in both of his hands felt comforting. His fingers tightened around the leather wrapped grips as if he were embracing long lost brothers.

"Thank you, Toksu." Zen wrapped the belt around his waist and fastened the silver buckle. "I was not sure I would see these again."

"The Oraibi found it in their temple. They're most grateful for your victory over Cheng." Toksu's grin faded. "I hoped that we'd find your sword too, but we didn't."

Zen's heart beat wildly against his chest. All hope disappeared. "It is my fault. I should never have brought it to Agrios. The important thing is that your village is safe."

Toksu sighed. "You and Enapay are leaving with Neva tonight?"

"Yes. He is finishing the necessary modifications to one of the transports the raiders had left behind."

Zen began walking, and Toksu followed at his side.

"You know," Toksu began, "with your long black hair freed from its knot, you might pass as a Nabeho brave."

Zen chuckled.

"Chief Ohitekah is going to display his spear you had used to defeat Cheng," Toksu said, keeping pace with Zen's slow steps. "He will hang it from a wall in the War Room. He said our people will look upon the spear and know the story of Zenjiro, the Warrior of Nihon who came to help defend the Nabeho."

Zen felt a shimmer of pride.

"That is a great honor," Zen said. "Please be sure to thank

him for me."

They arrived at the modest wooden hogan that once belonged to Enapay's uncle. Toksu initiated the goodbye by extending his large arm. Zen grasped it with tight fingers.

"Good journey, young one. Take care of Enapay, and I hope you fulfill your quest." Toksu gave Zen's much smaller arm a slight shake. "I will see you again."

"It has been an honor fighting alongside of you. I will remember the Nabeho always."

Toksu released Zen's arm and turned towards the Spirit Hall where Chief Ohitekah and the Elders entertained the visiting Oraibi tribe. Zen watched the hulking Nabeho disappear around a corner. When Toksu was gone, Zen entered the small cabin to gather his things.

NEVA DESCENDED THE STONE STEPS and found herself in the underground bunker called The Pit. The damp cellar housed three tiny cells, each crammed with a surviving raider. They looked up at her when she entered, but they remained silent.

She was confident Geller had sold the Iberian contraband to Cheng, and therefore he must have stopped in the Oraibi town to deliver the weapons. Maybe one of the raiders would give her the information she needed to catch up to her son. She paced up and down the humid and narrow corridor, building the tension. Out of habit, she took hold of her right pistol and twirled it several times before holstering it. Finally, one of them spoke.

"The Commander greatly underestimated you."

The raider might have been as towering as Toksu, but the man looked sickly and malnourished. His thinning white hair was greasy and fell straight down to his shoulders. The dirty beard failed to cover his hollow cheeks, and she recognized him at once. He had struck her with his whip and had stood guard outside her prison.

Neva kept her hand on her revolver. "Looks like your Commander did a whole lot of underestimating. Did you know that little boy from Nihon beheaded your leader? Isn't that a shame?"

It felt good to mock all of them. She wished she had been the one to cut the bastard's head off. "Funny how quickly the tables can turn. Two days ago I was the one in the cage, re-member?"

"I expect you'll be off to go rescue your son?" the man asked, finally lifting his face up to look at her in the eyes. Ne-va shot him a fierce look, and she wondered if he was teasing her.

The raider pressed against the metal bars, his pitiful face a thin sheet of flesh pulled tight against a jagged skull. "I hope you find him."

There was no trace of malice in his voice. Neva approached him. "What's your name?"

"Igor." He tilted his head as if he was tipping an invisible hat, and his gaze drifted far off as if he was searching for something.

Neva stared straight into the filthy man's dark eyes. "Wouldn't you like to do something decent before you die? That way, you will know right up until the end that your last deed was an honorable one."

Igor stood in silence, and she hoped he was considering her

offer of redemption.

"I believe Geller sold you the Iberian weapons," Neva pressed. "Where was he heading after his visit? Tell me what I need to know."

"Yes, Geller did provide us with the weapons." Igor's words spilled onto the dank floor without effort. "You missed him by only one day."

Neva dared to step closer. "Did you see my son?"

"No. I never even saw Geller himself. The Commander dealt with a representative instead. Geller remained in one of the passenger cars, behind dark windows. I only saw his employees when we took possession of the weapons."

"Do you know where they were going?" Neva took a step back.

"South."

"South where? Mexihco?" That had been Neva's best guess all along. "Tell me."

Igor kept his head up, his eyes shut in concentration. "I heard a couple of Geller's hired hands grumbling about having to cut through Mexihco on their way to Azincaya. They said something about a coastal city called Caru."

This made sense. Mexihco was the doorstep to the world's darkest underworld, a haven for pirates and other criminals. But Azincaya was worse. If Agrios was called the Wild Land, its southern sister continent was the Dead Land.

"I'm sure of it. That's where they were going." Igor let go of the bars and leaned back against the slimy wall of his cell.

Neva looked at him for several moments, satisfied that he had been truthful with her. "Thank you, Igor."

She turned from him and began to go up the steps. Before opening the heavy wooden door, she bent low to see Igor weeping into his slender hands. "Now I will do you a favor," Neva whispered.

Igor stood up and closed his eyes. He stretched out his arms, his palms facing her. He murmured something, a prayer perhaps. Neva slid her revolver from her belt and cocked the hammer back. She raised the gun and fired. Her bullet shot straight through his heart. Igor's eyes winced, and his lifeless body collapsed onto the grimy floor. The remaining raiders both gasped.

"One favor deserves another." Neva exited The Pit and slammed the rusted door behind her.

THE LOCOMOBILE'S CABIN BECAME CRAMPED with the three of them inside, and Zen felt the heat coming from behind a steel hatch near his legs. Enapay had laid down straw mats to soften the floor. In the other corner lay several auto guns, which Neva detested, but she couldn't dismiss their usefulness.

Zen's rucksack was in the other car, along with crates of dried food and other supplies. Enapay decided to leave the small cargo car coupled so they could take turns sleeping in any one of the several sleeping cots inside as only one pilot needed to remain in the locomobile cockpit.

"Are we all ready to go?" Enapay got the vehicle's engine to idle.

Neva took the co-pilot seat and snatched up the map. "Yes. We will head east towards the Oraibi town, then south through Mexihco, and continue on to Azincaya."

Zen bent over and glanced at Neva's map. He had read

about Azincaya briefly during his studies with Master Kyta, but the land was an even bigger mystery than Agrios. It was an ancient continent, where its people long ago plundered their own land.

The amulet pulsated against his skin again. Zen felt his spirits rise with the affirmation that he was doing the right thing by joining Enapay and Neva. His eyes were heavy, and his body betrayed him by yawning.

Enapay turned to him from the pilot's chair. "Rest up, Zen. You deserve it. Neva will fetch you when it's your turn to pilot."

With a nod, Zen went out the sliding door and walked along the narrow catwalk towards the rear of the locomobile. He hopped onto the coach car's steel platform and entered through a sliding door. He found his pack on the floor and dragged it to the back of the car.

Zen threw it onto a top bunk before crawling onto a bed below it. When he removed his belt and holsters, a sharp tug on his leg wound made him gasp. The bandage felt tight. When the pain subsided, he swung his legs onto the bunk.

He lay on his back. The engine roared from outside and the gush of steam filled the air. After several rough jerks, the locomobile was on its way. The gentle rocking reminded him of the rolling ocean, and he was soon swallowed by the eclipse of sleep.

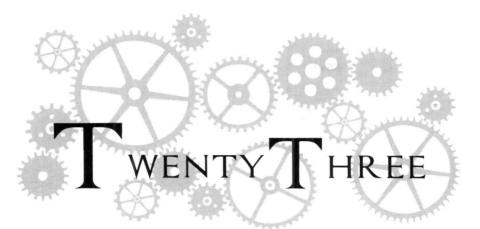

TWENTY THREE

Under the Atlantica Ocean...

"WE ARE FORTY-EIGHT HOURS FROM reaching the Azincayan Coast, Professor," Shannon McMillan reported.

The old man the crew called "Professor" was at his desk in his private chamber, mulling over several maps and a stack of open books. McMillan didn't know her employer's true name when she accepted the job, and she never bothered asking.

"Slow her down to ten knots," the Professor said without looking up. "Coming all the way to my chamber to tell me this is unnecessary. You could have told me through the talking horn."

McMillan turned to the brass horn connected to a thin metal tube going into the wall and running the length of the underwater boat. "Actually, I did try. You did not pick up."

The Professor looked up from his books. His white bushy eyebrows twitched in bewilderment. He followed McMillan's gaze to the horn hanging on its brass bracket right next to him.

"I apologize, McMillan. I was preoccupied." The old man went back to his reading. "Be on the lookout for pirates."

McMillan nodded, but she secretly wished to engage with sea bandits so they could test the power of the boat she piloted. The waters off of the Azincayan Coast swarmed with unlawful raiders, notorious for attacking vessels venturing into their territory. The Azincayans were seafaring masters and easily defeated all trespassers. There lacked any semblance of central leadership in these parts, and each city along the coast took what it wanted from outsiders and each other.

The Professor had designed and built this submersible boat, the *Triton*. The craft contained no cannons or guns, yet the *Triton* was the deadliest sea craft in the entire world. Stealth was the boat's main defense, and the sharp ramming prow at the bow was a formidable weapon, able to pierce the strongest steel. McMillan was eager to test The *Triton's* capabilities on any enemy.

"Of course, Professor." McMillan continued to stand at attention. "Is there anything you need, sir?'

The Professor opened his antique pocket watch. "It's supper time. Did you know that?"

"No sir."

Having been underwater for five days straight, she didn't know day from night. Her concept of time became nearly nonexistent since taking this job.

"Although my belly has been a little vocal in the last hour or so," she added.

"Mine too."

The crew of four, not including the Professor, worked in pairs. McMillan and her partner Simon were due to have their meal and leisure shift soon.

"I will join you for supper in fifteen minutes," said the Professor, tucking his pocket watch into his vest.

"Very good, Professor." McMillan did an about face. "I will see you in the galley shortly."

She left the chamber and closed the steel port door behind her. The passageway was narrow, a tough fit even for McMillan's small build. She ducked her head beneath the network of riveted steel beams running along the low ceiling.

The *Triton* held many secrets. McMillan had no idea how the boat was powered. The craft had powerful screws propelling the craft through the waters, and she had seen the various ballast tanks allowing the *Triton* to submerge or rise to the surface. The cockpit's controls took more than thirty days to master, but she still didn't know what a few of the levers and buttons did.

The biggest mystery to her were the little glass spheres throughout the boat, illuminating every corridor and chamber. McMillan couldn't figure out their mechanics. They were warm to the touch, and if she stared at them long enough, she noticed they pulsated to the rhythm of the boat's engines. The engine room was directly behind the Professor's private chamber, and he didn't allow anyone else back there. Large vessels needed an entire squad of engineers to keep it running, but the fact that the *Triton* only needed two pilots made it the most advanced machine in the world.

McMillan reached the empty kitchen galley. She took one of the seats at the square table in the center and wondered where Simon was.

Simon was the Professor's countryman, and the two of them had met McMillan in Haven City in Agrios months ago. Simon was a lean, quiet, but thoughtful fellow. He and McMillan were paired up, therefore she spent most of her waking moments with him. She was the type to keep to herself, so there was little to no conversation when they piloted the *Triton* or ate together. Simon was an enigma. McMillan knew he hailed from Francia, was involved with their rebellion as a military surgeon, and traveled to Agrios with the Professor. She wondered if he and the Professor were kin.

Simon seemed to be privy to the old man's secrets, so she considered him to be second in command. That suited her fine, and even early on, she noticed how he carried an air of silent strength.

The Professor and Simon had hired the crew after a lengthy interview process and offered a hefty salary for their services. There was a handsome upfront fee, and the rest would be paid upon completion of their mission, whatever that was.

McMillan leaned back in her chair, but her drifting mind was interrupted by a ruckus echoing down the corridor. She was sure she heard the other two members of her crew, Orsini and Lopez, laughing in the direction of the cockpit.

She assumed Orsini and Lopez had relieved Simon at the controls. The two shared a loud and lively personality, a nice change of pace while being stuck underwater for days at a time.

McMillan was fortunate to be working with some good people, and this would be her final job. The Professor all but guaranteed they'd all make enough to give up their hard lives after completing this mission. From the way the old man doled out cash during their training, it left none of them with any doubt they would be wealthy at the completion of their yet unexplained mission.

The Professor didn't mince words when he gave McMillan

the terms of her employment. The old man spoke of risk and extreme danger. Only a small amount of information would be disseminated to the crew as was necessary for them to carry out their duties. They were kept in the dark until it was absolutely necessary for them to learn bits here and there about their actual mission. Again, McMillan agreed to this, as long as she was getting paid.

Their job required specific training in the beginning, and mastering how to navigate and pilot the exotic boat took two months. Becoming accustomed to being submerged underwater for three to five days at a time wasn't easy either. When the Professor was satisfied with the crew's honed expertise, they received a more than generous paycheck as a reward.

Before setting off on their mission, the Professor had requested each of them to write down their next of kin and their addresses. He gave them each a signed contract that promised to personally deliver their pay to surviving family members, but McMillan was dumbfounded. She had no family or friends. She told the Professor she had no intention of meeting any such demise, and she would wager her salary on that.

The years had been hard on her, and she was ready to experience a little bit of the good life. Her brown hair sprouted wisps of gray. She longed to sail only for herself. Or perhaps take up piloting an air vessel and flying away. Somewhere quiet. Maybe somewhere tropical.

Life for an ex-soldier was a difficult one, but after this mission, it would be nothing but smooth sailing, or flying, thereafter. McMillan closed her eyes, immersed in her daydreams of the good life to come.

THE NIHON SUN BEGAN ITS ascent, lighting a clear blue sky and bringing a warm glow to the windows of the large chamber. Emperor Hideaki was elated. He had received the signed agreements from Chancellor Song of the Sui Faction only an hour ago. This official declaration made half of Xia a vassal state. Hideaki was confident the Jin Faction would soon follow, and all of Xia would be under Nihon rule.

Staring at the imposing hand painted map of the world on the wall behind his desk, Hideaki traced the borders of the Iberian Empire with his fingers. As he did so, his mind retraced Iberia's conquest of Europa country by country.

The latest reports confirmed an Iberian buildup along Xian's western border. Despite his plans progressing ahead of schedule, Hideaki wondered if all of their preparations would be in vain. He hoped to have everything in place before they invaded.

"It is official," said Takeo as he skimmed the signed treaty Hideaki had left on the desk.

Hideaki jumped, startled by his shogun's voice. He hadn't noticed Takeo enter his private study. "Yes. The Eastern Sui has signed our agreement."

Takeo said, "Do not worry, Emperor. With Sui support, we will have the manpower we need to fight Iberia. Western Xia is difficult terrain. Iberia will not rush to invade, and they will find the mountains difficult to navigate."

Hideaki took his seat. He wished he carried his Shogun's confidence and composure. That is what he trusted most in Takeo. "I cannot ignore my instincts. I know Iberia will cross into Xia, and they will do it soon."

"I am going to the Koreyan peninsula today. I want to see the experiments for myself," Takeo said. "This will be an unannounced visit so I can get a true assessment of our progress there."

Hideaki nodded.

"Why not join me?" Takeo suggested. "With the Sui Faction's submission, a visit by their new ruler would be a great way to build morale and gain support from your subjects. You are popular in Koreya."

"I think not." Hideaki felt his neck muscles tense.

Takeo bowed. "I will confirm the progress in Koreya is on schedule, my Emperor."

The Shogun hurried out of the study.

Hideaki had no desire to witness the gruesome experiments being carried out on the peninsula. The work being done there was a means to an end, and if Iberia did dare to set foot on Xian soil, Hideaki would make sure to unleash death upon the invaders.

THE NIHONESE STEAM GALLEON WAS two days from reaching Azincayan territory. Kai stood at the bow of the ship, and he inhaled the salty ocean air. Although he had never traveled to this part of the world before, he was aware of the dangers lurking in these waters. Pirates were like sharks circling their prey along the Azincayan coast.

Kai kept his left eye searching the tumbling ocean through his brass spyglass. Emperor Hideaki had hired him to do a strange job. It was a unique mission for a Shadow. Kai was accustomed to working in the dark, completing only clandestine tasks. His new directive brought him out in the open, and it required skills he had never employed before. Kai was to act the part of a diplomat of Nihon and purchase a child from the lowlife merchant Olaf Geller.

Down on the bottom deck of the ship, several crates of gold were stored in a locked room. It was more gold than Kai could count. The mission would go two ways. If Geller were to accept the gold for the child, Kai would simply hand over the crates in exchange for the boy. If not, he was to take the boy by force. Secretly, he hoped Geller would refuse the gold. That would give Kai a reason to slit the merchant's throat and take the child. Kai was a killer, not a negotiator.

Riches meant nothing to him.

Emperor Hideaki gave explicit instructions not to harm Marcel Bouvier, but he had the freedom to do whatever it took to get the job done. Kai had no idea why a child would be so important and worth nearly a ton in gold, but Hideaki did say the future of Nihon depended on this boy. At first, he thought this was a joke, but he knew the emperor was serious when he gave Kai his orders and all that gold.

Kai continued scanning the ocean with a wooden and brass spyglass, but there was nothing but an endless expanse of water in front of him. With only two days of traveling separating him from his destination and every member of the crew smelling rancid, Kai was more than ready to get off the boat immediately. Being able to tolerate the discomfort was easy for a trained Shadow. Only the mission was important.

However, for once, this secret assignment might not involve any killing if Olaf Geller was agreeable. This could all end up being a simple transaction. Exchange the gold for the child. It would be his first mission ever without bloodshed.

Kai's experience didn't allow him to assume any mission

was simple. His mind stopped its wandering and slipped into a light meditation when the heavy boot steps of one of the crew members approached him.

Without saying a word, Kai whirled around. The stumpy sailor's name escaped him, and if the man tried to be stealthy, he had failed. Maybe the man's name was Ako. Everything about the man was round, and the sailor's jowls jiggled when he spoke.

"Master Kai..."

Kai was not accustomed to being called by his name by anyone other than his own people and Emperor Hideaki. But it didn't matter since Kai would have all sixty-eight men on board killed once they returned to Nihon.

"The men and I were talking in the galley during dinner," the-man-that-might-be-Ako said. He bowed his head and averting his eyes towards the wooden floor. "And we..."

This didn't sound good. Some of the crew came up the steps onto the top deck to watch the scene unfold. The twenty or so men looked just as nervous as the fat sailor, and Kai understood they must have volunteered poor Ako to address him.

"What do you want?" Kai asked directly to the men below.

Ako shivered, making his chubby cheeks flap. "We are concerned."

"Concerned?"

"Yes, Master. We do not know why we are going to Azincaya. Our ship usually carries cargo to the western harbors of Agrios."

Kai felt the static charge of energy surrounding him. The crew was anxious, and Ako seemed to be on the verge of tears. He turned and looked the man in the eyes. The sailor wiped the sweat from his forehead, and Kai waited for the sailor to continue.

"Rumor has it this ship is carrying more gold than any of us could ever spend." Ako drifted off, waiting for a reaction from Kai. "We are in strange and perilous waters, and we are not accustomed to such danger. Why risk our lives? If there is gold in all those crates we carried on board..."

"What are you asking?" Kai's right hand twitched.

"You would get the most of it, Master. The rest of us would divide whatever you felt was fair."

Kai smiled, which Ako mimicked. The crew seemed perplexed for a moment until Kai let out a light chuckle. The men whispered to each other. Their relieved surprise cut the tension and they laughed. Some even slapped each other on the back. Ako joined in, and his body relaxed when he threw his head back in delight.

"I knew you would be agreeable," Ako said.

Kai unleashed his *katana* in a backhanded swing. He seared Ako's throat, and a crimson fountain sprayed from the gash. The splashing blood was carried by the wind towards the frozen sailors, staining their uniforms. The round and limp body fell backwards before crashing at the feet of the aghast crew below.

It took fourteen days for one of the men to even show a glint of treachery, and Kai was surprised by this. He had expected it much sooner.

TWENTY FOUR

ZEN JOLTED HIMSELF AWAKE WITH a vague memory of a dream about his mother. For a moment, he forgot where he was, but the constant rumbling of the steam locomobile lifted the fog in his brain.

He slid out of bed and went to a dusty window. The ache from his leg made him groan. It was still dark and only hints of morning light penetrated the feathery clouds overhead. The land looked bare, and it lacked vegetation or any sign of civilization.

When Zen exited the passenger car, the humid and musty air shook away any remnants of sleep left in his head. His feet fought to keep his balance, and he noticed the soreness in his right leg subsided. Zen gingerly walked down the narrow footway along the edge of the passenger car and entered the locomobile through the sliding door.

Still at the controls, Enapay turned to him and waved. Next to him, Neva was seated and studying the map. She didn't look up. A crease burrowed between her brows as she read. Everything was as Zen remembered before retiring to the attached car, and now he wondered how long he slept.

"You could have slept for another couple of hours," Enapay greeted. "I'm wide awake, and Neva refuses to sleep."

Neva folded the map. "I won't sleep until my son is with me again."

At the mentioning of the boy's name, Zen couldn't help his curiosity about her son. He made his way to the front of the car. "Tell us about Marcel." He sat on the hard floor of the cabin and pressed his back up against the wall. "If you are not going to be able to sleep, you might as well talk about him."

"Little Marcel is nine, soon to be ten on the fifteenth day in the winter season. He's named after his father." Neva's face softened. "My boy shares more than his father's name. He's curious and interested in the way things work."

"How so?" Enapay asked.

"My first husband was a great inventor. He could build or fix anything." A smile crept on her face. "My son is the same."

"I can't wait to meet him," Enapay said. "Sounds like my kind of little man."

"Yes, you two would get along well I think," Neva said to Enapay.

Zen's amulet was hot again against his skin. He wondered if the enchanted stone was trying to tell him something related to Neva. His instincts told him there was more to her story. He and Marcel shared the same birthday, and maybe that was yet another sign. Despite Zen's desire to not bring her anymore pain, something about the child's abduction bothered him.

"A man who steals a child is without conscience," Zen said.

"I must know something."

Neva tensed. "What?"

"Why did the merchant take him?" Zen asked, almost regretting he had asked. "I apologize if I have asked an uncomfortable question."

Enapay must have sensed her hesitation and filled in the silence with useless chatter. "Child labor still exists in certain parts of the world. They put them to work in the fields, tending to the animals on farms, in fact..."

"There is something you should know," Neva said to Zen. "My first husband was a genius, and the people of our small town marveled at his mechanical abilities. One day, a merchant brought his steam cycle into the workshop we owned at the time. Marcel placed his hands on the machine. Without having to take the cycle apart or unbolt any of its components, Marcel could feel precisely what was wrong with it."

Zen felt lost. He replayed her words in his mind, but the pieces failed to come together. Without saying a word, he looked up at Neva whose eyes were now full of threatening tears.

"What are you saying?" Enapay asked while looking through the dusty windshield. "Did you say your husband could *feel* the cycle's malfunction?"

Neva wiped her face. "Yes. He was a military volunteer, charged with maintaining our vehicles. I would watch him work. Marcel would place his hands on the machine, close his eyes, and within seconds he knew exactly what was wrong with it. His gift wasn't relegated to only transport. He fixed any machine, even if he had no prior knowledge of its mechanics."

Zen swam in a sea of confusion. Maybe he didn't have the

knowledge to fully appreciate this talent Neva's husband possessed. He looked over at Enapay, hoping for clarification as to what Neva revealed.

Enapay shook his head. "I've never heard of anything like that in my life. What you're saying is that your late husband had the power to commune with machines. Do you know how absurd that sounds?"

"You don't believe me?" Neva whipped around to face Enapay. "You think I'm making this up?"

Zen needed to intervene. He pulled himself up and put a hand on Neva's shoulder. "He can be infuriating. It is like arguing with a wall."

"It defies the laws of nature," Enapay said. "There's no such thing as someone having the ability to neuropathically connect to machines." He turned to Zen. "Just like there's no such thing as an all-powerful sword forged from a star rock that can cut through iron."

Neva tightly folded her arms. "Sword?"

Enapay looked disgusted. "Never mind."

"I don't care if you don't believe me, but I swear what I've told you is true," Neva shot back. "After Iberia crushed our Resistance, we fled the front lines and married. Because of the work he did at our shop, word of his abilities spread."

Enapay kept his lips tight in disbelief, but Zen listened with an open mind.

"Geller came to our workshop on many occasions, bringing all kinds of things for my husband to fix after he observed my husband repair his cycle," Neva continued. "At first, Geller would drop off Iberian vehicles and other everyday machines. Then he started bringing in strange weapons, like none we had ever seen. Yet Marcel was able to repair them. His beautiful mind talked to machines and understood how every component, clockwork, or gear should work."

The clouds were slowly beginning to lift, and Zen began to realize the implications. "Your son inherited his father's power," Zen said under his breath.

"Yes. One day, we found our boy in the shop, and he was fiddling with a small artillery cannon. Little Marcel didn't quite know which were the right tools for some of the tasks, but he managed to dismantle its main assembly and repair the breach-loading mechanism. His father and I watched him for a long time until we made him stop. It was unnerving."

"How old was your son at the time?" Zen asked.

Neva replied, "Four years old."

Enapay remained silent, but Zen was certain he saw him shake his head again.

"After that incident, we knew we had to close the shop. Cut ties with villains like Geller. We had made a lot of money, but we feared for our boy's future. We moved out to the country and bought a farm. I made my husband swear to me he would never let another soul know of his ability."

Neva paused to scowl at the unmoving Enapay before continuing. "Things were perfect for a year or two, but Marcel was a horrible farmer. Later, he became ill, unable to work the fields and tend to the animals. When he died, my boy and I lost the homestead. We were practically destitute. I had no family to turn to, and we survived with whatever assistance old friends offered us."

Zen couldn't imagine such desperation. "How did you survive?"

"Pierce and his family fortune came to the rescue," Neva replied. "I made Little Marcel promise to never reveal his powers to anyone, especially to Pierce, but I am sure Geller found us from my second husband."

The mood in the cockpit remained heavy, and Zen was relieved to see Enapay reach over the control panel and touch Neva's hand in a show of support.

"It doesn't matter what I believe about your son," Enapay said. "He is your child. That's all that matters to me. Machine powers or not, I will help you get him back."

Zen knew this was Enapay's way of apologizing, and Neva seemed to accept it.

"Now you know everything about Little Marcel," Neva said. "I must save my Machine Boy from Geller and however he plans to exploit my son's abilities."

Zen's ears grew red hot and tingly. He felt dizzy, and the blue fire from the stone underneath his shirt seemed to burst forth with intense energy. His mother's face and her words reverberated in his brain with such ferocity, he saw stars. Zen worked to regain normal breathing and keep from passing out.

"Something wrong?" Neva bent down from her seat to touch Zen's clammy face.

"Could you repeat what you said?" Zen murmured.

"I asked if something was wrong."

"No, before that." Zen's head was about to explode, but at least his lungs were able to fully expand again. "You called Marcel a *Machine Boy.*"

The corner of Neva's eyes wrinkled. "Machine Boy. Yes."

Zen pulled himself up to his feet. He tried to balance himself. He stumbled and slammed into the cabin wall. When the sensation of everything spinning returned, Zen had to sit back down.

"What's wrong with you?" Enapay said over his shoulder.

"I thought her mind was drifting; she spoke nonsense." Zen closed his eyes and willed the dizziness to go away. "For years, deep down, I knew it had to be significant."

"What are you talking about? Whose mind was drifting?" Neva left her seat and plopped down next to him on the floor. "You're scaring me, Zen."

Zen struggled to swallow, as if stones were lodged in his throat. "My mother. She died seven years ago. Her last words to me made no sense. But now..."

"What were her last words to you?" Neva took hold of his shoulders.

"She said I must save the Machine Boy."

Without warning, Neva and Zen were thrown to the other side of the cabin when the locomobile veered off the dirt highway and drifted into the rough edge of the road. Enapay lost his grip on the steering wheel and struggled to get the locomobile back onto the highway. He grunted an apology as he regained control of the vehicle.

"Machine Boy?" Neva's cheeks glistened with fresh tears. She threw her arms around Zen and nearly squeezed the air from his chest. "That's what his father and I nicknamed him, using his initials. M.B. Marcel Bouvier. Machine Boy. Your mother was talking about my boy?"

"Yes," Zen said in her ear.

"How? H...how is that possible?" Neva pressed her forehead on Zen's shoulder. "How could she have known?"

"As she was dying, perhaps she was able to straddle our world and the spirit realm simultaneously. She experienced a moment of complete clarity of past, present, and future. My mother saw what was to come and what I must do."

Zen's eyes stung. His mother's face, her beautiful countenance, became clear in his mind now, just as her words had become. Zen felt Neva's body quiver as she sobbed, and the intense and steady heat from his glowing amulet brought him comfort.

"My mother foresaw this. I am supposed to be here," Zen said. "I am supposed to save your Machine Boy."

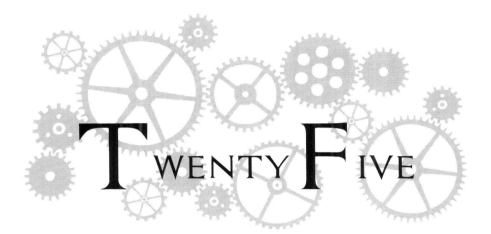

TWENTY FIVE

IT WAS DIFFICULT FOR GELLER to imagine Mexihco as the grand and awe-inspiring country it once was. The kingdom was ruled by a worthless king. There was nothing but crumbled ruins to remind the natives of how much their kingdom has deteriorated the last thousand years.

Mexihco bordered two worlds: the Wild Land to the north and the barren wasteland to the south. The locals were desperate, unscrupulous people roving in small tribes and bands. Targets of these bandits were usually travelers using Mexihco as a bridge from Agrios to Azincaya. Geller had come prepared, however. His bodyguards, their deadly weapons, and their reinforced vehicles were enough to deter even the most ambitious raiders.

Geller's caravan had finally reached the Capital after two days, and the oppressive heat greeted them when they rolled onto a brick-paved street. Marcel had fallen asleep at the desk with his head propped by a small stack of books. While Geller changed into a fresh white shirt, a wonderful idea struck him.

Shortly after taking possession of the boy, he had tested Marcel. Before crossing the Atlantica Sea, he wanted proof of the boy's machine power. The child was given a broken pictogram projector. It was an expensive and rare piece of technology, and something Marcel most likely had never seen before. The boy cried incessantly since being taken from his stepfather but was immediately fascinated with the damaged machine.

Geller said it was broken and he wanted Marcel to fix it. The boy's hands explored all of the moving parts, his fingers touching every gear and spindle on the outside of the rectangular machine. He found the small crank on the side and turned it. Nothing. Marcel closed his eyes and planted both of his hands on the projector's metal casing.

When the boy's brows crinkled in deep concentration, his right index finger found the small button on the side and pushed it. The casing popped open, exposing the projector's myriad of gear-works and components. Without even asking for tools, his tiny fingers worked furiously.

In a few short minutes, Marcel shut the casing and turned the crank. A ghostly image appeared a few feet in front of the machine's glass projection lens. While the boy continued to operate the crank, the pictogram sharpened. Geller grinned at the image of an ocean, a beach, and an ancient castle overlooking the surf. The footage was recorded on a small island in Oceania. Soon, he'd retire there.

But that had been an easy test. Its defect was a series of misaligned gears, easily repaired in minutes without tools. Now Geller wanted to see how Marcel would perform a more difficult task.

Geller went to the talking horn and yanked the brass cone from its station. A long metal cable ran from the horn to the wall. He pulled on the slack so he could sit on the long couch while he spoke. He brought the horn to his face and called out, "Boris."

After a short pause, Boris' voice emitted from the horn. "Sir?"

"I need you to go into the capital and request a meeting with King Tlacatl." Geller paused for a moment before continuing. "Also, inquire about getting a piece of machinery. It must be broken or damaged. Get something big."

"Sir?"

Geller tightened his lips in impatience. "Tell Tlacatl I would like something mechanical that no longer functions. Maybe a damaged vehicle or a steam generator. Something large. Is that clear Boris?"

"Yes, sir."

There was still a trace of doubt in Boris' voice, but Geller placed the horn back onto the wall and got up from the couch. He looked across the way, to the far side of his car. Marcel still slept soundly at the desk, and Geller wondered if the boy dreamed of automatons, moving gears, and bringing machines back to life.

THE IMPERIAL CHAMBER WAS A shadow of its former self. Geller noted the rotting marble columns that guarded the two arched entryways. The once awe-inspired domed ceiling no longer glistened with gold paint. King Tlacatl kept the furnishings plain. He probably didn't want to make the blatant atrophy of his kingdom even starker.

At the far end of the chamber, Tlacatl sat on his throne, which was nothing more than a large wooden chair elevated on a marble platform. It looked antique, but its flimsy construction matched the decay of his country.

The king's guards, armed with the Iberian auto guns Geller had sold them a year ago, escorted Geller and his large entourage through the chamber to the foot of Tlacatl's throne. The old man looked sickly. His long beard had grown longer since Geller's last visit. Directly following Geller was Marcel, being closely guarded by Kamau.

Kamau had changed into a loose shirt and light pants, just as the rest of Geller's men had. Geller noticed his most trusted bodyguard's dark skin through the man's damp white shirt. Mexihco was humid and stifling. Smelly and unbearable. Geller himself was already sweating when he approached the king.

"Welcome, Olaf Geller," Tlacatl greeted with a show of his brown teeth. He drifted from his chair, lifting his long brown robe to prevent tripping over it. "I didn't know you were paying us a visit. Otherwise, I would have prepared a feast."

Geller forced himself to bow his head. "I apologize for this unannounced visit, but I do come bearing gifts."

Two of his men brought a large wooden crate forward. They pulled the lid off to reveal two dozen Iberian auto rifles. Tlacatl's eyes grew large. He reached into the crate and caressed a gun as if it were gold. Geller didn't know why Tlacatl continued to buy weapons; no one in their right mind would ever invade this rat-infested country.

"This is an unexpected surprise." Tlacatl inspected the

weapons. He peered into the box, likely searching for the drum magazines and ammunition for the rifles. Geller threw in three Iberian grenades to sweeten the offering, and the king gasped when he held one of them.

Geller wiped his forehead. The humidity was thick, and even in the dim light of the chamber, the heat remained oppressive. "I never come empty-handed. I ask only for safe passage through your great country."

Tlacatl placed the grenade back into the crate. "Of course. You are a friend to Mexihco. My men tell me of another request you have."

"Yes," Geller began. "I need a piece of sophisticated machinery. Intact, but non-functioning."

"This is a strange request." Tlacatl's forehead wrinkled. "May I ask why?"

"Since today is a day of pleasant surprises, let's keep with the theme, shall we?" Geller was tiring of this game, and he wished Tlacatl would take a hint. It would be easy to simply kill this pathetic king where he stood, but a small part of him felt pity for the old man.

Tlacatl pretended to think it over. "Yes, we shall. On the condition that upon delivery of the machine, you tell me what you're up to." The king smiled, trying to lighten his tone. "Curiosity. It is a great weakness of mine."

Geller wiped his face with a cloth. "I will not keep you in suspense for long."

Tlacatl signaled his guards. "If you will follow me, I believe I have a machine that meets all of your requirements."

Geller and his group followed the king and his soldier from the chamber and through a series of dim corridors. The walls were deteriorating stone, but flecks of gold reflected the flickering light of the gas lanterns. The hall sloped downwards as they continued, and Geller found relief when the air cooled.

Tlacatl led them to a set of steel double doors. The guards pulled them open. The enormous chamber was filled with antique tools and discarded machines. They entered, and the smell of burning ore came to Geller's nose. Several engineers working with broken equipment and outdated tools snapped to attention as Tlacatl passed by.

They walked to the rear of the spacious workshop until they came to what looked like a giant metal spider. Geller approached it first. He placed his hand on one of its dusty iron legs. The machine was a transport with eight legs, and the body of the spider only allowed one operator.

The pilot's seat towards the front of the spider was surrounded by various levers and other controls. Geller went to the rear of the metal beast and tried to imagine this machine creature on the battlefield. It must have been frightening for the enemy to see a giant iron spider marching towards them.

"Have you ever seen anything like it?" Tlacatl asked, obviously taking pleasure in showing off this mechanized monster.

Geller exhaled. "It's an Iberian spydread. Where did you get this?"

"I bought it from an Azincayan pirate," Tlacatl replied. He wiped dust from the machine's legs. "He said he found it abandoned on the Caobana Islands."

Geller circled the spider one final time. "Intimidating. It looks like there might have been guns attached to both the bow and stern of the machine, but they've been removed." He turned to Marcel. "Come forward."

The boy was in his own world. Marcel looked captivated by

the broken spydread already. Kamau stepped aside and allowed the boy to approach. Marcel rushed to the giant spider. His hands ran along each leg methodically and slowly.

"Who is this boy?" Tlacatl asked in almost a whisper.

"This is Marcel," answered Geller. "He has a special gift with machines. Your spydread is the perfect test for him."

Marcel finished inspecting all eight legs. With his eyes closed, he climbed up into the pilot's seat and his hands wandered over every inch of the control panel. He hopped out of the cockpit and crawled towards the rear along the narrow platform, finally coming to the spydread's boiler and other vital organs.

"The child doesn't talk much, does he?" Tlacatl asked.

Geller ignored the question as he watched Marcel jump down from the machine. "What do you think, Marcel?"

The boy looked up at the spydread. His eyes were full of the sympathy a surgeon might have for his dying patient. "I need tools."

Geller gave Tlacatl an impatient glare, and the king shuffled back to the engineers on the other side of the chamber. Bending low to meet Marcel eye-to-eye, he whispered, "Can it be fixed?"

"Yes."

"Better question is: can you fix it?" Geller got down on one knee and studied the child's pleasant face. The boy seemed quietly confident. "Are you the man for the job?"

"Yes."

Geller felt giddy. "Please get him the tools he needs," he said to the king.

Tlacatl grumbled orders to his engineers who retrieved a pair of large leather cases. They placed the bags at Marcel's feet. The child opened them and studied all the wrenches, clamps, and other tools.

"You believe this boy can repair this machine?" Tlacatl muttered, sounding as if he was already bored. "Impossible."

"This is no ordinary boy," Geller said as he watched Marcel sift through the cases of tools.

Tlacatl weakly shrugged his shoulders. In his Origin tongue, he commanded his men to provide seats for everyone. After they brought in cushioned chairs, Geller attempted to get comfortable in his stiff seat. The audience sat quietly, preparing to watch a nine year old boy perform a miracle. Geller could hardly contain his excitement, but he contemplated what he would do if Marcel failed to repair the spydread. Even if he sold him off to labor in a factory, the proceeds wouldn't even come close to covering the two hundred thousand ibers he had paid the boy's stepfather.

Before beginning his surgery, Marcel approached the king holding a large wrench in each of his tiny hands. "Your tools are terrible." Marcel thrust the metal tool up into the air. "I hope I can work with this."

Tlacatl was unable to respond. His mouth fell open and his eyes flashed distress. He stirred in his chair. It looked like he wanted to leave the chamber. Instead he nodded and shooed the boy away with his thin wrinkled hands.

Geller laughed at the absurdity of the moment. He concluded he would kill Marcel if he failed to fix the spydread. Keeping the boy alive for the duration of his trip back home wouldn't be worth the trouble.

TWENTY SIX

NEVA HAD PILOTED THE LOCOMOBILE for several hours straight until the morning sun sizzled in the clear sky. The desert was dusty and hot, and the small trade city at the southern tip of Agrios was a good place to stop. She and Zen wallowed in silence all morning, drowning in their private thoughts.

Once the locomobile stopped, Zen climbed out of the vehicle and walked out into the hot desert. Zen replayed the final moments of his mother's life. Despite his reliving her passing, he found solace knowing her cryptic final words now made sense. His resolve solidified, and he treasured this new connection to his mother.

Enapay emerged from the passenger cabin with his eyes still heavy from sleep. He jumped off the car and joined Zen on the hill overlooking the small town. The simple native buildings were made of stone and wood. The market was already bursting with activity from the many vendors preparing their makeshift shops. As a border town, Zen assumed the locals depended on travelers for their livelihood.

"Did you sleep well?" Zen asked.

Enapay rubbed his face. "I sure did. I need another five or six hours, but it's hot in that car."

Zen's Nabeho shirt billowed from the hot wind sweeping from the west. He watched the marketplace come to life. A few of the vendors down below looked up at them with hopeful eyes, eager to sell their goods to new faces.

Enapay cocked a thumb at the locomobile. "Neva coming out?"

"I believe so." Zen took a deep breath. "Much has happened to her in a short amount of time."

"You both have turned my world upside down," Enapay remarked. "I'm a man of science. In my travels, I have seen many strange things. I think if you look long and closely enough, you start to see patterns all around you. To me, these patterns are mere coincidences. To others like yourself, the world is full of intentional and deliberate design. Make sense?"

Zen nodded, although Enapay seemed bent on dismissing the obvious.

"About that *Dragonfly* thing..." Enapay continued. "Sure, that was a strange coincidence. Neva's son with the ability to somehow understand the inner workings of machines by simply touching it? Defies commonsense. Looking into her eyes, however, I see truth there."

He put a hand on Zen's shoulder. "How did your mother have knowledge of future events? Telling you to save the Machine Boy? And the initials match up. M.B. This child must be the one your mother was talking about. How is all of that possible?"

"I do not know," Zen replied.

This was the sort of thing he would normally ask Master Kyta about. She always provided guidance and understanding of such matters. For now, he simply accepted it.

"I'm not able to dismiss any of this so quickly," Enapay finally said. "I look at you and I look at Neva, and the weight of it all is too real. Everything is upside down."

"It is understandable." Zen gathered his long loose hair and let the wind cool the back of his neck.

Enapay gazed at Zen's face for a moment. "I know you Nihon warriors are trained to control your emotions. I saw something stir inside of you earlier."

Zen felt his left eye twitch. "Even warriors have mothers."

"You wear a hard exterior, Zen, and I know your culture regards such control of emotions to be a show of strength. But I understand how you feel." Enapay leaned in. "I lost my mother, father, and sister by the time I was your age. I know your pain all too well."

Zen nodded solemnly. "Yes. You have mourned for many loved ones. I forget your pain because of your nonchalance."

"It's how I cope," Enapay said with a hint of a smile.

"Maybe I too must learn your humor," Zen said.

Enapay laughed. "You are a mystery."

"Life is full of mysteries." Zen closed his eyes and remembered something Master Kyta had once taught him. "We are not supposed to solve all of them. The unknown is what reminds us of our humanity. No need to know why. Just accept what is."

"How old are you Zen?"

"Twenty years. Soon to be twenty-one."

Enapay cracked a small smile. "You speak like an Elder. You're an old man in a young boy's body."

"I had a wise teacher. I am fortunate Master Kyta has passed some of her wisdom on to me," Zen said. "She taught me to relish the mysteries of life. Not to be in such a rush to know everything."

"Ah, maybe that's why I'm always getting into trouble," Enapay said.

"Maybe my quest for the Sky Blade does not seem as absurd to you now?" How open had Enapay's mind become? The blue medallion emitted a soft glow, and Zen saw Enapay glance down at it.

"Not so much. I will admit, it does feel like I'm where I should be. It's nice having a little direction in my life again." Enapay threw a quick look behind them. Neva exited the locomobile at last. "I owe it to this woman to help her save her little Machine Boy. She did save my life, and I always pay my debts."

Zen watched Neva give pause on the car's metal walkway. He waved to her, and she gestured back. "It is good you are opening your mind to such possibilities," he said to Enapay. "It is a start."

Enapay gave him a sharp look. "Speaking of possibilities, it's refreshing to see a little emotion come out of you. Makes you seem more human."

"Even warriors have mothers."

MOST OF THE PEOPLE IN the marketplace had tan skin with chalky black hair. Their gregarious voices rose and filled the hot desert air. Zen and Neva decided to traverse through the narrow aisles. Maybe they could pick up some information from the townspeople. It was most likely Geller and his group came through here if they were indeed heading south towards Azincaya.

Enapay stayed behind to guard their iron vehicle. He requested that they buy a barrel or two of water for the boiler and bread to go with the salted pork he was cooking.

Zen closely carried the leather bag of gold coins, which Enapay informed him was worth much more than the one thousand ibers he had owed him from their wager. After opening the pouch and glancing at the treasure, he was pretty sure the contents were worth five times that. The marketplace was undoubtedly filled with thieves and pickpockets, and Enapay warned him to not let anyone bump into them or stand too closely.

Neva led the way, as there wasn't enough width in the thick of the market for them to walk side-by-side. The vendors were much louder here compared to the marketplace in Agrios. The natives were all smiles. They acted like the passersby were long lost friends. Neva stopped to talk with three merchants, but they had no answers for her.

They came to what looked to be the largest merchant stand in the marketplace. The aroma of sweet flower petals came to Zen's nose, and he noticed the vendor sold various soaps. All the items were placed neatly on large wooden tables, and Zen took refuge from the sun underneath the massive canopy. The owner was a short woman of wide girth. Although the deep lines in her brown face gave away her age, she spoke with a childlike quality Zen found disarming.

"Can I interest you in any of my goods?" the woman asked them. "I have the best castile soap. Made from laurel oil. I also sell various canteens and other survival gear in the back."

Neva sniffed at a white bar of soap before approaching the woman. "I am in need of information."

The old woman leaned over her table. "What kind of information?"

"We are tracking someone, and we were curious if he passed through this way recently," replied Neva. "I expect if he had, it would've been quite a spectacle."

"I see." The woman retreated, her eyes conveying exactly what she was wanting in return.

Zen opened the heavy pouch and grabbed several coins. He flashed the woman the gold, and her wrinkled eyes blinked before growing wide.

"Did they come in a massive procession of steam loco-mobiles?" the woman asked, her dark eyes trained on Zen's treasure.

Neva nodded. "Probably. Yes."

Zen slid one of the gold coins across the table, and the old woman quickly snatched it up.

"Passed through here two days ago," she continued. "Their iron trains shook the ground, and we hoped the wealthy pas-sengers would stop to buy our merchandise, but they didn't. The entire caravan thundered right past us, but it did finally stop about a mile south of here near the town's main plaza."

"Were you able to see any of the passengers?" Neva asked, her voice sounding slightly constricted.

The woman thought for a moment. "No. The windows were blacked out. I couldn't see in. My niece, who was in the town square, watched them roll in. She said they made a stop in front of the government building and several men briefly met with the town's chief magistrate. Then they went to the orphanage across the street and took several young boys with them before leaving."

Zen got a hand signal from Neva and handed the old woman another coin.

"Can we speak with your niece?" asked Neva.

"Sure."

The woman paused and glanced at Zen once again. He jingled the bag to confirm he could pay, and when she smiled, she revealed perfect white teeth. The lady strained to turn her head towards a small tent behind her and called out to someone in her native tongue. A girl, maybe Zen's age, ran out and came to the woman's side. She was more robust, but her skin and long hair was the same hue as her elderly aunt.

"This is my niece, Izel." The lady turned to Neva. "She can help you."

Izel nervously gripped the display cart with both hands, but she managed to make eye contact with Neva and Zen after her aunt nudged her hip with the point of her elbow.

Neva's face and voice softened. "Izel, your aunt tells me you saw a caravan of steam transports rumble into town two days ago."

Izel nodded. Her left hand reached into her satchel and produced a large leather bound book.

"They stopped by the orphanage?" asked Neva.

"Yes," Izel said. "They grabbed some boys from there and threw them into one of the passenger cars."

Neva flashed Zen an expression of alarm in her eyes before returning her attention to Izel. "Can you describe any of the men? Or maybe any of the boys you saw?"

Zen stepped forward to give Izel's aunt a pair of gold coins. The old lady bumped the girl again with her bony elbow. Izel hesitated for a moment until her aunt threw her a coin.

"I drew them." Izel brought her book up against her chest.

Neva pointed to the book. "Drew them? There?"

The old lady chimed in proudly, "Izel is a gifted artist."

"May I take a look at your drawings of the men?" Neva asked gently.

Izel turned to her aunt and received a slight nod of reassurance before flipping through the leather portfolio and handing it to Neva. Zen studied the drawings over Neva's shoulder while she studied each page carefully. He was in awe at the girl's immaculate pencil drawings.

The first sketch was of a locomobile identical to the one Enapay was now piloting, and the drawings of the smaller roadsters with the mounted machine guns were exactly as Zen imagined. The fifth page Neva came to was of the men. They were warriors, armed with the same auto guns Geller had sold to Cheng's raiders.

"Gifted, yes?" the old lady said with a smile.

Neva turned the page. The next drawing was of a line of boys being dragged into one of the passenger cars. Although the picture was done in pencil, Izel captured the faces of terror on each abducted child. Neva wiped a renegade tear running down her cheek and turned another page. She let out a gasp.

"Are you okay?" Izel asked her.

Zen sidled up to Neva to take a look at the drawing for himself. Izel had drawn a small boy with brown hair. The child wore a blank expression. Dressed in a light colored shirt and dark pants, his thin body seemed helpless against the stocky man standing next to him.

The man looked like a bull. He was balding on top of his head, and his strong shoulders gave him a menacing appearance. Izel's pencil made him look almost dignified, his face wearing the look of arrogance. The sharp brows, narrow eyes, and half-grin gave the man's countenance the air of superiority.

Surely the man was Geller, and the boy was Marcel, Neva's Machine Boy.

"This boy here, he is my son." Neva pointed to the drawing of Marcel. "Did you see him?"

Izel nodded. "The man there kept your son at his side the whole time. They went into the orphanage and back out together. Then they boarded the middle car before the entire caravan left."

"In which direction did they go?" Zen asked.

"They continued south, down this main highway. It's the only road to Azincaya," replied the young girl.

"Can I have this?" Neva asked Izel as she regained her composure. "Just this one drawing."

Izel didn't get permission from her aunt before replying, "Yes."

Neva carefully tore the page from the leather book and handed the portfolio back to Izel. She scrutinized the drawing one final time before folding and putting it in her pocket. "Thank you."

Zen gave the young woman one gold coin before leading Neva away towards the center of the market. "Only two days behind. We can make that up." He stopped, wondering if Neva was listening. "Do not worry. We will catch them."

Neva seemed to be looking through Zen, her eyes and her mind were elsewhere. He recognized the look on her face, as it was the same expression she wore just before she defeated the raider during her duel. She was like a shark tasting a drop of blood in the water.

"I'm going to kill that bastard for taking my son."

TWENTY SEVEN

THE SHORT VOYAGE ACROSS THE Sea of Nihon was a welcomed respite from the long days and short nights Takeo Yoneda had endured since becoming Shogun. Although the steamship could easily transport a company of two hundred soldiers, Takeo brought only a skeleton crew of twenty with him on his trip to Koreya.

The ship's engine slowed down, and the two smokestacks blew gray steam in rhythmic bursts until slowing to an occasional coughing. When Takeo looked at the wispy trail of exhaust in the air, he thought of Zen. He prayed his prince was alive and hadn't fallen prey to the crooks and thieves populating Agrios. That was not how Zen should die. Nihon's greatest warrior should perish on Nihon soil, not on some faraway foreign land.

The ship carefully maneuvered to dock, and Takeo took a deep breath to prepare himself for this impromptu yet important mission. Since it fell upon Takeo's shoulders to make certain the entire Sun Nation could of withstand an Iberian invasion, this visit held special importance. The experiments secretly taking place on the Koreyan peninsula were central to their defense should they not be able to contain the Iberian advance.

It was four days after Takeo's inauguration as Nihon's Shogun when the Hideaki had told him of the secret facility in Koreya. It took every ounce of strength he had not to betray his true feelings about the emperor's plans. In all of history, Nihon had always faced its enemies with honor. Despite his oath to obey, he knew there was nothing honorable about Hideaki's covert operations on the peninsula.

Two of his men jumped onto the dock, which broke Takeo from his wandering thoughts. They carried the scroll containing Emperor Hideaki's official orders and met the Koreyan official waiting for him.

Takeo joined the commander on the wooden pier moments after the ship finished docking. The morning air was cool and humid. Takeo stepped through the fog, and he noticed that the nervous Koreyan officer kept shifting his weight back and forth between his feet. Two lines of Xian soldiers stood at attention lining the walkway from the pier to the shore. The area was nearly deserted. No banners flew, and no fanfare greeted the Eastern Sui's new rulers. The silence was eerie yet peaceful. Takeo wallowed in the fleeting moment of serenity before business began.

The officer finished reading the royal scroll. With a quick bow, he addressed Takeo with a low and authoritative voice. "Shogun Takeo Yoneda, I am Commander Tai Kwan at your service. Your presence here is a welcome surprise."

Takeo returned with a bow, careful not to bend too low.

"This will be a short visit. The emperor wishes for assurances that the experiments are being completed on schedule."

"Of course, Shogun." Tai escorted Takeo and his dozen men to shore. "Your scientists are efficient. This morning's report shows they are in fact ahead of schedule."

Waiting for them was an antique locomotive sitting on railroad tracks and pulling three passenger cars. The black smoke puffed from the single smokestack, impatient to begin its journey. Commander Tai climbed the steps of the middle car and opened the door for Takeo.

Once inside, Takeo sat on a long, comfortable sofa placed near the center of the car. Six of his men took positions within the cabin. They went to the seats positioned at all four corners, and the rest of his soldiers climbed into the third car.

Tai sat on the sofa opposite Takeo's. "Have you ever been to Koreya before?"

The long seat was almost too soft. Takeo exhaled deeply, and his muscles loosened as he sank into its cushions. "Once before. I took several brigades with me to do joint trainings with the Xian military. That was two years ago."

The entire car jerked when the locomobile surged forward, gaining momentum on the iron tracks. It had been years since Takeo rode in a steam train on rails, and he found the rhythmic metal clanging almost hypnotic.

"We held a grand celebration when Supreme Chancellor Song declared our alliance with Nihon," said Tai. "We tire of fighting the Jin. They are our brothers after all. We hope they will stand with us in defending our new Sun Nation. My brother-in-law enlisted with the Jin years ago. I am relieved to not have to hate my own kin anymore."

"Civil war is an ugly thing," Takeo said.

He found Tai's enthusiasm to say the right things suspicious.

Tai leaned forward. "Xia will be one soon."

The two hour long trip to the Koreyan region was spectacularly boring. Takeo spent all of it nodding his head and offering little words to Commander Tai during their one-sided conversation. The commander talked of how the Jin and Sui Factions came to hate each other, tearing the once great country in half. Commander Tai's history lecture didn't interest Takeo in the least bit. Tai himself was Koreyan, and that was the only thing that caught Takeo's ear in those two hours.

The train came to a long drawn out halt, and Takeo shot up from his seat to look out the car window. Koreya was a beautiful country with small towns and cities nestled between jutting mountains and forests. It was much like Nihon, but with an even rockier terrain.

The morning fog burned away from the rush of bright sunlight. They stopped in Daegu, and Takeo noticed the large bubbling pond near the foot of the tall steps leading to the old building. To his right were two smaller buildings being used as barracks for the soldiers. For now, the Xian, Koreyan, and Nihonese soldiers were segregated. Takeo would integrate them slowly.

After stepping off of the train and walking down the steep hill, Takeo stopped at the fountain. He watched the white and orange koi swim peacefully in the clear water. It brought a sense of normalcy to the grounds. Fish were a symbol of life in Nihon. Ironic, since nothing but death surrounded him here.

This used to be the government building of Daegu, but the Koreyans abandoned the site years ago for one closer to the center of the city. The main level and top floors were hardly used, but the lower level housed all of the scientific works.

Movement at the side entrance of the building caught Takeo's eye. An old steam truck with a long flatbed sat idling at the open doors. He saw two masked Xian workers carry a stretcher and dump its contents onto the bed. Takeo caught a glimpse of a mangled and charred human body roll onto the truck and slide underneath a canvas tarpaulin.

Abruptly turning away, he motioned for Commander Tai to lead the way.

Takeo and his men marched up the steps, passing through several stone columns and through a heavy door before entering the building. Commander Tai kept droning on. He enlightened them on the history of the building and the work it took to get the lower level to the Nihon scientists' specifications. By this time, Takeo felt annoyed. Two hours was too long to have spent listening to Tai ramble.

The lobby was empty. Brick walls surrounded them as they continued towards the back of the deserted chamber and stepped carefully down a chilly and steep stairway. The temperature drop made Takeo shiver.

They came to a solid iron door guarded by two Xian soldiers in gold armor. The two guards bowed and slid the heavy door open. Takeo followed the commander into a large chamber that must have been a prison a long time ago. There were five jail cells on each side of the wide hallway, and all but one was empty.

"We keep the test subjects in these cells prior to the experiments," Commander Tai said, pointing to the barren jail. "As you can see, we need more recruits."

Takeo swallowed his dread. In one cell, a man dressed in dark blue lay on a bench. The prisoner remained asleep and didn't acknowledge their presence when they walked past him. He expected to see men rotting in this facility, but from what Takeo could tell, this test subject looked to be in good shape. It seemed a waste to use strong and robust bodies for these gruesome experiments.

At the other end of the hall, Commander Tai opened another heavy sliding door. This was the heart of the facility, the main laboratory. Takeo stared at a multitude of glass beakers, small burners, and an army of scientists in brown overalls hovered over thousands of multicolored chemicals being measured and mixed. It was controlled chaos. The work of ingenuity creating death.

One scientist abandoned her station and stood at attention after bowing to Takeo. He assumed she was Dr. Sanu, a revered scientific mind of Nihon. Emperor Hideaki had personally appointed her as chief of this project. She was petite with white streaks running through her jet black hair, and her face looked stern.

This was their first meeting in person, and the impatient look in her eyes let Takeo know she was taking time away from her work and didn't appreciate this interruption from even the Shogun.

"Commander Tai informs me you are progressing faster than expected," Takeo said after giving a slight bow.

Dr. Sanu's irritation rose to her face. "We had our greatest challenges in the last three seasons, but we have made extraordinary progress. There is more work to be done. The delivery method of the toxin is the most difficult phase of our work."

"Doctor, would you be so kind as to give me a complete report on your progress with exact time lines?" Takeo requested. "The emperor is depending on all of us to complete this project on time."

The woman frowned. "Of course, Shogun. Make sure Emperor Hideaki understands the inherent dangers of handling deadly bacteria. Twenty days into our second season of work at this new site, thirteen of my scientists died from infection. It was a major setback."

Takeo felt the urge to leave, but he fought to maintain control. "The emperor fully acknowledges the demanding and delicate nature of your work. He appreciates how safety and extreme care are paramount when dealing with such a fragile and deadly pestilence."

Dr. Sanu slowly nodded, but Takeo knew she still wasn't satisfied. "The key was to find a material that would hold the bio toxins, yet remain stable enough to handle the installation into an explosive device. We designed special ceramic containers for this reason." She held up a cream-colored box that easily fit in the palm of her small hand.

"Excellent," Takeo managed, feeling a bead of cold sweat forming on his scalp. "Emperor Hideaki will be most pleased with your ingenuity."

"We are continuing to test this delivery method, but as you might have noticed on your way in here, we have nearly run out of test subjects," said Dr. Sanu. "We would like to test the pestilence on more appropriate subjects."

Takeo felt his jaw twitch. "Appropriate?"

"Since we are developing this weapon to defend against Iberian soldiers, we need test subjects with a similar physical make up. Up until recently, we tested it on beggars and criminals. That is why I asked you to provide more suitable bodies. Perhaps soldiers. Prisoners of war or other condemned men.

We need strong, healthy subjects."

Takeo nodded, not able to speak. His mind recalled the lone prisoner in the jail cell on the main floor of the building. He possessed the physique of a warrior, and that's what got his attention. The man was a soldier.

Dr. Sanu pointed with her hand. "This way, Shogun."

A bullet or a blade could easily take a life. But there was no defense against the invisible pestilence. He stared at the ceramic box. It was hard to believe that a harmless-looking object had the power to kill an entire army. When Takeo followed Dr. Sanu to her office, he longed for the simple and straightforward struggles of the battlefield. At least there, he could see the enemy coming.

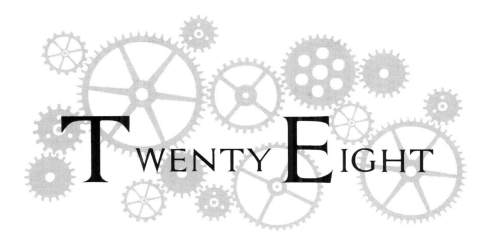

TWENTY EIGHT

THE HUMID CHAMBER HAD GROWN more unbearable in the three hours they watched Marcel work on the spydread machine. The audience, except for Geller's bodyguard Kamau, stripped down to their undershirts. Geller smeared the sweat from his balding head, feeling the sting of salt poke at the corners of his eyes. Marcel, however, was relentless and never paused to even relieve himself or ask for water. Large metal gears and other parts littered the floor around the spydread, and the boy foraged through several large wooden bins full of spare parts.

"This is a colossal waste of time." King Tlacatl wiped his face and threw his damp handkerchief onto the ground. "He's mutilated the machine's innards. If it was broken before, it surely is beyond repair now."

If Geller had not been so wilted, he would have scolded the king of garbage, but he dismissed Tlacatl with a shake of his head instead. He got up from his sweat soaked chair and approached the spider-like vehicle. Marcel was sprawled on the machine's main hull. His lower half lay on the metal shell while his upper body was deep inside the spydread's guts.

"How much longer, Marcel?" Geller asked.

The sound of a cranking wrench stopped, and Marcel's metallic voice replied, "Soon. Very soon."

"Can you hurry it up?" Geller felt himself on the verge of snapping. Marcel represented more than an entire life's worth of money to him, and he was ready to throw it all away to escape the oppressive heat of the chamber. "Finish it now."

Marcel pulled his head out of the spydread. "The governor valve was completely shattered. I had to find another one to replace it. The condenser was broken, and the pump was too. It was a mess."

"And?" Geller's head was throbbing.

Marcel's face was covered in soot and grease. "I'm practically finished."

Geller's arm dropped to his sides and he went back to his moist chair. Nineteen of his twenty men grumbled as they watched Marcel climb up and plop behind the controls of the spydread. Kamau sat absolutely still, the drops of sweat raining down his dark bald head. Geller envied his bodyguard's ability to withstand the heat, but of course Kamau had Nubian blood.

"What is the point of all this, Olaf?" Tlacatl's thin hands fanned his long face. "The boy is only fooling around. He has no idea what he's doing."

A sharp hiss made them jump. Marcel sat in the cockpit. When he pulled various levers, the iron spider shifted. All eight of its legs jolted to life until the engine died. Geller saw the boy smile, and his long lost excitement returned to his belly. The child jumped off the machine and grabbed a tank of water. Marcel fell backwards, unable to lift the barrel.

"Kamau," Geller snapped, turning to his bodyguard.

The dark warrior snapped to attention. He sprang from his chair and lifted the barrel of water for the boy. Marcel climbed back to the spydread's main hull, and with Kamau's assistance pulled the container up to him. Carefully, the child poured the entire contents of the barrel into the boiler. Kamau tossed the empty container aside and went back to his seat.

"Is it done?" Geller didn't care that his armpits were raw from his wet skin rubbing against his shirt.

"Almost." Marcel twirled a wrench. "Just one more thing."

The child jumped off the machine and went to the rear of the spydread. Geller couldn't see exactly what the boy was doing, but he heard the clang of a metal door opening and then shutting. When Marcel came to the head of the giant spider, his shirt was covered in blue dust. He climbed back into the cockpit and pulled the same levers as before. A heavy whoosh of fire bellowed from the spider's belly, and the rumbling filled the chamber. Geller was both elated and horrified.

Two of the metal legs stretched forward while the remaining metal limbs twitched. Marcel flashed his teeth in jubilation and he continued to manipulate the levers and buttons in the front cockpit. Its legs labored to move, the crusted rust having penetrated its joints. The boy pushed a red lever, making the spider lurch towards the audience.

Tlacatl let out a womanish scream. He threw himself out of his seat and retreated towards the exit. The spydread's front two legs pulled the rest of its iron body forward again while Marcel let out a high-pitched cackle.

Geller was mystified, and all doubt of the boy's power

washed away with the long strands of sweat streaming down his face. The machine took another two steps towards him, and all of his men abandoned their seats and cowered in the corners of the workshop. Marcel's face sharpened; his eyes narrowed.

The spydread raised its front right leg, the metal foot looking more like a harpoon. Dazed, Geller's legs refused to move. Confusion filled his cooked brain, and his ecstasy melted into terror.

Before Geller could shake his foggy mind from its inertia, Kamau lunged at him, grabbing his limp body and slamming both of them onto the hard concrete floor. The spydread's leg crashed down, smashing Geller's chair into splinters.

Geller's mouth flew open, but his throat was too dry to produce any sound. The machine plowed through all the empty chairs. Although the legs and its fat metal body looked cumbersome, the spydread moved at a deceptively fast pace. In seconds, Geller only saw the rear of the machine. Bluish steam hissed out from its small exhaust pipe.

Kamau jumped to his feet and drew his pistol.

"No!" Geller's throat cracked. "Don't shoot him!"

Geller's men lowered their guns. They watched Marcel maneuver the deadly spider through the chamber, up towards the corridor. Kamau slid his sidearm back into his belt and ran towards the spydread. His powerful legs bent and uncoiled, propelling his stout body upwards onto the iron spider. He let out a deep grunt as he crawled from the rear towards the cockpit of the machine. His large hands gripped the sides of the iron spider's torso to keep the rest of him from sliding off. The machine was in mid-stride before coming to a halt.

"Don't hurt him!" Geller got to his feet and sprinted towards the now motionless spydread. "He's worthless to me dead."

Kamau leaped off the machine. He held Marcel up by the back of the shirt. The boy flopped like a fish before being dropped onto the floor. Geller bent over the child. Although the boy had nearly killed him, he felt like kissing Marcel at that moment.

"Clever boy. You're lucky the heat didn't diminish my wits, as my man Kamau was ready to put a bullet through your precious head." Geller wiped the grime off the boy's face. "You are special indeed."

Tlacatl was still breathing deeply. He approached the spydread with apprehension as if it might come back to life on its own. "I can't believe it. How did he do that?"

Geller touched the rear leg of the spydread, the metal still hot to the touch from the hydraulics. "I told you, the boy is gifted." He turned to Kamau. "Take the boy back to my car and get him cleaned up."

With a click of the heels, Kamau took Marcel by the arm and whisked him under one of the spydread's outstretched legs and exited the chamber. The spider hissed a final burst of steam from the rear exhaust pipes.

"Leaving so soon?" Tlacatl said, his thin body slithering up to Geller. "Why in such a hurry?"

Geller fought the urge to give his men the order to dispatch the useless king, but he let it go. Geller was in a merciful mood, so he simply smiled and said, "I'm leaving at once."

"I would like to make you an offer for the boy," Tlacatl called, his quick little footsteps following behind.

"You don't have the means." Geller pointed to the giant spider partially blocking the corridor. "Keep the repaired spydread, compliments of Marcel Bouvier. Enjoy."

With a quick hand signal, Geller's men escorted him out of the stifling workshop and back to his car. Riches would soon greet him south of the Mexihcan border in Azincaya, the land of the dead.

T WENTY N INE

THE SCARY DARK MAN STOOD in the corner of the car and watched Marcel change shirts. The beige one Marcel removed was covered in grease, sweat, and blue residue. He trembled while he slid the new shirt over his body. Kamau stood as still as a statue with bulging crossed arms. He wondered if the bodyguard was going to strike him for his failed escape attempt.

Geller had remained in the other car. A third passenger car was coupled to this one, and Marcel was sure that's where Geller was keeping the other boys he had picked up three days ago. He could hear the merchant yelling at them.

Marcel made his way to his small desk. He craved to read any one of the books stacked high in three separate piles. The large volume on metallurgy was especially fascinating. He felt Kamau's hard stare, and panic overwhelmed his tired body. The bodyguard looked as if he could spring to life at any moment and cut his throat.

"You read all of them?" Kamau asked, his voice deep and rich.

Marcel never heard the man speak before, and the warrior's speech was coated with an accent that sounded otherworldly. He turned to Kamau, his constricted throat not allowing him to reply.

"How did you make that machine come to life?" Kamau leaned back, his menacing posture relaxing.

Geller still hadn't returned, and now Marcel half-wished the old man was back in the car so Kamau could go back to being the guard. He recalled how swiftly Kamau had pounced on the spydread and lifted him up out of the cockpit, ending his escape. The man emanated raw power, even when at ease.

"You won't speak to me, boy?" Kamau said, flashing his white teeth against his dark lips in a playful manner. "You are mad at me, huh? Mad that I foiled your plan?"

Marcel couldn't help it now. "Yes. I would have gotten away if it wasn't for you."

He felt himself stiffen and recoil at his own words.

"I couldn't let you go. You are worth a fortune to all of us," Kamau said. "What you did was a miracle. It would have taken Tlacatl's engineers several seasons to do what you did in a mere hours. I am in awe of your talents."

A shot of warmth filled Marcel's cheeks at the compliment. It sounded sincere. He played with the cover of the metallurgy book nervously, unsure of what to say. His apprehension ebbed away.

"How did you do it? I saw you touching the machine for a long time, with your eyes closed. What happens when you do that?"

Kamau seemed genuinely interested in Marcel's ability.

Geller was interested too, but it was more out of how much profit he could make. How the merchant was going to make money was still a mystery. He was going to ask Kamau what they intended to do with him, but he didn't want the bodyguard to get angry.

"It's difficult to explain," Marcel finally answered. "When I touch a machine, it speaks to me. I can read its thoughts."

Kamau chuckled. "Machines don't have thoughts, little one."

The hiss from the steam outside made Marcel jump. With a few hard jerks, it seemed the train was moving again. Confusion lingered in Marcel's mind.

"Master Geller is going to be riding in the car behind us for the final leg of our journey. He is overseeing the young boys' training." Kamau looked away, turning towards one of the windows. "In Azincaya, the people like to watch the children fight in the arena before the main contest."

Marcel's throat constricted. "Is that what he plans for me?"

"No, little one. He would never dream of you even suffering a paper cut," Kamau sat on the fancy bench across from him. "How can machines have thoughts?"

"They don't have thoughts like people," Marcel said. "Machines can be in different...conditions. When I touch a machine, I can feel every little piece inside. If it's broken, I can see how all the pieces are related to one another."

Kamau lay his head all the way back, his neck cradled by the arm of the couch. Marcel stared at the metal sliding door, and he wondered if he should make another run for it. Jumping off the train and hoping he didn't kill himself wasn't a sound plan, however. Marcel's fear paralyzed him. One act of stupid bravery per day was more than good enough for him.

"That sounds complicated," Kamau said while staring at the ceiling.

Marcel opened the metallurgy book and skimmed the table of contents. "It isn't. It's simple. Simple to me."

Kamau sighed. "I understand how difficult this is for you, being away from your home. I met your stepfather in Francia. Pierce was a moron that talked too much."

A snicker escaped Marcel's mouth. It felt good to laugh. There hadn't been much to laugh about in a long time. "You're right about that."

"Believe me, you are better off without him as your caregiver."

That was true, but he didn't want to waste one single second thinking about Pierce. Marcel missed his mother. Would he ever see her again? It had been days since he last cried, and keeping his agony to himself was taking its toll. The pit of his stomach hurt, and he felt like he had been thrown down a dark well. Falling and falling.

"You miss your mother. I see it in your eyes." Kamau said. "That pain will pass in time. You will be busy fixing machines, building them. Inventing them. You will one day create something that will change the world. With your genius, who knows what wonderful things you can do?"

There was some truth in this. Marcel had kept his power a secret all of his life. Once in a while, he would wander to a piece of machinery so he could talk with it. Until only several days ago, he wasn't sure of the full extent of his abilities. Repairing the broken projector Geller first presented to him was simple, but it did give him confidence.

Talking with the spydread machine was more complicated, but it too felt easy to him. Maybe someday he would use his power to reunite with his mother. Until then, he'd fill his days and nights working with machines. He'd yet to discover the limits of his power. Maybe the pain would go away as Kamau said it would.

Even while he began to absorb the contents of the metallurgy book into his brain, he knew in his heart the ache would always be there. No machine could make him feel better.

Marcel wanted to think his mother was out there looking for him. But he was so far away now. No matter how strong she was, she could never find him. His eyes glossed over the words in his book, but all he could do was think about his mother.

THIRTY

IT WAS ZEN'S TURN TO pilot the locomobile, and Enapay seemed relieved to get more sleep. Neva decided to stay in the locomobile. She sat next to Zen with her boots propped up on the console. Once in a while, she'd sigh and stare at the pencil drawing of Geller and Marcel before tucking it away. When Neva finally spoke, it startled Zen.

"You know, I don't know the reason why you left your home to come to Agrios." Her voice was warm and motherly. "Why did you leave Nihon?"

Zen kept his eyes and hands steady. The dirt road was rough, and the locomobile's rigid wheels were unforgiving. Without looking up, he replied, "I told you, I was sent on a quest."

"What's that?" Neva swung her boots off of the control panel.

"You have firsthand knowledge of Iberia's growing power," Zen replied. "You said you fought for your homeland in an uprising against them."

She nodded.

"Iberia is building up their forces along the western and northern borders of Xia, our neighbors to the west. They plan on sweeping east, and eventually, Iberia will invade Nihon. We have evidence they have developed even more advanced weapons to use against us."

Neva showed understanding with her eyes.

"Xia is mired in a civil war. With the country in such disarray, they will be unable to put up any kind of resistance against Iberian forces. Once Xia is under Iberian control, the invaders will continue their march towards Nihon and the other countries of the Orient."

Neva leaned forward. "Okay, but what does this have to do with your quest?"

"I have been sent to Agrios to search for the Sky Blade. It is an ancient weapon, forged from the ore believed to have fallen from the heavens. The sword is supposed to possess otherworldly properties. More importantly, the legend says that the one to find the Sky Blade shall rule all of Xia. Possessing the Sky Blade would be the final step in reestablishing the entire Sun Nation."

"Oh, that's what Enapay meant when he spoke of a sword made from star rock," Neva remarked.

Verbalizing his mission to her made the mist of doubt settle on Zen's skin, like a slow acting poisonous cloud. Neva was silent, and Zen wondered if she was trying to find the right words to describe how foolish his quest was. Even with all the signs of being on the right path, Enapay's doubt caught fire in Zen's mind.

"Do you need a sword to resurrect the old Sun Nation?"

Neva asked finally.

"We are an ancient society, and our ancestors have documented its history in exquisite detail. Xia and Nihon, and all the kingdoms of the Orient, still believe in the old ways. To the rest of the world, it is only a legend. To us, it is real. I must find the Sky Blade and make the people of Xia stop their bloody war."

Neva touched his shoulder. "Then what? Will it be you who leads them against Iberia?" She wore a teasing smile on her face. "Why did your nation send *you*?"

This woman bared her soul yesterday, and maybe it was time for him to do the same. He trusted her, and so he decided to share his secret.

"My father, the king of Nihon, sent me on this mission."

Neva slapped him jokingly on the shoulder. "So we have royalty on board. I knew there was something about you." She squinted at him. "If you're the prince of Nihon, why not bring an entire army with you to find this Sky Blade?"

"For my people, the sacred quest is a spiritual pilgrimage and must be carried out as such. I traveled alone, bringing only my barest essentials. The Sky Blade must only be found by one with the purist of hearts, and the sacred quest insures this."

She stared at him, her eyes barely blinking.

Zen found himself smiling. "It does sound like a fantasy, does it not?"

"It sure does," Neva said. "What if the wrong person finds the Sky Blade?"

Zen shook his head. "I am not entirely sure. One version of the legend details death and destruction once when the enchanted sword fell into the wrong hands. It has the power to enhance what is inside your heart. It can bring everlasting peace or never-ending-suffering."

"Hopefully, you won't have to worry about that," Neva said, getting up from her chair. "If there's anyone with a heart pure enough to have the Sky Blade, it's you Zen. I sincerely mean it."

"So you do not think I am foolish for believing in my quest? Enapay thinks I am naive. I must admit, at times, I too have my doubts." He noticed the warmth of his amulet under his shirt pulsating in rhythm with his heartbeat.

"Your mother's message about my boy is enough for me to believe in you," Neva said. "Who am I to question your story anyway? Look at me. My son talks to machines."

Zen kept his eyes on the dirt highway. "It does sound farfetched."

"It's unexplained, but that doesn't make it untrue." Neva started for the door. "Don't worry about Enapay. He's already reexamining his thinking."

Neva slid the door open, the warm wind from the desert filling the cabin. "The stone medallion you wear around your neck is lighting up. What does it mean?"

Zen turned to her for a moment. "It means I am on the right path with keeping my promise to *two* mothers."

Neva returned to his side, bent down and embraced him. Zen kept both hands on the steering wheel, but he imagined the arms around his shoulders were his mother's. The warmth of Neva's motherly gesture seemed to outshine even his glowing amulet, and Zen felt confident he was following the course foreseen by his mother.

MARCEL HARDLY SAW GELLER DURING the next three days of their journey through the desolate land. Kamau stayed in the passenger car with Marcel the entire time. The bodyguard asked him various questions concerning his ability with machines. Marcel was curious about Kamau's sincere interest, but it was a welcome change to Geller's cold and hungry stares.

Whenever Kamau seemed to sense Marcel's tongue had tired, he took over the conversation and talked about his home. The only things Marcel knew about Nubia were from books and maps, but Kamau painted vivid images of his homeland from his descriptive stories.

While Kamau talked about his three brothers and one sister and about growing up in a family steeped in military history, Marcel closed his books and listened with attentive ears. Maybe it was the longing in the warrior's voice that drew Marcel into the bodyguard's narrative about life in Nubia.

The continent was divided among twenty-two kingdoms, and war had been a way of life for Kamau's family. His father was a renowned military leader. Amidst politics and jealousy, a trusted comrade betrayed Kamau's father. One night, the traitors invaded his home and killed nearly all of his family members.

Only Kamau and his little sister were able to get away.

Not all of his stories were horrific. In fact, most of what he talked about was happy memories. When he spoke of the fun times he had training in school and playing with friends, the dark warrior smiled and spoke lightly. Nubia's kingdoms eventually forged a long lasting peace. Marcel was captivated by Kamau's storytelling, and it made the three days of being stuck in the passenger car slip by quickly.

The caravan made only seven stops along the way, and

Marcel felt uneasy being out in the alien and barren landscape. Even the sunlight felt eerie. In Mexihco, it had been desert followed by swamps. As they continued traveling, the everlasting doldrums gave the journey a nightmarish quality, as if the world wasn't real anymore. The land in Azincaya felt dead. When Marcel exited the passenger train to relieve himself, he saw Geller's men pacing in circles. They looked just as nervous as Marcel felt. Nothing grew from the earth here.

They continued down a highway of well-trodden dirt, and the landscape transformed dramatically. It went from a dull gray to green within an hour of traveling. They left the land of death behind. Soon, Marcel caught the familiar scent of the ocean again. Eventually, the caravan was surrounded by the everyday life of what looked like a comfortable, coastal town, much to his relief.

They veered onto a narrow path. The engine of the locomobile roared and shook when they climbed uphill. The road seemed to snake, and Marcel felt himself getting a little motion sickness. When it seemed he might lose the contents of his belly, they came to a slow stop.

Kamau got to his feet and opened the door, allowing cooler and fresher air into the car. The rushing of the ocean breaking on the large rocks below was a welcome lullaby. Marcel longed for sleep, despite the bright sunshine.

Marcel jumped off the car railing, immediately in awe of the ancient castle towering in front of him. Two main towers with pointed roofs dominated the building, and in the center was the fortress' tall iron gates. Buildings like this in Francia existed, but they had either deteriorated or suffered extensive damage from the war. This castle, however, looked intact. Geller exited from the car directly behind him and gestured towards the old palace.

"This will be home for the next few days," Geller said.

Behind Geller was a long line of boys, all of them older than Marcel. They appeared downtrodden and empty. With hollow eyes and blank stares, they followed the armed men through the front gates and disappeared behind the iron doors leading into the castle.

"Since you are the guest of honor, Kamau will give you a tour of my palace later if you'd like." Geller's smile was full, showcasing his big, white teeth. "I have all kinds of machines inside. I'm sure some of them are so unique and rare, you will fail to find them in your books."

Marcel tried to read Kamau. The warrior's face hardened, his stance like that of an alert guard. The talkative friend he had made during the last three days disappeared.

"Kamau." Geller motioned with his hand. "Escort Marcel to his room. After he has bathed and changed his clothes, take him to the kitchen. Whatever he wants, give it to him. Take him through my private collection. That should keep him happy and busy the rest of the day."

After an obedient bend at the waist, Kamau took Marcel by the shoulder and led him into Geller's palace.

EVERYTHING ABOUT THE CASTLE WAS extravagant. The ceiling stretched to the heavens; Marcel felt as if he had suddenly shrunk. Geller's guards were everywhere, and he decided to take a mental picture of every stairway and corridor that he and Kamau took.

His private room had enough space to house several families. It contained several sets of windows, but he was on the fourth level up. He couldn't survive such a fall if he were to try to climb down.

Kamau knocked before entering. He laid a bundle of new clothes on the bed and disrupted Marcel's thoughts of escape. "Get cleaned up, and I'll show you more food than you've ever seen in your life."

The playful smirk returned to Kamau's face. Marcel rushed to clean his body in the regal bathroom and put on the new clothes. The warm water from the bath soothed his skin, and he lay in the tub until his fingertips wrinkled. Any remaining grease and grime from working on the spydread washed away.

Marcel put on the clothes. The shirt was too loose, but the black pants and shoes fit perfectly. When he opened the door to leave, Kamau was already waiting in the corridor.

The kitchen was on the first floor of the tower. It was lined with long, rectangular tables, and a handful of servants in white uniforms scrambled all around preparing various dishes that looked alien to Marcel. On the far table, the cooks had placed several silver platters, each showcasing a mountain of meats, fruit, and figs. Kamau did not sit down with him, nor did he eat anything during Marcel's quiet meal. After Marcel filled his belly with exotic foods, Kamau decided to give him a tour of the palace.

According to Kamau, Geller owned several galleries designated to house various ancient and rare collections up on the third floor. There were five chambers displaying various pieces of art. Another room displayed Geller's hunting trophies from all over the world. Geller was an avid hunter, and his prize kill was a monstrous white shark. That sounded intriguing, but Marcel chose to see the main gallery near the stairwell first. Kamau called it the ancient artifacts room, and it was filled mostly with antique weapons from all over the world.

With his belly full, he followed the bodyguard back up to the third floor.

Glass cases protected the artifacts, said to be thousands of years old. Geller had bought many of them from markets during his travels to faraway lands. Relics ranged from pots and other handmade furniture, to various suits of metal armor and hand held weapons. From the chamber's main aisle, a labyrinth of displays filled the space from wall to wall.

A gigantic ax displayed on a far wall captured Marcel's attention when they approached the far end of the gallery.

"That weapon weighs more than you, little one." Kamau approached the display. "An ancient weapon from Norde. Scholars believe that it belonged to a man they called The Ice King. Look at the carvings on the handle."

The grip was at least three feet long; the images of strange animals were forged into the metal. Marcel's fingers danced, the urge to touch the weapon was unbearable. But he kept his hands to his sides. As he turned around, an intricate display to his left caught his eye.

Marcel turned and walked down the short corridor, ignoring the other display cases surrounding him. Gas lanterns hung on the walls and cast dancing light on the enclosed artifacts. The flickering lights created moving shadows in between the exhibits. Was someone moving behind them? After a few seconds of panic, Marcel realized that the light play had fooled him.

Marcel came to the end of the hall, and he felt drawn to one display near some large hanging tapestries. Kamau grinned and followed closely behind him.

Unlike the other weapons' protective casing, this glass case lay horizontally on top of an ornate wooden table. Inside were broken pieces of black metal. This was a strange thing to display, and he looked at Kamau for an explanation. Whatever was inside was the victim of both time and the elements.

"This is truly a strange relic." Kamau's hands went to the glass, stopping short of touching it. "Master Geller found it at an old blacksmith's shop in the Orient."

Marcel knew it had been some sort of weapon at one time, but it had degraded past the point of recognition. The metal pieces lay broken on the red velvet inside, entombed forever inside airtight glass.

"What is it?" he asked.

Kamau smiled. "It is the Xian king's magical sword. The Sky Blade."

Thirty One

There was only one road suitable for the steam locomobile to get through Mexihco City, and Enapay drove down the empty street with heightened apprehension. He brought the lumbering locomobile down to a slow roll. Neva sat in the co-pilot chair while Zen held on to a metal bar behind them and bent down to look out the window.

Even in the dimming twilight, Zen could see that the city stood in disarray. Enapay said the massive war that erupted in Azincaya had spread as far north as the capital of Mexihco. Nothing grew from the ground, and all the stone buildings were still covered in thick brown dust.

Enapay had traveled through the old capital on only a few occasions, and he feared King Tlacatl, master of this forgotten nation. In order to secure safe passage through the city, one had to offer a significant tribute to the king. Zen suggested the bag of gold coins given to him by Chief Ohitekah, but Enapay dismissed the idea, saying the king was crazy.

Neva reminded them of the Iberian auto rifles and ammunition they had brought, and Enapay still wasn't satisfied. The crazy King Tlacatl would surely want to take their transport and the passenger car it towed, along with the gold and auto guns.

Zen caught movement somewhere on the perimeter of the dusty street, and the strong sensation that they were being scouted made him pull his pistol from his belt. Neva noticed this and drew her own revolver.

"There's something up ahead," Enapay whispered.

Zen kneeled between the two pilot seats and squinted his eyes. He gazed through the dirty windshield. It took only a few short moments to realize what Enapay had caught. Roughly fifty feet in front of them, towering tree trunks were stacked atop one another, forming a formidable wall blocking the only route through the city.

Neva pointed out the window with her pistol. "They are all around us."

All along the decrepit buildings on both sides of the road, Zen spotted the silvery glint of rifle barrels pointed at them. Enapay cleared his throat and gave Zen a quick eye wink to acknowledge he must have detected the poorly concealed enemy too.

"Looks like Geller's been here for sure. Those are Iberian guns they're aiming at us." Enapay grabbed a red lever in front of him. His grip tightened and he pulled it back, guiding the creeping vehicle to a halt.

Outside, a solitary figure walked in front of the barrier. He carried one of those deadly guns in his hands. "By the order of King Tlacatl, you must pay tribute to guarantee safe transit through the holy city!" The soldier was dressed like a peasant in his torn pants and a dirty shirt, and he whispered commands to unseen soldiers behind the log barrier.

Enapay gave Zen a determined look. Zen knew he had no intention of honoring the soldier's command. Enapay pulled a black lever on the control panel, and Zen noticed the building heat from the firebox behind him roar to life. Neva twirled her pistol anxiously.

"Ready?" said Enapay, his voice full of grit.

Neva nodded, and Zen got a solid grip on the metal bar on the wall near Enapay's pilot seat. Enapay wiped his forehead before leaning forward and took hold of a red lever coming up from the floor. Peering out the small side window, Zen noticed more frantic movement in the shadows. The Mexihcans were no longer attempting to stay hidden now; their restless stirring became bolder. The air was thick with boiling heat and anxiety.

The rapid flash of gunfire from Zen's side lit up the window, and he hit the floor. Enapay let out a yelp and pushed the red lever all the way forward, bringing the locomobile's pistons to full power. A flurry of bullets slammed into the locomobile's metal armor from all directions as Enapay got the vehicle to accelerate. Zen took a split second to look up through the front windshield and watched the menacing blockade of trees ahead rushing at them.

"Hold on!" Enapay screamed as the front windshield exploded in a shower of glass.

Zen's body tightened before impact. With clenched teeth, his head wobbled when the wedge-shaped prow of the locomobile punched through the barrier. The eardrumblowing explosion of force threw him across the deck. Neva let out a scream when she flew out of her chair and tumbled onto the floor near Zen. The staccato blasts of bullets continued from behind, and Zen was relieved to see Enapay still in his pilot chair trying to regain control of their rumbling vehicle.

Neva did a quick check of her body. She winced and rubbed her left shoulder. Zen felt a sharp pain in his right thigh. The stitched up wound throbbed, and Zen was sure it was bleeding. The rumbling of the transport's engines sounded labored, and he watched Enapay fight the vibrating steering wheel.

"We're not in the clear yet," yelled Enapay as he steadied himself in the chair.

The front of the locomobile burst with more ricocheting bullets, and Zen caught sight of the blossoms of muzzle sparks coming from at least two dozen rifles in the distance in front of them. Neva struggled to her feet and staggered towards the co-pilot seat, and Zen noticed the auto gun in her hands.

She lunged forward and got low to the ground next to Enapay. She raised her gun and fired a wave of bullets through the open front windshield. The force of the auto weapon threw her backwards, but Enapay grabbed her left arm and steadied her. She planted her feet and prepared to fire again. Neva's mouth stretched into a menacing grin as she unleashed a curtain of bullets.

Zen crawled to the rear of the cabin and found another Iberian rifle. When he took it, its heaviness surprised him. He staggered towards the blown-in side window. He stuck the rifle out and blindly squeezed off several shots. The power from the sudden bursts of the rifle took his breath away, his hand nearly losing its grip on the weapon. He took a deep breath, held the rifle in both hands, and emptied the entire magazine of bullets in mere seconds. Zen lost his footing when his boot stepped on a pile of empty brass rounds the auto gun had spilled onto the floor.

The lumbering locomobile continued its path down the dirt road, and Zen wondered why the Mexihcan guns fell silent all of a sudden. Enapay looked ready to celebrate while helping Neva back into her seat.

"Looks like we made it." Enapay did a quick check of his controls. "All systems are still functional, believe it or not."

Half of the front windshield remained. Where it remained intact was covered with large cracks, but Enapay managed to dislodge the remaining glass by kicking it while keeping his hands on the steering wheel.

Zen stared through the now open front windows. "Something is up ahead."

It took several moments until the sight of a Mexihcan soldier waiting for them up the road became clear. He held something in his hands. Either the man was suicidal, or he was preparing to unleash a terrible weapon in his possession.

"What the hell is he doing?" Neva asked.

"I believe he has a grenade." Zen leaned forward. "That is my best guess."

Enapay's knuckles cracked from gripping the steering wheel tightly. "This locomobile has decent armor, but if he somehow tosses that thing into the cockpit, we're dead."

Neva opened her pistol's cylinder before slapping it shut. "I'll have to take care of him." She went back to the open side window and swept away any remaining broken glass. "Try to keep this thing steady," she said to Enapay.

"I'll try."

Neva climbed up and wiggled through the opening while

Zen held onto her boots to keep her from falling out. The road was rocky, and she struggled to keep her arm steady. Zen clutched her feet and watched the ominous figure of the Mexihcan growing larger in front of them until he was sure he saw the man pull the pin.

Zen was about to tell Neva to hurry when she fired her revolver. The soldier cocked his arm back, ready to launch the bomb at them. Neva cursed and fired again. Her second bullet hit its mark. The Mexihcan fell backwards and collapsed to the ground.

"This is going to be close!" Enapay pushed the throttle lever all the way down.

Zen pulled Neva back into the cockpit and pushed her down onto the hard floor. Three seconds later, a metallic explosion rocked the other side of the locomobile, nearly tipping it. Neva let out a shriek, and Zen's tailbone struck the metal floor when the entire cockpit shook.

Enapay dared to turn around. "You two okay?"

The locomobile steadied, and Neva holstered her sidearm as she stood up.

"Only you could have made that shot," Zen said. He rubbed his sore back. It felt bruised, but he was relieved to leave Mexihco behind them.

Neva took her place in the co-pilot's seat and thanked Zen with a smile. "I know."

T HIRTY T WO

T HE *TRITON'S* COCKPIT CONTAINED ALMOST enough room for at least seven people, but since the submersible boat needed only two pilots, it easily became the group's meeting room. Technically, it was Shannon McMillan's downtime. She assumed the Professor was finally prepared to brief the entire crew on the details of their mission.

Piloting the underwater boat at the moment were the two other mercenaries, Orsini and Lopez, joking around as usual when the group filed in one at a time. Orsini was a short and stocky man, and although he was normally jovial, he looked irked that his shift was being interrupted by the meeting.

Lopez, who could easily be mistaken for Orsini's brother, sat next to him at the controls. Both were always ornery and boisterous, and McMillan enjoyed their ability to find levity in any situation. This time, however, their laughter stopped when the old man entered.

The Professor shuffled to the center of the control room

while Simon and McMillan stood near the rear door. The old man looked rather uncomfortable when he revealed his real name, Lionel DePaul, but if the crew wanted to continue to call him "Professor," that was fine with him. He also confirmed that Simon was DePaul's nephew, and the young man was a military surgeon.

"With that out of the way," DePaul continued, "I must now reveal our mission." He looked across the small table at Simon before wiping his large forehead. "We are rescuing a boy."

The control room was silent except for the constant low humming of the *Triton's* rear screw propellers whirling. DePaul studied McMillan's face as if expecting a reply. She wasn't quite sure how to respond, and before she could start asking questions, someone else spoke up finally.

"All of this for one boy?" Orsini turned around in his pilot seat and stroked his curly mustache. "Seems like overkill."

DePaul took a deep breath, his face droopy and solemn. "The boy, Marcel Bouvier, has a special ability. He can communicate with any kind of machinery. Even if the machine is unknown to the boy, he is able to sense exactly what is wrong and how to fix it. I call it mechapathy."

Lopez, still seated next to Orsini, laughed weakly. "This Marcel can do such a thing? Sounds crazy, Professor. Are you sure somebody isn't playing a cruel joke on you?"

"I know for a fact this child possesses such a gift. I knew his father, and he had the power as well." DePaul tapped the table in the center of the room to emphasize his point. "In the wrong hands, the boy's abilities could be dangerous. Imagine the monstrosities someone might build with that kind of power."

McMillan felt like laughing. She had traveled to nearly every single continent on the planet, and she'd seen many mysterious things. Anything even remotely resembling mechapathy sounded like a farce. "Professor, I believe you."

She saw Simon do a double take, and DePaul shook his head, seeing through her fib. "Whether the boy has this ability or not, you three stand to gain a tremendous payday once we return the boy to a safe house on the Albion Isle."

Orsini and Lopez exchanged looks before turning their attention back to their pilot controls. McMillan could hardly argue with the old man's point there. Who cared if this Marcel boy truly had this power? "Money is money," she said, cocking her head in Orsini and Lopez's direction. "Besides, only a couple of seasons ago, the idea of driving a boat underwater for four or five days straight seemed impossible."

The two pilots shrugged their shoulders before nodding.

The Professor had warned them about the risks that came with accepting this job, but McMillan hadn't taken the old man seriously. "Something bothers me, Professor. You brought along your nephew-surgeon on this job. That tells me you're expecting some of us to get hurt."

DePaul replied, "The boy is being kept at the estate of a dangerous crime lord, Olaf Geller. He plans to auction Marcel among a select group of dignitaries." He once again wiped the moisture from his forehead and slid his glasses upwards. "This will not be easy. Otherwise, I wouldn't be paying you so much for your services."

"I knew there had to be a catch," McMillan said before sighing.

Orsini nodded. "If the boy does have this power, he is certainly worth a lot of money. I bet Iberia would pay a fortune for him."

DePaul's thin lips scrunched. "They would, if given the chance. The good news is Geller will not sell the child to Iberia, as he has a deep grudge against the Empire. His parents were slaughtered by the Iberians. He is selling Marcel to representatives from other nations, however."

Simon stepped forward. "The bad news is the boy is heavily guarded. The Professor and I have carefully thought this out, and we both agree we stand the best chance of keeping the boy safe if we take him before the auction. With only four of us, we will have stealth on our side."

"I have a contact in the coastal city of Caru where the boy is being kept, and he will give us the blueprints to Geller's fortress," DePaul added. "We will study the layout, and from there we will devise our strategy."

Lopez shut his eyes tightly. "Child slavery. So much for my wish for a more civilized world."

McMillan was no saint, but she did have one shot in her life at being a mother years ago. She lost that chance when her son died at birth, and her marriage quickly deteriorated thereafter. It was long ago, and so deeply buried, she couldn't remember the last time she thought of that tragedy.

"How do we know your intentions aren't the same as this man Geller?" she asked. "I might be a mercenary, but I don't necessarily want to be a part of stealing a child." She leaned back against the metal wall. "I do have some sense of morality."

Simon raised his head. "My uncle has been highly selective about whom he's brought on board the *Triton*. You've proven to be a highly intelligent and capable sailor. All three of you." He turned to McMillan. "We know all the details of your past military histories. We are confident you would not abandon a child."

McMillan didn't like how Simon was talking to her, and she immediately backed away. "Who exactly are you?" she asked, looking the Professor straight in the eyes. "I wasn't going to pry, but I also don't enjoy feeling like a puppet on a string."

DePaul replied, "I am part of a secret society of scientists known as the Enlightenment Guild. Our goal here is to make certain that Marcel Bouvier does not get into the wrong hands."

"So you and your Guild are the *right* hands?" McMillan asked him.

"Yes," the old man replied quickly. "I have something personal at stake here. The child's father was my friend."

Despite the sincerity of the old man, McMillan found it difficult to believe him. "All of this is a lot to take in, Professor."

"It sounds far-fetched, I will admit," DePaul said. "Had I not seen it for myself, I too would not have believed. Marcel Senior's talents became legendary and gained the attention of Geller, a powerful and dangerous smuggler. Marcel became fearful of the dark world that employed him. He had a wife and a new baby. So, they ran away, never to be heard from again. Eventually, he sought me out. We corresponded, with Simon here as our secret courier. We exchanged ideas and kept in touch. One day, he wrote about his son exhibiting the mechapathy ability too."

"Runs in the family," remarked Orsini.

"Later, Marcel fell ill and couldn't leave his rural hiding place to seek treatment," DePaul continued. "He was sure Geller was looking for him. In my final letter to him, I promised to watch over his wife, Geneva, and their son, Little Marcel. When Simon arrived at their homestead to help treat him and deliver my correspondence, his wife and son were nowhere to be found."

"Disappeared? So how did the child end up in Azincaya?" McMillan asked.

DePaul replied, "One of my friends, a diplomat from Russiya, received a written invitation from Geller to attend an auction for the boy. The letter went into great detail about Marcel's ability and vowed to prove it the night before the event."

McMillan felt her face twist in disgust. "Selling a child at an auction?" She still doubted the mechapathy bit, but she felt a flicker of her old maternal instinct kick in. Her mind tried to relate to the mother's point of view. "Whatever happened to the boy's mother? Is she dead?"

"Geneva Bouvier fled Francia after she killed her second husband. He most likely helped Geller abduct the boy. So who knows," answered DePaul.

McMillan knew what she would do in such a situation. Nothing would stop her from finding her own child. "So Geller plans to make a fortune from auctioning this child?"

"With the boy's mechapathy, one would profit greatly in many ways from using the child's power. Marcel's comprehension of machines and technology, of how things work, is beyond even my own abilities. There is no telling what the boy will be able to create as his grasp of science catches up to his powers."

McMillan said, "Even if another nation were to win the boy in an auction, you can guarantee Iberia will eventually learn of Marcel's power and take it for themselves."

The misery in DePaul's face lingered. "We live in troubling times, Shannon. Iberia is consuming nations whole. Their technology is already far more advanced than any other nation's. I dread the idea of them capturing Marcel and exploiting his gift. It would tip the balance even more. That is why the Enlightenment Guild will go to extreme measures to help keep the boy safe once we rescue him."

Lopez turned his head and gave them a nod of confidence. "I have a son back home. This is a worthy mission, Professor. McMillan is right, selling the boy like he's a farm animal is disgusting."

"Yes, it is." DePaul straightened his back and winced as he rubbed his hip. "From what my sources tell me, the countries bidding are all members of the Union of Nations. Human slavery was outlawed over three hundred years ago."

McMillan felt satisfied with DePaul's answers. "What's your strategy?"

"Once we grab Marcel, we will have little time until the entire castle is alerted to our presence," Simon said to the group. "McMillan will stay on board the *Triton*, ready to make our getaway once we return."

Orsini let out a low grumble. "How do we know she won't take off once we're on land?" He gave her a sideways grin. "No offense, McMillan."

McMillan was about to get up and slap Orsini across the face, but she kept her cool. "Simon is right, I will not abandon the boy," she said, keeping her fists clenched. "I'm no traitor. I've been a lot of things, but a traitor's never been one of them."

DePaul paced in the control room. "I have intimate knowledge of your temperaments, your past achievements, and even much of your personal lives. Iberia keeps detailed records of its military personnel. The Guild has the means to gain access to those records. As Simon said, I know none of you would ever abandon a lost child."

"Sorry, Mac," Orsini whispered to her from behind his seat.

"People can be unpredictable, I suppose," DePaul added. "I will have a special device in my pocket. If McMillan decides to leave us and profit from selling the *Triton* and its secrets to the Iberians, I can disable the boat from afar, insuring it won't get further than three miles from shore. It will sink to the bottom of the ocean, where it will remain forever."

McMillan slapped the wall in disbelief. "You can do such a thing?"

"Yes he can," Simon answered. "We're both confident that it will be unnecessary."

"It's settled then," Lopez said. "This is a child we're talking about. Special power or not. But, I hope he does have this mechapathy stuff. I've got a steam skiff back home that could use some fixing. Maybe Marcel can modify my boat to run on carbsidian."

McMillan smiled and interrupted DePaul's pacing by moving directly in front of his path. "You can just go ahead and throw that little gadget away, as far as I'm concerned. This is a noble mission."

"Indeed it is," DePaul said. "One that will reward you well."

Lopez gave Orsini a playful slap on the back, and both men laughed. Orsini tipped his flat cap in McMillan's direction, as was his way of apologizing again.

IN THE MIDDLE OF TAKEO'S visit in the Koreyan province, he received urgent news. He learned a diplomat from the Jin Faction of Xia was on his way to Nihon. He was to deliver their supreme chancellor's signed agreement to join the newly formed Sun Nation.

The historic treaty came as no surprise to Takeo. He knew about the two Shadow assassins being sent to Western Xia fifteen days ago; their orders were to kidnap members of Chancellor Zhi's family and force his hand to sign the treaty. For every day Chancellor Zhi hesitated to proclaim obedience to the Nihon Crown, a family member would be killed.

Politics was ugly business, but having Jin support was crucial. Their territories held much needed resources, while the greater populated Eastern Sui regions gave them the manpower they needed to fight Iberia.

It was now only a matter of days until the reunification of the entire Sun Nation as one solidified force, with Nihon as the sole ruler, was to be made official.

At receiving the update from an official Jin courier, Takeo left Koreya in haste. He was more than happy to leave the peninsula. It had been a difficult visit despite every facet of the project proving to be successful. Even as he stepped off his steamship and found himself back on Nihon soil, the heavy dread of what he had seen in Koreya weighed on his mind.

Sitting in Emperor Hideaki's private study, Takeo quickly reviewed his notes. The short trip to Koreya had not been short enough. The clear rules of warfare he had lived by for years were now muddled and cast aside. Takeo felt off balance.

"The scientists have made great strides in the last two seasons," Takeo managed to convey in an even tone. "They have finally created a suitable container for the pestilence. Ceramic capsules. We will be able to drop them from above in airships, or even launch them from power catapults. The sickness for which there is no cure will come upon the enemy fairly quickly, in four to six hours. However, we must remain cognizant of the winds if we are to use these weapons, as we could be killing our own."

Hideaki stood in silence for a long time. His emperor had been filled with angst ever since he sent Zen away to the Wild Land, but there was contentment now in his eyes. He turned to Takeo as if he sensed the Shogun's dark mood. "Tell me, Takeo, is something bothering you?"

Takeo struggled to answer, and his obedience struck down all the rebellious words threatening to come from his mouth. Hideaki leaned forward as if he expected to be told a secret.

"No, your Excellency. I am lacking sleep. Even to this day, I find it difficult when traveling abroad," Takeo replied.

Hideaki seemed satisfied with his answer. "I must admit, I had my doubts in the beginning. Seeing all of the pieces fall into place, I am now sure that I have done the right thing."

Takeo assumed he spoke of Zen. "I agree, my Lord. It is all for the best."

Hideaki's eyes turned upwards towards the ceiling. "If Zen were here, I imagine we would have a serious problem on our hands."

The emperor sought affirmation, and Takeo had no choice but to offer it. "The people adore and admire Zen. It would have created a potentially dangerous situation had he learned of our work. We would have had a revolt on our hands. A war with your own son is unthinkable."

With eyes closed, Hideaki nodded slowly and repeated,

"Unthinkable."

KAI DISPATCHED TWO OF HIS crew to Geller's castle to announce his arrival. As an official diplomat of Nihon, an invitation to stay in luxurious accommodations within Geller's estate was guaranteed. But Kai didn't see himself as a diplomat at all. Although his original orders came directly from Emperor Hideaki, Kai was free to do whatever it took to achieve his objective. As a Shadow, all that mattered was the job. If killing people was involved, it was a nice added bonus. Kai was still going to offer Geller the gold for the boy, but the old merchant was sure to refuse. Once Geller refused to exchange the child for gold, the simple mission would turn complicated. Kai was at his best when he needed to revise his strategy. Geller wouldn't give up the boy without a fight.

It was hot in this part of the world, yet Kai decided to keep his long-sleeved blue shirt on. Being uncomfortable was a good thing, as it kept his senses sharp. Compared to prior missions, this one seemed not only easy, but most enjoyable. Kai had been chosen for this mission, because out of the five loyal Shadows, he was the most comfortable with conversing with others. But that wasn't saying much.

His two men returned to the ship much sooner than Kai had anticipated. He waited patiently for them to catch their breaths.

"We showed Geller's assistant your official invitation for the auction," the tall one on the right said. "He verified the seal was authentic. They are inviting you to stay the night at the estate where all of your needs will be taken care of. Dinner will be served shortly."

The portly one on his left was still struggling for air. "Shall we get your things for you, Master?"

Kai shook his head. "Tell them I respectfully decline their generous offer. I will stay here, on board the ship with my crew. However, I will attend dinner. I do request a private audience with Geller tonight. After our meal, I have an official message from Emperor Hideaki I must deliver."

The two men bowed and scurried together back towards Geller's palace.

Kai started for his cabin below deck, as there was much to do before finally meeting Geller face-to-face.

Thirty Three

When morning came, Enapay stopped the locomobile to assess the damage. He complained of having to struggle to keep the vehicle straight since barreling through Mexihco. Neva and Zen exited the cockpit, eager to take in the fresh air, but the barren world that greeted them offered no relief from the growing heat.

Zen scanned the desert all the way to the horizon. "What happened to this land?"

Neva shrugged. "Lots of speculation. Some say a devastating war killed everything. Others believe it is cursed."

Before Zen could ask her which theory she believed, Enapay came from around the locomobile to find them sitting on the rocky ground.

"Bad news," Enapay reported. "The passenger car is damaged. I'm going to have to uncouple it from the locomobile. Otherwise, it's going to make steering this thing impossible."

Neva stood up and dusted herself off of the red clay. "How

far are we from Caru?"

"If we push it, we can get there about three days," Enapay replied.

"Then push it," Neva said. "My Machine Boy needs me."

GELLER WAS PREOCCUPIED WITH MAKING final preparations for the arrival of the invitees, but something new was bothering him. He had been in such a good mood since returning home. Representatives from several nations already made their initial appearances, with more to come in the next two days. The arrival of his most recent guest made him nervous, however. Geller had never personally met Emperor Hideaki or any of his dignitaries before, but the man who called himself Kai did not fit his preconceived ideas of Nihonese nobility. Kai had refused to lodge in the comfort of the castle, which troubled Geller immediately. And now, the Nihonese representative was requesting a private audience after dinner. He initially agreed to meet with Kai, but when he finally met the man in person in the dining hall, he regretted that decision.

Even with the sun sinking into the ocean, the air was still humid and soggy. The other representatives were dressed appropriately, wearing light and loose fitted shirts. Kai, however, looked out of place in his long sleeved navy blue shirt with dark pants and boots. His hair was not long and put up in a top knot, as was Nihonese custom for noblemen. It was cut short and looked ragged. Kai was menacing despite his attempts at smiling courteously.

Prior to dinner, Geller had warned Kamau to watch Kai

closely. In fact, he planned on making sure his best bodyguard was at his side when he was to meet with Kai in private.

Nihon was still a mystery to Geller. There were rumors of the nation gathering strength, creating an alliance with the other Eastern Powers of the Orient. The most striking report was of the eastern half of Xia pledging support of this new alliance, with the western faction soon to follow.

This was all speculation, rumors that lacked confirmation. If true, then Nihon came to win the boy. With Marcel's powers, even Nihon could stand toe-to-toe with Iberia's new weapons.

THE DINING HALL WAS FULL of useless chatter. It took strength for Kai to endure the banal talk and banter between representatives at the long rectangular table. The food was equally unbearable, but Kai ate what was put in front of him. Wine flowed freely for the guests, but he kept his mind clear by drinking water instead. One by one, the chamber eventually emptied, until only the sound of the ocean crashing against the rocks far below filled the hall.

During dinner, Kai had noticed Geller's scrutinizing gaze. The merchant might be greedy, but he was not foolish. In fact, despite the man's growing belly, Geller still held solid muscle on his thick frame as if he had been a warrior before becoming an arms dealer.

Kai was sure his own quiet demeanor must have struck Geller as strange compared to the other boisterous dignitaries. His suspicion was confirmed when the stalwart bodyguard with dark skin remained standing behind the seated merchant in the dining hall. Kai had tried his best to socialize with the foreigners, but he didn't understand the subject matter of their meaningless discussions.

Kai tried to wear an earnest smile as he slowly approached Geller's chair while remaining careful of the dark bodyguard's movements. Geller himself looked uneasy, and Kai was eager to get on with it. How the next few moments unfolded would dictate his next move.

"Honorable Master Geller," Kai greeted with a bow. "I thank you again for your hospitality and for taking the time to meet with me."

Geller motioned for him to sit, which he respectfully declined with a slight wave. Kai noticed the guard move slightly, and the tension was building even as the ocean's breaking waves sang a peaceful lullaby around them.

"I know you requested we meet in private." Geller pointed to his mercenary. "But Kamau goes where I go. I hope you can appreciate my safety measures. In my line of work, it's necessary."

Kai nodded. "Understood." He swallowed the urge to leap across the table and strike Kamau in the neck with the blade of his hand.

"Your men said you had a message directly from Emperor Hideaki himself," Geller said with one eyebrow raised. "I am but a lowly merchant, and to be addressed by your mighty ruler is a great honor."

Kai glared at Kamau once more before saying, "My Lord is preparing for an inevitable Iberian invasion."

Kamau shifted once again behind Geller's seat, and Kai felt the bodyguard's reciprocal hunger to kill.

"I have heard such rumors of Nihon leading the Sun Nation

once again," said Geller. "If a simple merchant can catch wind of Nihon's expansion, you can be sure Iberian spies have reported these events to their ruler as well."

Kai ignored Geller's warning and controlled his voice as he continued. "Emperor Hideaki feels it is important for you to understand the balance of power in this world is now solely in the hands of the Sun Nation. With the fall of Russiya, now no one stands in Iberia's way."

Geller's eyes narrowed. "The kingdoms of Nubia would disagree, but I understand what you're saying." He looked up at the bodyguard. "Right Kamau?"

Kamau kept his arms crossed and his eyes on Kai.

"This boy is important, and Nihon is willing to pay you handsomely for him." Kai still didn't know why this child was so vital to the world, but he pretended to be in on their secret. "Nihon's motives are honorable. My king knows of your distaste for the Iberians."

Kamau's arms uncrossed and lay at his sides. This made Kai nervous, and he prepared for Geller's man to charge at him at any moment. Kai had come to dinner unarmed, as the merchant's soldiers confirmed with a revolting body search before being allowed to enter the gates. However, the bodyguard wore holstered revolvers around his belt, which Kamau made sure Kai could see.

Kai said, "On board my ship are several crates of gold, worth more than ten million ibers. If you give me the boy, you can have all of it. This is Emperor Hideaki's private offer."

Geller cleared his throat. "Do you know why Marcel is valuable to your king and to the other leaders of those that are represented here?"

Kai was thrown off for a moment.

"I can see you don't." Geller smirked. "If you did, you would see how laughable your ruler's offer is."

Kai stepped back, feeling as if he had been slapped in the face. "Master Geller, you dishonor Emperor Hideaki's benevolence with those words."

Kamau drew his pistol level with Kai's chest. Kai decided to play along and threw his hands up in surrender.

"Marcel might only be a child, but he has the power to put any nation on equal footing with Iberian technology," Geller said. "The boy talks to machines, and what would you know, the machines talk back to him! This is why your emperor is willing to circumvent my little process."

Kamau brought his weapon down, and Kai did the same with his hands.

Geller continued, "I am a greedy businessman with maybe a shred of decency. I will not sell the boy to Iberia. I refuse to do business with those people. Other than that one caveat, profit is my sole purpose in all of these matters. I appreciate your offer, but I respectfully decline. I hope you are able to gather more resources for the auction in two days, as several suitors here are willing to give me more than double Emperor Hideaki's offer."

Kai felt great relief in Geller's refusal.

"I understand, Master Geller. I will indeed attempt to make a serious bid for the boy. In the name of Emperor Hideaki."

Geller looked satisfied, and Kamau holstered his sidearm. "Until then, my invitation to you remains. If you should change your mind, I will make sure you have proper lodging here at my estate."

Kai couldn't help glaring in Kamau's direction. "I will not trouble you any longer, Master Geller. You shall not see me until the day of the auction."

They exchanged slight head bows before Kai exited the dining hall. When he went through the guarded iron gates of the castle, he found his entire body covered in cool perspiration. The rushing sound of the ocean below was inviting, and Kai decided he would bathe in the tropical waters before retiring for the night.

Killing Geller and taking the boy was fulfilling Hideaki's orders. Beheading Kamau, however, would be a pleasure.

Thirty Four

MARCEL HAD NOTED THAT HIS room was in the western tower, one level above the floor with all the artifacts. Guards lined the corridors everywhere he went, so escape seemed impossible. After spending most of the day studying all of the exhibits, he felt exhausted. Kamau was his shadow, being replaced by another guard in the evening. Later that night, Kamau returned, and Marcel was surprised to find himself relieved to be in his presence again.

"You must get sleep." Kamau pointed to the elaborate four poster bed. "Tomorrow is a big day."

Marcel tugged on his sleeping gown. It was at least two sizes too large. "What's tomorrow?"

Kamau went over to help lift him onto the high bed. "Master Geller will give you another broken piece of machinery for you to fix. Important people from all over the world will be there to watch you work."

"What kind of machine?"

"I think it is a steam car. Maybe a roadster."

Marcel put his head on the soft pillow, and his eyes felt heavy. A spasm of bravery and delirium came over him. "Why should I do this? I don't like being here. Can't you help me escape?"

The words flew from his mouth, and Marcel immediately regretted it. Kamau was the closest thing to a friend he had, but the bodyguard was still loyal to Geller. In fact, it was Kamau who foiled his first attempt at freedom only days ago, but he hoped the bodyguard would change his allegiance.

Kamau's eyes narrowed. "You know I cannot do that."

"They want me to create things to kill people," Marcel said, his eyes threatening tears. "My mother wouldn't want me doing this."

Kamau shook his head. "You have a gift. You have the power to create new technologies that could help any of these nations defend themselves against invaders."

Marcel didn't care about other nations' sovereignty.

"Will I ever see my mother?" he asked.

"I don't know."

Marcel's heart lost its rhythm, and it took his breath away.

"Maybe someday," Kamau said with a quick grin.

Kamau extinguished the gas lantern sitting on a small table near the bed. The room contained large windows, but a heavy curtain covered them. Only the small flickering of a candle sitting on another table near the door provided enough light for Marcel to see Kamau turn and walk towards the door.

"A guard will be outside." Kamau bent over to blow out the candle, but he straightened up again. "You want to let this candle die on its own?"

Marcel pulled the light sheet up over his chest. He was too

upset to answer. Although asking for Kamau's help was the longest of long shots, he still felt betrayed. Any glimmer of hope was gone forever. Despite wanting to defy Geller, he knew once he saw the broken machine tomorrow, it would be too irresistible to not lay his hands on it to fix it.

Without saying a word, Kamau pinched the flame with his fingers, extinguishing the candle and allowing the night to consume the room.

MOST OF KAI'S CREW HAD retired for the night by the time he reached his ship. The sailor he considered his lieutenant gave him a quick nod before heading to the lower deck.

Kai's body felt energized after swimming in the shallow waters near the pier, and his mind was already sharp with focus. After returning to his ship, he strolled along the side of the vessel. His eyes wandered to the planks stained with blood. He never did confirm if the fat man's name was Ako, and even now he decided not to pray for the man's soul. Spirits failed to haunt him, as he believed his strength protected him from their curses.

Two men sat in the center of the main deck and kept guard. Kai waved to them before heading down a narrow stairway. He followed it all the way to the bottom to check on the crates of gold. The door to the vault was secured with a heavy padlock, and Kai was the only one with the key. With quick and swift movements, he unlocked the door and inspected the sealed crates.

Geller had refused to negotiate this evening, leaving Kai only one course of action to take. He would go back to Geller's fortress tomorrow evening with gold and bribe one of his guards to divulge the boy's exact location. Then he would steal the child away and kill anyone who got in his way. He hoped to kill Geller in the process, but a showdown with Kamau was inevitable.

This would be a most satisfying mission after all.

Kai felt his lips curl into a smirk as he left the room and locked the door with his key. Tonight, he would sleep soundly in his private quarters. At first light, Kai planned on doing his normal meditation and exercises, exactly as he started any ordinary day. He was sure Geller had assigned guards to watch him now.

Let them watch. It did not matter. No one was going to stop him from taking Marcel Bouvier back to Nihon.

ENAPAY WAS RIGHT. ZEN FOUND that the small city of Hunza possessed luxurious accommodations, if a person was willing to pay for it. It had been an easy two-and-a-half days of travel, and the swampland wasn't as perilous as Enapay had originally planned. After leaving the passenger car behind, the locomobile felt much lighter and faster. Hunza was a mere four hours away from their final destination, Caru.

When Enapay had suggested they stop in Hunza, even Neva agreed. They were hungry, as their provisions ran out, and Zen desperately wanted to take a bath. Their first stop was a large tavern on the outer part of town. It was empty save for a handful of patrons enjoying their expensive meals. Zen devoured several plates of cooked meat and several hot rolls of bread.

They found an ornate bath house in the main downtown area. The hostess took Neva to the women's section of the building. Enapay and Zen were led to another wing where they got out of their dirty clothes and wore only large towels into a room filled with invigorating steam. Large tubs filled with hot water for bathing awaited them, and it felt good to get the sand and grime off their bodies.

Zen's stitched up leg wound was no longer swollen, and even Enapay looked surprised at how quickly the gash had healed. Zen gave credit to the Nabeho surgeon and medicine man for their work, and he was thankful he hadn't re-injured his thigh when their locomobile was struck by the grenade in Mexihco.

Zen didn't feel any remorse about spending some of his Nabeho gold during the quick respite in Hunza. The food, bath, and new clothes were well worth it. His clean cream-colored shirt was loose fitting, and his tan trousers needed no alterations, thankfully. When he looked at himself in the mirror, he hardly recognized himself. He chuckled at the sight of his long straight hair settling on his shoulders. Toksu was right, he did look a little like a Nabeho with his hair removed from its knot.

When they reunited back at the locomobile, they all seemed energized and ready to get back onto the dirt highway. The land here was home to some vegetation, and Zen smelled the ocean.

Neva offered to drive, and Zen was happy to get a chance for a little more sleep before reaching Caru. Enapay said something about being relieved their quick visit was without incident, and went on about the last time he came through Hunza and stole a small chest filled with gold bars. The last thing Zen remembered hearing before falling asleep on the floor of the cabin was Enapay telling Neva about being run out of town by a local mobster.

When they came to a jerky stop, Zen pulled himself up and noticed it was nearing dawn outside. He thought that he had dozed off only for a few minutes, but he apparently had napped much longer.

"Where are we?" Zen rubbed his eyes.

Neva was still in the pilot's seat. "We're here."

Enapay was up, scanning the street in front of them through the open windshield. "It will be light soon. Let's find a good place to park and head into town once the markets open."

The fog of deep sleep lifted, and Zen felt alert and ready. "The markets? Why? Are we going shopping?"

Neva pointed to Zen's leather pouch near his backpack. "You still have some gold left?"

"Yes."

"Good. We're going to need it," she said, her eyes focusing on the road ahead of them.

Zen was still perplexed. "For what purpose?"

Enapay plopped down onto the co-pilot's chair. "I'm going to see if I can find someone who can give us a layout of Geller's castle. Knowing what kind of folks I'll be dealing with, money is the only language they understand."

Zen grabbed the bag from his satchel, tossed it across the cabin to Enapay, and smiled at Neva. "Let's go save your Machine Boy."

Thirty Five

THE MAZE-LIKE MARKETPLACE WAS busy, but DePaul was easily able to lead his group through the buzzing crowds and navigate to an old associate's place in the northwest corner of the open center. His friend was Anton, an ex-Francian patriot who had fought the losing war against Iberian occupation. He commanded a light artillery division and took a keen interest in DePaul's early work in developing smaller cannons that were quicker and easier to mobilize. During a skirmish near Francia's southern border that it shared with Iberia, a shell blast left Anton alive, but without his left leg.

Anton's storefront was plain, with only a young lanky man at the front greeting potential customers. There were no signs, nor any products advertising Anton's specialty. With Azincaya being the land of anarchy, all the criminals knew if you needed to get special contraband in this part of the world, you came to Anton's store in Caru.

Before addressing Anton's adolescent employee outside,

DePaul motioned for Lopez and Orsini to bring his heavy crate forward. It was always a good idea to bring a little offering when asking for an important favor. Simon stood at his side as if he were keeping watch.

DePaul approached and leaned forward. "Tell Anton that Lionel is here to see him."

The young man nodded and scurried away into a doorway leading to the small brick building.

"Professor, what's in here?" Lopez asked as he pointed to the cargo crate at his feet. "It's heavy."

"It's a gift. Never visit old friends without one," replied DePaul, his white brows dancing.

The employee came back out from the building with a smile on his face. "Master Anton is eagerly waiting for you in his office. Please follow me."

Lopez let out a low grunt as he and Orsini each lifted an end of the heavy box and followed the man and DePaul through the open doorway. Simon was the last to enter, signaling to his uncle that no one was following them. DePaul was led to the end of a dark corridor. The young man knocked twice and opened the heavy wooden door before allowing DePaul to enter the large office first.

Anton was already standing, his posture straight and smile wide. His hair was long and thinning on top, and his gray mustache twitched when DePaul gave his old friend a quick embrace.

"Leg's still working," Anton said with a grin. He lifted his left pant leg up and showed off the tiny moving gears and minuscule mechanisms clicking and spinning. "Miracle of science, huh?"

DePaul helped design Anton's biomech leg, which started

306

above the knee and went all the way down to the foot. The alternative would have been a wooden leg, which had sent Anton into a depression while in the infirmary. DePaul and two other engineers had designed the prosthetic, and its original design was still in use all over Europa more than ten years later. Simon had taken a keen interest in bio-mechanical work, and his surgical expertise led to new scientific possibilities that DePaul wished he had more time to explore.

"Excellent. I'm glad. It has been a long time," said DePaul as he took the seat directly in front of Anton's desk.

Anton moved gracefully as he offered the other chairs to the rest of the crew and took his own seat. "What brings you to Caru this time of the year? The mosquitoes? The oppressive humidity?"

DePaul ordered Orsini to show Anton the contents of their crate. Anton lifted himself up from his seat to inspect its contents, the flash of his white teeth broadening at the sight of new weapons that would bring a nice healthy profit to his business.

"These are new. I call them choke bombs," DePaul explained. "Non-lethal. You wind them up, adjusting the length to detonation, and with an explosion comes a nice gas cloud capable of knocking five or six full grown men out for ten minutes. It's a nice way to clear an area without making a mess."

Anton's approval was easy to see on his squarish face. He pushed back his greasy dark hair from his eyes and relaxed into his leather chair. "They will be easy to sell. Although, most of my customers enjoy making messes." He leaned in. "What can I do for you, my friend?"

DePaul drummed his fingers on the old desk. "A famous

smuggler lives here in Caru. I hear he owns the largest estate in town, overlooking the sea."

"Yes," Anton whispered. "I know him well. We are competitors. He handles large international orders while I'm only a small arms dealer. I sell only to locals and passersby. Still, I have to pay a non-competition fee to Mr. Olaf Geller. If not, I fear my livelihood would easily go up in smoke."

"That sounds fair," said DePaul, allowing his sarcasm to hang in the air. "Geller is holding a young boy captive at his palace, and I fear he intends to sell the child to the one with the most gold in his pockets."

Anton frowned. "Yes, oftentimes, Geller returns from Agrios with several young boys to fight in the arena. Grotesque, but wildly popular down here."

"Pitting children against one another to the death for sport is deplorable," DePaul said. "There is one boy in particular I want to rescue. The child belongs to another old friend. I made a promise to him, which I intend to keep."

"Promises to friends. The strongest of bonds. What do you need from me, Lionel?"

"I need a map or blueprints of Geller's estate. I must know the layout and deduce where he's potentially keeping the boy so I can devise a strategy of rescue."

Anton's strong jaw line pulsed. He suddenly looked twenty years younger, and he resembled the young soldier DePaul once knew. "I know someone who will have this information. Geller purchased the estate from another well-known businessman who still lives here in Caru. He's but ten minutes from here. He carries a line of credit with me, and I'm sure he'd be interested in doing a deal to lessen his debt. I will have one of my people fetch him immediately, as he never does businesses at his residence."

"Thank you, Anton. I am grateful." DePaul wiped his brow. Even in the dim office protecting them from the blazing sun, the air was thick and sweltering.

His friend got up and walked over to a metallic horn attached to the wall. He pulled it to his mouth, allowing the flexible metal tube to pull taut from its base. He spoke his orders into the horn and returned it to its place after finishing.

"You are all welcome to remain here as long as you need. My building has an underground level, which provides relief from Azincaya's merciless sun. Down below, I have a swimming pool."

Anton opened the door and allowed the cooler air of the hallway to stream into the office.

DePaul stood, more sweat pooling at the small of his back. "How do you stand it here? It's not even high noon yet and the heat is already unbearable."

"You get used to it," answered Anton as he led DePaul and the others back into the main corridor. "Besides, I don't have to worry about the Iberian Empire down here. Even they are not stupid enough to try to conquer these lands. Their naval fleet is afraid of the pirates swarming these coastal waters. In fact, I'm relieved to see you were able to navigate around our coast safely and without incident."

DePaul smiled to himself. "Yes. Well, I've been able to employ a little ingenuity in order to avoid trouble. Miracle of science, you could say."

A GUARD BROUGHT MARCEL'S BREAKFAST into his room. The radiant sunlight beamed from the open door and illuminated the entire chamber. It took Marcel several moments for his eyes to adjust to the light. The wooden tray was full of apple slices, grapes, and a giant omelet. Kamau stepped inside, his dark face even and calm. Any trace of their temporary friendship gone.

"It's going to be a long day," said Kamau, his deep voice echoing throughout the room. "I learned you will be tasked with doing more than repairing a broken steam car. You must somehow improve upon its original design using only spare parts and other junk."

His words were meant to be a warning, but it only intrigued Marcel.

"Fill your belly and be ready to come with me in thirty minutes."

Marcel slid his legs to the edge of his massive bed. His stomach rumbled as he stared at the food in front of him. "Are you mad at me?"

Kamau stepped back, and his intense eyes softened for a moment. "No, child. I remember when I was separated from my own mother. I understand what you're feeling. Remember who you are, what you are capable of doing. You are destined to do great things with your power. Be proud."

It was difficult to not think of his mother every moment, but knowing a strong warrior like Kamau survived being separated from his own family gave Marcel some hope. Maybe he too could be strong someday.

"If you perform like you did in Mexihco with the metal spider, you will surely impress the audience today. When they bring you to their native country, you will be treated like a king. Like their savior."

Kamau seemed sincere, and Marcel found comfort in that.

"After you've served your new masters well, perhaps they will reward you with helping you find your mother and allowing her to stay with you. Wouldn't that be nice?"

Hope rose from Marcel's belly. "Yes."

Marcel hopped off the bed and grabbed the purple grapes. He stuffed them into his mouth. The burst of flavor made him wince and his tongue tingled from the tart fruit. Kamau laughed before leaving the chamber, and Marcel was relieved to hear his guard's hearty chuckle again. He still had a friend in this place, and it would make it easier to face whatever fate held for him in the coming days.

ANTON'S CUSTOMER BROUGHT MORE THAN enough sketches and maps of his old estate. For a fleeting moment, DePaul hesitated leaving the cool waters of the underground swimming pool, but he was eager to study the blueprints.

After a warm goodbye, they left Anton's building and walked back out into the heavy sun. With sluggish strides, they began their three mile journey back to the docks where the *Triton* lay partially underwater. The massive rocks on the shore provided more than enough cover for his boat as only a portion of the single conning tower penetrated the ocean's surface.

They came to the eastern edge of the marketplace when DePaul nearly fainted from what he saw. First, he caught a glimpse of a stunning woman with auburn hair, followed by a small boy of the Orient. Emerging from between the two was the native young man he had taken in years ago. Enapay still walked with confidence many mistook for insolence, but De-Paul knew better than to think that of his old apprentice.

A split second before calling out his name, Enapay spotted DePaul.

"Professor?" The Nabeho's dark eyes grew wide with recognition as he ran over and threw his long arms around him.

"Enapay," DePaul cried, his breath pushed from his lungs from the native's powerful embrace. "What are you doing here?"

After a quick scan of their surroundings, Enapay moved in closely. "We are here to rescue a child."

DePaul felt his breath leave his chest again, and he wasn't able to speak for a moment. Luckily, Simon stepped forward to react on his behalf.

"We too are here for that same reason," said Simon, his voice low yet full of determined intent.

The woman and the young boy seemed alert, their hands near their holstered pistols. Enapay motioned for all of them to put some distance between themselves and curious people hovering about from the busy market. Without saying a word, Enapay led them to a more private spot behind a towering dead tree.

"What do you want with my son?" the female asked, her tone sharp and on the edge.

"Your son?" DePaul studied her face.

The woman must be Geneva Bouvier, Marcel's mother. Without warning, her revolver's barrel was pressed against DePaul's forehead. Her face was flushed with rage when she cocked her pistol's hammer.

DePaul's crew gasped behind him, and Simon began to reach for his own weapon when the young man with the wild black hair rushed in. The youngster left Enapay's side and moved like lightning when he ripped the pistol from Simon's belt, leveling the gun at his nephew's chest. Orsini and Lopez raised their weapons.

"Now hold on here!" Enapay threw his arms up in the air. "This is not necessary. This is Lionel DePaul, the man who taught me...everything." He turned to Geneva and bent his body to look her straight in the eyes. "DePaul is an honorable man. He's here for your Machine Boy too, and I'm sure that's a good thing. Right Professor?"

Geneva jabbed her gun against DePaul's head. "Tell your two men behind you to throw their weapons down, or I will kill you where you stand."

DePaul had no doubt she was ready to pull her trigger.

"Neva, there is no need for this," Enapay pleaded.

DePaul heard Lopez and Orsini toss their sidearms onto the sandy ground, but he dared not even take a breath. He now felt foolish for ever having dismissed Little Marcel's mother. He assumed she had run away after killing her second husband. The woman was on a mission to save her son after all.

"Answer my question, Monsieur DePaul." Neva's pistol remained steady.

It took a moment for DePaul to gather his thoughts before replying, "I am here to rescue your son and keep a promise I made to the boy's father." Her eyes softened, to his relief. "Marcel Senior was my friend."

Neva blinked before removing the revolver from his head. The exotic boy looked at her for assurance before handing the gun back to Simon. DePaul finally took a deep breath and relaxed his body, followed by the rest of his crew doing likewise.

Enapay took hold of DePaul's shoulder. "Sounds honorable to me. Let's bring this boy back to his mother."

They all agreed with quiet murmurs, but DePaul remained a bit on edge. He still felt the sting on his forehead where Geneva Bouvier's pistol had been, although the ferocity had vanished from her lovely face.

"I was able to get our hands on detailed drawings of Geller's entire estate and palace," DePaul whispered. "Let's get out of here and study the prints in private. I don't like being out in the open like this. Geller has eyes everywhere throughout the city."

The foreign boy stepped forward. "Our vehicle is down the road, hidden in the brush."

DePaul shook his head. "I have someplace better. More private. Let's go to the docks. The *Triton* is there. We'll be quite safe."

Enapay's black eyebrows crinkled. "*Triton*? What's that?"

T HIRTY S IX

W HEN THEY REACHED THE EDGE of the dock, Zen spotted the long, metallic boat partially submerged in the ocean. He was at a loss for words, and he wondered how such a craft could stay underwater for that long. Enapay said something about air tanks and was about to explain how they worked when the old man revealed a small metal box in the palm of his hand. He turned a tiny crank on the gadget's side with his bony fingers several times and pressed the small brass button on top three times.

A tall rectangular structure emerged from the water like a whale coming up for air, and the gigantic boat seemed to be slowly rising up. The water crashed all around the hulking transport. Zen wondered if the hand held device DePaul manipulated actually commanded the boat to rise, but Enapay explained that it was called a tele-relay. With it, the old man was able to transmit and receive a coded signal to the pilot of the *Triton*.

315

The water continued to chop and bubble as the ship surfaced. Eventually, a small circular hatch in the center of what the old man referred to as the boat's conning tower opened. A dark haired woman poked her head out from the opening and disappeared again. DePaul and his crew crawled into the tower's open door hatch and led the way into the *Triton's* main cockpit. One by one, they descended down a narrow ladder into the belly of the craft.

The chamber was a tight fit with all eight of them gathered around the small center table. The front of the cockpit housed all of the *Triton's* main controls, but other foreign instruments lined the entire space. Zen gazed at the hundreds of levers, small wheels, and buttons surrounding him. He noticed Enapay hovering around the front control panel until the female pilot shooed him away with her glaring eyes.

DePaul went through quick introductions. The intense woman at the controls was named McMillan. The two dark-featured men with mustaches that looked like brothers were Orsini and Lopez. Simon, the old man's nephew, was tall with pale skin and had a quiet demeanor.

Neva handled her end of the introductions while asking to see the layout of Geller's estate in the same breath. Without hesitation, DePaul unrolled the various blueprints and drawings onto the tiny table. Neva grabbed a few of them, holding them up to one of the strange orange glowing orbs lighting up the ship's interior.

Zen bent over the large blueprint on the table and traced the perimeter of the entire property with his finger. He came to a stop at the architectural drawing of what looked to be a castle. It held two jutting towers from the facade of the fortress, and the main body of palace was rectangular and spacious. From studying two other prints, Zen confirmed the center section of the castle held three levels with various open chambers. The two towers each contained six levels.

"My guess is Marcel is being kept in one of the towers," Zen said, breaking the silence. He held up a large map showing a side view diagram of one of the tall structures. "The chambers are closed off, easy to defend."

Enapay took the same parchment and glossed over the drawing. "I agree. There's a winding staircase and six full floors in each tower. This one has at least three or four separate chambers on every level. If you were to keep the boy safe from greedy hands, you'd put him in one of the towers and place guards on every single floor and a dozen outside the room. There's only one way in and one way out, and you'd have to get through all of those guards."

Neva placed one of the scrolls on top of the others on the table. "I don't see any other points of entry except for the front gate."

Enapay put his hand to his chin. "That's impossible. There has to be an underground level of sorts. Aristocrats don't like servants parading in and out of the front gates."

Each person picked a map and studied it in silence. Several minutes ticked away until Enapay clapped his hands in celebration, making them all jump. He turned his scroll over and revealed the reverse side of the thin paper. On it, a crude drawing had been etched onto the parchment.

"This is underneath the castle," said Enapay. "It's a tunnel system. Most likely made for servants. It'd also make an easy way to smuggle things in and out of the castle without detection."

DePaul patted him on the back. "Brilliant, my boy. You

were always one of my brightest apprentices."

Enapay's smile evaporated, and he stepped away from the old man. "What happened, Professor? Why did you abandon your workshop? Why did you abandon all of us? We came into work one morning, and you were gone. Everything was gone."

DePaul looked embarrassed. His cheeks flushed, and his eyes fluttered. "I had received a warning from one of my associates in Europa that Iberia planned to take me back to their capital and work for them. Create new weapons. They were going to steal all of my work. I had to go."

"Why didn't you tell me?" asked Enapay. "Why didn't you at least bring me with you?"

DePaul exhaled deeply before answering, "Because I wanted to protect you. That's why I kept all of you in the dark about the work you were doing that made the *Triton* possible. The less you knew, the less of a threat you were to Iberia."

"If you trusted me enough, I could have helped you. Helped you put this boat together, for example. I didn't need your protection. We were doing such important work with you." Enapay's shoulders slumped. "You shouldn't have left us like that."

Zen saw the anguish in Enapay's eyes, and he could feel the unresolved pain underneath his usual flamboyant and jovial manner. Fate had brought him full circle with his old teacher.

"All of you would have paid for my sins," DePaul said. "After my homeland was crushed by Iberia, they forced me to make new weapons for their kingdom. When they were satisfied with the weapons I designed for them, they let me go. When I came to Agrios, I wanted a new life. I was done with building instruments of destruction. When Iberia came for me again, I had to run away."

Enapay stood in silence, the ember glow of anger disappearing from his eyes. The mood in the room was awkward, and Zen felt the group needed to focus on devising a strategy for saving the Machine Boy. He started to speak, and he wanted to remind everyone of their mission when Neva slammed her fist on the metal table.

"How do we access this underground passage?" she asked the group. "I'm sorry Enapay, but time is of the essence here."

Enapay looked unable to focus, so Zen slid the hand drawn map towards himself. He followed the winding path leading to the tunnel's entrance with his finger. "It looks like it comes from a small building in the rear courtyard."

"There is a small building, towards the rear of the estate," Simon said, holding up the largest blueprint. "Servants' quarters. Inside, there must be a door or gate leading to the passage straight to the western tower."

Either Orsini or Lopez, Zen wasn't sure which, spoke up. "We can't go searching for the boy without knowing exactly where they're keeping him. We'll walk right into Geller's soldiers."

Zen did a swift scan of all the maps while the group pondered in another round of silence. "That is why I must go and find him."

DePaul objected with arms crossed and mouth agape. "Nonsense."

"No way." Simon reached over and snatched the scroll from Zen's hands.

"I'm not sending another boy into Geller's castle. I will most certainly not," the old man said while shaking his finger.

There wasn't any time for debate, and Zen felt his face

flush. To DePaul and his crew, he was only a child after all.

"Zen can do this," Enapay said, tearing the map from Simon's grasp. "Don't underestimate my friend."

It looked as if both Orsini and Lopez were going to intervene, but the sound of Neva's gun being drawn stopped them before they could even take a step. Enapay flashed his signature grin when he handed Zen the small drawing.

DePaul put his hands up. "Please, let us all take a deep breath."

Neva dropped her pistol back into her holster. "I appreciate all of you being here." She turned to DePaul. "I am especially grateful you made a promise to Marcel's father and aim to keep your word. This is a dangerous mission, and I am thankful you are willing to help. But I trust Zen with my life, and my son's."

"Geller has an entire army guarding every corridor, every corner of that fortress," said DePaul. He turned to Zen with his gray eyes. "Even if you find Marcel, the soldiers will prevent you from taking him. You and Marcel would be in danger."

Enapay tapped the old man on the shoulder. "Don't bet against this kid," he said with a sideways smirk. "Believe me. You're sure to lose."

⋆⚙⋆

MARCEL'S HANDS ACHED. EARLY IN the morning, Kamau and Geller had brought him to an elegant theater on the second floor of the castle. There were enough seats for hundreds of people, but the audience comprised of only a handful of strangers seated and scattered throughout the auditorium. Sharing the stage with Marcel was an old steam car, a four-seater. Kamau was right. He was going to have to prove his powers to the observers. Marcel had to not only fix it, but he must enhance it using only the leftover components stuffed inside several large crates.

Geller faced the audience. He used large and elaborate arm gestures as he spoke. He assured his audience that Marcel had never seen this steam car before, and no one had fed the boy knowledge of any sort prior to this demonstration.

Despite his queasiness, Marcel swallowed his anxiety and went to work right away. He put his hands on the vehicle, and instantly he felt the car speak to him. Instead of perceiving words, images flashed in his mind. Foreign and familiar components and small parts passed through his vision, and he felt how every single piece worked in harmony with all the other pieces. It was as if the machine spoke to him and showed him every single aspect of its mechanics. Marcel kept his eyes closed and allowed his hands to be led by his intuition.

When Marcel lifted his eye lids, he saw Geller join his guests in the audience. The merchant whispered to a fellow next to him in a tall, funny hat, and Marcel fought the urge to blindly bolt from the stage. Kamau stood at one end of the stage and another guard minded the other. Escape remained at the forefront of Marcel's mind.

He couldn't get far in the steam car on the elevated stage platform. As he stared at the vehicle's gray and brown exterior, he felt drawn to the thing. It was begging to be repaired. Marcel found several cases of tools beside the front of the car, and he sorted through them to decide which size wrench he would use to begin his surgery.

"What is wrong with the car?" Geller's voice echoed across the theater.

Marcel found himself trembling. "The fly wheel is stuck, and the chain powering the governor is broken."

Geller stood up and put his hands to the sides of his mouth. "Can you fix it?"

It took strength to hide Marcel's annoyance. Geller was putting on a show for his friends. Of course he could fix this stupid car. It wasn't much of a test. The difficult part was in modifying the craft somehow.

All along the rear of the stage, Marcel spotted the mountains of spare parts. He recognized pieces of old artillery, another steam car, and various gears and drive chains. His mind raced, visually putting a design together.

"Yes. I can fix the car," replied Marcel. "It won't take too long."

Geller stood from his seat. "How will you modify this machine?"

All of the audience members were dressed differently from each other, and Marcel presumed they had traveled from distant lands. Each one of them stared at him, anticipating his reply with open mouths.

"I'd like to keep that a surprise for now." Marcel forcing himself to grin. He had only a couple of vague ideas, and all of them centered on his escape. He knew he possessed the right spare parts behind him to create something that would kill Geller in his seat. "I promise, it will be something no one has ever seen before."

The audience applauded, and Geller's belly jiggled when he chortled and took his seat. Before getting to work, Marcel turned towards Kamau, who was not laughing or applauding, so he bent over the tool boxes and decided to get to work.

KAI WAS CAREFUL TO FOLLOW a normal routine the following morning, and he spotted Geller's men watching him from shore. The ship's crew had kept out of Kai's way all afternoon, and he spent the rest of daylight in his quarters below deck preparing. When the sun set, Kai perched on the bow of the ship.

Two armed men stood guard more than one hundred yards away near a small building. They leaned against the brick wall, not bothering to conceal their presence. When Kai turned to them, he smiled and waved his hand at them. When nightfall came, he could still make out the dark forms of Geller's mercenaries holding their rifles and smoking cigars.

Kai exhaled his nervous energy. It was almost time. Time to have one last meeting with Olaf Geller. Geller had squandered his only chance to escape this with his life and several crates of gold in this matter. Kai would enjoy killing him more.

MARCEL WAS LOST IN HIS work. It felt like only several minutes passed, but he was sure that several hours had elapsed before completing the steam car. Repairing it was simple and only took about an hour of labor to finish. Doing the modification was more complicated, and the majority of his time was spent searching through the mounds of junk. He carefully chose the vital components before installing them into the vehicle. The final step included pouring the paraffin fuel from a handful of old broken lanterns into the glass tank he had attached to the car.

With his throbbing hands covered in grease, he pulled himself into the car and started the engine.

The boiler came to life, and soon the exhaust stack in the rear spewed bluish steam. Marcel made the car move forward, and he saw Kamau jump as if he was preparing to thwart another escape attempt. He maneuvered the vehicle into turning a tight circle to the left, facing the audience.

Marcel raised his chin in order to see over the wooden dashboard. His hand felt for the small lever on the left side of the steering wheel he had installed. The front of the car was lined up perfectly with Geller, who was once again on his feet cheering.

All of the guests stood up and clapped their hands. Only three bystanders near Geller were in the line of fire, as the other audience members were seated further away. Out of the corner of his eye, he spotted Kamau rushing the stage yelling something.

With a deep breath, he pulled hard on the lever and pressed a small button on the front console. He felt heat burst from underneath him and then rush towards the front of the car. A rumbling fireball spewed from the wide hose he had placed inside the steam car's front grill. The shooting flame roared towards its target. To Marcel's dismay, Kamau leaped off the stage and shoved Geller to the floor.

Marcel gasped. Harming Kamau was the last thing he wanted to do, and panic rose from his chest. He climbed out of the car and ran towards the end of the stage. His boots pounded against the wooden planks, and he didn't dare turn around to see if his flame-thrower had successfully killed Geller or Kamau.

He dove behind the heavy red curtain, and his eyes found the small door only a few paces away. When Marcel took his first step, his feet slid out from under him, and he felt something hard strike the back of his neck. He nearly fell flat on his face when something yanked him upwards by his collar.

Marcel was shoved backwards, and he stumbled before collapsing on the floor. When he looked up, he saw Kamau. At first glance, the bodyguard showed no evidence of injury from the fire, and he was sure Geller remained safe too.

"You failed again, little one."

"Why did you save him?" Marcel said, his fury bubbling inside of him. "Please, let me go."

Kamau bent down, his eyes like black steel. Marcel wondered if he was going to strike him. He winced and prepared for the punishment.

"Listen to them," said Kamau. "It's all for you."

It took a moment for Marcel to decipher what he was saying, but when he quieted his heaving breaths, he heard it. Wild clapping and jubilation. Marcel's flame thrower had inflamed their frenzy.

"You did well today. I will escort you to your chamber where you will get a bath." Kamau pointed to the open side door with his eyes. "That stunt more than impressed the buyers."

Marcel tasted the acid in his mouth. He meandered to the open doorway and began the long journey to his chamber. The cries of the celebrating men in the auditorium felt like kicks to his gut, and his failure was almost impossible to bear. He would never escape. Never see his mother. Slavery was in his future.

"Master Geller will want to show you off at his grand dining hall tonight. You will meet your potential masters. Take this opportunity to further impress them with your knowledge and your loyalty. It will make your new life easier."

Marcel struggled to lift his heavy feet. Defeat was difficult to swallow.

And he was choking on it.

THIRTY SEVEN

I̲ᴛ ᴛᴏᴏᴋ ꜱᴇᴠᴇʀᴀʟ ᴛᴇɴꜱᴇ ʜᴏᴜʀꜱ, but they finally came to an agreement. With Neva's insistence that they follow Zen's lead, even DePaul and his furious objections eventually surrendered. Zen was to go into Geller's palace alone and locate the Machine Boy.

Inside a cramped and dim cabin, Zen put on his armor deliberately and with purpose. He took the time to follow his normal ritual before a mission, and he made sure to quiet and focus his mind. He concluded his prayer to his ancestors aloud in a soft whisper.

Those who embrace life, only find death. Those who wish for death, defy it.

Zen's mother would be proud, and he was still in awe of her foresight. This was destiny, and she knew this day would come.

On a small table next to his loaded revolvers was the hand held tele-relay. DePaul had instructed Zen on how to use it.

Although the plan called for Zen finding Marcel alone, the others would be following closely behind, waiting inside the underground tunnel connecting the servants building to Geller's palace. Zen was to locate the boy, turn the small crank on the side of the tele-relay, and press the brass button three times. DePaul would have a receiver with him, and the old man would be alerted to bring reinforcements.

Or if the situation deteriorated, Zen was to signal the rest of them to come to his aid. However, Zen was sure that transmitting for help would not be necessary, and he had no intention of bringing the others into harm's way.

Zen studied the blueprints for hours. He memorized every room and corridor. His leg was free of pain, and his body felt rested. Zen allowed the confidence to fill his chest, pushing aside any fears and doubts. All of his training, all of his experience prepared him well for this new quest. He was ready to fulfill his unspoken promise to his mother.

The *Triton* rumbled and shook, which meant it was surfacing. Zen pressed his hands against the walls to keep his balance. He slid both of his guns into their holsters and tucked the tele-relay into his pocket. When he opened the oval door, he found Neva already waiting outside in the dimly lit hallway. She smiled, but her eyes hinted of the motherly fears he easily recognized.

"We'll be right behind you," Neva said as she entered the room. "If things begin to fall apart, you transmit the signal. You understand?"

Zen nodded. "I will not hesitate."

Neva bit her lip and threw her arms around him. Zen took a deep breath and held her close. For the briefest of moments, he felt as if he was embracing his own mother again.

"I only ask that you promise me two things, Zen."

"What is that?"

"First, you make sure my little Machine Boy is safe and stays that way. Second, you promise to not kill Geller. You save him for me." Neva's arms loosened, and she stepped back. "He is mine."

ENAPAY WALKED SLOWLY ALONG ONE of the metal walls of the cockpit. Only McMillan was with him, busy at the controls as the *Triton* broke the ocean surface. During the last several nervous hours, Enapay had spent his time studying the *Triton*, amazed at the pure number of controls needed to pilot the submersible boat. In his estimation, a craft as sophisticated as the *Triton* needed at least ten crew members to handle all the functions. After this was all over, he would like to spend more time in the engine room of the boat and see what made it work. He suspected it was powered by carbsidian.

He walked toward the center of the control room and found the periscope. When he put his right eye to the monocular lens, he spotted the empty dock outside. McMillan must have maneuvered the *Triton* right up against it.

"You think this is right, sending that boy in there?" McMillan's eyes narrowed while her hands remained at the controls.

"You don't know him," Enapay replied. "Do not let looks fool you. Take it from me when I say Zen is the right man for the job. He's the only one who can do this and not get killed."

He watched the woman at the controls. She reached for two levers without hesitation, despite an entire panel of at least a dozen of them to choose from. He wondered how long McMillan trained to even get a basic understanding in piloting the *Triton*. She was a master pilot.

Enapay stepped away from the viewer after making sure the dock remained clear. "Trust me on this one. If we're to get Marcel back to his mother, Zen is our best chance at making that happen. Besides, we're one tele-relay buzz away. We'll be waiting in the tunnel for his signal if he needs us."

McMillan turned away. "This is all a big mistake. Geller's men are highly trained mercenaries. I don't know why you insist on placing your friend straight into danger like this."

Enapay shut his mouth and pressed a finger against his lips when he heard hollow boot clacks approaching the cockpit's hatch. The lever turned, and Zen opened the door to step inside. From the look in Zen's eyes, Enapay knew he had heard their arguing.

"My name is Zen," he said to McMillan without a hint of spite. He was still fastening his fancy, red armor when he entered the chamber. "I am accustomed to danger, but I do appreciate your concern."

McMillan left her pilot's seat and went to the periscope. "I don't agree with any of this, Zen." She pressed her right eye into the viewer, rotating the periscope before stopping abruptly. "I think someone has seen us."

Enapay dashed over and took a turn with the viewer. "It was clear a second ago."

Through the periscope, he made out the figure of a man walking towards the dock. The *Triton's* conning tower was visible to anyone nearby, and now the person was approaching them for a closer look. Enapay squinted his eyes, trying to sharpen the image. It was definitely a man armed with a rifle.

330

"He's got a gun, and he's coming this way," Enapay said through tight lips while keeping his eyes up against the glass viewer. "He's likely one of Geller's men."

Zen grabbed one of his revolvers from his belt. "Then it is time." Zen was up the ladder and nearly to the conning tower's hatch when Enapay called out to him.

"You watch yourself out there." A rush of doubt filled his lungs, and Enapay felt his mouth dry up. "We'll be waiting for your transmission should you need us."

Zen saluted with his pistol before he went up the final two rungs and opened the hatch. From the corner of his eyes, Enapay saw McMillan rush back to the periscope. He could tell her mouth was stifling another protest as she watched.

Without another word, Zen closed the round hatch behind him and slipped outside. Enapay took another shaky breath and leaned against the wall, watching McMillan stare into the viewer. Her mouth contorted with anxiety, and her feet wouldn't stop shuffling. Maybe if the woman saw for herself what Zen could do, she'd stop barking in his ear.

Knowing the Professor, he kept an arsenal on board, and it was time to get ready. Enapay pushed himself off of the wall, but he kept watching McMillan remain planted onto the periscope's viewer. The echo of a single gunshot rang out, and McMillan's body jolted as if she herself had been struck by a bullet.

"You get used to it." Enapay made his way to the cockpit's door.

"He..." McMillan slid away from the periscope, dragging her feet away before flopping into her pilot's chair. "Incredible. I've never seen anything like that."

Enapay chuckled as he swung the hatch open. "I know the

feeling."

"Zen moved so fast." Her eyes focused and turned to him. "Is he even human?"

He had one foot out the door when he said, "Be happy he's on our side."

S<small>UPPING IN THE MAIN DINING</small> hall was nothing more than an opportunity for Geller's guests to interview Marcel and ask him all kinds of questions about his abilities. Some questions were thoughtful, like the man from Roma inquiring if using his machine powers drained him physically. Marcel replied it wasn't the power that drained him, it was his need to get no rest until the machine was fixed. This solicited a warm applause from all the guests, and Geller seemed pleased with the answer.

Geller, in fact, looked jovial despite nearly getting incinerated by Marcel's spit-fire car. He looked invigorated by having escaped death without injury. His voice boomed louder than ever, and his eyes gleamed with greed. He stood to make a lot of money, and it made Marcel sick.

Kamau sat next to Marcel, quietly listening to the chatter during the entire dinner. Even he seemed a little uncomfortable with the setting. The old man from Eran kept staring at Marcel, and Kamau must have noticed it. The bodyguard watched the Eranian with intense scrutiny thereafter.

The entire affair lasted more than two hours, and when the guests began retiring one at a time, Marcel felt relieved. Having to put on a show all day was exhausting. He watched Geller whisper into Kamau's ear before dismissing everyone.

Kamau signaled it was time to go, and Marcel felt like he could finally breathe.

In his chamber, the bed never felt so comfortable, and Marcel plopped onto the soft mattress while still fully dressed.

"Master Geller was extremely impressed with how you handled yourself this evening, without incident this time." Kamau sat in the chair next to the bed. "The guests are more than satisfied that your gift is authentic."

Marcel stretched his limbs, and he let his sore muscles relax. "He's going to sell me to one of his friends. Make a fortune. That should make him happy."

Kamau paused. "One day, you will be in a position to get your freedom back. With your abilities and your intelligence, you will devise a way to get the upper hand. Some, like myself, are not so lucky."

Marcel was about to ask why he serves such a crooked man, but he thought better of it. "You are free to do what you want, right?"

"I'm a disgrace to my family back home," Kamau replied in a faraway voice. "I often disobeyed my commanders' orders and was dismissed from the military. In Nubia, being a warrior is everything. Geller gave me the opportunity to be my own kind of soldier and rewarded me for my loyalty."

"I hope I'm as smart as you think I am," said Marcel.

"Oh, you are." Kamau chuckled. "You will outsmart your masters, and who knows. Maybe you'll carve out your own kingdom someday. If you are able to create and build new machines, the kind no one has ever seen before, imagine what kind of power you could have. You could have whatever you want. Look what you did today with a rusty old car and piles of junk."

Marcel turned to him. "What if I come back for you? You could be my protector."

Kamau flashed his white teeth in a smile. "Now that would be something."

"I would reward you handsomely. Pay you better than Geller does. I wouldn't have you doing bad things like kidnapping children or keeping them from escaping."

"I'm sure you would."

He wondered if Kamau was being his friend again. "Are you mad at me? I nearly broiled you today."

Kamau reached over and touched Marcel's head. "No, I am not mad. You are a sly one, that's for sure. It helps keep me employed. That marks the twenty-third time I've saved Master Geller's life. The second time from your clutches."

Images of giant machines toppling empires filled his mind, and Marcel wondered if it was possible. Power meant freedom. Kamau was right. One day, he would make it so he was no longer a victim. He'd find his mother, and he would create powerful machines to protect them from whoever intended to hurt them.

"You can be the king of your destiny," whispered Kamau. "Take advantage of the situation you are in, no matter how bleak it seems right now. Learn all you can and gather all the resources you can. You'll have your freedom eventually."

They talked about being masters of their own dominions for several minutes until Marcel began to drift. The last thing he remembered was Kamau putting his hand on Marcel's forehead and whispering something in his ancient native language.

KAI FOUND HIMSELF IN THE basement of the palace when he emerged from a small metal door. The corridor was extremely narrow, filled with the echoes of distant workers in the kitchen somewhere beyond the short hallway. The underground tunnel system was easy to find, and it had been described in great detail by one of Geller's men. It only cost Kai a sack of gold bars.

These mercenaries were poor soldiers. They lacked loyalty.

He reloaded his pistol, having used three bullets already on the employees he encountered while using the passageway. Kai took no pleasure in killing these innocents, and having to hide the bodies took up precious time. As he pressed his body up against the wall and slid down the corridor, it became clear the kitchen was some distance away.

There were no windows, and only dying torches lit this level. The main corridor was slightly wider than the one he left, amplifying the voices of Geller's servants. He scanned the area, despite the darkness, and knew there were two stairways he could take, one at each end of this main hall. The kitchen was to his right, so Kai chose the less traveled stairs to his left.

Sounds reverberated too well in this castle. Kai relied on silence and surprise, so he put his gun away and slid his sword from its sheath. His eyes were fully adjusted to the lack of light, and he felt all of his senses amplify while he maneuvered in silence up the stairwell. His body's vibrations increased in frequency, and the energy was both stimulating and calming. Kai immersed his whole being in the state of *Ishen*; his muscles twitched, ready for anything.

Time was against him, as the two soldiers Geller had assigned to spy on him were likely due to check in soon. He had slit their throats shortly after getting off his ship, and when they would fail to return, Geller would put his entire personal army on high alert. Kai climbed the steps. He led with his sword. After gliding up three more flights, he realized he was on the floor housing a museum. Ancient weapons stood on display, protected in glass boxes. Kai now doubted if the child was being kept in this tower, as it seemed too quiet here.

Heavy footsteps thundered above him. Kai closed his eyes, letting his acute hearing take over. He surmised that two men were coming his way. He reached over and snuffed out an already dimming lantern, giving his eyes enough time to adjust to the dark.

The two men were conversing about spear fishing as they made their way down the stone steps. After taking a final deep breath, Kai emerged from the shadows and sliced through both men's necks with one fatal slash of his *katana*.

REFERRING TO THE MAPS HE had memorized, Zen easily navigated his way back to the main marketplace and followed the dirt road towards Geller's estate. He came to a fork in the road. He knew the one to the right lead directly to the front gate of the castle, and the road to the left was the way to the servant's cottage. Without hesitation, he went left and continued down the cobblestone path.

Zen hoped to avoid Geller's employees when he reached the modest cottage stationed at the rear of the grand estate. Thankfully, the cottage was deserted. The door wasn't locked, and the main room contained only a large table and bench and an ancient and empty gas lamp.

Finding the door to the underground tunnel was easy, as the square wooden hatch on the floor was already open. He supposed the servants came and went from there, and he made sure to listen for the sound of approaching footsteps. Using the peering moonlight to see, his feet found the thin rungs below, and he lowered himself into the tunnel.

The brick-lined tunnel was much wider than he expected, and Zen was relieved to find old, lit lanterns lining the brick walls. He kept a tight grip on his revolver and followed the winding passageway until the scent of gunpowder brought him to a halt. Zen inhaled deeply, and the lingering, acrid smell indicated that a firearm had been discharged recently. He cocked the hammer of his own pistol before proceeding through the damp tunnel.

Zen felt for the tele-relay in his pocket, hoping he wouldn't have to use it. The edges of anxiety tugged at his throat, and he led with the barrel of his pistol as he traveled deeper within the underground path to Geller's castle.

The closer he got to the palace, the wider the tunnel grew. Zen noticed shallow paths veering off of the main passage. They were filled with old crates and served as small storage areas. Referring to the map in his mind, he quickened his pace. Zen kept his guard up, but he let out a panicked breath when his boot caught on something while in mid-stride.

Zen nearly lost his balance as his momentum made him stumble forward. When he regained his footing, he turned back to see what had tripped him. He tapered his eyes and spotted a brown leather boot protruding from one of the short storage alleyways.

He retreated backwards when he spotted a dead body dressed in servant's clothing laying on the soft earth. When

Zen peeked his head inside the tiny outlet, he discovered a second body stacked on top of the first one.

Zen removed a lantern from its hook and brought it into the opening. The two dead men appeared to have been Geller's hired employees. As he lifted his light, he noted both men had been shot straight through the forehead. One of them twice.

Someone else had come here before him and was likely after the Machine Boy too.

T HIRTY E IGHT

Z EN'S PREMATURE ENCOUNTER WITH ONE of Geller's men on the docks had amended their original plan, and DePaul was obviously shaken by it. He uncharacteristically began barking orders at everyone.

Enapay found the well-stocked arsenal near the entrance to the control room, and he already found boxes of cartridges compatible with his rifle. The weapons DePaul kept were not the Iberian auto guns, but comprised instead of standard Francian rifles and sidearms. That was a good thing.

There was one surprise, however, and DePaul pushed aside his panic long enough to instruct Enapay on the proper use of his strange looking grenades.

"Choke bombs," DePaul explained as he held one of the spherical grenades in his hand. "Wind it up, and it'll give you up to a three second delay. It releases a toxin that can render five or six full-grown men unconscious for about ten minutes."

"Those will come in handy," Enapay said as he took two and stacked them in his leather satchel.

"We must hurry." Neva stood near the ladder stretching up to the exit hatch. "We were supposed to go to the underground entrance with Zen. He's alone out there. He could be in trouble at this very moment."

Orsini and Lopez rushed to get their gear together. They pulled a pair of bandolier belts filled with bullets around each of their torsos. Meanwhile, DePaul continued his nervous pacing. Simon finished up with stuffing his own satchel with medical supplies and tried to calm his uncle down. Enapay and Neva exchanged anxious looks while they waited beside the steel ladder.

"This was all a big mistake," DePaul stammered. "We should never have sent your friend Zen in there. I don't understand why you insisted, Enapay."

"Calm down, Professor." Enapay threw McMillan a quick look. "I'm pretty sure he's fine."

"Professor, Enapay is right." McMillan left her pilot seat and interrupted DePaul's pacing. "I saw it for myself. I watched Zen kill one of those mercenaries with little effort."

Neva took hold of one of the ladder rungs. "I'm tired of waiting. Let's go."

DePaul double checked the hand held receiver once more, giving it another three or four cranks. Enapay wondered what the range was on the gadget, and a stone of hysteria formed in his throat. He followed Neva up the ladder to the surface in haste. Although it was only four miles away, Enapay couldn't get to Geller's castle soon enough.

KAMAU LINGERED IN MARCEL'S CHAMBER for a moment, retreating gradually while watching the child sleep. He said an old Nubian prayer over him, a blessing of protection. It surprised him that he remembered it after so many years.

At the conclusion of dinner, Geller had ordered him to double the guards outside of the boy's door. Kamau handpicked the eight soldiers himself, and his mind now turned to finalizing the security details for tomorrow's transport of the child to the winning bidder's ship. That would be when danger would be at its peak. The stakes were high, and a sore loser might try to steal the child from the rightful winner. He most certainly did not want Marcel trapped in the middle of a gunfight.

The representative from Nihon who was absent at dinner was Kamau's top suspect. Geller refused to deal the child before the formal auction, and Kai looked like he had murder pouring from his slanted eyes. The fact that Kai didn't attend Marcel's demonstration made Kamau even more suspicious.

Kamau's hand touched the door's lever when he heard a thump come from the other side, followed by a wet gurgle. His body jolted to action. He drew both of his pistols and pressed his body flat up against the wall adjacent to the door's hinges. The intruder's footsteps were light and erratic, as if he were stepping over bodies.

Shards of splintered wood burst past Kamau's head, and several gunshots punched fist-sized holes through the door. Marcel let out a shriek. Kamau motioned for the boy to hide under the bed, but Marcel hesitated until the wooden door began to open. The child scampered onto the floor and took cover. The tip of a bloody sword crossed the threshold first, and Kamau dared not even take a breath. He was about to extend his left pistol when the dark figure swooped inside the room and struck the gun out of his hand with a flash of his blade.

Kai had come for the boy.

The speed of the intruder shocked Kamau. He managed to raise his other pistol, but Kai kicked his right arm, sending the bullet up into the high ceiling. Kamau threw himself off the wall to avoid the next swing of Kai's sword.

Kamau felt the whirl of the blade above his head as he spun away. He pulled his gun's trigger. Kai staggered and grasped his left shoulder before leaping out of the room and using the damaged door as cover.

Taking advantage of the opportunity, Kamau scanned the floor for his other pistol. His hands shook, and he felt his heart crashing against his chest. He gave an exasperated groan when he spotted his lost weapon. It lay about twenty feet near the center of the chamber. He needed to draw Kai away from the child to give Marcel a chance to flee. Kamau pumped another two rounds at the door.

Kai blindly returned fire from his own weapon and tore more holes through the door but harmlessly struck the wall above Kamau. He knew Kai's next round of bullets would surely find their mark from such close range.

The room was bare except for the small chair and nightstand beside Marcel's bed, and the dread sank into the pit of his gut. He couldn't risk hiding behind the furniture and putting the boy in the line of fire. Kamau had one desperate move left.

With two bullets remaining in his pistol, Kamau launched

himself from the wall and sprinted towards the center of the room. He spun around for the briefest of moments to fire once again towards the door. A searing sizzling stab through Kamau's left leg made his body seize and stumble onto the hard floor.

When Kamau raised his head and opened his eyes, he expected Kai to be leveling his pistol at his head, but instead the sweet symphony of a squad of boot steps and distant gun blasts came from the corridor. More of his men had come to the rescue, and Kamau heard Kai grunting and returning fire from the other side of the door.

He noticed a flicker of movement where Marcel was hiding. With struggling breaths, he endured the excruciating fire smoldering in his left thigh and staggered towards the boy.

"Are you hurt?" Marcel cried from underneath his bed.

"Stay down. Don't worry. My men will get him."

He had only one bullet left. His other pistol still lay ten feet away. The gunfight outside continued, and he fought to get his legs pumping again.

Out of his periphery, he saw Kai shove the door open and dive into the room with the barrel of his gun lighting up. The hammering punch to Kamau's abdomen made it impossible to breathe, and his weakened body collapsed to his knees. He heard Marcel cry out again, and he wanted to scream at the boy to stay hidden until his men took Kai out. But Kamau was unable to fill his lungs with air.

Kai rushed at him again, and with his final burst of strength, Kamau raised his revolver and discharged his final bullet with a pull of the heavy trigger. The sound of his own gun never reached his ears as blackness consumed his vision. He saw Kai's eyes bulge. But his sight failed him. Kamau didn't even have the chance to see if Marcel was safe when he surrendered to the dark veil overcoming him.

At the exact moment Zen placed his hand on the underground door to Geller's castle, he heard a wild commotion coming from the other side. He backed away. Zen hid in another storage outlet seconds before the first hurried footsteps of what sounded to be an entire brigade came crashing into the main artery. Zen remained immobile as dozens of Geller's servants rushed into the passageway and stampeded past him. It was mass hysteria, and Zen knew he was running out of time.

Whatever the reason, security surrounding Marcel was going to be escalated. Zen considered using his tele-relay now, but he decided against it. This was going to be a bloodbath, and he needed to get Marcel out of there as quickly as possible. The fastest way to do it was alone.

When the mob of retreating servants finally stopped, Zen left his hiding place and hurried through the open door. Stepping into a tiny hallway, he listened to the distant yells and the angry smashing of boots against the stone floor.

The frenzied sounds of Geller's mercenaries echoed from up ahead. Against his own logic, he decided to follow the sounds. He breathed a short prayer and hoped Marcel was safe.

Zen visualized the blueprints once again to get his bearings. He was in the western tower, standing next to a spiral staircase on the first floor. A kitchen and an adjacent stairway were to the right. He shuffled to the nearest set of stairs to his left, and the sounds of gunfire thundered from above.

Zen kept his pistol steady as he lunged up the steps to the second floor, but he paused for a moment. A group of men were hurrying downstairs, coming from one flight above him. He left the stairwell and ducked into a large dimly lit chamber. He flattened up against the wall flanking the threshold. Zen waited until the group of men scurried past him and continued their descent to the first floor.

More gunshots rang out from above. Zen rushed up two more flights of stairs, once again stopping to make sure the way remained clear before proceeding. This third level held a gallery, he recalled. The sounds of battle were much louder now, followed by the shattering of glass.

Zen prepared himself to enter the fray. He commanded the sea of calm to engulf his body, and the brisk awakening of *Ishen* took over.

The first thing he noticed in his altered state was the overwhelming fumes of discharged gunpowder. With short bursts of muscle twitches in his legs, he leaped up the final handful of stairs.

NEVA LED THEM TOWARDS THE abandoned servants' cottage, but she signaled for them to take cover behind the trees. She peered from behind her hiding spot to watch more than fifty servants bust the door open and pour out of the building in a crazed frenzy. They continued fleeing up the dirt road cutting through Geller's estate.

Enapay shrugged his shoulders as the uniformed men and

women screamed past them. Even if Neva and the others had stood out in the open, she knew that the servants would have ignored them during their flight.

"What do you think?" Enapay came out from behind a tree. "You think it's Zen?"

"He hasn't given us the signal," DePaul cried in a shaky voice. "I thought he said he specialized in stealth."

Neva said, "I'm going in. Signal or not. Something's wrong, and I'm going to get Marcel and Zen out of there."

She had been patient long enough, and no one was going to stop her from going into Geller's palace. Neva's grip on her pistol's pearl handles tightened. She approached the small building's door, only to get out of the way of two women in white uniforms shrieking and running past them as if they weren't there. Neva's spirit sank, and she hoped Zen and her Marcel were alright.

Simon, Lopez, and Orsini checked their weapons before following behind her.

"Let's go," said Enapay. "We're going to find your boy."

KAMAU WAS LIFTED BY HIS surviving comrades who brought him over to Marcel's bed. His wounds were already bleeding through his clothing, saturating the sheets underneath him. From Marcel's quick examination, Kamau was shot at least three times. The one to the stomach looked fatal.

Geller was in the room carrying an auto rifle. "Go find him! He could not have gone far."

Marcel hung back. He listened to the men replay the violent

events. Apparently, the intruder was wounded by Kamau too, and when reinforcements came, they had nearly cornered him. Marcel heard one of the men saying something about jumping through a window, but a weak tug on Marcel's sleeve made him jump.

"You are safe," Kamau managed, his eyelids barely open and his teeth covered in blood. "I'm glad."

Marcel took Kamau's large hand with both of his, grasping it. "The bad man is still out there. He jumped out the window." He saw Kamau wince. "Are you in a lot of pain?"

"I would be lying if I said that I'm not." Kamau's eyes fixed on Marcel's. "I sure wish you could fix people."

Geller rushed over and grabbed Marcel by the shoulders to do a quick once-over. "Good, he's not injured." He bent low to Kamau. "You have done an excellent job in protecting the child. Kai would have most certainly taken Marcel if it wasn't for your actions."

Kamau slid both feet off the bed, wincing again as he sat up. "I will stay here with the boy. This is still the safest place for him. We must make sure to gather as many men as we can to guard this chamber. That door is the only way in and out of here."

"Except for the shattered windows," Marcel said.

"Get someone to man them," Kamau told his employer.

Geller nodded and barked orders to his soldiers.

Kamau exhaled a deep grunt when he stood on his feet. Marcel couldn't help but stare at the growing clouds of blood on Kamau's midsection and left thigh.

"Don't worry, child." whispered Kamau. "Kai will not take you. I struck him at least twice before I passed out. He will either die slowly, as I will, or my men will finish him."

"I know." Marcel took a hold of his left hand, and the dark warrior held on with loose and blood-covered fingers.

Kamau leaned against one of the tall bed columns, his eyelids flickering. "Do me a favor. Go get my other gun."

ZEN WAS STUCK HIDING BESIDE the entrance to the gallery as two more of Geller's soldiers flew by him and rushed down the stairs. Gun shots echoed from below now, and he heard the two mercenaries give one final cry before hitting the ground.

The victor was coming up the steps, heading straight for him. From the sound of it, however, Zen felt sure there had to be at least four people ascending the stairway. He brought his pistol up and waited. The cacophony of quick steps grew louder. He took advantage of the dark. He used his acute sense of sight to see the moving shadows floating upwards towards him.

The first thing he saw was a pistol with a pearl handle, followed by what looked to be auburn hair. He slid his own firearm back into its holster with a mix of relief and annoyance. He felt a slight pop in his inner ears and *Ishen* washed away.

"Neva?"

She hurried up to the third floor and entered the museum to give Zen a brief embrace before the others filed in.

"What are you doing here?" Zen asked, letting his irritation take over. "I did not give the signal." He turned to Enapay. "Remember the last time you failed to follow my instructions?"

"Something's going on here," Neva said. "We watched all

the servants run out of here as if the place was on fire."

Enapay gave Zen a playful punch to the shoulder. "I thought for sure you were behind it all."

"Not me," said Zen. "I found two bodies in the tunnel. Both were Geller's privateers. Someone had been there before me."

"We saw the bodies too," said DePaul with a frown. "Who could have done that?"

"Whoever he is, he's raised the alarm," Enapay said, peeking out the entrance and looking straight up towards the top floor. "I think more of Geller's clowns are on the way too."

Neva pointed upwards with her gun, and the thudding of heavy boots reverberated from outside the gallery. "I'm getting my son back."

Before Zen could stop her, Neva left the safety of the museum and sprang onto the stairs. She fired her revolver twice. The bodies of two more of Geller's men rolled down and crashed at her feet. Zen sped up the stairs to catch up with her.

"Body count's up to four," called Enapay from behind. "Never agitate an angry mother."

"Wait, let me lead," Zen pleaded. "You are full of blind fury and it puts our rescue operation in danger. Stay behind me."

Neva ignored him. She lunged up the final steps and strode around the corner to shoot her pistol into the corridor. Neva shoved her empty sidearm into her left holster.

Zen stayed low and tried to get a clear view of the enemy around the corner. He felt Enapay right behind him, and the rest of the group protected the rear. Geller's men returned fire with their auto guns, sending Neva back as chunks of stone broke away from the wall and pelted Zen's face.

"There's at least twenty up here," Neva yelled over the

gunfire.

Zen wiped his eyes and spit out a few chalky fragments of the wall before saying, "Your Machine Boy must be up there."

Enapay and Simon crawled up towards Neva and Zen on the landing, stopping just short of the disintegrating corner.

"Make sure to watch our rear," Zen said to Orsini and Lopez below. Zen noticed DePaul was out of his element. He clutched his tele-relay box up against his chest and his whole body quivered while up against the stairway wall.

"This is a good time as any." Enapay reached into his satchel slung around his side.

"For what?" Zen asked. His ears rang from the blasts of machine gunfire.

Enapay produced two strange black grenades. He pulled their pins, wound their keys, and hurled them around Neva into the hallway. Zen pulled her away from the corner to protect her from the inevitable explosions. He heard the bombs clank on the floor before rolling, and the soldiers let out a collective yelp as they scattered.

"Those don't go *boom*," said Enapay.

Before Zen could ask, both grenades burst with a hollow and harmless thud. Zen assumed the grenades had somehow malfunctioned. He hated those damn things. A high-pitched hiss filled the area, and DePaul pulled on Zen's leg.

"We must pull back, the gas will knock us out too if we're too close."

Neva and Enapay led them back down to the gallery on the third floor with Zen covering the rear of their retreat. He heard the dull thump of bodies hitting the floor above them as he followed them down. Several escaping footsteps sped towards the stairway, and Zen readied his pistol.

Three men bounded from the fourth floor, covering their coughing faces with unsteady hands. Zen unloaded three shots, cutting down the men immediately.

"Excellent shot," said DePaul.

Enapay pointed a finger at the old man. "Told you."

Zen remained on the stairs, prepared for more mercenaries fleeing the gas-filled hallway.

"When will it be safe to go up there?" Neva asked as she reloaded.

DePaul sat on the steps, taking deep breaths while he opened a brass pocket watch. "In two minutes. We'll have about seven minutes thereafter until most of the men awaken."

"I'm not waiting two minutes," Neva said as she shot past Zen and made her way back up to the fourth floor.

Zen followed, and the smell of metal and rotten eggs attacked his nose. For once, he was glad his senses were not heightened by *Ishen*. Neva hurried into the corridor with gun drawn. She stepped over the unconscious soldiers and approached a large wooden door.

"I'm a little light headed," either Lopez or Orsini remarked from behind. A whitish fog lingered in the corridor, and Zen felt queasy. Neva stopped at the only door near the end of the corridor, which looked to have suffered from more than a dozen gunshots.

The others stood back. Neva flanked the left side of the door, while Zen and Enapay remained with the others on the right. Despite Zen's protesting with his eyes, Neva reached down and turned the lever. With her revolver raised, she pushed the door open.

Zen waited for gunshots to bang from inside the room, but

a moment of heavy silence hovered in the air. There was a click, followed by blasts from an Iberian auto gun from inside the chamber. The door was further torn to splinters, only an outline of wood remaining intact. From the sound of it, there was a single gunman firing at them.

The shooting ceased. Zen heard the shooter struggling with his rifle and cursing in a foreign tongue. Zen raised his pistol, ready to throw himself into the chamber. However, Neva beat him to it. She stepped into the doorway and fired a single shot.

Zen peeked inside and watched a stocky, balding man with a single gunshot wound to the head wane before crashing onto the floor. He recognized the fallen man from the pencil drawing. Geller lay face down with his legs twitching. Neva got her kill after all.

To Geller's right was the boy, but a bleeding soldier with dark skin grabbed him with one hand and held an unsteady pistol aimed at Neva with the other.

"Mama!" Marcel cried, still in the clutches of the wounded soldier.

She stepped into the room, her revolver steady and aimed at the wounded man sitting on the bed. "You let him go, or I will kill you where you stand."

Zen and Enapay came from behind and aimed their own weapons at Geller's man.

"Let me go," said Marcel, looking up at the soldier. "She's my mother. She came for me!"

The man released him. Marcel sprinted to Neva. He leaped into her arms and began to sob on her shoulder. Zen kept his gun aimed at the soldier who dropped his weapon and collapsed onto the bed. The dark-skinned man's shirt was blood-soaked, and a horrible bullet wound blossomed on his upper left thigh.

"Don't hurt him!" Marcel cried while still in Neva's embrace. "Kamau is my friend."

Neva slowly released her son, but she pointed her pistol at Kamau. "He works for Geller. He took you from me."

Marcel pushed her gun aside. "He did work for him, but Kamau protected me from another man trying to take me." The child looked his mother squarely in the eyes. "Kamau is on my side."

Kamau lifted his head. "You need to get out of here now, all of you."

Marcel dragged Neva to the dying man. He grasped Kamau's bloody hand and tried to yank him from the bed. "We're taking you with us."

"No. You are with your mother again," Kamau said. "Everything is as it should be. You should never have been taken from her in the first place, so this is my punishment." His body tightened in pain. "Now go."

The Machine Boy whispered something in the man's ear before letting go of his bloody hand. Marcel's cry grew louder as he grasped Neva's pant leg.

Kamau turned to the others. "There is a faster way out. It leads to the underground tunnel without having to go down all the stairs. You need to go back down to the floor below us, the artifacts museum. There is another exit there, at the end of the main gallery corridor. Underneath the brown tapestry you will find a doorway. It leads to the passageway to the tunnel system." Kamau winced and clutched his stomach wound. "Kai is still on the loose, and he will not stop until he has the child."

"Kai?" Zen took quick steps to the fallen soldier. "A man named Kai did this to you? He tried to take the Machine Boy?"

Kamau tried to respond with words, but could only manage a slight nod before his head slumped.

"Some of the men are already starting to wake up," DePaul cried from outside the room.

Although he didn't recognize the name, Zen knew Kai was a Nihonese surname. Kai had to be responsible for the two dead bodies he had found in the tunnels. His countryman had also been in this room in pursuit of the boy. Kai must have broken through the window during his escape. Zen felt a light tap on his shoulder.

"We need to go," said Enapay.

Zen hadn't noticed Neva and Marcel approach the dying man's bedside, both bent over him. The boy shuddered as he wept, and Zen saw Neva take Kamau's hand. She reached down with her free hand and caressed the man's sweaty forehead, and Zen knew the man's body no longer held his spirit.

It is in dying you are born into eternal life.

Zen finished the quick prayer and exited the chamber. Neva and a still-crying Marcel followed him, and they joined the rest of the group into the corridor. The gas in the air completely dissipated. Several of the mercenaries on the floor stirred, slowly breaking free from their unconsciousness. Simon, Lopez, and Orsini kept their rifles nervously trained on them.

"What should we do? Go the way we came? Or believe Geller's hired hand?" asked Enapay.

"Grab the privateers' weapons," Zen said to Simon before turning to Enapay. "We do as Kamau said. We go down to the gallery."

T HIRTY N INE

T HE FLURRY OF GELLER'S MEN searching the castle for Kai reverberated throughout the stairwell. It was difficult to
tell whether the sounds were coming from above or below them; therefore, Zen set a slow pace as he guided the
group down two flights of steps back to the third floor. When
he reached the museum, he caught sight of three mercenaries
inside with their weapons already drawn. Zen lunged backwards as the bursts of machine gun fire tore large lumps of
stone from the walls.

"We got more coming up from the second floor," Enapay
cried as pointed down towards the stairway.

Neva huddled with Marcel and DePaul in the center of
their group, her anger surfacing on her flushed cheeks. "We're
trapped, Zen."

The now familiar hollow click of a failed Iberian rifle came
from at least one of the gunmen inside the gallery. After silently thanking Iberia for making such ineffective weapons,

Zen threw himself into the doorway and fanned his revolver. He caught one of them uselessly trying to unjam his gun, dropping him first. Zen's next bullet found its second target, slamming into the chest of the man in the middle. However, the mercenary on the far left was able to squeeze off three rounds before Zen got him between the eyes.

Before the final soldier's body fell to the floor, a bullet tore through the top of Zen's left shoulder, the impact throwing him off balance and leaving a sizzling laceration searing his shirt. Neva and Marcel both shrieked, and Simon climbed down to help Zen back to his feet. The bloody wound burned a new kind of pain throughout his body, but the metallic barrage of enemy gunfire from the level below shook him from his agony.

Ignoring the biting gash on his shoulder, Zen entered the gallery. Simon offered to examine the wound, but there wasn't time. Neva, still holding onto Marcel, followed. Enapay returned fire down the stairwell, holding off the advancing soldiers so the rest of them could take refuge inside the gallery. Orsini and Lopez flanked the open doorway to provide cover fire for Enapay as he opened his pack.

"We need breathing room," Enapay said, dropping his weapon and fumbling in his leather satchel.

Zen's whole left side ached, and he felt the warm dripping of his blood trickle down his shoulder and tickle his side. "Another gas bomb?"

Enapay's mouth formed a sinister line. "No, this one goes *boom*."

DePaul took Neva and the boy deeper into the gallery, away from the firefight. Zen formed a fist with his left hand, double-checking that he still had function on that side. He stepped away from the museum's threshold to make room for Simon, Orsini, and Lopez who kept the mercenaries at bay on the stairway with their constant rifle bombardment.

Enapay jumped out of the gallery as he pulled the pins from two grenades and heaved them down the stairwell. Uncoiling his long legs, he dove back into the room. Zen reached out to help the other two men, but another stray bullet zipped past his ear.

Gunfire erupted from below, and one of DePaul's employees was struck in the neck by a ricocheting bullet, but Zen didn't know if it was Orsini or Lopez. The man's limp body buckled before falling to the floor. The soldiers below screamed at each other when the sound of Enapay's grenades bounced off the stairwell walls.

From below, the mercenaries unleashed a final short burst of gunfire, striking yet another one of DePaul's men. Zen narrowed his eyes to try to discern who was shot when two earth-shattering explosions filled the entire area with flames and debris. Simon and Enapay were thrown backwards, and they nearly slammed into Zen just as a fireball engulfed the stairway.

It took a few nervous moments until a voice finally called from the heavy smoke consuming the entrance to the museum. Zen clutched his left shoulder and struggled to stand.

"Everyone alright?" Simon emerged first from the billows of smoke and staggered further into the gallery.

Enapay brushed the dust from his long, black hair. "I'm still in one piece."

With most of the smoke rising upwards, Zen saw the huddled bodies of Orsini and Lopez just outside the chamber. The stairway below them had been completely annihilated. On the landing, only one of the men was moving, and Zen felt a pang of regret he couldn't distinguish which man was which. He was sure one of them was dead, and the other was at least wounded.

Simon rushed towards both men on the smoldering platform.

"It's Lopez. He's dead." Simon next examined Orsini who writhed silently next to Lopez's body. "Can you make it?"

Orsini clutched his midsection, unable to reply. Enapay went to the fallen man to help him up, but Orsini went limp and stopped breathing. Blood pooled underneath him, and it was obvious he had received a fatal shot to the gut.

Enapay took the pause in action to reload his rifle. More of Geller's men were yelling below. "Someone needs to tell these hired guns their boss is dead." He glanced towards the museum. "Where is everybody? They're safe, right?"

Zen turned to check on the others inside the gallery. He was about to take a step towards the chamber, but a piercing scream followed by a gunshot sliced through the blackness. With pistol in hand, he ran inside.

Marcel screamed from ten feet away, and his mother stood next to him. There was something odd about Neva's posture. Her right arm held out her pistol, but both her legs were bent at awkward angles. Someone moved in the shadows on the far side of the gallery, and Zen raised his gun and squeezed off two shots in a harried attempt to keep the attacker away. When he turned his attention back to Neva, he saw her struggling to stay on her feet even with Marcel's help.

Enapay burst past Zen. He snatched Neva and Marcel and pulled them to safety behind one of the large exhibit cases. Zen's eyesight caught subtle movement beyond the reach of the gas lanterns' flickering light, proving Zen's shots had missed. He kept his weapon raised. He hoped to catch even a glint of the man he knew must be Kai.

Zen spotted a dance of shadows from afar, but there wasn't enough time to dodge the silver knife whirling at him. The blade plunged into his left leg, right above the knee. Zen pitched backwards but managed to drop to his right knee and yank the knife from his flesh. He lost his breath. His lungs shuddered from the new pain overwhelming him.

Simon, still carrying his rifle, ran and shoved the old man behind another large wooden case. They crouched low to the floor directly across from Enapay. Zen heard Neva gasp. Enapay held Marcel's head down while clutching Neva's shaking body with his free arm.

Zen wanted to take cover as well, as he was still out in the open. The flowing rage rose up to his mouth, and if he was going to die today, he wanted to make sure he killed Kai first. He remained on one knee and scanned for his target.

He was sure Kai was still lurking somewhere in the dark side of the gallery, and Zen detected more subtle motion from behind a glass exhibit about fifty yards in front of him. The longer he glared into the murky side of the museum, the more he thought the flitting lantern light was playing tricks on him.

"Get over here," Enapay called out from Zen's right.

Zen turned to him but seeing Neva lying on the floor with the throwing knife jutting out of her chest made him lose his breath. Acid burned on his tongue. Despite his body's protests, Zen stood up; the stabbing pain made it difficult to walk. He ignored Enapay's plea and advanced deeper into the gallery. He lifted his gun and unloaded another three bullets at what he guessed was Kai's fluid movements in the dark.

He was sure he missed again, as all he heard was the explosion of glass and wood from his wild shots.

"Take cover, damnit!" Enapay wildly waved a bloody hand at him. "Neva's wounded!"

Zen couldn't swallow the dry lump in his throat. He glanced at Neva again. Her legs were stretched out as if her entire body was immobile. Her head lay in Marcel's lap, and her eyes fluttered open. Neva looked up at her son who hovered over her and cried silently.

Blind fury took over, and Zen pulled his trigger again. The pistol was empty. He holstered it while pulling his other gun from its holster. His eyes fully adjusted to the dark, and this time, he saw the twirling glint of metal spiraling towards him. Somehow, he threw his body towards Enapay's position in time to avoid Kai's spinning knife. He landed flat on the cold stone floor. Sharp stabs of pain attacked his body from the clumsy belly flop.

Zen remained on his stomach, and it hurt to move. Enapay bent forward. He grabbed Zen's hand and pulled him to safety behind the antique display case. While fighting Enapay's tugging, Zen raised his revolver. Without even aiming, Zen fired four more bullets into the darkness.

"I can't see him," Simon yelled from directly across from them. He lifted his rifle and pointed it towards the far end of the gallery, firing three blind shots. "It's like trying to kill a ghost."

Zen got to his knees. The sharp pinch above his left knee made his whole body tremble. He looked down at Neva who struggled with every rattling breath.

"It doesn't look good," Enapay whispered. He jerked his head towards Zen. "You're not looking so great right now either. Why don't you use that *Ishen* stuff and kill this bastard already?"

Neva's body convulsed, the still embedded knife in her chest quivering. "Can't breathe..." Her voice was barely audible. She kept her eyelids open and looked straight up at her whimpering son for a few seconds before closing them again.

"I cannot," Zen said while trying to exhale his anger from his chest. Clarity. Focus. Serenity. These were the prerequisites needed to bring his mind to the proper state, but he found none of those three in his heart. Hatred consumed him. "I am too angry."

Neva tried to speak. Her mouth moved, but Zen couldn't hear her words. Marcel looked up at Zen, his flooded eyes full of pleading desperation. For one ephemeral second, Zen wondered if his own eyes looked that way at his mother's deathbed.

"Just have to do it the old-fashioned way. If you can stay on your feet, draw him out. Just don't get killed." Enapay lifted his rifle. "Get me a clear shot."

Zen pushed all of his pain aside. He allowed the healing breaths he took to fill his entire body. He pulled himself up to his feet and leaned up against the exhibition stand. Zen readied his second pistol. He caught a glance of the growing pool of blood on Neva's chest, and a wave of hopelessness filled him, settling into the back of his throat.

Zen slid the cylinder of his pistol open, confirming what he already knew. He had two rounds left. When he stepped out from behind the exhibit case, he saw Simon across from him wave his arms wildly.

"Get down. Are you crazy?" Simon yelled at him.

DePaul reached up to yank Simon back behind their cover.

Smoldering anger remained, and he knew bringing his mind into conjuring *Ishen* was impossible. His mind wouldn't relinquish the image of Marcel helplessly watching his mother die. Zen's only option was to use his hate to fuel him.

Zen's eyes caught a flash of metal in the distance to his left. He saw the flying knife only after it penetrated the shadows and came into the light. Zen slid to his right to avoid it. The twirling blade hurled harmlessly over his already wounded shoulder.

Raising his revolver, Zen went into a slow jog towards the dark end of the gallery, leaving the light of the gas lanterns behind him. He spotted movement to his right, and Zen squeezed off a shot. It struck a tall exhibit holding a colossal ax, the glass exploding into a thousand shards. The low strained grunt met his ears, and he knew he at least wounded Kai.

A growl echoed from that same direction. "Prince Kanze Zenjiro."

Boots scraped glass, and Kai shuffled out from behind what remained of the display case. The ancient ax it once protected, however, was still held upright by its metal stand. Kai was in agony. He flashed his teeth in a tight grimace and glared at the ax as if he contemplated taking it in his hands.

Kai looked as if he were ready to collapse. The man had short cropped hair and wore a uniform the hue of dark indigo. He bore no clan emblem on his chest armor, but his dark pants were soggy from fresh blood spilling underneath his clothing.

The man looked familiar to Zen. It took only a few seconds for him to recall meeting this solider on his way to his father's study the day of Nihon's Unification Day celebration. He knew Kai was a Shadow, a member of the secret army Zen believed existed but never discussed with his father.

The stone Zen wore under his shirt was burning his skin, the blue light penetrating his white shirt. He ignored it, and he forced his attention to return to the wounded Kai.

"Who are you?" Zen pointed the barrel of his gun and cocked the hammer back. He had one round left in the chamber, and that's all he needed.

Kai's shoulders drooped. His arms hung loosely at his sides. He opened his bloody hands to reveal that they were empty. "You know what I am, but not who I am." The Shadow removed the *katana* from his scabbard before throwing it on the floor. His mouth flashed a gloomy grin.

"I know *you*, Zenjiro. The most honorable warrior of Nihon. You would never kill an unarmed opponent. That is not your way. That is not the way of the *samurai*." He spat a spray of red from his mouth. "Honor first, right?"

Zen's insides caught on fire. The need to pull the trigger was overwhelming.

"You look like your mother." Kai dropped his head. "My beloved sister."

Zen froze. "What?"

Kai's eyes rolled back as if he was going to pass out. His body lost all tension and started to go limp. Instead of collapsing in a heap, he steadied himself. Kai raised his right hand, flashing another throwing blade that had been concealed in his sleeve.

The crack of gunfire came from behind Zen, followed by another. Zen remained still, unable to move his aching body. Kai's dark form jerked and jolted from the two bullets punching through his torso. He let out a weak exhale before dropping his knife and crumbling to the floor.

Zen struggled to stay on his feet. He nearly dropped his pistol, and he fought to stay upright. The room felt like it was spinning, but he kept his gun trained on Kai's unmoving body. Had the Shadow tried to distract him?

If so, Kai had succeeded. His mother never spoke of having a brother, or any other family. She was an orphan. Zen felt dizzy with humiliation, ashamed of his moment of weakness and foolishness. His moment of hesitation had nearly cost him his life.

Enapay stood at the edge of the shadows, the light still revealing his rifle's smoking barrel. He ran to Zen's side and poked Kai's body with his gun.

"Are you okay?" Enapay asked him.

"I will be fine." Zen turned around and looked towards the open entrance to the museum. "How is Neva?"

The dread in Enapay's eyes answered him.

Zen shuddered in a silent rage. The full realization that his own father had hired Kai made him sick. Hideaki had also conspired to take the Machine Boy. Abducting children broke the *samurai* code. His father's dishonor hurt far worse than his bloody wounds.

The stone around his neck continued to emanate hot energy, more intense than ever before. Enapay caught a glimpse of it before leaving his side to run back to Neva. Zen bent over Kai's body and took the sword and wooden scabbard from the floor. His instinct was to say a prayer for Kai's spirit, but instead he turned to where Neva lay. He hoped she was still alive.

The heat from his medallion was almost unbearable, and the stone seemed to be moving by itself. He pulled it from underneath his blood soaked shirt, and it immediately felt like it was pulling to the left. The chain was taut, the stone nearly levitating in mid-air. When he turned to the direction of the stone's pull, he allowed himself to be led by the amulet.

Zen reached an artifact in Geller's gallery, protected inside a long horizontal glass case. The entire weapon was of a strange black metal and lay broken in several jagged pieces. It looked long eroded by nature and the passing of centuries. His eyes welled with tears, and the stone continued to rattle. It seemed to nearly catch fire against his skin.

With whatever strength Zen had left, he slid the glass off the wooden case, and it shattered on the stone floor. He removed the medallion from his neck, keeping the stone hovering above the broken sword. The pull downward was strong, and when he let go of the chain, the stone clung onto the once-ornate hilt of what he knew had to be the Sky Blade.

Enapay and Simon shared Neva's weight on their shoulders, her head lifted and her breaths remained rapid and shallow. Marcel clung to her and held her up from her waist. The old man followed, peeking around them to stare at the exhibit.

"What is that?" Enapay asked, looking at both Zen and De-Paul for an answer.

"The Sky Blade," Marcel said between quiet sobs.

Zen's normally steady hands continued to quiver. "Yes, Machine Boy. You are correct."

When Zen swallowed, it was as if the sharp fragments of glass on the floor were now in his throat. His world tumbled upside down. All he had ever known were revealed to be nothing but lies. The Sky Blade was nothing more than a rusty useless antique, a display purchased by a greedy, and now dead, merchant.

The veil of mystery and mysticism of the universe evaporated, and all Zen could find was cold reality. The world lost its color. Zen reached over and pulled Enapay's leather satchel from his free shoulder. Enapay straightened his arm, allowing the strap to slide off.

"It is the Sky Blade." Zen's words were hollow, which is exactly how he felt inside. "Not so mighty after all."

Enapay was about to speak, but he shook his head instead. He had been right all this time, but he looked as if he took no joy in being so.

Zen picked up the pieces of the sword and threw them into the bag. Drying his eyes, he slung the pack over his wounded shoulder and scanned the gallery for the large tapestry Kamau had described. On the wall directly in front of them hung the earth-colored woven rug.

Zen pulled the tapestry from the wall, revealing a small wooden door. "Let's get out of here," he said as he pulled it open.

The warmth of the stone stuck to the Sky Blade's hilt penetrated the leather satchel on his back, mocking him. Zen carried with him a bag filled with broken promises. He silently cursed his father as he led what was left of his group through the hidden doorway and into the pitch-black of the underground tunnel.

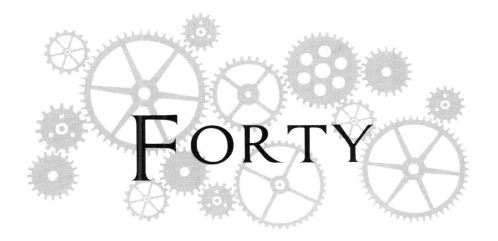

FORTY

DePaul led them to his friend's building, hidden underground in the center of the now empty market. The man with the mechanical leg named Anton brought them to a simple chamber resembling a small bedroom. He supplied Simon with the medical materials he needed.

Simon had been a surgeon in the Francian army, DePaul explained. The old man's nephew worked furiously to save Neva. He worked with determined skill and urgency. DePaul remained at Neva's bedside, his wrinkled face full of gloom. Everyone wallowed in horrible silence as Simon continued to work on her.

Marcel's cries eventually subsided, his face void of any color. Zen and Enapay sat on the floor up against the wall. After noticing Zen's bloody injuries, Enapay got up and snatched several cloth strips and a small bottle of yellow disinfectant from the table at Simon's side. Despite Zen's initial protest, Enapay tended to Zen's wounded shoulder and leg.

"I cannot help her," Simon whispered to DePaul. "Her injury is too severe. I cannot stop the bleeding. I gave her something for the pain, but that's all I can do." He turned to Marcel. "She has little time left, and she wants to speak with you."

Simon and DePaul left the room. Marcel tiptoed up to Neva's side. He leaned over the bed and kissed her cheek. Zen watched Neva's flickering green eyes stare at the top of her son's head, her expression eerily identical to his own mother's during her final moments.

When Marcel lifted his face to hers, Neva forced a thin smile on her grayish face.

"My little Machine Boy. You're safe, and that is all that matters to me." Her voice trembled, and the sound of bubbling fluid filled her throat.

Enapay stopped dabbing the medicine on Zen's shoulder and motioned for them to join the boy. As they approached, her hand gestured for them to come closer. Enapay and Zen leaned in; Neva focused on them for a moment.

"Please take care of my son," she gurgled. Her eyes rested on Enapay as if to confirm her wishes. "Watch over him."

Marcel buried his face into the crook of Neva's arm. Enapay took a long time in composing himself. He gently touched the boy's chestnut hair and looked into Neva's eyes. "Are you sure? I'm not the best influence. I might corrupt him."

Neva's lips tightened. "I trust you, savage."

She slowly turned to Zen, and he felt a familiar pain fester in his chest. This was to be a good death, as Neva had proved herself to be both brave and honorable. One of the best he had ever met, but this was little consolation. He was watching another mother leave her son in this unforgiving world.

"Zen," she breathed. "Your mother is proud of you."

Forgetting proper decorum, Zen allowed the cold tears to run from his eyes. "I know she would be."

"No." Neva took another shallow breath, pausing for a moment. "She. Is."

Zen said a silent Nihon prayer and bowed. He placed his hand on hers.

The brilliance of former glory is now dimmed. While mortal men pray for tomorrow, your spirit runs free forevermore.

He opened his eyes and stared at the Machine Boy, knowing intimately every ounce of despair the child felt.

"My son, please." Neva's chin pressed tightly against her chest. She waited for Marcel to look up at her again. "Come close to me."

The Machine Boy put his face close to hers. Neva whispered something in the boy's ear. When she finished giving her final message, Marcel nodded and wrapped his arms around her shoulders.

"Don't be afraid," Neva told him.

With her final words to her child, Neva slipped from the known world.

EARLY STREAKS OF SUNLIGHT CLIMBED from the horizon when Anton led them to the local funeral parlor where they properly burned Neva's body. Marcel's weary eyes looked empty during the entire funeral.

The five of them said goodbye to DePaul's old friend and hiked back to the *Triton*. When they arrived, Simon offered to properly address Zen's injuries, which he graciously accepted.

McMillan piloted the *Triton* to stay close to shore, but still hidden under the depths of the ocean to avoid detection by the pirates who lurked along the coast. Simon proved to be an excellent surgeon. He stitched up his left shoulder and leg and changed the dressing on the healing wound on his thigh.

During the three days of being submerged underwater, Zen did little else other than sleep and eat. He had lost a lot of blood, and he was content with doing as little as possible in order to regain his strength. Enapay and McMillan took turns taking care of the child, who continued his quiet mourning.

The entire group finally came together on the third afternoon, congregating in the control room to decide what would be done next.

Simon and McMillan sat in the cockpit chairs to pilot the craft, while Zen and the rest of them gathered around the small table. An awkward silence permeated the room. The old man took a sip from his steaming tin coffee cup before finally speaking.

"I have financial obligations to Lopez and Orsini," DePaul said. "My associates are assembling on the Albion Isle. There, I can dispatch couriers to make sure Lopez and Orsini's kin receive their promised salaries."

Enapay asked, "What about me and the Machine Boy? I don't think it's safe to bring Marcel to any country in Europa. Iberia would love to get their hands on him."

Marcel wiggled nervously in the corner of the control room.

"I've already thought of that," DePaul replied. "We will stick to my original plan. On the Isle, outside the capital of Londin, we have built a well-protected safe house."

"Who is *we*?" Enapay's right eyebrow arched.

"The Enlightenment Guild. We're a secret society comprised of some of the greatest thinkers and scientists in all the world. In fact, the Guild financed this whole operation. The members all realize how important Marcel is to the world, and they have pledged to insure he is no longer exploited for his powers."

Enapay crossed his arms, seemingly satisfied with the old man's reply.

"Zen, I grossly underestimated you. I apologize," said De-Paul. "Would you consider accompanying us on our mission to the Albion Isle? We could use your talents."

Zen's canvas backpack carried the remnants of the Sky Blade. The sour taste in his mouth had refused to dissipate one bit in three days. In fact, his anger swelled with each waking moment. If his mission had been to find the enchanted sword, he would bring the feeble remains home.

"I am sorry, Professor. I cannot go with you. I have a new mission of my own."

Enapay raised his arms in mock resignation. "What could that be?"

"My quest was to bring the Sky Blade back to Nihon, to my father. I will get the truth from him before I throw the shards of the worthless relic at his feet."

"Your *father*?" Enapay looked bewildered.

Zen's insides twisted at having to admit his lineage. There was a time when such a declaration would have made him proud. "Yes. My father is the king of Nihon."

Enapay threw his head back. "If you're the prince, why didn't you come to Agrios with a whole armada and platoons of troops? Or at least with your kingdom's riches? That kind of power could have come in handy, oh, maybe a couple dozen times."

"I was put on a Sacred Quest, stripped of my royalty and privilege." The shame felt too much to bear. "I must return to Nihon."

DePaul stepped forward with a grave look in his eyes. "Young man, your father is King Hideaki?"

Zen nodded.

"You *must* come with us," DePaul said. "The Guild believes your father is engaging in dangerous scientific experiments in Koreya. He's committing atrocities. We are formulating a plan of action to stop him."

Zen had no time to contemplate his father's scientific transgressions. His father's secrets were indeed dark, and he intended to learn all of them. "I am going home."

"What for? Those ragged pieces are hardly the magical weapon you were bestowed to return to your people." The constant grin Enapay wore slid away. "Like your enchanted amulet. It glowed every time you were near carbsidian, and it's also reacting to the dark metal of the Sky Blade. That sword might have been forged from star rock, but it's not mystical. Your quest is over."

Zen felt his fists tighten. "I was sent on this fool's errand. I fought and killed for my country. I need to know why my father rewarded my victories by casting me out. Nearly everything I believe in, everything I know...has been a lie. This is not over for me." He turned to DePaul. "If my father is committing further sins against mankind, I will stop him."

Enapay leaned forward, his eyes glaring. "Zen, don't go home. Maybe someday you can return. Stay with us. Help me protect the Machine Boy. Neva would have wanted you to stay with us."

"I am sorry. I cannot."

"How will you get back to Nihon?" DePaul asked Zen.

"I saw foreign ships in the main harbor on the way to Geller's estate. I am sure Kai's ship is still docked there."

Zen pivoted to face Enapay, the ache in his left shoulder throbbing when he moved. He took hold of Enapay's reluctant arm and gave him the traditional tribal handshake.

Marcel remained hunched in the corner of the room. Zen stepped over to the child and bent down. "I am sorry, Machine Boy. I too lost my mother. It hurts now, but it will become easier with time." He saw himself in the child, and the fire in his chest flared again. "I will avenge you, Machine Boy. I promise you."

ENAPAY KNOCKED ON THE METAL door before opening it. Marcel didn't move as he continued lying on his back with his hands folded behind his head. The boy stared up at the ceiling, his vacant eyes drifting and failing to focus on anything above.

"We're going now." Enapay approached with apprehensive steps before sitting on the bed.

"I know." Marcel kept his soft gaze upwards. "I can feel the boat moving. Is Zen gone?"

Enapay replied with a nod. "Are you hungry?"

The Machine Boy remained silent.

"I can ask McMillan to cook something. You don't want me near a stove. I'm liable to burn the *Triton* down." Enapay waited for a response, but got none.

Enapay's doubt hung in the air like a bad stink, and he struggled to find the right words to say to a child who only days ago lost his mother. He opened his mouth and blurted the first thing that came to his mind.

"You know, your mother and I met under the strangest of circumstances. She and Zen were both captured by a menacing pirate. I swooped down from my airship and saved them by blowing up a bunch of stuff."

This seemed to break Marcel from his trance, and the child looked at him with familiar emerald eyes.

"Later, the raiders shot my airship right out of the sky. Neva came to rescue me when the pirates came to finish me off. Your mother saved my life."

Enapay blinked to prevent the tears forming from his eyes. The kid's face was still red and swollen from crying, and maybe it was too soon to talk about Neva. He sighed, unsure if he was breaking the ice or making things worse for the boy.

"My mother was a soldier," Marcel finally said. "Pistoleer in the Francian army."

"That's what I heard. When she and Zen were captured, she was forced to fight in a duel. I wasn't there, but my tribesman witnessed your mother dispatch a nasty bandit in a deadly contest."

Marcel sat up, and he smiled.

Enapay felt relief; the kid didn't seem to hate him after all. The future seemed uncertain, and he questioned if he was ready for the responsibility of raising a child. In the meantime, he was thankful that Shannon McMillan was there to help him. She possessed the motherly instinct he lacked, and Marcel seemed naturally drawn to her even shortly after meeting her.

Despite his uneasiness of having to be the boy's custodian for life, he considered Neva's trust in him an honor. Enapay secretly longed to take him back to his village, where his wrecked *Dragonfly* remained. If Marcel did have mystical powers with anything mechanical, he would love nothing more than to see just how real the child's abilities were.

Marcel said, "My mother was fast."

Enapay nodded. "She had a dead eye too."

The boy's chin dropped. "She told me something before she ...died."

"I remember that she whispered in your ear."

"She wants me to help him to stand."

Enapay watched the Machine Boy's chin quiver, and he considered Neva's cryptic message. "Who needs help standing?"

Marcel shrugged. "I don't know. It doesn't make any sense."

"Life is full of mysteries," Enapay said. "It must be important. Whatever Neva meant, I'm sure it will become clear in time."

For the rest of the night until they both fell asleep, they exchanged stories of the great woman that brought life to Marcel and saved Enapay in more ways than he could count.

THE DOCKS WERE PRACTICALLY EMPTY save for a few merchants traipsing back and forth between their small boats. At the far edge of the shore, two formidable steam galleons remained. The one on the right was distinctly from Nihon, despite the lack of normal emblems or flags depicting its nationality.

When he climbed on board the ship, the startled crew

stopped their work and stared at him. Low whispers of doubt among the crew floated up to Zen's ears.

"I am Kanze Zenjiro, your prince. I am taking command of this ship, and you will take me home to Nihon." His voice was full and confident, but he felt awkward from their incessant stares. "We depart at once."

The men were frozen, unsure of what to do. It took several moments for one of them to step forward. The crew member looked sturdy and strong, and he shrugged his shoulders before addressing Zen.

"I'm sorry, but you don't look like the warrior prince. You look like a pirate."

With Zen's long hair loose and wild and his dirty clothing, the sailor's assessment was probably accurate.

"What is your name?" Zen asked him.

"Maeda. I am the navigator." Maeda's thin brows furrowed. "What of Master Kai?"

Zen tore the *katana* from its wooden scabbard. The crew, including Maeda, recoiled with a gasp. "You no longer serve that dog." He held it up for display. "Kai proved to be a villain, so his death will please you."

Maeda looked unmoved. "You could easily have stolen it. Maybe he got himself killed. All the foreigners fled the castle and rushed back to the harbor. They spoke of a bloody massacre." He spun around to gather the muttering support from his crew. "Prince Kanze Zenjiro is the greatest warrior in all of Nihon. He is known as the *Dragonfly Warrior*, he who bears the crest of the Kanze on his armor." He scrutinized Zen with squinted eyes. "You look like a beggar, more fit to clean the latrines than be the prince of Nihon."

The crew broke into wild laughter. Maeda tossed his head

back to release another hearty bellow; Zen slashed the sword across the man's waistline. It would have been a deadly blow had he fully extended his arm.

Instead, the leather belt holding up Maeda's pants tore in two, dropping his blue trousers. Thankfully, the navigator saved further humiliation by wearing thin shorts underneath the pants now lying around his ankles.

This made the crew roar even louder, and even Maeda laughed at himself after pulling up his pants.

"I have a new quest," Zen said. "We leave for Nihon right now."

ACKNOWLEDGEMENTS

W HERE DO I BEGIN?
I'm pretty sure I'm going to forget some people, but I will try my very best to thank everyone that's played a part in helping me get *Dragonfly Warrior* out to the world.

To my long time blogging buddies that read my early drafts and offered their expertise: Mary Pascual, Kimberly Wadycki, Cynthia Clubbs, Michael Ignacio, and Michael Offutt, I thank you from the bottom of my heart.

The blogging community is my home away from home. I appreciate all the love and support you give me and all the other writers out there.

Big thanks to my editors: Matt, Martha, and especially Neely Bratcher. Thanks for smoothing the rough spots and making this book all spiffy and shiny.

I must acknowledge Jennifer Howard, Mary Pax, Cambria Hebert., and Jennifer Pringle. When things fell apart, you were all there to give me the encouragement and advice I needed. To all the authors at Hydra, I'd like to give all of you a big high-five.

I'm amazed by the artistic talent of Enggar Adirasa. Thank you for bringing my story to life with your amazing skills.

And finally, I want to thank fellow writer J. Maria for her telling me like it is. Your ideas helped me out when I had painted myself into a corner.

ABOUT THE AUTHOR

Jay Noel was born in New York but lives in Missouri with his family. He received a degree in English from Southeast Missouri State University. Jay is a prolific blogger, and he's a contributor to CultureBrats.com and inkPageant.com.

Find Jay Noel online at www.jaynoel.com.